[illegible] is the author of two novels, *Habitus* and *52 [illegible] Magic America*. He has written features and reviews for many national newspapers and magazines and his short fiction has appeared in collections published by Penguin, the New English Library and the ICA. In 2002 one of his stories ('The Nuclear Train') was made into a short film for Channel 4, directed by Daniel Saul. *The Book of Ash* was a winner of a 2003 Arts Council Writers' Award.

The Book of Ash

JAMES FLINT

PENGUIN BOOKS

PENGUIN BOOKS

Published by the Penguin Group
Penguin Books Ltd, 80 Strand, London WC2R ORL, England
Penguin Group (USA) Inc., 375 Hudson Street, New York, New York 10014, USA
Penguin Group (Canada), 90 Eglinton Avenue East, Suite 700,
Toronto, Ontario, Canada M4P 2Y3
(a division of Pearson Penguin Canada Inc.)
Penguin Ireland, 25 St Stephen's Green, Dublin 2, Ireland
(a division of Penguin Books Ltd)
Penguin Group (Australia), 250 Camberwell Road,
Camberwell, Victoria 3124, Australia (a division of Pearson Australia Group Pty Ltd)
Penguin Books India Pvt Ltd, 11 Community Centre,
Panchsheel Park, New Delhi – 110 017, India
Penguin Group (NZ), cnr Airborne and Rosedale Roads, Albany,
Auckland 1310, New Zealand (a division of Pearson New Zealand Ltd)
Penguin Books (South Africa) (Pty) Ltd, 24 Sturdee Avenue,
Rosebank 2196, South Africa

Penguin Books Ltd, Registered Offices: 80 Strand, London WC2R ORL, England

www.penguin.com

First published by Viking 2004
Published in Penguin Books 2005
1

Printed in England by Clays Ltd, St Ives plc

For my parents

For two hundred years we've lived in the future, believing that tomorrow would be better than today and today would be better than yesterday. I still believe that. Together, we can begin the world over again. We can meet our destiny. And our destiny – to build a land here that will be for all mankind a shining city on a hill. I think we ought to get at it.

Ronald Reagan, TV Debate, September 1980

You can't make this shit up.

James L. Acord, in conversation, Wasilla 1998

Custoditus

The Facility

I'm standing outside in the Yorkshire rain, ducking to keep dry beneath the pink-tinted bell of Liz's see-thru fashion umbrella. Ducking because Liz is holding the umbrella by its stem and Liz is somewhat shorter than I am. She should give the umbrella to me to hold. Me being the taller, larger and all round sturdier of the two of us, it's my argument that I'm altogether better suited as an umbrella trunk. But Liz says the primary objective is not the overall efficiency of the system. Liz says the primary objective is the maintainance of Liz's hair in its present, perfectly dry condition. If I do not understand the reason for this primary objective, Liz explains, it's because I do not use hair straightener, and therefore do not understand that the application of moisture to one's straightened hair will result in a transformation of said hair from current state of straightness to a state of sudden and unrestrained frizziness. Which would not be good.

But this, I try gently to point out, would not occur under my scheme. Under *my* scheme we would the both of us stay dry. Taking 'the both of us' to mean Liz, Liz's hair and me.

'Maybe so,' says Liz, 'but the hair situation is far too critical and delicate.'

'Too critical and delicate for what, exactly?'

'Too critical and delicate to even think about messing with. Too critical and delicate to allow another authority input and control. The potential for disaster is just far too great to contemplate.'

When Liz talks like this I know she's doing it deliberately, to wind me up. It winds me up.

'Too critical and delicate to allow this person's input and control,' I say, thumbing a thumb in the direction of my chest (a chest Liz once unforgettably described as 'cuddly').

'Maybe.'

'Right. Precisely. Meaning I have to stand here, without a coat, getting soaked, while you get to have dry hair *and* a dry body.'

The dry body bit is an issue here, as Liz is not wearing her own coat but one that Andrews threw over her shoulders as he co-ordinated the evacuation of our floor. If you can call it coordination. Andrews is our department head but if you ask me he couldn't supervise a goldfish bowl let alone a military-grade satellite control systems coding operation, which is what our department is. Standing in the corner, calm as an air steward and about as camp, chanting: 'Please leave the building and assemble at the assembly points,' and: 'Please remain calm,' and: 'This is not a drill,' while smiling the kind of worried smile you'd expect to find hanging off the face of a stressed-out kindergarten teacher and clenching his buttocks with delight that he's got yet another chance to order us around . . . it doesn't exactly take a genius, does it? It doesn't *exactly* call for gallantry of the coat-unfurling variety? And it certainly doesn't merit the grateful and downright simpering looks certain female members of our staff were giving him. I mean, it's not like he's a fucking fireman or war hero or anything.

'It's not my fault you don't keep a raincoat at work,' says Liz. 'You should be grateful I'm letting you get any umbrella space at all.'

I'm seeing red. I am. I am literally seeing red. Liz is smiling, I know that. I can't see it through all the red I'm seeing, but I can sense it.

Fuck this, I think, and removing my head from beneath the plastic carapace I stand up and face the weather.

'You know, it's not that bad,' I say as raindrops sting my face, though all I get by way of response is a theatrically indifferent cough.

'It's not, it's really not.' Water bombs explode across my glasses and obscure my view. Some kind of bunker-seeking precipitation missile tunnels down inside my collar and obliterates secret forces bivouacked along the wind-scoured cliffside of my neck.

'Why d'you think there are so many goddamn guards?' Liz says quietly. 'They're everywhere. I've never seen so many. Where do they keep them all? It's like they've drafted in a whole extra division.'

'I think they have.'

'No wonder we pay so much tax. Is it really necessary?'

I laugh at this because the answer is so obvious. 'Er, like, given recent events, I'd say that's a yes.'

Perhaps wisely, Liz ignores the patronizing sarcasm. 'But so many?'

'What I want to know is,' I say, ignoring back, 'if they could please turn off that fucking alarm? Or at least turn it down. It's driving me insane. Why does it have to be so loud? It's not like we haven't got the damn message. I mean, we're all standing out here getting pneumonia aren't we? Do they have to rupture our eardrums too?'

'Calm down, will you? What's got you so worked up, all of a sudden? I hope you're not going to sulk because I won't let you hold the umbrella.'

'I'm not sulking! Christ. I've left my inhaler inside, that's all.'

'You can live without your inhaler for a few minutes.'

'No, Liz, I can't. That's why I've got one, see? Because if I have an attack I might not last a few minutes.'

'So don't have an attack.'

'What d'you think it is? A decision?'

'No, of course not. I just think you're getting worked up for no reason. Just breathe. And while you're breathing think about this. Even if a grand mal epileptic seizure reduces you to a quivering heap on the floor at my feet, I'm still not going to give you the umbrella.'

I sniff a bit at this and go quiet. It's not defeat – I'm just biding my time. While I'm doing that I take a look around.

You'll have gathered by now that Liz and I are not alone out here. We are not the only ones standing around, miserable in the rain and cold and wet. Out here in the car park with us are the entire staffs of Sectors 7 to 10. Here are all the people I work with, all the people I see from day to day. Here is Pauline. Here is Simon. Here is Josie. Here are Suhail, Damian, Bruce. Suhail, Bruce and

Damian are programmers, Simon is a sys admin, Josie's personnel and Pauline's too important for me to know exactly what it is she does. Alongside them are maybe two hundred faces belonging to people I've never met. A few I vaguely recognize but the vast majority I've never even seen before, which is not exactly impressive when you consider I've been working on this site for three years now. But RAF Featherbrooks is hardly a magnet for the socially gregarious, which I suppose is one reason I've been so happy here.

And you couldn't say that mixing in the ranks is actively encouraged. Quite the opposite. My bet is that these tight groups in which all of us are standing, talking in low voices, looking miserable, smoking cigarettes, rubbing hands and stamping feet perhaps, but mainly just blinking like freshly woken moles in the wan excuse for daylight that's being served up as an accompaniment to this tediously energetic late-September rain, all these groups are made up of the six or eight people who happen to sit together at adjacent desks. That's all anyone really gets to meet, round here. Those are your colleagues. That's your team.

And fair enough. The only difference I can see between most of them and me is that they are carrying umbrellas. Why is that? How come they're all so damn *prepared*? Maybe that's why they all seem so calm, the bastards, while I'm in a state of some distress. Look at them. They could be waiting for a fireworks display.

'What are we doing out here?' I ask of no one in particular. Some of the faces turn towards me. Most of these faces are smooth. Most of the butts are fat. Most of the accents are American. Liz is American. Bruce is American. Pauline is Anglo-Dutch. Suhail is Indian-American (as opposed to Amerindian, or Native American, or whatever the correct term is these days). Damian and Simon, they're English. They're the odd ones out, like me.

The facility is a little piece of America in England. The cars are American. The clothes are American. People have no choice but to live in English houses scattered in and around the nearby town of Whitby, but they waste no time in replacing everything they can with imported American fixtures and fittings: refrigerators the size of mortuaries, specially wired 120-volt electrical sockets, waste-disposals, jacuzzi bathtubs, power showers. Their kitchens are stocked with the American groceries you can buy from a special supermarket here on the base. Satellites beam in special American TV. It's a home away from home, is the idea.

All of which is just fine by me. The way I see it, these days we're all Americans. I mean, I might have been brought up in this country, but I don't consider myself English, not particularly. I don't consider myself anything. And you know what? I do not have a problem with this. I'm just not interested if you want to stand up there and tell me this is somehow wrong of me. You want to do it, you go ahead. I'm just not going to listen.

'Does anybody know *anything*?' I say again, marvelling (as I've done many times before) at my companions' apparently innate ability to ignore me. 'Someone must know something? Surely?'

'It's just a drill,' says Simon, who takes it as a point of honour to never let anything bother him.

'Could be a fire,' suggests Pauline.

'So where's the smoke?' Simon again.

'I just hope they sort it soon. I'm totally freezing.' Typical Liz, that is – always thinking of herself.

Then, as if on cue, the sirens stop.

'That's it,' says Simon. 'All over. A false alarm. Another fifteen minutes, we'll all be back inside.'

'Fifteen minutes! Jesus.' Liz. Moaning.

The crowd falls quiet as individuals align themselves with the growing mood of optimism and anticipation, keener than ever to get back inside now that the rain has turned into an unseasonal icy sleet. We wait bravely, all facing towards our building, trumpeting small cornets of condensing breath, looking up at the nearest of the eleven geodesic spheres that are clustered in the centre of the facility like God's golfballs on some kind of preposterous eighteenth tee as if an answer will be transmitted to us directly, psychically, from within.

Then an answer comes, albeit in a somewhat more prosaic fashion. It comes over the tannoy, in the form of a digitized female voice, in the form of 16-bit sound waves that propagate with tiny overlaps, interferences and delays into the gaps between the buildings, into the gaps between the domes, into the gaps between our ears.

'Will employee Cooper James please report immediately to Security Office D. That's immediately. Without delay.'

I'm not sure who they mean at first and look around to see. What I see is Liz, giving me a 'wakey wakey' wave six inches from my face.

'Go on then,' she says. 'Go and find out what they want. Then maybe they'll let us back inside.'

She's right, you know. I'd better go. Because 'Cooper James', that's me.

I can't tell you what my job is. The reason I can't tell you what my job is is I don't know myself. That's one of the things that having a security clearance means. You may sign a security agreement form but it doesn't put you in a position where you have knowledge. What it does is put others in a position where they're permitted to keep you in ignorance. But that's a prerequisite for the job. And it's not as if it's a major secret that we're all working on either electronic surveillance or Nuclear Missile Defense. All those giant spheres – they sort of give the game away.

The only one who makes any kind of a fuss about all this is Liz. Liz is a cynic – or at least she likes to think she is. Only this morning she was going on about how we are all peons on the Death Star. That we're exactly the kind of people Timothy McVeigh regarded as expendable. Which is easy for her to say; being an American she's got a higher security clearance than me and therefore has access to actual information. She denies this of course – it's in her contract that she has to – but it's true. It must be true, she must know stuff. Why else would she have to file a PS-6 (a lemon-yellow security form to you) every time she has an off-base conversation with any person (yours truly, for example) with a lower clearance than the one she's on? Time, place, interlocutors, content. It all has to be logged. The files must be groaning with conversations we've had about *ER* and *The X-Files*. Especially *The X-Files*. I must like her, or I wouldn't put up with it. But it drives me nuts all the same. I mean, can you imagine having to write down every chat you have with one of your friends? And you wonder why no one on the base talks to anyone who's not on their team.

The only consolation to this ridiculous practice is that you only have to do it when you're off-site. This presumably means that we're so heavily surveilled when we're at work that it doesn't matter, what we say is all logged and recorded anyway. But one of the things Liz no doubt knows is that no one's likely to look at anything but a fraction of the footage, so she takes the opportunity to pretend she's cooler and more anti-establishment than we all know that in fact she is.

It really annoys me when she does this. Hence my somewhat belligerent response. 'McVeigh was an madman,' I said. 'A rabid animal who deserved to die for what he did.'

She gave me her matter-of-fact face: eyes square as square things, lips straight and flat as strips of Sellotape. 'When Luke Skywalker got his missiles down the air intake, don't pretend to me that you didn't cheer.'

'I hardly think there's a comparison to be made between McVeigh and Skywalker.'

'Okay then. You're from Nottingham. How about bin Laden and Robin Hood?'

I glanced around the office and suppressed the urge to ask her to lower her voice. 'You are joking, right?'

'You tell me. All I know is, if Robin Hood were alive today, he'd be cluster-bombed. They'd napalm Sherwood Forest. They'd smoke him out, him and his evil band of Merry Men. The argument, see, would be that all that feeding-the-poor stuff is not only a sinister plot, a prelude to seizing power. Worse than that – it's short-termism. This Hood guy, what he's in fact doing is destroying the long-term interests of the poor by disrupting the mechanisms of the state. He's damaging trade routes, breaching mead pipelines, impeding tax collection and hindering the successful promotion of the crusade to cleanse the Holy Land of barbarian influence. We have to take the long-term view, the Sheriff says. It's only by ensuring the free functioning of the markets that the poor willl ever be helped to clamber from the mire. Hood is an enemy of the people and we will stop him at any cost. It will be total war. Justice will be done. Sherwood will be freed of this menace. If it means cutting down each and every tree, the forest will be saved. Whatever it takes.'

'If that's the way you feel I don't see why you're working here, of all places.'

She shrugged. 'Maybe they like me for my ability to think outside the box.'

I started rearranging the coloured Post-it notes stuck around my screen, suddenly deciding that the three lime greens belonged together, that they shouldn't be broken up by the pinks and blues like that. But after I moved them I couldn't seem to get them perfectly realigned, plus one of the limes had lost its stick and kept floating loose onto my desk, meaning it would have to be rewritten. 'Or maybe you're an agent provocateur, trying to entrap me into saying something I shouldn't,' I said.

She smiled back, teeth white and fine as expensive bathroom fittings. 'Maybe.'

I hate offices; no job or conversation ever gets properly concluded, everything you do is always left half undone, hanging in the air like a half-built bridge and leading nowhere. Case in point: this is the moment that Andrews chose to walk in on us and interrupt. 'What's bugging you, Cooper?' he said. 'Someone rearranged the pencils on your desk?'

Liz sniggered. I blushed. I knew that somewhere out there in the space of all sentences there was a killer retort waiting for me, but I was too upset to search for it. Instead I made the elementary mistake of actually answering his question. 'Liz has been talking crap about Robin Hood. But she's got it all back to front. She's making the guys who build the castles out to be the villains, but it's thanks to them that there isn't complete anarchy out there.'

I'm like this with conversations. If I start off on a topic I'm not happy till the topic has been argued through. I can't settle down. I can't let it go. I don't know why I should be that way – other people don't seem to care. It used to make me angry but it doesn't any more; now it just worries me. Perhaps I'm missing something. Being around Liz sometimes makes me feel like this. Being around Andrews always makes me feel it.

'Well that's a very admirable sentiment, Coops,' Andrews said, then let out this sighing little laugh. *You are pathetic*, this laugh said. *You are pathetic, with your plans and schemes and your ideas. You'll never amount to anything. You're so small and limited that I can read you like a book. I know every move you make before you make it, every thought you're going to think, every word you're going to speak. Every moment you're in my presence you reveal yourself. This is why putting you down comes so easily to me. I don't have to think about it, it comes so naturally. And the only reason that I do it is it amuses me.*

'Piss off Andrews,' I muttered. But he and Liz had already left the room.

'He is such a creep,' I said, when Liz returned.

'I don't know why you just don't stand up for yourself,' was her considered analysis. 'If you let him walk all over you, of course he'll take advantage. You make it easy for him.'

'He's a bully.'

'You ask for it.'

'I don't see why I should have to lower myself to his level.'

'You're scared of a fight. Doug's actually a decent guy, if you get to know him.'

'Yeah, well, you seem to like him well enough.'

'What's that supposed to mean?'

'The way you laugh at his jokes and all, the way you are around him . . . you fancy him, I know you do.'

'I do not.'

'You do too. Look. You're blushing.'

'I am *so* not blushing. How can you tell I'm blushing?'

'You've gone a darker shade of black.'

'What total crap. I do not fancy Douglas Andrews.'

'You said he was a decent guy, when you got to know him.'

'Exactly, I said he was a decent guy. I know a lot of decent guys. I don't want to sleep with all of them. Or most of them. Or hardly any of them, in fact.'

'Except for Andrews.'

'Cooper, fuck off.'

'See. Now you're swearing. You wouldn't be swearing if it wasn't true.'

'Look. I do not fancy Andrews. I'd sleep with you before I'd sleep with him.'

'You'd sleep with me?'

'It's a figure of speech. Don't get any big ideas, okay.'

'You'd *sleep* with *me*? I'll remember that.'

'You'll remember nothing. It meant nothing. It was a figure of speech. Get back to work.'

'I remember everything. I'm stupid that way.'

'I know you are. Get back to work.'

Even though I know Liz would never sleep with me, I sensed I'd scored some kind of victory. But Liz is my direct superior so ultimately I have to do whatever she says. I turned my attention to the code I've been working on. It's very complex. I know that it's a servo-motor control sub-routine, but beyond that I don't know what it does. It could be designed to control the electric sunroof on a car or change the focus on the laser range-finder of a military satellite. I wish this made debugging it more difficult, but the sad truth is it doesn't. To do my job I don't need to know which of these it is. Though I have my suspicions, obviously.

Two minutes and thirty seconds later the alarm went off.

Before I even get to the security office two guards fall in to accompany me. They step up the moment I walk forward from the crowd, my right hand raised in a limp *mea culpa*. One minute I'm totally, horribly alone, the next I've got a pair of brand-new friends. They say nothing but the way they shadow me, one at either shoulder, it's a bit like I've just sprouted a pair of giant blue wings. My body starts to feel all tingly and light and I begin to feel that at any second I might float away – and preferably not come back.

I've no idea of the way to Security Office D. I ask the right-hand guard and he motions straight ahead with the muzzle of his gun. For some reason I am scared, which is completely irrational seeing as how I've done nothing wrong. It's Liz they should be arresting if they're arresting anyone, for all that nonsense she was spouting back at our workstation. Maybe that's why they're calling me in, to inform on her. Or maybe they're going to give me some kind of award for not taking any of her shit. Or maybe a promotion. Maybe they're so impressed they're going to give me a higher clearance level. Then when I talk to Liz outside the base we'd both be equals and she wouldn't need to fill in forms reporting on whatever we've been saying. Then we could relax.

Inside Security Office D are several men I haven't seen before, plus Andrews. None of them look at all pleased to be there except for him. He's trying to look serious but it's obvious that he's pretending. So. No promotion then. The man sitting facing me I also recognize. He is Chief Security Officer Daniels; on the facility his word is law. I know this because he reminds us of it at our regular weekly security briefing session. These briefings were only monthly until 9/11, since which time CSO Daniels has been very busy what with the increased risk of air attack and all the new protesters who've joined the camp outside the gates. Heat is rising off his cheeks in waves and his eyes hover and bounce like water droplets on a stove. I've got this urge to try to turn down the heat, stop them burning up, but that's a crazy person thinking, my secret inner me. I can't say I've ever liked CSO Daniels very much, though I certainly admire him; he's like someone in a Gap ad, the sort of perfect human specimen you can't help but hold in a minor kind of awe. If he hauls Liz in for questioning, she'll probably come back and tell me he's a decent guy as well.

To my rear the two members of my personal entourage are standing tight-faced and to attention; Andrews is hovering over to my right. He's set his teeth in this peculiar way I've never seen before, I think to try to make his jaw look squarer, which presumably means that Daniels's presence is making him feel insecure. Daniels is in uniform; the two suits sitting either side of him are not. They are either middle managers or lawyers, it's difficult to tell. The one on the right has sharp features, waxy; the other's face is rubbery and swollen like a basketball – or like he likes a drink. I presume they're both American – that self-righteous glow, it's unmistakable. They couldn't look more serious if they were stepping up to impeach the President. Suddenly I feel quite important. I wonder what I've done?

'Are you Cooper James?'

'That's correct.'

'This anything to do with you?' Daniels's voice is calmer than his face. Daniels's face is funny; his voice is not. His voice says: *Take me seriously*. It also says: *Do not fuck about*.

'What?' I say. I have no idea what he is talking about.

'This!' he says, pointing to a silver canister the size and shape of a freeze-dried-coffee tin of the kind they stock in the General Stores here on base to make the Americans feel at home. I think, in fact, it *is* a freeze-dried-coffee tin. Any label that there was has been removed, revealing the spaced corrugations common to such tins. The lid isn't the original lid. It's a metal one that's been fixed with three neatly soldered catches like mini versions of the ones you get on bottles of Grolsch. A simple symbol – a sort of square inside a circle – has been crudely engraved into its centre, a symbol that looks like this:

'I don't drink coffee,' is what I say. It's true. I don't. Coffee gives me stomach cramps. If I want caffeine I have a Coke. When it comes to hot drinks I'm strictly a tea man.

'What do you think this is, James? Do you think this is some kind of joke? We've had to run evacuation drill for the entire facility because of what's in this canister.'

'Whoever sent it has committed a major offence under US Federal Law,' says one of the lawyers, the sharper, thinner one.

'Why? What's in it?'

'Why don't you take a look-see for yourself?' Daniels says this like I am a child. I am not a child. I may be an employee but I am not a child. I am, however, beginning to feel more than slightly short of breath.

I walk forward to the desk and pick up the canister. It's pretty heavy, heavier than you'd expect a coffee canister to be. At a stretch I can just about hold it in my left hand without help from my right. Tucking it into the crook of my arm, I unclick the catches one by one. After that the lid's still quite tight and, again, unaccountably heavy. Gingerly, trying to keep the opening pointing as far away from me as possible, I start to ease it off.

The looser it gets the tighter my lungs become. I don't know what I'm expecting to find inside. Maybe a dead man's finger, or a tarantula, or a joke jack-in-the-box that will give me a minor heart attack when it springs out into the room. But the lid comes away and nothing happens, so I unscrunch my eyes and untense my neck and take a look at what the canister contains. Which is nothing really, just this weird and lumpy dust. Sort of grey in colour, like dirty sand. With orange streaks.

'It seems to be some kind of dust,' I say.

One of the guards takes the canister, replaces the lid, and puts it back down on the desk. The irises in Daniels's eyes spin like twin propellors. 'Some kind of dust?'

I don't know whether or not I'm angry. Certainly I'm feeling scared. 'What's this got to do with me?'

Perhaps Daniels is not in charge, perhaps's he's psychic, perhaps the lawyers are capable of independent thought. But one of them – the left-hand one – now holds up a huge and battered Jiffy envelope. On it is the address of the facility, handwritten in purple marker pen; three Airmail stickers, randomly distributed; a grimy mosaic of US stamps; and my name. 'It came in this,' he says, as he places the envelope on the table.

'Someone sent this canister to me?' I ask pathetically.

Andrews has been bouncing around on his toes during all of this. Now he speaks. 'Anthrax hoax,' he says.

Daniels's irises stop spinning and ratchet back to reveal the nose cones of twin ICBMs. He points them first at Andrews and then at me.

'Who do you know in the United States who might have sent this package?'

'Nobody. I've never been to the United States.'

'So the name Jack Reever means nothing to you?'

My lungs, which have been struggling with the task of breathing anyway, now try to swallow themselves. 'Did you say Jack Reever?' I say.

'Jack Reever. That's correct.'

My lungs are full of sand. 'I need my inhaler,' I manage to say.

But Daniels doesn't seem to hear me. At least, he doesn't answer me. He just repeats the question.

'Yes,' I gasp. No one reacts to this except for Andrews, who nods violently, sticks his hands into his pockets and flexes his thighs like he needs to take a piss. I feel terrible. I think I'm going to pass out. Daniels signals to one of the guards who grabs my hand and bicep and holds me rigid and upright. Then he whispers something to the lawyer who'd produced the envelope.

'What about the initials DECD? Do you know of any organization going by this name?'

I shake my head. Daniels leans across to the skinny lawyer and confers again. Then he picks up the canister and holds it towards me so that I can see its base. On it, written in the same purple marker pen as used on the envelope, are the words:

REEVER, Jack
D.E.C.D.

'Dad,' I say. And faint.

On the Cliff

Liz can't believe I fainted like I did. She keeps on mentioning it, and long before we get to Bempton Cliffs I'm already wishing I hadn't told her that it happened.

'I'm bringing you along for emotional support,' I say. 'Not to take the piss.'

'I'm not taking the piss. Honestly. I'm not. But still. *Fainting*. I mean, that went out with the Victorians, right? And even then it was just for girls.'

'So you don't think that not to see my father for twenty years then have him turn up inside a tin of instant coffee does not qualify as a limit experience, emotionally speaking?'

'But you always hated him, is what you told me.'

'I don't care. He was still my father.'

'I don't know,' says Liz. 'It strikes me that fathers earn the name by being there.'

Typically, the only space left in the car park is next to the short row of turquoise Portaloos. I don't want to leave the car there because I don't think it's properly reverential but Liz says don't be stupid, I should be thankful there's any spaces left at all and we don't have to park half a mile back down the road. So we leave the car there and walk out along the path that leads towards the cliffs. It's a Sunday and the paths are busy. Discarded crisp packets and empty cans of Fanta decorate the gorse.

We follow in the wake of a pikey-looking family. Mum, dad, three kids. Dad is wearing a cap with a minature sheep-doll mounted on its brim. I've no idea why. Maybe it's some kind of portable memorial for all the deaths caused by last year's foot-and-mouth. Mum's a blimp, clingwrapped in jogging sweats and a mauve windcheater, tiny white Reeboks on her feet. Snared back with a rubber band into a thick lank wad, her hair looks the colour and consistency of liquorice. The two small boys bob and bounce behind her, their bobble hats and padded jackets transforming them into characters from *South Park*. Bringing up the rear, teen daughter walks in a slouch, head hung low, a scowl of bitter resignation on her face. She has her mother's figure, that's obvious enough, despite the ankle-length rubber trenchcoat. Her hair is over-washed and cut into a bob. With that and the purple lipstick she's wearing she looks like a lifestyle columnist. This family, I want to machine-gun them from defensible positions. I want to strew landmines in their driveway. I want to tie up dad and ravish girl and brown the two kids like sausages over a crackling fire of mum. Then I want to say I'm sorry and fly backwards round the world like Superman and place my own body between them and the bullets I've just fired, across the Claymores I've been planting. Then I want to marry girl and play football with the boys and share a laugh with mum and drink beers with the patriarch out in his little triangle of garden with the Flymo and the barbecue.

I don't know what I want. But I do think it's funny when a seagull swoops down suddenly from out the sky and grabs an orange lollipop off one of the kids.

'God, did you see that bird?' says Liz, astonished. 'That was so vicious.'

'Interspecies rivalry,' I say. 'Revenge against these creatures who've been stealing eggs for centuries and now have started poisoning the sea.'

'That poor kid. He's really upset.'

'Oh well. I'm sure mummy'll comfort him.'

'Don't be so heartless.'

'Why not? I don't see what it's got to do with me.'

We detour around the fractured family, stopped in the middle of the path to attend to this disruption in its ranks, and walk on for a while in silence.

'Thanks for coming,' I say eventually, not because I'm feeling guilty about being cynical about the seagull ambush but because I'm feeling stupid about getting upset at Liz's teasing me about my fainting fit. 'I didn't want to have to do this on my own.'

She takes my hand and squeezes it. Gives me a smile. And now I'm feeling happy again. What percentage of me, I wonder, is using this whole ashes thing just to get Liz alone, all to myself.

'Let's go this way,' she says, and we fork off down a sheep track towards an area where there are fewer people. It's a bright October day. Clouds have been described too many times to make it worth doing again, but I'll do it anyway: the ones overhead are curdled like the egg in egg-drop soup and moving fast, while on the horizon, out at sea, a static log of beancurd lolls. Gulls dip and caw about our heads, becoming more belligerent in proportion to our proximity to the edge. After what happened to the little boy I'm a bit afraid of them.

Already I'm wondering if coming here to cast the ashes was such a good idea. I share this fear with Liz. She asks me if it's possible I could be any more neurotic. So I turn the fear around and tell her that what I'm really worried about is that the ashes will get blown back by the wind towards the cliff and suffocate some day-old chick hidden in a fissure down on the rockface. But she just laughs at this, like I can't possibly be serious.

I want Liz to treat the occasion with a bit more gravity. If she isn't serious then I don't think I'll manage to do this thing and this whole outing is quickly going to deteriorate into some kind of farce. I can feel it. Since I received the ashes I've been suffering what I think are mood swings. On balance I should consider this an improvement, since as a rule I'm just depressed. But there's something undermining about feeling joyous because your father's dead.

We arrive at the cliff's edge and peer over the lip of turf down to the sea. Instantly I get vertigo. 'I don't know if I can deal with this.'

'Try lying down.' We do that thing, feet pointing inland, heads jutting out into space. Even now I have to clutch at the grass, growing here luxuriant as polythene. The impression of being about to dive head first into the blue is an almost overwhelming one. Cooper + Freefall onto Rocks = End of Problems. I worry that my glasses are going to fall off. I wish I had one of those sports things, made of neoprene, that fix around your head. I make a mental note to buy one the next time I see an outdoor sports outlet and carry it with me always.

'Look.' I point across to an outcrop of rock a couple of hundred metres to our left from which three dayglo figures hang neatly backdropped by the beancurd cloud and miso-coloured sea. 'Maniacs. You've climbed here, haven't you?'

'It's good, but the chalk's rotten at the top, so you have to watch it. And you're only allowed to use ice-screws and pitons so you don't damage the ascent.'

I've no idea what a piton is nor am I in the mood to care. 'It looks difficult,' I say.

'It's an E4,' she answers breezily.

The coffee can is digging into my ribcage so I pull it out and hold it over the precipice.

'It would be easiest just to drop this into the sea.'

'So maybe that's what you should do.'

'I need to think about it first.'

'Do you want to talk about it?'

'I don't know what to say.'

'Can I ask a question?'

'Shoot.'

'What's with you and your father having different names? How does that work?'

'Oh, that. It's sort of complicated.'

'I've got all day.'

I don't answer straight away. Instead, I watch the climbers. They are moving very slowly. It's weird the way they seem glued onto the cliff face by their wrists and ankles. I'd say they look like insects, but they don't, not really. They look more like . . . I don't know. Like fridge magnets, or something.

I didn't see a fridge magnet until I was eleven. Don't worry – I realize this doesn't make me a total victim or anything. It's just one of the things I remember about going to live with my aunt and uncle, after my father had left Stasie and me.

Where I grew up before that, it was this commune down in Cornwall, a few miles outside of Newquay, on the northern Cornish coast. We lived up in this old farmhouse on a cliff that overlooked the sea, which is partly why I thought Bempton Cliffs would be a good place to scatter Jack's ashes. There were about twenty of us in all, though numbers varied as people came and went. There were lots of kids, which was cool – and useful too, because whenever we came in for shit at the school, which was all the time, we could find safety in numbers.

Mum and Jack had met at the Isle of Wight festival in 1969 – listening to Blodwyn Pig, if you believed their stoned and much recycled version of the great event. Jack's twenty-three probably looked pretty impressive to Stasie's nineteen; he had facial hair and a good line in boho rhetoric which was somehow made much easier to swallow by the fact of his being American. He was going to save the world through art or something, the logic being that someone had to, seeing how science was doing such a good job of wrecking it. Nuclear deterrents, flush toilets, suburban housing, central heating, fast food, personal hygiene – these things were the enemy. Strung out on speed and dope and acid, Stasie wholeheartedly agreed, and the two of them 'built a boat of love and floated it away', as one of her better songs described it.

They spent a couple of years roaming around Europe on Jack's motorbike before they got round to having me. Mum used to tell me I was conceived on the beach at Le Lavandou when it was still a quiet and unknown backwater. Once when I was seven or eight and a group of us were driving down through France to Spain she insisted we make an impromptu two-day detour and try to find the place, so she could show me the exact location of the great event. I of course was mortally embarrassed, and my privacy and pride were saved only by the fact that since my parents' last visit the area had become a heaving tourist trap and virtually unrecognizable. As we drove up and down the coast, exploring multitudinous side roads while Stasie railed and bitched about tourists and plastic waste and the 'so-called march of progress' and everyone's tempers wore ever more thin, I alone was happy, sitting quietly in the back sending up silent prayers to whatever higher power I believed in then and getting a full-on buzz of wish fulfilment every time one of my mother's excited hopes soured into yet another false alarm.

Jack Reever was a sculptor. And a pretty good one too, I'll give him that. He worked in wood and was always on the lookout for stuff to carve. Anywhere we went with him, he'd have us lugging bits of bush or tree he'd snagged from some hedge or beach or roadside spinney. These would go into the wood store behind the 'studio' he shared with Tom, i.e. the biggest and oldest of the various barns and farm buildings arrayed around the house itself.

Tom was quiet, from Lancashire I think. His beard was long and blond and all twisted up and he wore his hair in a slim ponytail. He had pale and smoky skin and his eyes were always rimmed with pink, like at any moment he was going to cry. Tom never said much; when he did almost the only thing he ever talked about was trees. Everyone teased him because of this, but he was the one person in the commune who never fell out with anyone.

Jack and him, they'd walk around the woods near where we lived hunting out oaks and chestnuts and dying elms and junipers, weighing up their merits, discussing how long it would be before they were 'ready'. When the right time came they'd go and lop off a couple of branches – usually at night, since this activity was invariably taking place on someone else's property – and haul their booty back to the barn, where they'd peel off the bark and season the wood with different oils before wrapping it up in plastic sheets sliced out of ancient fertilizer bags and putting it away.

And then they'd wait. Sometimes they'd wait for four or five years before they'd get round to carving a particular piece. They had some pieces they'd laid down before I was born, like wine. To test if a particular piece was ready they'd peel back the wrapper and sniff the wood and test it with their thumbnails, and then sometimes Dad would carve off a sliver or two using the little silver pocket knife he always carried with him. If I asked him what he was doing he'd say he was getting the 'feel of the material', and then pass the piece to me. And I'd touch it and sniff it and put on a concentrated expression, like I understood what he was saying, like I was already started down the road of being a serious carver just like him. But Genetics + Desire ≠ Talent, and the fact is that I was never quite able to grasp what he was getting at, beyond its being a nice-looking sliver of wood. Maybe that's all there was to grasp, maybe that's what I was missing. I was certainly missing something, that's for sure.

However wonderful and beneficial the sensibilities and principles my father was trying to instil in me, I was generally far happier fooling around on the beach with the other kids than listening to him. That was the absolute best thing about where we lived, the beach. It was an absolutely perfect place, a private cove pebbled with disc-shaped skimming stones and walled in by cliffs all cavey at their bases with kid-sized cracks and runnels that the ancient English sea had obligingly gnawed away. The only access was by the steep path than ran from our back gate (unless you came by boat, of course), and so the place was effectively our private playground, a perfect theatre in which to act out endless intersecting scenarios of piracy, shipwreck and war.

These games, they were our reality. They were certainly more real than what happened at school. I still blame my complete inability to speak more than three words of French on the intricate battle plans I compulsively drew up while Mr Speight droned on about tenses and prepositions and how *Monsieur et Madame Camembert et leurs deux enfants ennuyeuses aiment la nouvelle voiture*. The games infected everything. We ate school meals in character, stole food for hidden caches, fashioned weapons with bits of wood and metal filched from CDT, passed notes written in secret codes during lessons and assembly. At the end of the day we'd spill out of the bus that dropped us at the end of our lane, race back through the farm hurling our satchels and sports bags over the wall into the garden, and bypassing the house completely charge straight off down the cliff path to pick up where we'd left off the previous evening. We'd play until we were called in for for tea and then packed off to bed, where the games would continue in our dreams.

It's funny. All those games, so important and absorbing at the time – these days I can hardly remember them, at least not in any detail. And my strongest memory of the beach isn't a game at all, but something much more tangible, much more real, something that I suppose, looking back, was one of those events that arrive in your life with increasing frequency as you grow up and the essential dullness of existence slowly and surely displaces games for ever.

One day at breakfast Tom burst into the kitchen to announce he'd found a young orca, a killer whale, washed up in the surf. Of course we all hurried out the house to look at it – about thirty of us in all, I think, what with the friends and randoms who had come to stay for the holidays. The whale lay on the beach like a collapsed balloon; we could see it as soon as we reached the cliff edge. As he turned off onto the narrow path that led down to the beach Jack wondered aloud what it was doing in these waters this time of year. It was Mum who answered him. 'It's a message from America,' she said, a non-joke at which I remember laughing loudly and automatically even though – or maybe, thinking about it now, actually because – I had no idea what it was she meant.

Shouting and whooping we crashed across the pebbles, us children running on ahead, the wind raking at our eyes and faces as we ran towards the yellow crusts of surf. But when we got to our destination it wasn't clear what we should do. No one wanted to touch the creature. The corpse was already partly putrid and stank terribly unless you stayed upwind of it. What if whales had ghosts? As it lay there on its side all pale against the shingle, skeins of foam gurgling in and out its mouth, this looked more than possible. The effect was so strange, so ectoplasmic that Jake, the eldest of what we thought of as 'the kids' and old enough that he liked to think himself an adult (and therefore superior to the rest of us – he didn't believe in ghosts), announced that the animal was still alive and ran back to tell the others that this was so. Believing him, they quickened their pace a little, expressions set, beards and hair and skirts and shirts billowing and blowing, like actors trying to recreate the nineteenth century on a location film set. Which, I suppose, is pretty much exactly what they were.

When they reached us it was explained to Jake that whales

breathe through their blow holes not their mouths and that the the noise he thought was breathing was being caused by the movement of the surf. '*I* knew that,' Jake insisted, then pointed to the rest of us – Max, Moon, Jaycey, Otter, Leaf and me – and said we were the ones who thought whales breathed through their mouths. On hearing this Max, who was only a year Jake's junior and the great pretender to his throne, called him a liar and started trying to wrestle him to the ground. The two of them scrapped until Jack grabbed them by their jacket hoods and threatened them with a dunking in the ocean if they didn't behave.

That seemed to settle it and everyone calmed down again and focused on the whale. The men talked about its shape, its 'lines', its perfect evolutionary fitness, the women about the radiance of its being, the kids about how its skin looked dark and tough as tractor inner tubes and how even Jake's farts couldn't out-compete its smell. Summer, who was in reality called Celia, birth mother to Moon and Leaf (male, ten; female, six) and notoriously sensitive and highly strung, began to cry. Jake, intent on reimposing his superiority in the face of Max's attack and the sudden barrage of fart jokes, started scudding pebbles at me.

Mats – a bisexual Swedish freak who'd been with us about a year – said why didn't we take a plaster cast of the carcass, in order to preserve its shape. Though it wasn't his idea Jack quickly took it up, I think mainly because Mats had just finished having an affair with Stasie and Jack was trying to prove he had no hard feelings.

But Jack had no right to hard feelings anyway, seeing how it was entirely his fault that Mats and Stasie had got together in the first place. Although partner-swapping wasn't actively encouraged within the commune, it was 'allowed' under the rubrics of self-growth, friendship and personal fulfilment. What was definitely forbidden was casual sex with random outsiders. The community had originally been formed by five couples, and the theory was that if a new couple wanted to come and live with us (singles weren't allowed, though we had two lesbian couples and one supposedly homosexual, one half of which was Mats) then for the sake of stability and harmony partner-swapping was not allowed between the newcomers and more long-standing members until a grace period of six months had elapsed. There were lots of rules like this. There always are. The commune was an enclave like any other, and the sets of codes and regulations it erected around itself worked like a missile shield to keep the big bad world from butting in. And like all the rules this one got bent. Still, I don't remember it being seriously challenged, not until Jack brought Shannon in.

Shannon was the perfect all-American hippie, from somewhere in Vermont. Pretty in a Calvin Klein kind of a way she was also young – eighteen, nineteen tops. She and her friend Deborah had been hiking along the Cornish coast that spring, and Tom and Jack had discovered them camping in the woods behind the farm.

Shannon got along with everyone (or all the men at least) and ended up staying with us while the more conventional Deborah moved on. After Shannon had been with us about a month Stasie left the commune for a few weeks to play some European festivals. Jack stayed behind – he was working on a sculpture he said; it was at a crucial stage, he couldn't leave. But with Stasie gone his work suddenly seemed mainly to consist of long walks in the woods alone with Shannon, walks which were instantly the subject of almost every adult conversation – and quite a lot of the kids' conversations too.

Everybody knew, everybody talked. But it was Moon who blew the whistle. The night of Stasie's return, right in the middle of the impressive 'welcome home' dinner that all the adults had fussed and stressed to prepare like it was some kind of expression of their collective guilt, as if they were all responsible for what had happened and not just Jack, Moon came out and said it in that matter of fact way children have, especially children like us, who'd been brought up to be used to things like that.

'While you were gone Jack and Shannon have been having sex together.'

Silence descended on the table. Then Stasie freaked. She ran upstairs and Jack ran upstairs after her and the rest of us (except for Shannon, who rushed out to the barn, and Moon, who started crying, unsure quite what he'd done wrong) sat and finished our dinner in stony silence while my parents' muffled shouts descended through the floor.

According to Jack it was just a fling and Stasie had no reason to be jealous, but obviously she was. There was a whole series of major rows, screaming matches; Jack got up on his high horse about the English obsession with conformity, about how the whole point about living the way we did was that everyone should be free to do exactly what they liked. But the others didn't agree and soon enough he found himself isolated – a situation he wasn't used to and didn't like.

Much to the horror of his then partner Ralph, a fey Cambridge drop-out, Mum then started screwing Mats to get her own back. This widened the conflict so much that for a while it looked like threatening the existence of the commune itself. But in the end it was Shannon who cracked first. Partly upset by the trouble that she'd caused and partly annoyed because Stasie's tactic had got Jack worried that he might lose her for good, one day she could stand it no more and left – along with Ralph, who'd had his faith in communal living completely obliterated by Mats's betrayal. Triumphantly Stasie kicked Mats out of her bed and let Jack, his tail between his legs, come crawling back. For a while things reached a sort of equilibrium. And then we found the whale.

It was hard work, taking the cast. We began by bringing ropes and pallets down from the barn and using them to haul the whale further up the beach, above the bladderwrack and bottle tide mark, beyond the reach of the waves. While Jack and Mats got down to constructing the mould and Angus – Summer's husband, a great big Scottish guy – took Jake and Otter into town in the VW to buy a couple of sackloads of plaster of Paris and a giant tub of grease Tom, Moon, Max and me carried the old paddling pool down to the beach and started filling it with fresh water we ferried down the cliff in a variety of cans and buckets.

They didn't make it how I thought they would. Instead of building a square box around the carcass, filling it with a vat-load of plaster of Paris and producing a giant impression of enormous weight – heavier, probably, than the dead whale itself, which had taken two dozen of us pushing and tugging just to shift a few metres further up the beach – they cut and rigged boards to form a close-fitting loop about halfway up the body, like they were constructing a life-sized wooden orca stencil. It was past lunchtime when they were done, and we had just set about building a fire from driftwood and the left over scraps of timber when a procession started down the cliff path towards us: Stasie, Margaret and Summer bearing sandwiches and a giant pan of soup; followed by Angus, sacks of plaster of Paris draped over his shoulders like enormous epaulettes; followed by Jake, who bounced down the path unable to see where he was going past the tall stack of empty buckets he was cradling in his arms. We watched him anxiously, half fearing and half hoping that he'd take a comical (but not too painful) tumble down the slope. But somehow he managed to make it to the bottom without major mishap.

After a break for food we started up a little production line of plaster mixing, churning and churning the gloop around in the paddling pool then passing pails of it to Jack and Mats for careful application. They'd already smeared the upper portion of the orca with an even layer of grease and now, using their pitted, craftsmen's hands as spatulas, they creamed the plaster on, like they were applying a mysterious ointment that would magically reanimate the giant beast.

It was almost dark when we were done and everyone was tired. Max and Jake had exhausted themselves by warring with plaster gobbets, a battle which had at one point widened like a bar-room brawl until everyone was flicking plaster at everybody else. This continued until Leaf took a chance hit in her eye and started crying, prompting Angus and Summer to step in and call a halt, by which time we were all dappled with leprous-looking patches that later on we'd peel off our arms like scabs to reveal miraculously pink, healthy and 100 per cent rejuvenated skin beneath. So one by one people left the scene until only Jack, Mats, Moon and me were left, the two men smoothing on the last of the plaster and checking for fissures and weak points while Moon and I watched them from over by the fire. It had been an incredible day and I didn't want it to be over; for the first time in months the commune had felt like a happy family once again.

That night after dinner (split-pea curry and black bread baked by Margaret on the collapsing Aga, with stewed plums and milk pudding for afters) Moon and I crept out onto the clifftop to have another look at our handiwork. The moon – the real moon – was bright and full and by its light we could see clear down to the beach where the body lay, all the more alone now the tide was out. With its flared white carapace tinted amber by the glowing embers of our fire, it didn't any longer look much like a whale at all, more like a strange kind of time machine or space ship that we were building to transport us to another place, another planet, another life.

The following afternoon ten or twelve of us returned to the beach to ease the dead creature from its shroud. Despite the cold the plaster had dried thoroughly and after a tense few minutes of probing and testing the men declared themselves pleased with the result. The idea was to upend the mould like a giant turtle's shell, flipping it over on to a makeshift cradle of ropes that Tom and Dad had rigged the night before. It wasn't going to be an easy job, even with four grown men and various small boys and girls to help: the construction was twelve feet long, the size and shape of a small boat, and initially it wouldn't budge. The layer of grease was making the mould cling to the carcass like a mussel to a rock and Jack and Angus had to lie down on the shingle and kick at the belly of the orca in order to break the bones of its ribcage and collapse it a bit in order to introduce some air beneath the mould and disrupt the suction. It worked – the next time we tried the whole thing came away with a phenomenal farting noise that was immediately imitated by Moon and me and Max and Jake.

I think I'd expected something pristine and perfect to emerge, something that would somehow help restore the lustre to the newly tarnished image of my father. But at first the cast wasn't much to look at, not with all the grease and filth and bits of timber hanging off it, and I remember feeling an enormous sense of anticlimax and disappointment. But the men, they seemed very happy. They trimmed it off, sluiced it with sea water, then hauled it up the cliffside and stood it in one of the barns to dry completely for a day or two before cleaning it thoroughly and generally tidying it up. And that's when the orca finally emerged: leaping from its death mask, luminant and graceful. I still think it was maybe the most beautiful thing I've ever seen.

Jack and Tom especially were very proud of it, and they rigged up a rope cradle and hauled the thing up into the rafters of their studio so it could hang above their heads as a source of inspiration while they worked, a negative that seemed suffused with all the life that had fled from the bones of its eerie positive, rotting into an unwholesome mess and being got at by seabirds and foxes where we'd left it on the beach. It was still hanging there when Reever disappeared from our lives for ever, not long after. For all I know it hangs there still.

'And he just upped and left?' asks Liz.

'Yeah. He said he had to go back to the States to renew his visa but we never saw him again.'

'But why? If things were all sorted out.'

I shrug, look away. 'Maybe they weren't,' I croak. 'Maybe there was other stuff going on I didn't know about.'

Liz shakes her head. 'I find that just . . . incredible. How could someone do that? It's just so completely callous. I'm so sorry Cooper. I don't know what to say. Didn't he even write you? Call you? Anything?'

'Not as far as I know. Stasie never showed me any letters. But she used to go on about him having gone to join Shannon and she seemed pretty certain about it so I think he must have done, once or twice at least.'

'And that's when you took your mother's name?'

'You already worked that out?'

Liz nods.

'After Reever left and the divorce came through Stasie insisted on changing both our surnames back to James, her maiden name. And she changed my first name too.'

'Cooper's not your real name?'

'It's my middle name. My real first name is . . . Ash.'

'Ash!'

'Don't *laugh.*'

'I'm not laughing,' she says, though she is. 'Jesus. *Ash.*'

'It was Jack's favourite tree,' I say, a little defensively. 'The wood is really good for carving, apparently.'

'Wow. They sure went for that hippy thing, didn't they just? Actually, you know, I think it's kind of cool.'

'Yeah, right.'

'Well it's better than Moon,' she giggles, presumably glad to be off the subject of Jack's incomprehensible heartlessness. 'Or Leaf.'

'Only just.'

I look over at the climbers, who've inched their way a bit further up the rock face. The colours of their jackets, I realize, correspond to the colours of the Post-it notes I've got stuck up on my monitor. I wish I hadn't noticed that. Now I want to change the way the climbers are arranged, spread them out a little, space them more symmetrically along the grey rake of the cliff.

'What about your mother?'

'She had her ups and downs. She tried going back to her music for a while, touring quite a lot. In the beginning she tried taking me with her, but that didn't work out so I went to live with my Uncle Matthew, back in Nottingham.'

'And what was he like?'

'Normal. Nice. An accountant, if you can believe that. Lived in a big house with Janet, his housewife wife, and their two daughters, Katherine and Vanessa. Stasie used to call them the cuboids, and they really were. They read the *Telegraph*, didn't let us watch ITV. The two girls were a few years older than me, though it didn't always seem it. Working hard at their exams, heading towards university, suburbia, the real world.'

'And where's your mum now?'

'Oh, she's been back in Nottingham for a while now, living in

Grandma and Grandad's old house, running a "Calm Centre" or "Spiritual Retreat" or some such rubbish. After the music gave out she discovered she had a gift as a faith healer, though if you ever met her you'd realize what a joke that was.'

'Do you still see her?'

'Every now and then. She doesn't have too much time for me these days. Too busy rushing around waving her crystals over some poor bastard's backache, or realigning the chakras of her neighbour's neurotic cat. It hardly seems worth it, most of the time. She's still one chip short of a motherboard, if you ask me.'

'And do you blame your dad for that?'

'Don't analyse me, Liz.'

'I'm not.'

'Yes you are. You're trying to get to the bottom of something there's no bottom to. It's not even that it's shallow. It just doesn't exist. I put family life behind me a long time ago.'

'I'm just asking you how you feel, that's all. You don't have to talk about it if you don't want to.'

'So I guess I don't want to. Okay?'

'Sure. Whatever.'

For a while we stare in silence at the sea. And then we hear a yell. It's the climbers. One of them, the middle one, is waving and calling out. Or that's what I think at first. Then I realize he's fending off a bird. One of the seagulls that use the thermals of the cliffs like a bank of speedy executive elevators is dive-bombing him.

Liz starts getting to her feet, worried that the climber's going to fall.

'I don't see what you can do,' I say. 'He's either been roped up properly or not. We'll soon know either way.'

'There might not be safety lines,' she says quietly. She stays standing, facing away from me. From where I'm lying I can see the muscles tensing in her neck.

I'm calm about what's happening because I'm assuming that the seagull is going to relent. But it doesn't. Knocked back by the climber's flailing arm it gyres around and comes again, diving first then flipping in the air and flapping a series of strong, hard downstrokes that bring its outstretched claws into contact with his head. His purple helmet proves no protection from panic: as we watch he lifts his second hand from the crevice in which he's had it jammed and uses it to try to fend the bird away. Pointless, of course; deprived of an upper-body hold he slowly peels away from the rock face and starts to plummet towards the small group of people gathered on the thin beach down below, a man-sized block of stone cleaved by a silent explosion from a quarry wall.

As quickly as his dive begins it ends. The climber falls about ten or twelve feet past the next bloke in the chain before jerking to a halt and hanging limply by his belt like a broken Action Man. There's a fresh moment of tension as he swings violently and catches parts of himself on the rock, spinning in and out of view. But then his feet kick out and he steadies himself into a cantilever, pats his body with his hands and signals a thumbs-up to his teammates, a result that leaves me feeling partly relieved and partly disappointed.

'See,' I say, as the leisure-seekers spangling the landscape resume their hikes and picnics, 'it was all to do with how well roped up he was.'

'Cooper, when did you last do any climbing? When did you *ever* do any climbing?' says Liz, looking at me for the first time since the beginning of the mini crisis. 'You don't know the first thing about it.' She shifts her gaze to the coffee tin I still have clutched in my two hands, perhaps noticing how white my knuckles have gone. 'Are we going to cast those ashes or aren't we?'

'I don't know,' I say, looking down at the tin and ordering my fingers to relax.

'You should think about it carefully. Is it what he would have wanted?'

'I don't give a shit about what he would have wanted! It's what I want.' I'm shouting, I realize, but before I have time to say something in a quieter, more considered voice a violent streak of white shrieks down from the sky, grabs at the silver can and knocks it from my grasp. I go one way, the seagull goes another. The can goes a third, rolling off enthusiastically towards the cliff's turfy lip.

I'm too stunned by the totally unexpected nature of the air attack to do anything but watch it go, as apparently is Liz. I flatten myself back in my original position just in time to see it gimbal down the lower slopes, heeling up little gouts of dust whenever its rims nip the scree. It comes to rest on the shoreline, less a beach than a limestone shelf, about ten yards from the sea.

For a moment neither of us says anything.

Then: 'Well the top seems to have stayed on, anyway,' Liz observes.

I purse my lips. There are no words.

'You could just leave him, abandon him to the waves,' she suggests. 'It would be sort of poetic. After all, that's pretty much what he did to you.'

I watch the waves unfurl themselves, happy in their nested families of threes and fours and eights, then I look beyond them, out over the psychotic vastness of the sea. But it's like a kind of blindness, a suffocation of my visual field, and within a couple of seconds I switch my eyes back to the dark zags of the footpath cut into the cliff face to our left, so much steeper than the cliff path I helped haul the orca cast up almost twenty years ago. My gaze is drawn back by the silver can, a tiny shape, meaningless beside that white front of foam lazing away in both directions to slowly constrict this tired old island and all the millions stranded on it in its soft, geological embrace. I think of the dead whale and how the surf got in its mouth, made it seem to breathe. Most of all I think of the whale-sized void that was my father's parting gift.

'I want him back,' I say. My cheekbones thrum as the muscles bunched around my tear ducts start to vibrate.

Liz nods slowly. 'Then we'd better go and get him.'

Andrews

My car is minging. It's a Maestro, aka a total piece of shite. The Maestro is the king of shite cars. The bodywork is the colour of dead skin. The gearbox is pants and even the door panels don't fit. Liz calls it 'the pony', a term she seems to find unaccountably amusing. Still, she rarely turns down the offer of a lift. She doesn't have a car and every day I pick her up and drive us both to work. She never gives me any money for petrol and sometimes I ask myself if she's taking advantage of the fundamental goodness of my heart. But I don't say anything because if we stopped sharing rides in the mornings she'd turn back into being my boss and I wouldn't be able to keep tabs on her and Andrews and whether or not he's spent the night at her place. He hasn't yet, but that doesn't mean he isn't going to.

When I pick up Liz the next morning it's pissing down. I pull up outside her house and beep the horn, and a minute or two later she comes tottering down the path towards the garden gate, huddled inside her raincoat like a geisha, leather satchel cradled in her arms, deploying that strange run of hers that seems to involve solely muscles located below the knee. When she reaches the car she plumps herself in the front seat and sits there for a while, looking straight ahead, hood still up. The heat from her body steams up my glasses and the windscreen, and I wipe both with my sleeve. The result is unsatisfactory, to say the least, but it's the best I can do without professional equipment. The smears interfere with my vision in an exciting and intriguing way, doubling up the scene in front of me. Taking a guess at which cars are real and which the ghosts I pull away and set off down the street.

'Horrible day,' she says. No *Hello Cooper*, nothing like that. Not that I feel taken for granted, or anything.

'It's not raining in here,' I say. This in reference to her hood.

'Oh yeah,' she says, and she pulls it back and pads it down behind her neck, taking care to keep any drips of water away from her precious hair. 'So. How are you today?'

Oh, okay. Now she's asking. 'I think I've got toxoplasmosis,' I say.

'What on earth is that?'

'It's a parasite that lives inside the brains of humans, rats and cats. I read about it in *New Scientist*. I think it might explain why I have difficulty concentrating.'

'When do you have difficulty concentrating?'

'When I'm driving, mostly.'

'That's because you're a bad driver. Not because you've got some kind of microscopic creature inhabiting your cortex. You're such a hypochondriac.'

I ignore this and continue to expound my theory about how I would've almost certainly got infected as a child, living in that commune, but after a while I realize Liz isn't listening. Instead, she's digging around in the satchel she's still clutching in her lap.

'I brought you a present,' she says. She passes it to me and I take it nervously, trying all the time to keep my eyes on the road ahead. The present is wrapped in stripy wrapping paper, so I can't tell what it is. It's small and book-shaped so it's a book, probably. Either that or it's a Game Boy cartridge, boxed. Perhaps it's *Zelda*. Liz knows I've been wanting *Zelda*. I've been going on about it enough.

'What have I done to deserve this?' I ask. I'm pleased, basically. I've got this warm feeling in my lower intestine. It's *Zelda*, I'm positive.

'You don't know what it is yet. For all you know it might be a small but effective anti-Cooper device.'

'For all I know it might be. But I've got a feeling that it's not. Whatever it is, thank you.'

'Why don't you stop being so fucking polite, Cooper, and unwrap it.' It always sounds strange to me when Liz swears, as if this girl who looks like butter wouldn't melt has suddenly been possessed by Bride of Chucky.

I take my hands from the wheel and wave them in the air.

'Uh, duh! In case you haven't noticed, I am in fact der-riving. Do you want us both to *die*?' This amuses me, to be like this. It's like I'm taking the piss out of being American and simultaneously becoming more American, both at once. 'Anyway, I've already guessed what it is. It's *Zelda*, right? For my AGB? You've bought me *Zelda*. Which is extremely nice of you.'

'It's not *Zelda*. And stop overreacting. You overreact to everything.'

'I do not.'

'You do too. Oh – just give it here.' Liz reaches over and takes the package from where it's resting in my lap and unwraps it with a series of tidy, origami-esque hand movements, not tearing at the paper like I would have done but carefully removing it in one relatively unblemished piece. Then she hands whatever it was wrapped around back to me.

She's right. It isn't *Zelda*. It's not new media in any shape or form, it's old media. A book, to be precise. An old book, squat yet slender. The dust jacket, if there ever was one, is long gone; there's only a hard, navy-blue cotton cover shiny with age and use. The title's not written on the cover but is stamped in small black letters along the spine. In Latin, I do believe. I have to turn it to the light before I can read it, glancing down in between trying to keep my eyes on the road. *Hydriotaphia*, I think it says. I open it one-handed while steering round a milk float and a Hello Kitty postcard tumbles out, a message inscribed upon it in a childishly perfect copperplate. *To Cooper, who needs help. Love from Liz.*

'Er, thanks Liz,' I say. 'Sounds thrilling.'

'It's not a science-fiction novel, Cooper. It's a monograph.'

'A monograph?'

'That's right.'

'I don't get it.'

Liz lets out a sigh, takes the book from me and reads from the title page. '*Hydriotaphia: Urne Buriall; or, A Discourse of the Sepulchrall Urnes Lately Found in Norfolk*. It's an essay on human burial rites through the ages. By Sir Thomas Browne. He wrote it in 1658. It's a classic text. I thought it might be useful.'

'Useful?'

'In working out what to do with the ashes, dufus. They say that Thomas Browne was the last man alive who had read every book that was ever written.'

'No kidding,' I say, without enthusiasm.

'Can you imagine that? Can you imagine what it must be like to have absorbed the entirety of existing human knowledge?'

I try to imagine this. I try to imagine what it must be like to feel in command of your own culture, to sit on top of it and survey it with a chieftain's eye. I try to imagine what it must be like to live in a world where a lifetime's worth of reading matter – books, periodicals, newspapers, scientific journals, websites – is not published each and every minute. I try to imagine what it must be like not to be completely walled in by data, not to have invisible mountains of the stuff all around you and reaching up for ever into the sky. I try to imagine this but I cannot do it. It's no longer even possible to conceive of such a situation. I can't work out if this is exhilarating, depressing or entirely unremarkable. I mean, before there were so many books – or any books – it wasn't like stuff wasn't happening. It was just that people weren't writing books about it. Right? Or was the world genuinely simpler then? I contemplate running this little stream of thought by Liz, but I know what she would say. She'd say that's like asking if a tree falling in a forest makes a sound when there's no one there to hear it. And then I wouldn't be sure whether she had actually said something quite profound or whether she was talking utter bollocks or whether she was just making fun of me. So I don't say any of this. In the end, what I say is: 'No.'

The word leaves what feels like a bullet hole, hanging where I used to have a mouth. This ashes thing. It's getting to me.

Still, the fact that Liz has given me a present definitely lifts my mood, until we reach Featherbrooks at least. Whereupon we have to drive through an avenue of placard-waving protesters who think it's within their rights to scream obscenities at us and pelt my car with mud.

'Fuckers!' I say, as a six-inch splodge of what looks like cowshit splats across the window inches from my face. 'There could have been a stone in that! I tell you, if one of them damages my car, I won't be responsible for my actions.'

'I think you're a bit outnumbered, unfortunately.'

'Yeah, well, where the hell are the police? I didn't mind when they were just camped outside the gates but this is beyond a joke.'

'Cooper, I don't think a day's gone by since they got here that you haven't moaned about them, even before they started getting so belligerent. Though I think I might be starting to work out why.'

'What d'you mean by that?' I say, though I know exactly what she means and it infuriates me.

'Well, you know. What you told me on Saturday. About your scene when you were growing up.'

'That's total bollocks. My attitude towards these idiots has got nothing to do with that.'

'So what has it got to do with?'

'It's got to do with the simple fact that they're morons, basically. I mean, their ignorance stuns me. They haven't the faintest idea of the issues at stake. Don't they understand what it is that guarantees their precious freedom of speech? Don't they?'

'I'm not saying anything,' says Liz, clearly crushed by the flawless logic of my argument, 'except that if you don't slow down we're going to crash into the gate.'

On this point if no other she happens to be right, so I stop arguing and concentrate on getting through the checkpoint – something that takes an age now they're insisting on checking under every vehicle that goes in or out (why out, for God's sake?) for concealed explosives. The protesters have pissed me off so much that I sit in silence throughout the whole procedure, trying to read the introduction to the book Liz gave me. But I can't concentrate. See what I mean about toxoplasmosis? It's not natural, this.

Finally we clear security and I park the car and we hurry through the weather to our building. Today the rain doesn't bother me because today – yes! – I have my *own* umbrella. Once inside the lobby I shake it vigorously to prove it, spraying droplets of water across the carpet tiles and the snack machine, where they cling to the perspex food-viewing window like perspiration, like the snack machine's been working out.

Our office was refitted two years ago and now it's much like any other. Though you wouldn't've said that previously it had a particularly distinct aesthetic of its own, it did have a bit more of a military feel about it. But now it's just white corridors, doors of ash veneer, workstations arranged in clover-leaves or hedged around by cubicles, undusted aluminium window blinds, ceiling tiles the colour and texture of cheese rind. If it wasn't for the magnetic passcard readers on every door and the fact that the idiot brigade is camped outside we could be vetting insurance claims or strategizing record company PR. Still, it's probably fair to say that winning the contract to orchestrate the campaign for Britney's latest single probably doesn't require you to have a sixty-metre Ballistic Missile Early Warning System stapled to the roof. Although it probably won't be long before it does, the way things are going.

I'm being facetious, of course. There are rooms on the base that are very different from what you'd see if you did your time at any normal company. They look like the kind of thing that NASA builds in Houston to monitor satellites and communicate with shuttle missions: vast wall screens showing maps of the world faced by terraces of terminals, stages for a non-stop ballet of technology. But I personally have never been inside these rooms; these rooms aren't for the likes of me. I've only seen them in photographs, some of which are displayed around the facility, some of which are posted on nuclear protest sites I've found on the web. Actually, that's where I get most of my information about Featherbrooks. Maybe one of the reasons I get so angry with the protestors is because of the growing feeling I've been getting lately that they know more about what's going on here than I do.

Where I work it's sort of semi-open plan, and as I walk in I can see that Josie, Pauline and Suhail are already at their desks. In this main area eight people sit; off it is a smaller zone which is home to Liz, Bruce, Simon and me. Off that is the soundproof office that is Andrews's lair.

I get to my computer and switch it on. At my feet the tower bucks and stirs like an old dog being chivvied out of bed. There's a sealed memo in my in-tray but I don't open it right away – for me the day doesn't begin until I've bathed my face in streaming rads.

The screen blurts awake and the familiar fragments of fossilized DOS crag up. White and ancient, they linger for a second or two before being smothered by the first Windows splash. Bravely, willfully, the command lines rattle back, but then Windows unfurls its backdrop of faked cumulus for the final and decisive time and marks the arrival of this theoretically fair and fulsome weather with that dumb thunder roll.

'Have you ever noticed the dragon hidden in the clouds?' I say to Liz, who's returning from the kitchenette with her customary cup of herbal tea.

'What?'

'The dragon. On the Microsoft cloud splash screen. Bottom third flying left to right.'

'Sometimes I wonder about you.'

'It's true! One of those Tolkien-obsessed Redmondites must have worked it in as a private joke, somehow got it through the system. Like the secret level of *Doom* hidden in Excel.'

'It's also true that seeing patterns in clouds past the age of eight is a good indicator of mental problems in later life.'

'If you don't believe me, look at your screen.'

'I can't. Too late. It came and went while I was making tea. I'll just have to wait till tomorrow to find out whether or not you've actually gone mad.'

Liz sits down and types in her password, then waits while the server executes her log-on script. I do the same.

'I can prove it to you,' I say. 'The clouds are on the system as a JPEG.'

'I have so much work to get through, you have no idea.'

'No, honestly – this is really imp . . . oh fuckpants.'

'What now?'

'Mistyped my password. Hang on a sec.'

I type it in again: ***********. Hit enter with a thwack. The hard drive chunters, the network cable hums, a message box blips up. *Password not recognized. Please retype.*

'Oh Christ! Give me Unix. Give me Linux. Give me Commodore 64. Give me anything but frigging Microsoft.'

I type again; this time I single-finger type. I do it deliberately and patronizingly, like I'm picking out a three-note tune on a piano keyboard for a tone-deaf child.

Password not recognized. Access denied. This machine is now locked. Please contact the nearest systems administrator before attempting to re-access this machine.

'I don't believe this,' I say to Liz, but she's already started working and she doesn't want to know.

'Oi Simon,' I say, calling over to where he's sitting hunched before his screen. He's got a giant pair of headphones that I've never seen before clamped around his head and his body language suggests that he's vaguely trying to hide, as far as that is possible in a space like this. 'What's this all about?'

Hiding definitely: without even looking up he jabs a thumb over his shoulder, indicating the door of Andrews's office.

Something's up.

Trying to contain my exasperation I tip myself forwards off my chair and stride across the room. Catching my sudden movement out of the corner of her eye, Pauline looks up from across the way and smiles, then opens and closes her hand in a little cartoon wave. I glower back.

I reach the office, pull open the door, stick my head in through the gap. I already know this is totally the wrong thing to have done. Andrews looks up from his desk. His face is different, somehow. Distant. Merciless.

'What's the problem, Cooper? Can't you read?'

I can read, that is just the problem. There's a big sign on Andrews's door, see, a sign saying 'Always knock'. Which is exactly why I didn't.

'Uh. Yeah. Sorry – I didn't think you'd be in a meeting or anything this early.'

'Is that the point? No, that is not the point. The point is that it's a basic tenet of base security that no private office is ever entered without permission.'

I can't win this battle; I lost the moment I came in. So I withdraw pointedly: hold up my hand, nod in apology, close the door, then knock. I feel like I am back in school. This, I realize, is what school is for – to prepare you for a life like this. I'm beginning to understand what my parents were trying to save me from, in their own, misguided way.

'Come,' he says. I come. 'Morning Cooper,' he says, without looking up.

'Good morning Douglas,' I say back.

'And what is it I can do for you this fine damp Yorkshire morning?'

'My password has not been recognized, Douglas. The system has frozen my machine. I need you to reactivate it. Please.'

'So I take it you haven't read your mail?'

'My mail?' Duh, *hello*? Is there anybody in there? Remain calm, Cooper. Don't patronize him. You know he won't rest until he's made you regret it. 'I can't *get* my mail until my computer is reactivated.'

'Not your email, Cooper. Your real mail. That memo in your in-tray. The memo that I placed there this very morning, precisely forty-seven minutes ago.'

Ah. 'Er, no. No, I haven't read that memo.'

'Well, I suggest you go and read it.'

'Can't you tell me what it says?'

'Go and read it Cooper.' I hesitate. 'Go on.' He waves me out of the room; returns his attention to the papers on his desk.

I leave and walk back to my place, retrieve the memo, tear it open. Five lines on a folded sheet.

FAO: Cooper James, Desk 11, Room 414, C Block, extension 714

Please note that your security clearance has been rescinded until further notice, effective immediately. On receipt of this message please remove any personal effects from your cubicle and report to your supervisor, who will advise you on the necessary procedure. Your cooperation in these matters is noted and appreciated.

Anne Matthews,

pp CSO P. J. Daniels

I have to read this several times before I can get the meaning to imprint on my brain. By the time I've managed this all the blood in my body has run into my feet. When I try to speak it comes out as a whisper.

'Liz,' I say, willing my voice over to where she sits. 'Liiizzzz.' I'm whining, I think.

I'm in my living room, where I've been all day, staring at one of three CD towers, talking on the telephone to Liz, who's on her mobile in the taxi she ordered to take her home from work. The tower is silver and metal and holds fifty CDs and sits on the grey carpet between the stereo and the TV. My life, by contrast, is black and shit and empty and disappearing down the nearest toilet.

'It must be because they thought it might be anthrax,' Liz is saying.

'But Andrews said it wasn't that.' I contemplate my hi-fi. I think it's probably the one truly good thing I have. I've spent years putting it together. The centrepiece is a pair of resprayed Quad II mono-block valve amps. These babies sit on their own private concrete slabs, have dedicated power supplies and never get switched off. Having them glowing away in the corner of the room – it's better than a pet. Though their comfort value is lost on Liz, who considers them a fire risk.

'What else could it be?' she asks.

'I think it's got something to do with my father.' The Quad IIs feed into a Quad 77 pre-amp which in turn drives a pair of Acoustic Energy AE2 Series 2 loudspeakers featuring Teflon-insulated twisted-pair silver-plated oxygen-free copper wiring crossover and custom-cast mass-loaded stands, along with an REL Acoustics

Storm III sub-woofer (cheekily positioned over by the sofa). My primary audio source is a Micromega Stage 6 CD player, linked to its accompanying Micromega DAC 3 by a Chord company 75-ohm digital interconnect. The other interconnects are Cambridge Audio Silver 60s; for speaker cable I use QED 'Silver 12' with Air-Loc™ terminations. All power cords are Jenving Technology AB Supra LoRad 3 x 2.5 Screened, which blocks electric and alternating magnetic fields to minimize radiating mains noise and RF pick-up.

'Cooper, are you even paying attention here? That's precisely what I'm saying.'

'No –' I say, forcing myself back from Planet Hi-fi to the task in hand, 'you don't understand. Not to do with his ashes. To do with whatever it was he was doing when he was alive.'

Liz pauses. I pause. I'm not really sure exactly what I'm saying. I'm stuck wondering if the Micromegas were in fact a particularly wise choice, if it wouldn't have been better to stick with something low end for a while – maybe a Marantz – and save up for an Audiomeca Enkianthus DAC (featuring the world's first totally independent input and output clocks) and Audiomeca Mephisto II CD Player with 32-bit floating point DSP, a combo possessed of virtually zero jitter, not to mention sublime chrome stylings. But I don't know of any supplier in the British Isles who deals in them, so on top of the already fairly astronomical price there'd be the cost of getting the things shipped over here from France.

'Have you asked your mother about it?'

'My mother? No, of course not.'

'Well I think you should.'

'Why?'

'It just seems sensible, that's all. Not to mention polite. I mean, presumably she'd be interested in knowing that the father of her only child has died. And maybe she knows something that would give you more to go on than just a hunch.'

'It's not a hunch.'

'What is it then?'

'It's the way they looked at me, in that room, when I said that Jack Reever was my dad.'

'I thought you fainted.'

'Well, yeah, I did faint. But only for a few seconds. A minute, tops.'

'And so what was this way they were looking at you?'

She is asking me a lot of questions, many more than usual. Perhaps she's just concerned about me. Perhaps. 'I don't know. It – it's nothing concrete. It's just . . . they were looking suspicious, that's all. Suspicious and kind of confirmed in their suspicions at the same time. Like it all made some kind of sense.'

'Like what made some kind of sense?'

Is this an interrogation? Is that what it is? 'It. Everything. Me. I don't know.'

'Nor do I. I'm not sure that *you're* making any sense.'

'Thanks Liz. That's a real vote of confidence.'

'I don't mean it like that.'

'Then how do you mean it?'

'There's no need to get snippy with me. *I* didn't lose you your security clearance.'

'Yeah, well, for all I know you might have done,' I grump.

Liz waits a beat or two before replying. When she does she sounds a little hurt. 'Okay, so just because I don't understand why you think it's got something to do with your father suddenly I'm the enemy.'

'I'm not saying that. That's not what I'm saying. I'm saying that for all I know you could be, that's all. Could be you. Could be Andrews. I don't know. I don't know anything. I'm completely in the dark here, except for this weird feeling I've got.'

'Is that weird feeling the same weird feeling you get when you realize you're being totally offensive?'

'Oh come on Liz. I don't mean it like that.'

'So what way do you mean it?'

'Jesus Christ! Why are you being like this? All I'm trying to say is that I think it might have something to do with whatever Dad was up to!'

'There's no need to shout.'

'Who cares if I'm shouting! Why shouldn't I shout? Don't you understand how scared I am? This isn't a fucking game, Liz! *I've lost my security clearance*. Next stage is I lose my job. I'll never find another job that good round here. I'll have to move away, I'll never sell the house. It's a disaster. This is not funny, okay? It's scaring me. I need to know what's going on.'

Liz says nothing. For a moment I wonder if she's hung up. Then I realize she hasn't, she just waiting for me to calm down again. She often does this, the silent thing, and usually it gets to me immediately. But somehow since the last time I seem to have developed an immunity. I go back to thinking about my stereo. I know I've spent a lot of money here, but compared to someone with real cash to burn what I've got is relatively paltry. I was lucky with my Quad IIs, I bought them at a bargain price from a house auction off this guy who didn't know what he'd got. But if I was really serious I'd junk them and buy four *original 1955* Quad IIs, designed by Peter Walker, reconditioned and refitted with 9th degree of purity slow-drawn silver wire, Black Gate electrolytic capacitors, WBT speaker terminals, Vishay resistors and Golden Dragon KT66 valves. These I'd use to bi-amp not my AE2.2s but a pair of early serial-numbered biwirable 11-ohm BBC Studio Reference Rogers LS 3/5as, originally designed for use as near-field monitors back in the 1970s and widely regarded as the best stand-mounted monitors ever made. 'I'm sorry,' I say, pretending to give in. 'I didn't mean to shout. I'm just . . . I'm just scared. That's all.'

'Well don't be. You're just being paranoid. None of that is going to happen, okay? I promise you. In a couple of days they'll give you a call and you'll be back at work like nothing happened.'

'You think so?' I say, wondering if she knows I'm testing her.

'I know so.'

Gotcha. 'How do you know so?'

She hesitates, like something's caught in her throat. 'Well I don't actually *know*, but I'm sure . . .'

'So you're patronizing me?'

'No I'm *not* patronizing you. God! What the hell's got into you?'

'Nothing,' I say, realizing with a shock that to get the most out of the set-up just described I'll also need a Michel Engineering Orca line-level pre-amplifier; a Trichord Research 1000 clean power supply (five hundred quid that is, for what's basically a plug); a plaster-rumbling REL Acoustics Studio III sub-woofer capable of dropping bass fully 11 hertz beyond the hearing range of the human ear; either Leider Spoor solid silver cables or Nordost SPM Reference (actually in an ideal world I'd have Nordost Valhallas, but at eight grand a metre even if money was no object I think I'd probably baulk); and on top of that a whole new living room, since what I've got isn't even good enough to do justice to my current set-up and really needs to be replaced with something resembling a padded concrete garage. And all this by way of not thinking about the consequences of saying the thing I've really been wanting to say, and which now, in an apparently non-sequitur kind of fashion but in fact not really, if you've been paying any serious attention to what's been going on, suddenly spills out.

'Just that I know you're shagging Andrews, and I know he's asked you to spy on me. You're sick, you hear me? *Sick*!'

This time she does put down the phone.

I sit. I stare. I don't call back. What I do do is pick up the Sennheiser HD 580 Precision headphones I bought last month and put them on. Currently they're rigged up to the Micromegas via the tube amp I also bought to drive them. The remote is on the coffee table; I lean forward and press play. The effect is awesome and instantaneous. It's like strapping my AE2.2s onto my forehead then having someone push them right into my frontal lobes *but using only love*. All I feel is sound. I am no longer a human being, I am only a reverberation, a spastic tuning fork harmonizing with the universe. I am beyond. Or almost.

What prevents me from completely crossing over to the sonic astral plane is the thought of what Liz happens to be doing, right this second. Right now she's sitting in the back of that taxi filling out a PS-6, concentrating on it like it's a fucking love letter. Right now she's writing down every damn word that I've said so she can lay it like an offering before Mr Right. Right now she's thinking that I'm an arsehole of the first degree. Right now she's contemplating never speaking to me again. Oh well so what. I'm glad I've said it – it needed to be said. And fuck her, anyway. Who the fuck does she think she is?

Stasie

Jack was a dog person. At the commune there were lots of dogs, mainly strays we'd taken in. Stasie was always more into cats. Here at her 'retreat' there are lots of cats; I'm not exactly sure how many. Neither, I think, is she. Only some of them are hers – the rest are opportunists on the lookout for company and food, delinquents playing hooky from surrounding households, chancers slipping thievishly across the high, damp tobacco-coloured wall that gives her garden the sullen atmosphere of a compound.

And for these cats food is always available. She leaves out dishes for them in what she calls the pantry – an old back kitchen or garden room, home to her washing machine and various boxes of assorted crap – rotating Whiskas and Go-Cat with frozen plaice fillets she defrosts in pans of water on the kitchen stove, boils and then leaves to cool, sometimes for several days, before deeming safe to serve. Unsurprisingly the cats are often sick. At least once on any given visit I'm guaranteed to skid in a unnoticed patch of scum-like puke, usually first thing in the morning, when I'm making my way through the chaos of the hallways in search of breakfast. Or last thing at night, when I'm stalking the small but complex network of garden paths in search of air free of the combined reek of feline vomit and Stasie's forty-a-day Benson & Hedges habit.

If they don't get you one way, these rancid familiars of my mother's, they get you another. Like warring tribes they long ago carved up the house between them. Walking along the corridors and stairways you're in constant danger of being caught in a cross-fire or ambush. Sit on a sofa and you're likely to find yourself being used as a human shield in some kind of complex covert op. Retreat to your bedroom, chances are your bed's been requisitioned and repurposed as a field hospital by a torn-eared mog who has used your pillow as a surgical pad and then retreated deep under your duvet to shed half its bodyweight in fur in the course of a sweaty and restorative soldier's sleep.

Personally, I'm not altogether big on cats.

Forget about toxoplasmosis for a moment, I'm actually allergic to the little fuckers. I arrive on the Friday evening, it having taken me an entire week of sitting in my house watching daytime television to summon up the courage to come down here and visit, and within twenty minutes of walking through the door my nose is streaming. The house is fully occupied, as usual – I think it's part of Stasie's life-strategy to surround herself with people at all times, presumably because she's terrified the void would swallow her completely if she experienced more than half an hour of solitude.

It's a decent-sized property, so there's lots of space available for spongers and malcontents – Janet would never have allowed Stasie to get her hands on it if it had been in a better part of town. There's this floor, then the ground floor (accessed by the main front steps), then the first floor with the big two-section landing and all those big bedrooms, and then the loft. But with all the bedrooms taken I get to stay in the library, which isn't really a library at all but a small, semi-subterranean room, about three metres by two, featuring a small cot-like single bed covered with one of those bobbly cotton coverlets, a small and broken chair, two sets of Do-It-All pine-effect shelves stuffed with a couple of hundred suspect-looking books, plus a window whose sill is coterminous with the snail-varnished crazy paving of the front garden and which leaks grimy water every time it rains. Oh yeah. And a cat, splayed across my pillow like a giant cockroach. It cracks an eye when I walk in, immediately discounts me as a threat and goes straight back to sleep.

I dump my bag and throw the window open, hoping to relieve the heavy fug of damp. In Granny and Grandad's day this part of the basement was shut off and forgotten, and in my opinion it should've stayed that way. I was at university when they died and Stasie was down in London, unable to hold down a job and living off social security. Matthew – generous as ever – wanted the house to go to her so she had somewhere decent to live, and it was his idea that she get the downstairs converted into a flat which she could then rent out to provide her with an income. Janet wasn't keen, to put it mildly – she thought that Stasie would turn the place into another hippy commune. And when she got bored of playing landlady and set up her retreat instead I suppose that's pretty much exactly what she did. This 'library' was one of the results.

As a general rule I avoid this room, chiefly because the books kept in it terrify me. Books like these, they could get you arrested back on the facility. Here is Norberto R. Keppe's *Trilogical Metaphysics*. Here is Robert Heinlein's *Stranger in a Strange Land*. Here are L. Ron Hubbard, Terence McKenna, Zecharia Sitchin. Here is David Icke. Here are books on crop circles, sex magick, how to awaken your divine Ka. Here is an entire shelf devoted to a genre I can only describe as prehistorical hyperspeculation.

I pull the Icke down off the shelf and start to skim. I've heard some conspiracy theories in my time, but this is on another level. Blood-drinking lizard men from the fourth dimension have taken over the world. Wow. This stuff is schizophrenic. I'm about to put it back up on the shelf when the page falls open at something I recognize.

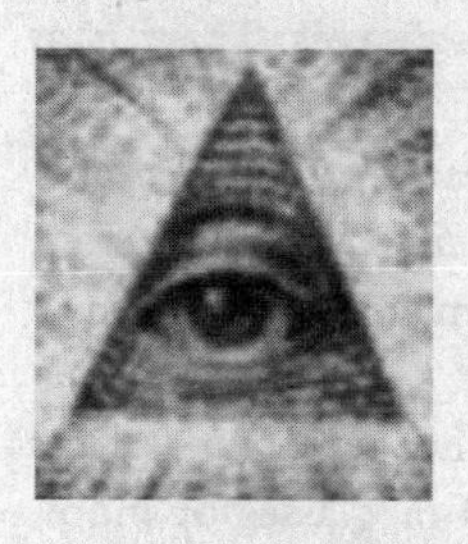

The caption says it's called the Eye of Horus and I realize now where I've seen it before (other than on the coffee canister) – it's on the back of every dollar bill. According to Icke it's something to do with the Illuminati conspiracy and all that balls. But unfortunately he doesn't say who Horus is.

I'm so engrossed that when it's time to go upstairs for dinner the book comes upstairs with me.

'Oh, you're reading Icke,' says Stasie, as she dashes past me with a steaming dish of something in her hands. 'He's a genius.' Her voice sounds a little strange, maybe because of how her nose is stuffed with flu and swollen like a boil, or maybe because she's got a smouldering Superking clamped between her teeth.

'It's certainly interesting,' I say, staying where I am while she disappears into the dining room. 'Who was Horus?'

The next sentence is delivered as a kind of broadside as she heads back towards the kitchen, pot delivered, cigarette switched to hand from mouth. 'Son of Osiris, the Egyptian sun god. Why?'

'No reason. I didn't know, that's all.'

'Nothing in there should come as any surprise to you, working where you do.'

'At Featherbrooks we have a slightly different world view.'

But she doesn't want to hear it. 'Are you going to stand there philosophizing or are you going to help me carry stuff through for dinner?'

Pulling domestic rank on me; now that's a low trick. Especially coming from her.

The buffet is arranged along the old oak sideboard in the dining room. There's a bowl of what looks like mixed frozen vegetables cooked in several tins of mushroom soup, which Stasie describes as vegan chilli. There's a pan of new potatoes (cold), over-cooked and exploding at their seams. There's a 'sweetcorn salad', meaning a bowl of sweetcorn niblets with some slices of cucumber laid on top. There is a dish containing nine Quorn sausages. There is a lettuce (whole) and a loaf of woodstain-brown sliced bread. There are five tomatoes and a catering-sized plastic jar of salted peanuts. There's a bowl of Sainsbury's brand prawn crackers. There's an atmosphere of despair and pointlessness. Or maybe that's just my contribution to the meal.

One by one the guests arrive. In between her hypomanic trips to and from the kitchen to fetch more food or glasses or more bottles of teeth-clenching Bulgarian wine Stasie introduces everyone. Tamsin is a poet from Derbyshire with a fanatic's gaze and tapering features straight out of Dr Seuss. Keith's an anger manager from Preston with a bouncy, chubby look. Chrys is a performance artist who mood-flips between distracted and indignant. Jemma's an aromatherapist from Goole who smells of patchouli oil and armpit. Simon is a garden activist from Devon who wears a stripy jumper that's two sizes too big for him and looks like it was knitted by his gran. Mary is a self-effacing medievalist studying at the University of Nottingham who has important exams early tomorrow morning. All of them are in their late thirties/early forties except for Mary, who I think is probably about twenty-three. By the time we sit down to dinner they all already hate me, because Stasie takes it upon herself to introduce me to them like this: 'And I'd like you to meet my son Cooper, who for reasons known only to himself helps the Americans spy on us and put weapons into space. He'll be staying the night.'

'So how did you get into that then?' asks Keith, dunking a fold of bread spread with non-dairy mayonnaise into his bowl of chilli.

'I'm just a programmer,' I say. 'It's not quite the way Stasie portrays it.'

'There's a reason, though, that it's called code,' says Chrys, enigmatically. I'm not quite sure what she means by this.

'Oh very good, Chrys,' says Stasie, who clearly does, though she doesn't deign to enlighten me.

After we've sat down at the table I notice there's an extra place. A few minutes later I hear the front door open and close, a cue for Stasie to leap up and leave the room in a manner that strikes me as distinctly girlish. The rest of us sit silently while she greets the newcomer, pretending not to be hearing what is clearly love-talk going on in the hallway. Jemma breaks the silence with a non-threatening comment about the benefits of Quorn, and Keith and Tamsin have just about managed to spin this thin thread into something approaching a conversation when a black-clad man with a Caesar cut and a goatee beard walks in.

Flushed and beaming, Stasie announces him. 'This is Moon,' she says. 'Cooper, you remember Moon, don't you?'

I do remember Moon, but not like this. Last time I saw him I think he was eleven. Last time I saw him I don't think he was sleeping with my mother.

'Moon, this is Tamsin, Mary, Keith, Simon, Chrys and Jemma. Moon's a druid,' Stasie says proudly.

Me, I'm busy choking on my sweetcorn.

Once Moon's been steered through the dangerous rapids of the buffet he joins us at the table. 'Moon and Cooper grew up together,' Stasie explains to the audience of innocents gazing at us expectantly. 'They've got a lot of catching up to do.'

I should say something but I don't know what. Moon smiles at me. His hair is neat, his beard perfectly groomed. He looks a little vain. He also looks embarrassed.

'Hey Moon,' I say.

'Hey, er, Cooper,' he says, his discomfort with the name (or perhaps the situation) quite obvious.

'No one calls him Ash now, Moon. We dropped that, Cooper, didn't we? A long time ago.'

'That's right. Long time,' I say, though I don't mean it as a repetition.

Moon understands, I think. At least, he nods. 'Indeed. How's things?'

'Oh. You know. Up and down,' I say. 'Jack died,' I say.

'Really? When?'

'Moon's very into divination,' Stasie says immediately. 'He's been mapping the major ley lines around Nottingham. He's discovered nine passing beneath this actual house. Tell them, Moon.'

'It's true,' Moon says, apologizing to me for the interruption with his eyes. 'The house is on a major node of power.'

People nod. 'Oh *really*?' Jemma says. 'You know, I was *sure* I could feel something.'

Chrys smiles as if she, too, had known it all along.

'And, er, how do you map ley lines, exactly?' I ask, perhaps naively.

'With divining rods,' says Stasie.

'That's right,' says Moon. 'With divining rods.'

'Divining rods? I thought those were for finding water.'

'They are. But you can tune them to other power lines in the landscape, too.'

'Tune them? Er, okay.' I cannot believe that Moon, my old friend Moon, has so completely bought into all of this. 'So, these ley lines travelling under this house. How can you be sure they're not water mains or something?'

'Different frequency signature,' Moon assures me. 'Plus I mapped the position of all the utility pipes as well – gas, water, electrics, phone – to ensure I didn't make exactly that mistake. It's standard practice.'

'Oh.'

Following a prompt from Chrys, Moon goes on to give us a short lecture on the subject. When he's done he asks Chrys to tell us about her performance art. What is it, exactly, that she does? Chrys, it transpires, dresses up as a hospital inpatient and wanders round nightclubs pretending to be mentally ill.

When she hears this Mary lets out a snort. It seems she's been too busy studying towards her exams to have had much contact with the other occupants of the house. It's hard to see, otherwise, why she's waited this long to express incredulity. 'And what's that supposed to achieve?' she asks a little scoffily.

Chrys looks dismayed, like Mary's just told her to go out and get a job. Keith rides valiantly to her rescue – but not too valiantly; he no doubt wouldn't want anyone to think that he was exhibiting unreconstructed male behaviour by stepping in. 'Is it necessary that it achieves anything, Mary? Does art have to be goal-oriented?'

'Chrys does aura paintings too,' says Stasie weightily, as if that fact somehow resolves the argument.

'What's an aura painting?' I ask, genuinely intrigued.

Seven of the assembled give me a look like I've just admitted not knowing the name of the President of the United States.

'It's a painting of someone's aura,' says Stasie. 'What do you think?'

'She's very good,' says Jemma. 'You're very good, aren't you Chrys?'

Chrys blushes modestly. 'I do my best.'

'She's done all of us,' says Keith.

'Not me,' says Mary. She sounds panicked, like she had no idea these people were living just over her head (she has the bedroom in the basement, next door to the library).

'Chrys has kindly agreed to do aura portraits of you and Moon,' Stasie says.

Chrys stares guru-like at the whorls of mushroom soup in the bottom of her bowl.

'When?' I say. I'm afraid. My eyes are moving wildly.

'Tonight. Now. Right after you've helped me clear the table.'

All I can think is how this would all be different if Jack had never gone away.

In the kitchen, dishcloth in my hand, I get my first proper opportunity to talk to Stasie. I've told her about the ashes on the phone, so she knows that they exist. But we didn't get as far as what to do with them. This being a subject that 99 per cent of me and 100 per cent of my mother does not want to discuss it's proving difficult to broach. So I decide to try and get to it sideways, hoping that at some point, more or less of its own accord, it will just appear and trip us up.

'I think there's a good chance I'm going to lose my job,' I say, 'on account of all the trouble I caused.'

'Well, that can only be an improvement.'

'Thanks,' I say, shoving first one feline and then another away from the pile of dirty plates. 'Thanks for the sympathy.'

'You know what I think about you working in that place.'

'Yes, well, even so, I thought I might be able to expect a little bit of family loyalty.'

She laughs so hard at this it starts her on a coughing fit.

'I don't like you smoking,' I point out, 'but you do it anyway.'

More laughter/coughs. 'It's not quite the same thing, is it?' she says, when her respiratory system finally starts functioning again.

'Er, I think you'll find that there's actually quite a lot of similarities,' I say, aware of a certain tensing in the muscles of my jaw.

'I'm not going to argue with you Cooper.'

This is the point that I'd usually break something – a glass, a cup, a cat – but I manage to remind myself that I'm here for a purpose and a row would not help me achieve it. But I might as well abandon any hope of reaching the topic in question via more subtle means;

there are simply too many minefields to negotiate. I'm just going to have to take the plunge and jump straight in. Dive-bomb.

'So what do you think we should do?'

Stasie passes me a food-encrusted casserole. 'Do with what?'

'What else? The ashes.'

'Do we have to talk about that now? We've only just finished eating.'

'It's what I've come to talk about.'

'It would be nice if you came a little more often.'

Still she tries to twist it into a fucking argument! It's intolerable! Do other people in the world have mothers like this? Surely it's not possible – within two generations the human race would simply cease to exist, drowned in wave upon wave of unremitting matricide.

'We have to talk about it some time.'

'We'll do it later.'

'When later?'

'Well, we've got the aura painting now, in the living room.'

'I don't believe you.'

'Don't believe me what?'

'It's just pure distraction, isn't it? This whole aura-painting thing. You've set it all up so you won't have to talk about what I've come to talk about.'

'Jesus – and I thought I was supposed to be the paranoid one.'

'Don't evade the question.'

Stasie's been drying the same plate for a good two minutes already, but now she begins rubbing it so vigorously with her dish-cloth that fag ash tumbles from her cigarette. 'I'm not evading the question, Cooper. The question is so completely ludicrous that it's evading me. I can't see a way to even begin trying to deal with you when you're like this.'

'Like what?' She doesn't answer. 'Like what? When I am like what?'

But she's ignoring me, busying herself with dishes and dish towels and general kitchen-type tasks. We do this kind of dance to and fro between the sink and the sideboard, me trying to get an answer out of her while she tries to avoid both my stare and the various cats darting to and fro between her feet. She's fucking difficult to intimidate, my mother. You wouldn't think I was a good six inches taller than her and one and a half times her body weight.

'So after that?' I say eventually, knowing that to say it is to admit defeat.

'After what?' She's all over me now. Really rubbing it in.

'After the aura paintings. We'll discuss the ashes?'

'My God, are you still on that? You're like a stuck record, you are. Alright. If we must. After that. Happy now?'

Now I'm feeling guilty. I can't believe she's made me feel guilty. Not only has she won the argument with an unbelievably childish and simple tactic, she's made me feel guilty in the process, guilty and suspicious. I haven't even got close to asking her what the hell she thinks she's doing, having an affair with Moon.

Chrys's aura paintings are not what I'm expecting. They're rather beautiful, in fact. Or Moon's is, anyway. A red-gold globule surrounded by pale creamy swirls rising gently on a background of even, azure blue, it looks like a cross between a human foetus curled up in the womb and a lava lamp. When they see it people cluck and coo.

'What's it mean?' asks Tamsin.

'It doesn't mean anything in particular,' Chrys explains, 'but it does show that Moon's aura is very peaceful and complete. This is the aura of an integrated person, of a person whose creative energy is resonant and focused.'

'What's this signify?' asks Keith, pointing to the spermy gloop that's curling in a yin-yang manner around Moon's primary auratic glob.

'Hmm,' says Chrys, 'it's difficult to say exactly; the pictures are non-representational. But it might be the echo of another person's aura, someone that Moon is particularly close to? Stasie, perhaps?' Everyone looks at Stasie; Stasie blushes happily and puffs on her fag. Jemma actually claps.

This all stands in marked contrast to what happens when my painting finally comes off the easel. Then there are no claps, no coos and ahhs, no enthusing compliments. All I get is one 'hmm' (from Keith), one sneeze (from Tamsin) and one suppressed giggle (from Stasie, naturally). The reason for this is simple. My painting – meaning my aura, meaning, by extension, me – looks like an abortion. *I* look like an abortion. To paint it Chrys has deployed a palette made up almost entirely of reds and blacks, with some pus-yellows and snot-greens daubed here and there for definition. My central globule is vast and exploded, like roadkill or a splatted baby-head. With this cancerous spectre no spermy auras venture to entwine. The few dark ribbons that do vein my essence look more like the infection vectors of some insidious disease than anything remotely wholesome.

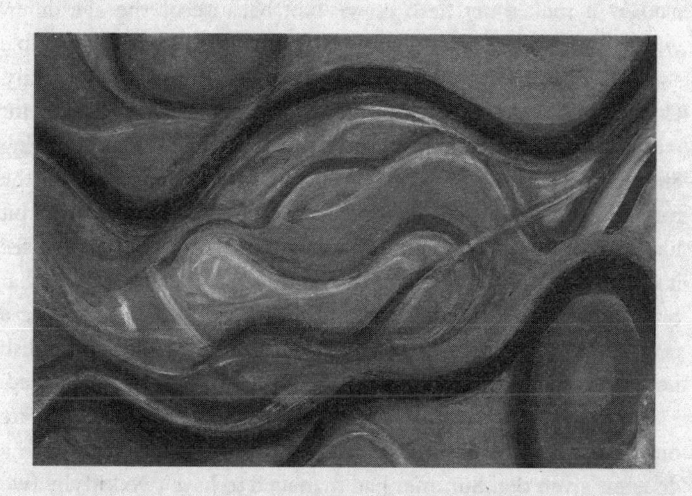

'So what does it mean?' I say, forcing the words past the suspicion that this is all some elaborately rehearsed routine engineered by my mother to belittle me.

Chrys, to give her credit, tries her best to wring from this pastel catastrophe a message of positivity and hope, but it's a lost cause, it really is. When it's over I admit defeat and say I'm going to bed. Everyone says good night and I hurry out the room, down the hall and out the house, desperate to get outside and breathe some air that isn't laced with smoke.

Outside in the garden it's cold and damp. I stand on the stoop and look out over the wall in the direction of the city, suck on atmosphere that's mildewy and stagnant. There are no stars, just a cloud-level bank of amorphous mist that glows softly, as if from the inside, with the energy radiating from Nottingham's millions of lamps and lights. I could be standing inside a giant section of poisoned lung. Through the window to my left and at my feet I can hear Mary trying to sniff herself to sleep. Up in the living room I can hear singing. Christ almighty. Stasie's got the guitar out.

It's too fucking weird about Moon. I mean, sleeping with my *mother*? It makes my flesh crawl. Not because of the age difference, though that's putrid enough, but because there's a horrible sort of logic to it, a kind of perverse emotional inevitability. Consider: Moon was the one who set the wheels in motion for Jack's departure when he blurted out that he'd been shagging Shannon. And now here he is, usurping my father's place in the marital bedchamber. It's almost Shakespearean – *Hamlet* was a bit like this, as far as I remember from an ancient school trip to see it at the theatre. Or is it *Oedipus*? Is that Shakespeare? Or is that one of the Greek ones? Or both? Or is *Hamlet* supposed to be a rewriting of *Oedipus*? Christ, you know, I can't remember. English never was my strong point. Miss Banner would've been appalled.

But then Moon did always have a thing about trying to infiltrate our family. It probably had to do with how his own was such a disaster, given that Summer had managed to have two kids by two different men and then lose track of both of them (the men, that is, not the kids). Whenever we played our games down on the beach he liked to pretend that we were brothers of one sort or another – long-lost brothers, brothers-in-arms, tragic brothers torn apart by circumstances and fighting on different sides. He was terribly upset when he realized the damage his comment had caused to Jack and Stasie's relationship. For ages afterwards he couldn't bear to be around them and he ran away in tears whenever either of them came into the room. It was only when we all got together to make the whale cast that he finally calmed down.

Jack knew how close we were and I think that must be why he decided to take us down to see the whale one day, maybe a week after the cast was done. The orca had really started rotting now and the seabirds were all over it, picking at the carrion. The flesh was completely putrid, the corpse bloated and swarming with maggots; to get a single whiff of it was enough to make you puke. But for some reason Jack wanted us to go right up close to it – he had something in mind, I could tell.

As we approached the thing I became more and more uneasy. The whale had taken on an almost holy significance for me since I'd discovered the beauty of the finished cast, and the stark contrast between the virtual perfection of this frozen image and the blunt unpleasantness of the mess left on the beach wasn't something I wanted to be confronted with. In a fit of filial contrariness I protested that it was disgusting and that I wouldn't go any closer, and I ran off down the beach in an attempt to get upwind, assuming Moon would follow my lead as he usually did.

This time, though, he didn't. For whatever reasons – curiosity, bravura, the sense that the two of them were laying something to rest – he stuck with Jack. As I watched from what I considered to be a safe distance the two of them approached the whale's head, Jack shouting and waving at the seagulls to frighten them away. Reaching into his trouser pocket he took out his clasp knife, I could see that much, but what I couldn't see was what he proceeded to do with it. Whirling birds obscured my view as well as the body of the whale itself, and my perception of the scene was restricted to Jack's bent back and the figure of Moon standing back from him and to one side, hands pulling his T-shirt up across his nose and mouth and torso bent away from the source of the awful smell but eyes black and bright as mussels and fixed just as firmly to whatever it was that Jack was doing.

A minute passed, and then another, and finally Jack stood up with a lump of something bloody in his hand that he quickly carried down the beach to wash off in the sea, Moon following so closely after as to be within the ambit of his shadow. They were moving upwind now, in my direction, so sensing that I was missing out – had already missed out – on something of importance I tentatively started to approach.

By the time I reached them Jack was halfway through dissecting his lump of flesh on a largish, flattish stone. T-shirt down, hands in pockets now, Moon stood gazing down at him.

'What is it?'

'It's a bulla,' Jack said, wrenching something free of the tangled sinews and rinsing it in the water lapping at his boots. 'A tympanic bulla. Part of the whale's inner ear. It's the smallest bone in the creature's body.' He scraped it with his knife again, rerinsed it, then scraped and rinsed it once again before holding it up for us to examine. It was a tiny thing, shaped like a half-sized monkey nut, but smooth and pearly white beneath the few streaks of blood and matter that still clung to it. 'The bulla was something Roman fathers gave to their sons when they were born. It was either the whale bone itself or a stone or metal amulet shaped like one, and you wore it as a pendant to ward off evil until you became a citizen, at which point you took it off and saved it, because one day, if you were heroic in battle or something like that, something that elevated you in the eyes of your fellow Romans, you were entitled to wear it round your neck again as a sign of honour and status and to protect you from the jealousy of men and gods.'

Moon and I absorbed this mini history lesson instantly. Thanks to these ancient connotations, couched in a form that ten-year-old boys could understand, the bulla was now a thing of awe, a totem possessed of magical properties that could endow its wearer with that most crucial of boyhood magics: the ability to enter the adult world. And, more importantly, what we both understood implicitly was that it was mine by right. As Jack's son, I would now be handed the bulla to wear and keep. It was what was expected. It was my natural right.

Which is why it came as such a shock when Jack passed the bulla not to me but to my friend.

'Here Moon, why don't you have this? Just to show you that there's no hard feelings, huh?'

This gesture clearly surprised Moon as much it did me. First thing he did was look my way, half thinking he should apologize, half worried that I was going to intervene. But I'd been stunned into silent immobility by what had just happened, and I wasn't saying anything. So Moon accepted Jack's gift along with Jack's forgiveness, and the smile didn't leave his face for over a week.

He adored the bulla, naturally. He asked Jack to attach a thong to it so he could wear it round his neck. But I was furious. I was so jealous I couldn't sleep. I couldn't work it out. Why had Jack given it to Moon and not to me, especially when it was Moon who'd gone and told Stasie Jack was sleeping with Shannon? I couldn't see why he couldn't just have straightened things out with Moon another way. All I could see was that Jack preferred Moon to me, that he wanted Moon to usurp my position in our little family. I can't tell you how truly overjoyed I was when one day Moon finally lost the thing. It was like all my birthdays had come at once.

And now he's fucking my mother! And all those feelings of anger and jealousy are coming back and all I can think is what a bastard, he can't do that. What a cunt. With his black polo neck and his bloody ley lines and his fucking perfect aura and all that crap. He usurped me and now he's usurping Jack. I mean, I know this is irrational and stupid, that I've got no right, that he and Stasie can do whatever they like, but it all seems so completely wrong somehow, like some kind of conspiracy to steal what's left of my family away from me.

I dig in my pocket, retrieve my mobile, scroll down through the phonebook until I get to *LIZ*. She'll be in bed by now, for definite, but that's actually what I want. Right now I don't want a conversation. Right now I just want to get all this off my chest.

'Hi, you've reached Liz's answer service. Go ahead, leave that message. You know you want to.'

What is it about the way she talks? How can the mere *sound* of someone's voice do all this to me?

'Liz, it's me. I know you're sleeping but that's okay. I'm in Nottingham. It's a nightmare, as predicted. But what I didn't predict was that, of all people, Moon has showed up. You remember I told you about him? Yeah, well, guess what. He's shagging Stasie. I can't fucking believe it. I mean . . . *Moon*. It's fucking weird, man. It's just not normal.' And I proceed to gabble out into her message memory the gist of what I've just told you.

When my little boil of hatred's been lanced I go back inside and make my way down to the library where I discover a new cat camped out on my pillow. I remove it and it scratches me. I go to the bathroom, disinfect the cut, wash my face and clean my teeth. Then I go to bed.

There's no curtain on the window and the glare from a single street lamp seeps across the garden and into my subterranean room like a cloud of mustard gas. I stare at the spines of L. Ron Hubbard, Zecharia Sitchin, David Icke. From upstairs comes the sound of my mother's singing. She still has a lovely voice, despite the cigarettes and everything. I know the song; it's one of hers. When I was a child she used to sing it to me when I couldn't get to sleep.

It seems like such a long long time ago.

The next morning when I wake I feel horrible. The room is cold and damp and pale, and a seemingly inexhaustible supply of scum-snot is running out my nose. Fourteen hours' exposure to cat hair and cigarettes, that's what that is. I'd like to get up but I'm frightened of the carpet, which is old and scabrous and possibly possessed of a proto-consciousness. A long time passes before I can muster the courage to risk bringing it into contact with my bare feet, worried that this is an act it might interpret as extremely hostile. It makes my slumbering mind hoop and boggle, this thought of how the world would be if all carpets suddenly decided to rise up and retaliate. I fall back to sleep and the thought converts itself into a vivid B-movie of a dream.

Next time I wake it's from fleeing down a suburban street pursued by several dozen undulating mats of needlepoint and contract velour beneath a sky dark with soaring floor tiles bent on violent vengeance. This vision is enough to drive me from my pit, but by the time I get up the stairs and into daylight it's already gone ten o'clock.

Outside it's raining. I pass Keith and Jemma in the hallway; they have their coats on and are going out. They say good morning and make some joke about the night before that I don't get. I ask where Stasie is and they tell me they haven't seen her but they heard her talking on the phone not long ago, so she's probably not far away.

I fled the nightmare downstairs too fast to bother with my shoes and this proves to be an error, as on entering the kitchen I step in a large puddle of a pungent briny liquid that bears more than a passing resemblance to cat pee. I remove the sock, chuck it in the sink, rinse it, then try to rinse my foot as well. I manage this without sustaining major injury, but then I can't find anything to dry it on. I sort of rub it against the leg of my jeans and then give up, meaning that I have to go about the business of making tea while collecting fluff and shards of diced onion and doughnuts of dried cat food between my damp and tender toes.

Tea made, I go in search of my mother. I search in the pantry and the living room and the dining room and then I meet her coming down the stairs. She too is wearing hat and coat.

'You're going out?'

'No – I like dressing up like this and staying indoors.'

'But we haven't had our conversation yet.'

'I'm sorry honey. My friend Pamela's got terrible problems with her back; I've got to go and treat her with my crystals.'

'But what about Dad's ashes?'

'What about them?'

'Well, like, you know, do you happen to have any idea as to who might have sent them?'

'Darling, I've no idea. Maybe that little bitch Shannon did.'

I stand open-mouthed. After twenty years she still hasn't forgiven her. Then again, nor have I, probably. I just haven't thought about it. My lip starts trembling a little.

'So what should I do with them?'

'Well don't leave them here, not unless you want them chucked out with the rubbish. Because that's what's going to happen to them if it gets left up to me.'

I'm getting angry now, angry and petulant. Why is it that being around their parents always makes grown adults revert to their childhood selves? Even if one of the parents happens to be inside a reinforced coffee canister. 'You really don't give a shit, do you?'

Stasie looks at me, unlit Benson poking like a thermometer from her gob. 'No, Cooper, you're right. I really don't. The day he walked out on us was the day I stopped caring about Jack Reever. I've got no respect for him or his memory, and if you had any sense, you wouldn't either. He wasn't a father to you. He wasn't helpful to you in any way. And he won't be now, whatever you think about the importance of honouring his memory. My advice to you is get rid of those ashes in any way you see fit and get on with your life. Are you going to be joining us for dinner tonight?'

I mumble something about wanting to go and visit a friend.

'Well then, make sure you lock the door behind you when you leave. And let me know if you plan on spending a whole weekend here, ever.'

And then she's gone.

Situation Normal: All Fucked Up

The friend I'm going to visit is my old friend Miles. Miles is rich. Unlike Stasie, who lives in a part of town that used to be a good part but has become a bad part, Miles lives in a part of town that used to be a bad part but has become a good part. He lives right in the centre, in the old lace-making district. When I was at school this area was all rotting warehouses, smack addicts, ranks of broken windows, squats. But then a century's worth of industry was sand-blasted off the gungy walls, the tarmac skin smothering the cobbles was flayed away and the warehouses were converted into studios and lofts. These days expensive cars sit poised in primly painted parking spaces like the stone lions beside the steps of an eighteenth-century country house, the broken windows have been filled up with glass bricks, cocaine has become the drug of choice and the streets look like something from a bathroom catalogue.

Miles and me were friends at school and then we went to university together – we both did computer science, at Warwick. After college we stayed in our student house in Coventry and started up a company designing video games. Just the two of us, coding 3D shoot-'em-ups for the Amiga and the Atari. We were just beginning to turn the corner profit-wise when we got approached by DERA. DERA is the Defence Evaluation and Research Agency (or was; it recently changed its name to something much more innocuous). Basically, it's the R and D arm of the Ministry of Defence. They wanted programmers to help code a tank sim, full networked VR, to let tank crews practise tactics in vast transatlantic online battles. It was an exciting project. Huge resources – much more than anyone in the private sector had back then, anyone in the UK at any rate. Job security, health care, pension and so on. I wasn't really making any money with Miles and I didn't like how precarious it felt, so I took the job. Miles stuck it out with the 3D engine we'd been working on. I moved to Farnborough and started work. That was about six years ago.

Three years later, just after I moved from Farnborough to Featherbrooks, Miles sold the 3D engine to Acclaim for three million quid. Miles has got his own company now. He always says that there's a job for me there if I ever want it but I never do. I think I've become institutionalized. Either that or I can't bear the thought of working for Miles. Not now he's moved so far ahead of me. Whichever way you look at it he'd always be the boss and I'd always be the worker. And I've got my pride.

I told Miles about the ashes over the phone. I also told him, slightly against my better judgement, about losing my security clearance and my subsequent suspension from duty. Against my better judgement because I rarely speak to Miles about my job. The ostensible reason for this is because I'm not allowed to, but actually that's just a good excuse. Even if I could I wouldn't want to – compared with his fast-lane existence as the head of a fast-growing games company my life is far too dull.

Fortunately, Miles insists on finding something James Bond and glamorous about the thin veil of secrecy behind which I live my life, and I make no attempt to relieve him of this misconception. Over the last few years I've sensed the need of something special to help make sure he stays friends with me. Even when we were still working together I got the feeling that our friendship was starting to look to him a bit like excess baggage. That worried me then and it worries me now. Fortunately, the fact that I write codes for top secret satellites has been enough to ensure he keeps in touch. I say fortunately because apart from Liz Miles is the only real friend I've got.

Miles lives behind a security door, up a brushed aluminium lift and along a maple corridor. He owns half of the top floor of this building, Grade II listed and built in 1873. His partner, Kristrún, greets me at the front door – Miles, she says, is having a jacuzzi bath and will be with us in a minute.

Kristrún leads me into the kitchen and offers me a Coke. The kitchen is fully Smeg. Kristrún is fully beautiful. She's blonde and Icelandic and an artist and I want to sleep with her so much it's terrifying. Her pictures don't help; there are several of them on the walls, all of them self-portraits. Naked self-portraits. It's enough to make a grown man cry.

I manage to hold back the tears but at the cost of being unable to look her in the eye – I'm afraid that she'll see the desire raging across my pupils like a porn movie in miniature.

'Come and talk to me in the living room,' she says, leading me through to where she's in the process of assembling some piece of upscale flatpack furniture that she tells me she ordered online from Heals. Strewn around the place are squares of smoked glass, rectangles of teak.

'It'll be a low-profile sideboard, when it's put together,' she assures me. She hands me a recent issue of *Wallpaper** magazine, open at a photograph of the finished product. 'I chose it because it looks just like the one in those seventies Bang & Olufsen ads, you know?' She speaks with this nice, slightly otherworldly lilt that perfectly matches the walls of sliding glass that let out onto the balcony. The balcony is paved with ash-grey paving tiles that hover on invisible steel risers above a bed of fishtank gravel, designed to absorb and transport the rain. The rain has no chance. Human beings are getting good at this.

I ask her if she needs a hand.

'No, it's okay, thanks. I think I've got it covered. You can just sit and talk.'

But I'd much rather help. Talking frightens me – I'm happier when I'm doing something with my hands. What if I say the wrong thing? What if I make an idiot of myself? Then she'll never sleep with me. Stupid, stupid. She's married to Miles. She's also several years his junior (and mine as well). So why am I so impressed by her?

'Have you ever seen the movie *Tron*?' I say. This is the only topic I can think of. That's how sad I am.

'Oh yeah,' she says unconvincingly, while contemplating a curious kind of squat, truncated screw.

'I saw it again the other day,' I say, 'on video. It's so cool.'

'Yeah?'

'But you know what I thought was really cool about it? It was how it was like completely prophetic of the computer industry in the 1990s.'

'Oh yeah?'

'Yeah – check it out. You know how you've got Jeff Bridges playing this long-haired whiz-kid video-games geek and how Bruce Boxleitner plays his mild-mannered supernerd friend, and how they end up getting trapped together in the cyberspace construct of the mainframe where they have to do battle with the master program in the middle of all those awesome vector graphics? And then how they eventually defeat it and take over the company, only to become the new computer hegemony? Well, tell me that's not a total template for how Steve Jobs's Apple and Bill Gates's Microsoft teamed up to displace the IBM mainframe culture with the personal computer, then divide up the spoils of the new market between the two of them? It's almost like the characters involved are exactly the same. It's weird.'

'Yeah?'

'Yeah, even down to how Bruce Boxleitner lets Jeff Bridges spearhead the attack while hanging back and developing his dodgy software packages, which he'll roll out later on when things have calmed down so he can totally clean up. It's exactly what Gates did with Apple, how he let them stick their neck out by actually building hardware and doing all this high-visibility cultural stuff like with that 1984 smash-the-system ad where the woman throws the hammer into the giant computer screen while all the time he was lurking in the background, writing operating systems and word-processing packages designed to make money out of whichever of the computer manufacturers won the battle. And that's exactly what *Tron*'s all about – about how, although it *seems* that Jeff and Bruce are the cool dude rebels out to smash the system, actually what they are is the system's *agents*, the guys whose actions end up helping it *survive*. Though in a much mutated form, of course.'

I stop because I've started ranting, I realize. Not that Kristrún's paying me much attention; most of her mind is taken up with the effort of concentrating on the correct assembly of the sideboard, the expression on her face that of a child putting together a complex Airfix kit. But it's just not that hard – I can see how to put the various sections together from here, without even looking at the instructions. It's such a fucking no-brainer. But I know that would be butting in and so . . . At least this way I can watch her body move without her looking back at me.

'Miles says your father died,' she says.

Ah. Yeah. I'd forgotten about that.

'I'm sorry.'

'Don't be.'

She looks up at me, her face an adult's once again. I realize I've already put my foot in it, gone too far in trying to be cool, come over like an idiot. To make things worse, having realized this I panic. 'No – I don't mean it like that. I just mean . . . I didn't really know him.' What am I doing? Can someone, can anyone, please please tell me how I should behave?

Fortunately, Kristrún takes back the initiative.

'Did your parents divorce when you were young, then?'

'Something like that.'

'God, mine too. It's so fucking hopeless, right? My mother kicked my father out when I was eight and I didn't see him for nearly ten whole years. But now we get along okay.'

Just as I'm wondering if this is a subtle way of asking me just exactly what my problem is in walks Miles, looking like a god.

'Hey Coops,' he says. 'How's it going?'

I stand up to shake his hand and spill my Coke, which I'd placed on the floor next to my fat and useless foot. Dark fingers stretch across the honey floorboards in the direction of a deep-pile white rug, thick and pristine as an advancing glacier. Instantly Kristrún is on her feet and gliding kitchenwards.

'Don't worry, I'll get it.'

Seconds later she's back with a folded wodge of kitchen towel. Miles notes that I'm still the klutz I always was and I nod agreement like a fool.

'Kristrún looks well,' I say, when she's finished mopping up and gone off to deposit the now sodden napkin in the bin.

'Yeah,' Miles sniffs. 'She's nesting. I read in the paper that it's a common response to September 11.' He sounds so blasé. If I had a lover like that, I'd be screaming thanks to heaven in between kissing the ground she's walking on. Which may go some way to explaining why I haven't got one.

'So what d'you think of the new place then?' he says. 'I don't think it was finished when you last came.'

'No, I don't think it was. It's nice.'

'Nice?'

'Yeah. You know. Nice. I'm jealous.'

'I know you are, you stupid sod.' He smiles at me. Kristrún comes in with fresh drinks for both of us then tactfully disappears again. 'It's good to see you, Coops,' Miles says, when she's gone. 'Are you okay?'

'Yeah. I dunno. I'm a bit disoriented by it all, I think.'

He nods, and neither of us says anything for a minute. Then:

'You know . . .' he muses, like he's building up to something.

'Know what?'

'Well, I hate to say it, but your old man and you, it's hardly like the two of you were close. I mean, you haven't seen him since you were eleven, right? And you hardly ever mentioned him.'

'Fuck you!' I say, surprised even more than Miles is by the strength of my reaction. 'Just because I didn't talk about it you think it wasn't there? You're as bad as Stasie, you are! She doesn't want me to mourn him either. She thinks I should just throw the ashes in the bin.'

Explosion over. Miles sits tense, expectant, bracing himself for the full force of the tempest. When he realizes the storm's already broken he takes a slow sip of his drink and sniggers slightly. But the snigger forces Coke up into his sinal passages so now he's sneezing and coughing too, which serves him right.

'Don't laugh, you bastard.'

'Well you've got to admit it's pretty funny.'

'Not to me it's not.'

'Oh come on, Cooper.'

'Come on bollocks. This is my dad, alright? Has your dad died? No, he fucking hasn't. Well mine just has, and even though I haven't seen him for eighteen years I feel like I should feel something.'

'So what do you feel?'

I turn away, toe the edge of the fur rug with my foot. 'That's just the problem,' I tell him quietly, 'I don't know what I feel. I don't even feel nothing. I just . . .'

'You just want some kind of closure?'

Thinking Miles is taking the piss again I examine his expression. But I don't think he is, not this time. This time I think he's trying to be genuine. But 'closure', though. It's the kind of annoying psychobabble I'd expect to hear from the Americans at Featherbrooks. What'd he do? Pick it up off the telly?

'Something like that,' I say.

Miles nods. 'Let's go down the pub,' he says.

That's more like it.

Eight minutes later I'm waiting out the back of Council House in Nottingham town centre while Miles stops in at the olde-worlde tobacconists that's been there for ever to get some fags. When he's done we walk around the building and past the fountains that we used to hang around as teenagers. They've been drained – Miles says some students put soap in them again and they overflowed with foam, an old old trick that was tired even in our era. It depresses me that people are still behaving so childishly when so much else round here has changed. In the six months since I last walked through the square a lot of new shops and stuff have opened up, and the place is beginning to lose the dismayed look it's had . . . well ever since I've known it really. A lot of the shittiest old buildings have been knocked down, stained concrete frontages have been replaced with steel and glass, the few historic buildings are in the process of being cleaned. There's a Waterstones, and a Gap, and a Coffee Republic. Cappuccino in Nottingham. Who'd've thunk it?

We head for the place at the intersection of King and Queen Streets, which used to be a scary biker's pub called the Crown. Now it's a Slug and Lettuce. The dark, heavily mullioned windows, smeared thick with beer and breath, against which I used to cower with my pint have been knocked out and replaced with giant sheets of glass. The walls inside have been stripped of their snot-like layers of lead-based paint and are smooth and unscarred, airbrushed a delicate shade of parchment designed to suggest nicotine staining rather than to actually be it. The smeggy carpet has been removed and the floorboards varnished and polished to a mirror sheen.

I like it. It's nice. It could've been put together by the same interior designer as did Miles's place. Probably was, in fact. We walk up to the bar, run our eyes along the racks of wine, the chalkboard menus, the vistas of brass and pine. Then we order Stellas and go and take a seat.

'Kristrún doesn't like me smoking in the flat,' Miles says, in between lighting up and twitching his head backwards in the direction from which we've come.

'No?'

'Women. They've barely got one foot through the door and they start acting like they own the place.'

'I wouldn't know,' I say, somewhat pathetically.

Miles gives me an amused look. 'Still not sorted yourself out with a bird, Cooper?'

I shrug, flick a couple of stray nuts in the direction of an ashtray.

'What about that whatsername, that Liz? I thought you were making moves on her.'

I bounce my head from side to side, non-committally.

'Come on! So what's the problem?'

'I don't know. She's my boss, for one thing. Or was, until those ashes showed up.'

'So there you are. Every cloud, right? You lose your job, but now the pressure's off. Now you can go ahead and get the girl.'

'Right Miles, my status has really changed that much. I'm no longer her underling, now I'm the cool and crazy dude who got thrown off the base because of his weirdo father's nutcase plans for his cremains. Very sexy.'

Miles sips his drink, considers this. 'When you put it that way . . .'

'She did give me a present the other day,' I say, aware that if I don't stop being wholly negative there's no way Miles can give me the encouragement I need, for which I've come.

'Oh yeah?'

'Yeah.'

'What, exactly?'

'Some old book about ancient burial rites. She thought it would help me work out what to do with them. With the ashes.'

'And has it?'

'Dunno. Haven't read it yet. But I think it means she likes me.'

'So what're you waiting for?'

More head bounces.

'Well, if you don't do something soon, you're never going to get the chance. You're hardly going to stay in Whitby, are you, if they don't decide to give you back your job. Sooner or later you're going to move away, and that'll be that. You'll probably never see each other again, whatever promises you make, and this Andrews guy will have her all to himself. Give her a month, she'll've forgotten all about you. "Cooper? Oh yeah, I think I remember him . . . Quiet guy, a bit nerdy, but kinda cute. I used to have a bit of a thing for him, you know, but he was too shy to make a move. What's a girl to do?" '

This is what I want, Miles to lay it out for me like this. I don't seem to have the simple ruthlessness necessary for analysing sexual situations by myself. 'So you think I should just go for it?'

'What've you got to lose? Give the girl a kiss! If she kisses back, then you're set. If she doesn't, then hell, it's her loss, right? You're outta there. Rolling stone. No regrets. Pastures new.' Miles downs the remnants of his pint. 'Right. Your round, I think. Same again for me. I'm off for a slash.'

While he's gone I get the drinks in and ponder his advice; when he's back I change the subject by telling him the full story of the security alert. I tell it minus angst, as a joke, like it's a prank I got away with. I fill it with details Miles will appreciate, even if in the process I do make myself sound like a total dork. Sure enough he laps it up, and that tight little smile he's been wearing ever since we got into death and mourning starts to melt away.

'What does my head in,' I hear myself saying, in what I promise myself will be my final mention of the subject, 'is how I can get into so much trouble over my father's ashes when it's okay for the fucking Americans to get pizza delivered in from the local Domino's.'

'No way?'

'Yeah – we're on this high-security base, right, and at least once a day someone orders takeaway and this bloke drives into the facility on his moped with a heatbox big enough to conceal a small nuclear device wobbling on the back.'

'Security must vet him, surely?'

'No! That's just the thing!' I say, warming to my subject. 'They give him a quick once over at the gate and then wave him through. I asked once why this was allowed and they told me it was the director's office ordering in the pizza, and he liked it that way because he'd got used to it at Cheyenne Mountain.'

'What's Cheyenne Mountain?'

'It's, like, the bunker that houses command/control for all of US aerospace, the place that tracks every object in orbit around the earth. This place can survive a direct nuclear-missile strike, is completely self-sufficient, has generators big enough to power a small city for a month. It's like the most high-security place in the whole of the US. And they order in!' I shake my head. Look how I'm shaking it. 'It wouldn't happen at DERA, I can tell you that for free.'

That's it, we're off. The big-tech button has been pushed and for the next two hours there's no more talk of dead people as the two of us swap tales about the arcana of technology – the more esoteric, the more extreme, the more wasteful, absurd and dangerous the better. This kind of chat is, after all, the rock upon which our friendship is founded. Neither of us want to talk about our dads or death, not really. Neither of us want to mention girls, as that's a minefield too. What we want to talk about are systems and their SNAFUs. What we want to do is get drunk and stumble through the streets trying to remember the entire script of *Star Wars* and talking Elvish and reciting the precepts of Discordianism. And, hopeless boys together, this is what we do:

The Story of the SNAFU Principle
(as recited [drunkenly] on the streets of Nottingham
by Cooper James and Miles Clayton)

In the beginning was the Plan,
and then came the specification.
And the Plan was without form,
and the specification was void.

And darkness was upon the faces of the implementors,
and they spake unto their leader, thus:
'It is a crock of shit,
and it smells as of a sewer.'

And the leader he hath pitied them,
and took aside the project leader and to him sayeth:
'It is a crock of excrement
and none may abide the odour thereof.'

And the project leader he believeth him,
and spake these words unto his section head:
'It is a container of excrement and 'tis very strong,
such that no one may abide it.'

And the section head he rusheth to his department manager,
and informeth him thusly of the news:
'It is a vessel of fertilizer,
and none may abide its strength.'

And the department manager he carrieth these words
unto his general manager, and in this manner they were
repeateth:
'It containeth that which aideth the growth of plants,
and it is very strong.'

And lo the general manager rejoiced,
and delivereth the tidings unto the Vice President.
'It promoteth growth,' sayeth he,
'and it is very powerful.'

And rusheth the Vice President to the side of the great
President,
where at once he joyously exclaimed:
'Here, see this powerful new piece of software,
that will expand our company and heap upon us untold riches!'

And so it was that the President looketh upon the Product.
And he saw that it was good.

But the words seem lost and hollow and I get the sense that Miles is humouring me, going through the motions for my benefit. And I can't help thinking, after he and Kristrún have gone to bed and left me lying cocooned in an expensive sleeping bag on their sofa, head spinning with more beer than I ever drink, that there's another game going on, one that I have somehow failed to learn to play.

I push in through my front door to the soft smell of a house that's been standing empty for a couple of days. In the kitchen, on the sideboard, the answerphone is flashing. Six messages. The first four

I've listened to already – they're old, from Liz, left over from before I left, when I was sitting in the house alone, not going out and not answering the phone, just listening a lot to Radiohead and Arvo Pärt and my extensive collection of minimalist German and Japanese electronica turned up very loud while trying to pretend I'd transcended body and emotion and family and job and all of base mundanity and was now inhabiting another, higher, altogether purer plane of being. In the end of course it didn't work; in the end my stomach forced me to drive up to the supermarket, and once I was out the house I realized that I had no choice but to go to Nottingham. But for a time staying in for ever seemed like much the better option.

The first new message is also from Liz. 'I got your message,' it says. 'And yes, you were right, it was unbelievably petty and small-minded. There was absolutely no way you could be justified about feeling that way towards Moon, the poor guy. It certainly wasn't his fault. Call me tomorrow at work. I'm going to have another talk with Andrews, see what he can do. Don't panic. It'll get sorted. Promise.'

Great. Fine. What's she going to do? Promise him she'll spend the day on her knees down inside his crawlspace if he'll reinstate me? Fat chance. You may be my superior, Lizster, you and Andrews may even want to shag each other stupid, but I know enough about the way things work at Featherbrooks to know that you've got no power in this situation, no power at all. Neither of you have. Andrews is just a fucking lackey, basically, just as much as you or I. Another jobsworth, promoted to management precisely because of his total lack of initiative and his wondrous inability to have an independent thought. Just because he's got a title and an office space you think he's something. But he's not. He'll do exactly what he's told. If I want to solve this thing, to sort it out, the first, most urgent step is to cut him out the loop completely. Build an Andrews bypass. With him working as intermediary between me and Daniels I might as well give up now. I've already lost.

I'd be happy to wallow onwards in this train of thought and spend the next hour and a half feeling sorry for myself, but then message two starts playing. And message two is the real surprise. Because message two's from Stasie.

Her voice sounds muffled – I think she's eating toffee. 'Er, yeah, Cooper?' she is saying. 'I'm sorry if I seemed like a heartless cow yesterday, but some wounds never heal. Still, despite appearances I do understand that he's your father, and if you want to know, then that's your right.' She swallows whatever it is that's been clogging up her mouth then lights a cigarette and takes a lip-smacking drag. 'Thing is, though, you see . . . well, I've been lying to you slightly, when I told you he never sent us any letters. He did send one or two, or quite a few, I can't remember exactly how many, but because they all had Vermont postmarks and that's where *she* was from I burned most of them unread. One of them I did bother to take a look at said he was living in some place not far from Woodstock called Granitetown or Graniteburg. Woodstock – you know, where they had the concert, the first one, I mean, not that ludicrous replay where all the corporate interests started cashing in. He was learning to carve gravestones or something equally dumb. But then he always was an idiot – remember that if nothing else: your father was an idiot.'

The machine clicks off and the new messages LED stops flashing. So. He did write, did he? And she never told me. What a bitch.

'Fuck,' I say, but it feels like nothing. 'FUCK!' I shout, bouncing the word around the walls. But it's still nowhere near expressing how I feel. 'FUUUUCKKKK!' I yell, and picking up the answering machine I dash it to the floor and jump on it before slamming through the door into the living room and walking round and round in a tight figure of eight, trying to calm myself.

What they don't tell you about impulsive and instinctively directed ultra-violence: it makes you feel much better.

It's later. It's late. I know nothing, I've realized. Only Thomas Browne knew everything. And he was the last man who did. Except for Miles. He knows everything too. Or acts like he does.

I pick up the phone, call his mobile.

'Hi,' he says. 'What's up?'

'Er . . .' I say.

'What?'

'I . . .'

'Cooper, are you okay?'

'No. Nothing. Yes, I mean. Yes, I'm fine.'

'So what do you want?'

'Erm, well, I'm thinking of getting a Palm, you know, to replace that Psion I've got?'

'Cool. Psions are shit. Palms rock.'

'Yeah, well, and I was just wondering if you knew of any, er, you know . . .'

'Conversion software?'

'Yeah, that's right.'

'You rang me up for that?' Miles doesn't sound convinced. 'Why didn't you just download it off the net?'

'No, well, I didn't just ring you up for *that*, obviously . . . I rang you up to tell you . . . er . . . I'm thinking of taking a holiday.' I spit it out, or a bit of it at any rate.

'Oh yeah?' he says. 'Anywhere nice?'

When I say 'America' I say it like a question, without meaning to.

'To find out what happened to your dad?' he says.

How come when Miles says it it sounds completely matter-of-fact, like the most natural thing in the world, but when I even think it it sounds impossible and ridiculous? How come when Miles has an idea it doesn't strike him as odd or weird or egotistical or perverse but useful, or not, or fun, or not, or practical, or impractical? He just makes a quick decision about it based on the facts he has available. He doesn't get hamstrung by all the terrible possibilities, by all the might-bes and might-have-beens. He doesn't chase every consequence and ramification down the endless dark alleys of the imagination. He sticks to the boulevards. That's right, the boulevards. That's the difference between Miles and me. He sticks to the highways while I skulk in the alleys.

'Something like that.'

'When you off?'

'Not sure. Soon, though.'

'Good. I think that's a good idea.'

There's a pause. Miles, I can tell, is wondering if I'm still saying what I want to say.

'Er, Miles?'

'Yeah?'

'. . .'

'What?' He's starting to sound exasperated.

'Nothing. It's nothing. Don't worry. I'll see you.'

'Sure. Send us a postcard, yeah?'

'Wilco.'

I can't sleep that night. I go to bed maybe more tired than I've ever been, but don't even get close to losing consciousness. I lie awake until finally, just before dawn, I can't stand it any more and get up, wander about the house a bit, then end up going for a walk.

My house is on a hill and I walk to the top and down the other side. Though the sun's not up yet the sky's already light, light enough to see that God's been up before me, driving around in his SUV, gouging tyre-tracks of purple cumulo-stratus across the loamy sky. Around and about, seven or eight stars blink lazily. Stars, or planets maybe. One of them is definitely Venus, I know that much. As for the others, a couple are definitely moving so that means satellites. Maybe they're military. Maybe they're streaming data down to the facility at Featherbrooks, making all the golf balls chirp. Probably.

I've come to a decision. Within twenty-four hours I'm going to be on a 747 bound for Boston. I'm going to go without saying anything to work. I'm going to go without saying anything to Stasie. I'm going to go without saying anything to Liz. I can't have her filling out a PS-6 and telling Andrews where I've gone. If Daniels is watching me, so be it. But I don't want Andrews to know. And you know what? I don't want Liz knowing either. I want to surprise her, show her that I can sort this mess out for myself. I'm going to go to the US, find out who sent the ashes, tell Daniels it's all been a terrible mistake and make him give me back my job. I'm sick of being the neurotic one, always at the mercy of all these other idiots in my life. I'm going to take control of the situation. That's what I'm going to do.

Take control.

That's right.

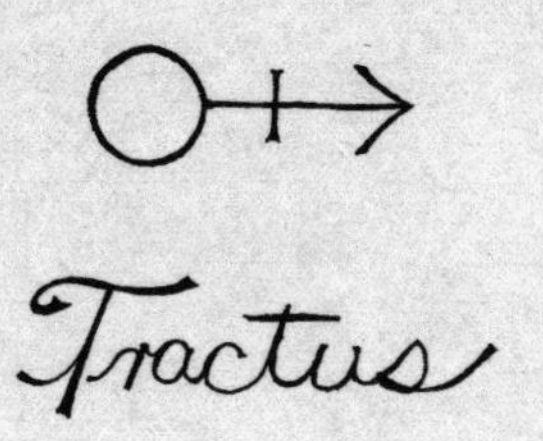
Tractus

Trouble at Customs

Dear Liz,

I've been on US soil precisely half an hour and I'm already in the shit. I'm sitting in a white room at Boston airport. Boston, Massachusetts, USA. This room – it's effectively a cell. It's quite a nice cell, with freshly painted white walls and a padded bench and a tangerine carpet on the floor. But it's still a cell and I'm still locked in. My luggage has still been confiscated. It was the coffee can, is what it was. No surprise there. From beyond the grave my father still manages to fuck with me.

Thomas Browne doesn't have anything to say about coffee cans. I already checked – I read Urne Buriall *on the plane. Can't say it was the most ideal of transatlantic diversions, death and interment not being the things I most want to think about while being carried through the sky at thirty thousand feet on fairly shaky principles of physics, but I suppose recent events have made it morbidly appropriate. Certainly I got some extremely worried looks from the American advertising executive sitting on my right. I think she found my reading of a book that didn't declare itself upon its cover a bit unsettling; she kept peering over from her copy of* High Life *to check it wasn't the* Koran.

Anyway. Point is that Browne has lots to say on the subject of cremation. He says the practice was, and I quote, 'of great Antiquity, and of no slender extent'. He says it was 'confirmable also among the Trojans, from the Funerall Pyre of Hector, burnt before the gates of Troy'. He says that 'as low as the Reign of Julian, we finde that the King of Chionia burnt the body of his Son, and interred the ashes in a silver Urne'. But he has precisely squat to to say about coffee canisters, unless I've missed something. Which I'm sure I haven't, considering all this extra time I've suddenly got on my hands.

I know you're probably thinking it's my fault, that I did something stupid to provoke them, that I lost my temper or something like that, but on this occasion when they asked me what was in the canister I swear I stayed completely calm. It was only when they said it didn't look like a funeral urn and that they couldn't let me bring it into the country, it was only then I lost my rag. Up till then I honestly wasn't paying too much attention – I was too busy listening to the recorded security announcements looping over the PA and looking at the other passengers and trying to take in the giant agribusiness ads hanging on all the walls, ads with big sunflower-yellow words and phrases in lots of different font sizes but no actual content, as I far as I could tell.

How was I to know the next thing that would happen was this snotty little official, this whiny little bureaucrat who'd been going through my bags, would tell me he was going to have to confiscate my father's ashes? How was I to know he'd hit the alarm when I tried to grab them back? How was I to know two female guards would swing into instant action and stick their M-16s practically up the inside of my nostrils before I had a moment to register what was happening?

You won't believe this, I know you won't, but the truth is that at that moment I didn't experience the remotest tinge of fear. I'm frightened now, I promise you – look at how my hand is shaking, I can barely hold the pen – but all I can remember thinking as they turned their guns on me was that it was all so totally absurd. That these ashes should be causing a major security alert for the second time in under a month. And that the guards both looked too little for their guns. Diminutive Hispanic women with Batman-style utility belts clipped round their foxy bellies, chubby fingers drumming sexily on the trigger-guards of their lo-slung M-16s; the image that sprang into my head was of Jill St John in Diamonds are Forever *when she picks up the machine gun on the oil rig and the recoil judders her backwards and right off the deck like she's some kind of wind-up toy. Because that's what looked like was going to happen to these women if they shot at me. They looked overwhelmed. Not so much people with guns as guns with people.*

'Place the canister on the floor,' said one of them while behind me my fellow travellers started backing off as quickly as they could manage. 'Put your hands upon your head,' said the other. 'Which first?' I grinned. See? I told you I wasn't feeling frightened, not right

then. But I don't think either of them saw the joke. The one on the left signalled to her partner and repeated the two sentences, one after the other and I stopped messing around, put the canister on the floor and then put my hands on the back of my head. Another guard – male, enormous, with a ginger crew cut and a broad moustache – inched forward and retrieved it. 'But you can't take that . . .' I tried to say. But no one was listening. Then they took my wallet and my passport and all my luggage and brought me to this room.

And now here I am with Thomas Browne. Thomas tells us cremation 'was in use with most of the Celtæ, Sarmatians, Germans, Gauls, Danes, Swedes, Norwegians; not to omit some use thereof among Carthaginians and Americans', so that's good. He says that 'Manlius the Consul burnt the body of his Son' and that in ancient Rome many conceived it most natural to end in fire because it was the main constituent in the composition of the body, 'according to the doctrine of Heraclitus'. He maintains that 'the Indian Brachmans seemed too great friends unto the fire, who burnt themselves alive', an opinion with which it's hard to disagree. But he has absolutely fuck all to say on the subject of dumping someone's funeral ashes inside a used coffee canister.

What if they think it's anthrax like in Featherbrooks and arrest me? What if they frame me with some trumped up terrorist charge? They've just passed that new law in Congress, the one that allows them to apply the death penalty without a trial. What if I'm the person they decide to test it on? What if they ransack my house and 'find' a file from work? Andrews would plant one for them happily – you know damn well he would. What if they find that copy of The Anarchist's Cookbook *I once downloaded off the net? Or all that porn on my computer? Or all that stationery I stole? What if they discover I got brainwashed by the Chinese as a child and I've been spying all along without even knowing that I've been doing it? What if they lock me up and throw away the key? Will anyone even remember me? You will, won't you Liz? Won't you?*

After three hours and twenty-two minutes in this room my fear and trepidation has reduced me to a level of inactivity that's almost total. I'm sitting in the corner, on the bench, back against the wall, trying not to do anything except breathe and blink. Breathing is something that has begun to require particular attention, seeing how I took the last hit on my inhaler more than an hour ago, so effectively I'm meditating. Which is just as well; having filled up all the blank endpages in my copy of *Urne Buriall* with that letter I just wrote to Liz I've got nothing else to do.

For a while I got onto trying to remember all the countries in Africa, then all the States in the US, then all the countries in the world, and for a while this makes me calm. Then it strikes me that I'm probably being watched on CCTV, that my behaviour's being monitored, compared to analyses and breakdowns of known patterns of criminal activity. I don't know how to respond to this. If I'm being watched, then how should I behave to convince them that I'm innocent? Should I cry, and rage and tear out my hair, mimicking the frustrations of the honest man? Or should I sit quietly and reflectively, gently laughing at my own jokes, like a man who has nothing to fear? What does the terrorist do when he's being watched? Does he act like he's being watched? Is the terrorist exactly the person who assumes he's always under surveillance and behaves accordingly, so appearing more normal than anybody else? While if I act normal, I'm certain to not be very good at it, meaning they'll know I'm acting, meaning that they'll have to ask themselves why I'm acting, meaning that they'll conclude that I'm acting to cover something up, meaning that they'll think that I'm guilty. Unless of course they're far enough advanced with their psychology to have understood that anyone who acts normal is innocent, while anyone who *behaves* normal is a terrorist. Which still leaves me with the question of what counts as a normal response to the kind of severely abnormal situation I'm in.

Maybe that's how they tell. Because if I *was* normal, presumably I wouldn't even have to ask myself this question in the first place . . .

Help me! I'm being held captive by US special forces, by a platoon of diminutive Hispanic girls with big fuck-off guns, girls who work out in the gym and who read only self-help manuals and who've mortgaged their entire adult life to pay for their education and who from an early age had to put up with absent or abusive fathers and overburdened, overweight and distracted mothers whizzed-out on the output of an industrial base devoted to the production of short-lifespan consumer goods and high-caffeine/high-calorie/high-addiction junk foods. Girls who are planning at some point soon to come in here and clap handcuffs on my wrists and lead me away to another cell exactly like this one but positioned deep below the ground in some facility not unlike the one at Featherbrooks and no doubt staffed by stupid, fatherless, programmer drones who are like me in every detail and who will one day through some small misfortune or quirk of fate discover that just like me they too are guilty though they never even knew it.

What was that?

The door.

Someone's unlocking it.

They have come for me.

Thank God for that.

I'm in another room, an office. Behind the desk a walrus of a man is talking to me in between trying to swallow his swivel chair with his arsehole. There are flecks of what I think might be doughnut on the heavy bristles of his moustache. He looks like a man I saw once on a documentary about these four freaks who lived in trailers out in the boondocks of one of those states like Utah or somewhere, one of the ones with bizarrely liberal marriage laws, who'd all got hitched to animals. The particular one I'm thinking of had a donkey for a wife.

The walrus speaks. I've missed the first part of whatever he's saying but the ending seems clear enough. 'Because it's the easiest thing in the world for me to have you put on the next plane back to Britain,' is the gist of it.

I don't like the way he says 'Britain' like that. Like he knows that because you're not American you can't help but feel ambivalent about wherever it is you come from. Like you're running an operating system that's long since obsolete. I've already asked him to get someone to fetch my spare inhaler from my hand luggage. I think I've got about two blasts left on the one I've got, at which point I will definitely start to panic.

'Yes, I know,' I say. I'm trying hard not to grovel but I know that's what he wants. What's it worth to you, he's thinking, what's it worth, to be allowed to stay? Come on now, it's got to be worth more than that, he's thinking. *I want to see you beg.*

'Would you like to go back?' he says. 'To Britain?' he says again.

'No. Well, yes, but not right now,' I say. 'In a month or so, maybe.'

'It'll take you a whole month to scatter a bunch of ashes?'

'Maybe. I don't know. I need to track down some of my father's friends. Work out what's best to do with them, you know?'

'But when I look here on your immigration form you haven't put in the names and addresses of anyone you might be visiting.'

I try to be patient. I really try. I visualize another Cooper, a miniature action-hero Cooper, beating back the fury that's clutching at my throat. 'That's because I don't know, yet, who they might be.'

'This wouldn't,' he says, his face tightening like a drum skin into a pig-eyed expression of such self-satisfied ignorance that it wouldn't surprise me if any moment he burst like a boil across his desk, 'have anything to do with you and he having completely different names, now would it? You being Mr Cooper James and he being . . .' he looks down at the spiral pad in front of him, hippocampus gasping at the effort of trying to recall the extra name, '. . . Mr Jack Reever?' He looks at me again like he's some kind of grand inquisitor instead of what he is, a braindead consumption unit programmed by a lifetime of advertising and media manipulation to sit gobbling industrial output as surely as if they'd come along and strapped him by his jaw to the end of one of their production lines and rigged a rubber conveyor to empty an endless stream of overprocessed shite into his gullet.

Slowly I explain again about not having seen my father for twenty years. Why I'm bothering I've no idea, as Donkeyman's clearly not listening to me. What he's doing is staring at my passport while making a strange noise with his throat.

It's quite a while before I realize that what he's doing is humming.

'Is that Eminem?' I say, meaning it as a sort of desperate joke.

'It's Kid Rock,' he replies. 'You like Kid Rock?'

'Oh yeah,' I lie. 'He's great.' Then I start to shake. Will he detect the sarcasm in my voice? If he does, I'm finished. I bring my inhaler to my lips and take its final hit. That's it, all gone, there's nothing left. Two minutes before I scream.

'You don't know much about music,' he says, 'if you can't tell Kid Rock from Eminem.' Then, and to my complete amazement, he flips open his little inkpad, picks up his little stamp, rolls it on the pad till it's good and wet, then stamps my passport. Bang. 'Two weeks,' he says, filling in the details with a ballpoint pen that looks like a toothpick against his giant paw. 'I'll give you two weeks but that's all I'm giving you. And the ashes or whatever they are stay here. You can pick them up on your way back through to Britain. Sounds like Mr Reever owes it to you to spend some more time over there.'

It takes me almost an entire minute before I can work out what he means by this. 'What if I can't get a flight?' I ask finally.

'You'll get a flight,' he says. 'And I hate to say this, but from what you've told me? It sounds like your old man was a true arsehole. If I was you, I'd forget about doing the right thing by him and take the opportunity to have yourself a real nice holiday.' Then reaching into a drawer he gives me a brochure guide to Boston, taking the trouble to especially recommend to me one of his favourite restaurants and also a strip club he frequents.

Boston's bigger than I imagined. Not just the city itself, but everything. Cars are bigger. Buildings are bigger. Roads are bigger. People are bigger, meaning both fatter and larger-than-life, like they're playing the part of themselves in a film. I respond by playing the confused Englishman back at them. They understand me okay when I do that. If I behave like I do I at home and speak quietly and quickly with an air of combined efficiency and truculence, they look at me like I might be dangerous and start edging away. It's odd. Are they always like this? Or are they just extra paranoid because of what just happened here? The latter, probably – I know Americans are supposed to be patriotic but I've never seen anything like the amount of flags they've got going on. They're draped from windows, over cars and down the sides of buildings, pinned to T-shirts and lapels and hung like curtains in shop windows as well as flying from everything that even vaguely resembles a flag pole. It's a bit like the whole city is trying to cover itself in Elastoplast. I wonder if, say, Manchester would have Union Jacks everywhere like this if someone had flown a plane into Downing Street. Somehow I doubt it.

My hotel is corporate and nondescript, as is the area that it's in. I go straight there, exhausted by my ordeal at Logan Airport, take a bath, then order a meal on room service too tired even to venture downstairs to the restaurant. Then I try to sleep, first with the aircon on (too noisy), then with the aircon off (too hot). Both times I fail. Is this what jet lag is?

Finally I give up and I lie awake trying to work out what I'm going to do now I haven't got the ashes. One thing I'm *not* going to do is send that letter to Liz. I wrote it when I was scared. I said stuff I didn't mean. And anyway, I don't want to rip the pages from the book and there's no way I'm copying the whole thing out again. I'll keep it as a souvenir, a reminder of what I'm like when placed under extreme stress by bureaucratic paranoia. Not that I'm likely to forget.

After a few hours lying motionless staring at the ceiling I decide I might as well carry on with my search for Jack. After all, I'm here now. And who knows, maybe Donkeyman was right and I'll end up wanting to scatter the ashes in England after all, just to serve him right.

I feel spacey, a little outside myself. It's unlike me to feel so positive about such a disastrous situation. I don't know what's come over me. It's weird.

Next morning I'm unable to work out whether I slept or not, but I feel okay so after breakfast (which I manage to consume down in the restaurant – and let me tell you that on the evidence of this meal American breakfasts are just what they're cracked up to be, i.e. the total biz) I go out and rent a car. National, I go to; the woman in reception having directed me to an outlet two blocks down the street. The office, a single-storey prefab sitting sulkily behind several rows of cars, is a run-down looking place. There are scuff marks on the entrance door, the carpet's got a greying sheep track worn into it, the green fabric cushion covers on the aluminium-framed foam easy chairs belch open where they've been burnt with cigarettes and bored customers have picked away at the peachy flesh inside. The once-white plywood counter has yellowed in the sun.

It's also odd because the assistant is so earnest about company policy, so life-or-death, that to begin with I think she might be making fun of me. But when I see the forms I have to sign I realize she's not joking. They want deposits, securities, credit cards, passport, the whole nine yards. They want me to sign my life away. I have to make a trip back to my hotel to get all the things I need. It's only a car, for God's sake. After I get back I try to be all jokey, but it doesn't help the assistant lighten up. 'I'm here to rent you a car,' is her attitude, 'and if I don't carry out my task to the letter, the fabric of society will begin to unravel and I'll be personally responsible for its collapse.' She seems very worried and afraid. Still, she gives me a car eventually.

My hire car isn't some extravagant machine like in all the myths of road-trip America. On the contrary, it's a tidy little Honda Civic in deep metallic blue with a turquoise-pool interior colourway. It's in better condition than the car-hire office, being almost brand new, and is certainly in better condition than my pony Maestro back at home. There's only four hundred and twenty-seven miles on the clock and I suspect most of those are actually factory miles as the interior is still powerfully impregnated with the heady scent of boxfresh packaging. I like it immediately and the next morning I pack my suitcases into the boot (sorry, trunk) and set out for Vermont.

If the car confounds the myths, the road does too. It's not a great and empty highway stretching like a promise towards discovery and the West but a car conveyor, a four-lane train you slot into, lose yourself for however many miles you're going among the thousands of red tail lights undulating around you in slow simplicity like the self-sorting components of a gigantic factory, and then slot off. One thing I did back at Heathrow Duty Free was buy a cheap digital camera so I could have some kind of record of my trip, but I'm not used to taking pictures and I forget I've got it with me so I don't get any photographs of how this looks. It's a shame, because it's really very beautiful – very lulling and hypnotic. Much less stressful than the frantic roads at home.

I'm not sure how much hope I hold out for this camera. I tried getting into photography once before, when I was a teenager, probably thinking that it might be a way to impress girls. Well okay, one girl in particular. Carol Banks. And for a couple of months I went around taking pictures and developing them in the darkroom at school until I had this album filled with stuff I was actually pretty proud of, which one weekend I showed her over chocolate shakes in the McDonald's in central Nottingham. And she flipped through all these images I'd taken so much time and trouble to collect, pictures I thought were filled with resonance and power and not a little meaning, and she said, 'How come you only take pictures of streets and motorways and buildings? How come you don't take any pictures of people, of your friends?'

And I didn't know the answer. And I stopped taking pictures after that.

So maybe now I'll try again.

Here's my first picture. It's of the Graniteburg Masonic Temple.

Here's my second, of a granite quarry.

I'm already getting the feeling that portraits still aren't quite my thing.

Graniteburg is in the mountains of Vermont, surrounded by towns that in the winter turn into ski resorts. It's the Granite Capital of the World, at least according to the big stone sign you pass as you motor into town. Granite-faced buildings line the streets, there's an all-granite bank, there are granite statues everywhere. Granite mining has disappeared big chunks from the hillsides – you can tell where they were from the gaps in the green carpet of trees. Granite dust chokes the river that runs through town: its banks, thick with powdered stone, channel an oily sludge away into the valley beneath the bridge that supports the passing highway.

I take a room in a Travelodge just across from a non-chain pizza parlour called The Magic Flame, and after I've checked in I go across the road to eat. The tables have red table cloths and split-cane table mats and candles stuck in bottles drenched in wax. While I eat I stare out the window at the corner opposite, where a hanging traffic light shuffles the few cars passing through here neatly back

and forth. Just across from it is a statue of a man with a heavy moustache, dressed in a flat cap and apron, holding a chisel in one hand, a mallet in the other. He looks a bit like the waiter who's been serving me. A stonemason, I suppose; it's a war memorial, I think. He's looking out over the valley at something, I don't know what. Maybe the future. Maybe the past. Maybe a particularly rich lode of stone extruding from a distant mountainside. Maybe the expressway that carries traffic to the north; that's what's over there these days.

When the waiter – who I think might also be the owner; he has this kind of proprietary look – brings me my crème brûlée I tell him I'm looking for someone who used to carve stone here, maybe fifteen or twenty years back. He tells me he doesn't know, suggests I try over at the toolworks over on the other side of town. So after I've finished eating and paid the bill that's where I go.

God's Own Rock

The man behind the counter at Donready & Sons is dressed smart-casual: pressed navy slacks and a clean white brushed-cotton shirt, open at the collar; his thick black hair crashes down in a long black wave across his forehead. Fretful is the word that best describes him. He's got this expression, looks like he's been dreaming of escape and I'm the prison guard come to remind him that it's hopeless. Through the door behind him I can see dark machines, large, the colour of bullets; glimpses of another century, another millennium. They're making so much noise he has to close the door and make me repeat Jack Reever's name.

'I don't know,' he says. 'It's a long time ago.' The place is immaculate. Pristine. Behind him tools hang in neat lines on labelled racks: cape chisels, hand tracers, mash hammers, striking caps, four-tooth rippers, shims. It's like a dentist's for mountain dwellers, devoted to the maintenance of golem teeth. Jack was here, I know he was. Not because of the last letter Stasie said he sent but just because it feels right. Though I sense it was dirtier, when he was here. Dirtier, rawer, more naked. Devoted less to orthodontics, more to brute extraction.

'How long ago did you say?'

'About fifteen years or thereabouts. I can't be exactly sure.'

That would be in his father's time, he tells me. His father doesn't live in town anymore, not since he retired.

'Oh, so you're the son,' I say, pointing to the Donready & Sons logo on a blue and silver tool catalogue. It's nerves that make me ask this question. What's it got to do with me?

'I'm the grandson,' he says, looking less than pleased about it.

His father comes and minds the store on Saturdays, he says, if I feel like coming back then. In the meantime maybe I could try up at God's Own Rock. Most carvers who've been through

Graniteburg have worked there at some point or another.

'What's God's Own Rock?'

'It's what's taken over,' he says. The best word to describe him now is glum.

God's Own Rock is situated just outside of town, in a campus-style industrial park attractively laid out on a landscaped bit of hill. The road up here flows between giant piles of stone – the way the trees grow all over them they look like the remains of a ruined city.

The first building you get to, the one nearest the car park, is a visitors' centre, housed in a single-storey timber prefab. Inside there's all sorts of stuff. There are big pinboards presenting facts about granite mining and stone carving, from which I discover that the big tree-covered heaps are waste stone called 'grout', useless for anything but landfills or crushing up for gravel. There's one booklet on the history of Graniteburg, two on the history of God's Own Rock. There are racks of little granite samples and all these cool crystals – quartzes and sulphur and amethyst and stuff – that the miners have found while quarrying. There are tables covered in little granite keepsakes and gewgaws: penholders and mini tombstones and that kind of thing. There are stuffed eagles and owls fixed to bits of branch set into the walls. There's a showroom dummy dressed in a stone-worker's outfit: yellow waterproofs, a helmet, heavy-duty gloves, a face mask, earmuffs, protective eyewear. All gear the man on the memorial in town didn't have. It's funny, though. You can't imagine putting up a statue looking like this in town. I mean, it could be anyone.

What there isn't is anyone behind the counter, so as I wander round I try to make it obvious – just in case there are hidden cameras and I'm being watched again – that I'm not here on the rob. I glide regally between the information displays, postcard racks and glass-topped tables making sure I don't bump into anything and whenever I pick up something I examine it at arm's length then put it down emphatically.

I'm about to go and explore the outside section out the back where they've got this ancient steam train that in the old days was used to haul the stone up and down the hill when a voice behind me makes me jump.

'Can I help you?'

She's standing behind the counter looking like a warning sign in tartan trousers and a ribbed scarlet polo neck, peering at me through turquoise plastic glasses. They magnify her eyes so much that along with her short-cropped and greying hair and her pursed but placid mouth she looks she's related to the stuffed owls staring down at us from their perches on the walls.

'I wasn't stealing anything,' I say idiotically.

'I didn't think you were,' the woman smiles. 'Are you English?'

I nod and tell her yes I am, though I don't quite manage to turn all the way around to face her.

'Oh how nice.'

'I suppose it's nice enough.'

'And are you on the hunt for anything special?'

'You could say that.'

'Which is?' She's hovering in the air with a saleswoman's anticipation, trying to coax my answer out from its hole so she can pounce. So I turn around and tell her I'm looking for my dad.

It's like I've squirted a big cloud of owl-oestrogen in her direction. Next thing I know she's fluttered to the ground and practically got her arm round me, like I'm this lost soul she's been detailed to protect. Ten minutes later I've told her everything and she's on the phone to head office further up the hill, putting the screws on someone in senior management to take five minutes to try to help me out.

She succeeds, and packs me off along the drive that winds through the pines up to the main building with instructions to go straight in through the main doors, follow the signs for the office and ask for Mr Berry.

The main building is a giant steel-frame barn about the size and shape of an Ikea superstore, but grey instead of two-tone yellow/blue. The road carries round to the back for the benefit of trucks and lorries, but a path strewn with woodchips splits off from the tarmac and leads pedestrians past a showcase memorial garden of sample grave plots with polished headstones and up to the entrance porch. And when I say up I mean up – the path's on quite a slope and then there are steps and by the time I get to the top I'm out of breath enough to have to pause before opening one of the twin glass doors beyond which, bathed in aircon, a rake-thin receptionist sits staring at a screen. She's wearing a green business suit and looks like a stick of asparagus in an otherwise empty fridge.

As I enter she looks up with a creak. I swear this woman's waist would slip happily down the inside of my thigh. 'Are you the son who's lost his father?' she says, all decorous and neat.

'That's right,' I say, wondering if someone somewhere's got their wires crossed. But I let it lie – I'm too busy guessing how many offers she gets from men whose wives have copped it. I'm sure she gets plenty, though she's too skinny for my taste.

She picks up her phone, talks to it like she would to a child while cleansing a graze on its knee. 'Mr Berry will be down in a few minutes. If you'd like, you can go see our visitors' gallery while you wait.' She angles a twiggy finger in the direction of a passageway. A little golden sign stands beside it, a sign which says 'Visitors' gallery this way'.

'Thank you, I will,' I say. I get this feeling I should probably bow, but manage to stop myself. What I do do is ask if there's a snack machine. Which there isn't.

At the end of the passageway there's a heavy, padded door, and beyond that there's another. Past the first door a sort of hum enters the air; past the second the hum becomes a shudder. This shudder becomes increasingly pronounced as I proceed along the corridor until I can feel the vibrations oscillating from my belly to my buttocks. Eventually I reach padded door number three, and when I open this one I'm almost knocked over backwards by a deluge of metallic sound.

I do believe I've reached the entrance to the stone shed.

I'm in a viewing gallery, a bit like the ones you get overlooking squash courts. A series of labelled photographs, laminated and fixed to the rail in front of me, tell me what I'm looking at. There are saws, sandblasters and polishers of various sizes and types, most of which are equipped with diamond-tipped cutting surfaces of one kind or another. Big chunks of mountain come in at the far end of the shed and begin a complex journey on a series of rollers and conveyors, during which they get sliced and diced into dozens of giant dominos. Grave markers, basically. God's Own Rock is one big tombstone production line. I take a couple of photographs and watch the handful of workers tend to the puzzle of machines until a figure hurries down the gallery towards me, trouser legs flapping an inch or two clear of his shoes.

'Chip Berry!' the figure shouts, smiling and extending a tiny hand. 'You Mr James?'

I nod.

'Wanna come through where it's quieter?'

Yes please.

Three minutes later we're sitting opposite each other on a pair of low, cream, linen-clad divans, listening to ultra-ambient mood music and watching the burbling water feature while a monster shag pile sets about the business of devouring our feet. The water feature's not much to write home about, consisting as it does of a metre of shallow pond filled with machine-cut granite pebbles and enlivened by a stubby water spout that spurts liquid about twelve inches into the air in the exact same shape as a human tongue, albeit a particularly pointed one – not unlike Miles's in fact, his being longer and more pointed than the norm and capable of actually reaching up inside his nose (a feat he used to perform to annoy me, though not one, I think, Kristrùn's been privileged enough to see).

'This is what we call the Sanctuary,' says Chip Berry. 'It's where we always bring our clients.'

I look around pretending to approve. The place looks like the sales office of an upmarket furniture showroom. Which I suppose is what it is. Last bit of furniture you'll ever need. 'Very calming,' is my comment.

He nods, smiles. His pupils dart around, scanning my face, taking it in.

'That's a lot of gravestones you've got out there.'

'Well that's our business!' He says it like he's not quite sure, like he's got certain doubts. He's got ginger hair, ginger sideburns, a ginger moustache and ginger glasses too. In his forties, with pale, freckled skin and limpid, mottled eyes.

'And is business good?'

'Better than good! Like the sign says, this is the granite capital of the world, and we're the capital of the capital! Statues, kerb-stones, bollards, benches, signage. If you want it and granite can do it, we can cut it!' I realize too late that this is supposed to be a joke and when my smile comes it's forced and weak, but it doesn't matter because Berry's already done my laughing for me. When he's finished he lifts his hands and puts them together as if about to pray. 'So. Sally tells me your father has recently passed away?'

I explain that this is true but that it doesn't put me in the market for a memorial. For some reason I apologize.

'Oh that's all right, that's all right! We can't cater to absolutely everybody, can we? Though we do have a wide range of granite urns. Perhaps you'd like to see? I could show you our brochures.'

'No, really, thank you. All I'd like to know is whether my father ever worked for you at any time in the last fifteen to twenty years.'

Berry works hard at trying to look like he's not at all put out even though he is a little put out, really.

'And what did you say his name was?' he says.

'Reever. Jack Reever.'

Next to Berry's divan is a small table on which are several brochures and a white plastic intercom. He presses a silver button on the latter, leans in towards its hidden microphone. 'Marcia? Could you check see if we ever had a Jack Reever working for us, anytime over the last . . . how long did you say again?' he asks in a dreamy, casual voice, though I'm quite sure he heard the first time round, '. . . any time over the last twenty years? When you've got it, could you bring it through? We're in the Sanctuary.'

He shuts off the intercom, gets to his feet, walks over to where some refreshments are laid out on a cherry sideboard. 'It'll no doubt take her a minute or two so we might as well have a quick flip through those brochures while we wait. There's some coffee here as well, if you like. Though probably you'd prefer drinking tea. Being a Brit and everything.'

When asparagus-girl enters about twenty minutes later it's into an uncomfortable silence. While we've been waiting I've learned a great deal about funeral urns and heard several stories of people Chip Berry knows who scattered their parental ashes and later on never forgave themselves for doing it. 'And you know what they always said to me?' all these stories end. 'They said, "Chip, what this whole experience has taught us is there's a basic human need to keep back more than a token, to keep some kind actual physical part of the loved one, so that in a genuine way they're always with us."'

After I hear this for the third or fourth time I tell Chip that my plan for Jack's ashes is to bake them in a big apple pie and eat it with his friends, once I've tracked them down. Hence the silence.

'So . . . John Reever,' Berry says, snatching at the piece of paper. He is now, I think, more than ready to get rid of me.

'Jack,' I say, still annoyed by the hard sell I've been subjected to.

'Jack then,' he says. He studies the paper for a second and twitches his head, like he's just remembered something he did once which he shouldn't have. 'Well, according to this, your father did work here, briefly, er, February through July 1984. Finisher and general labourer, six-month contract. That's all.'

'Why did he leave?'

Berry hands the piece of paper back to Marcia and nods. As she stalks out the room his two eyes grip her buns. It's the most intense expression I've seen in them since I arrived.

'Can't help you there, friend. I was here then, it's true, but I'm afraid to say I really don't remember him. And our records don't say, so . . . We have so many people passing through.'

'You've no idea where he might have gone after he left?'

He turns his wrists out in a negative. 'Sorry.'

I stand up to go and the shag wags at my toes like a giant anemone. 'So you can't tell me anything more?'

Berry shrugs. 'You might try asking down at old Max Depaoli's place,' he says suddenly, like he's just changed his mind about telling me. He's looking at me very carefully, leaning back a little, trying to work something out.

'Where's that then?'

He gives me directions. 'Thanks,' I say. 'Much appreciated.'

But as I turn to leave he grabs the brochures and passes them to me. 'Don't forget these!' he says. Then he grins a hesitant grin and gives me a wink. 'Because hey – that thing about the pie. That's the famous British sense of humour, right?'

Max Depaoli

Depaoli's place is only a couple of hundred yards from the motel where I'm staying. Right in the direction that statue of the stonemason's looking, in fact. Turns out there's a reason for that. It was Depaoli who carved it.

Follow the gaze, you find his studio. That's what Berry said and he was right: at the bottom of a short side road stands an old shingled barn with a modern, steel-frame extension built onto the side and the sound of steel on stone whining out through the gap between the sliding doors. A different sound from the diamond-tipped saws up at God's Own Rock. Not as loud, but more intense. Even before I've parked the Honda it's set my teeth on edge.

I walk up to the entrance and hover at the threshold. Inside is a dust cloud almost more substantial than the human shapes half hidden within it. A hazy glare penetrates a couple of grimy skylights and boosts the output of a row of epileptic neon strips; together they drench the room in a flat grey palette devoid of shadow. Large blocks of stone crouch in corners, chained and ready for the attention of the gantry crane squatting overhead. Between its rails, looking like the shed skin of a record-breaking python, a corrugated silver tube hangs limp; at its business end, hidden somewhere up among the spidery metal rafters, a set of powerful fans breathe out a throaty whirr. Down here in the studio the tube is sucking up air so fast you can see the vortex it's creating.

To begin with I thought there were five or six people at work in here, but now I see that there's only one; the other bodies are people too but they're carved out of stone. Tiny chips of granite hail down on the concrete as the lone sculptor coaxes the leftmost figure into being with a giant bushing tool the size of a small pneumatic drill. The chips pitter-patter against the walls, pile up on the workbenches in drifts. One even buzzes far enough across the studio to strike me on the shoulder.

The statues are of firemen, I think. Hauling on something. No, not hauling, pushing. It's not clear what – there's an absence there, a gap awaiting whatever it is that's going to be placed into their gripping hands. Full-sized Action Men, that's what they look like. They're pretty mad.

I wait. And I wait. And I wait. I even wave my arms over my head. But the sculptor is far too involved in his work to notice me.

'Hey,' I shout. 'Hey!' My voice is beaten back by waves of juddering noise. I wave my arms again, higher this time. Still nothing happens. 'Hey!'

I need to move in closer but I don't dare. It's the dust, is what it is. Already my throat feels like a drinking straw, my lungs like two dried peas. I pull my inhaler from the pocket of my jeans, take a hit. Oh, blessed relief. What did people do before Bayer Pharmaceutical?

Confident of having stolen another minute or so before I asphyxiate, I walk into the space and tap the man on the shoulder. It's like stone itself, the muscle there. As hard, as unforgiving. For a moment I think it's as unfeeling too and I'm about to prod him a second time when the sound of the tool in his hands starts to die away and slowly, very slowly, he turns around to face me.

'What in hell do you want?' Between the peak of a filthy denim cap and the 'O' of a grime-caked face mask twin gas-jets burn blue-hot enough with fury to melt the plastic goggles that are shielding them. Interrupting the master at work is clearly not the thing to do.

'You Max Depaoli?'

'Who wants to know?'

'Jack Reever's son.'

Something flashes in the eyes, not anger this time, something else. Without turning down the heat, Depaoli walks away, clanks his drill into a rack, powers down the compressor, pulls his face mask down around his neck and hawks up a gob of gritty phlegm. Grabbing a rag from a hook on the wall he removes his cap and goggles and wipes a ring of dirt and sweat from features that are older and more fragile than the eyes led me to expect. His skin is coarse and lined as a baked potato skin, his massive eyebrows unfurl left and right like twin grey Nike swooshes. But what I really notice are his hands. Pink and smooth with layers of ancient scar tissue, knotted like old, exposed tree roots, they're missing something. Fingers. One from the right, two from the left. Hardcore.

He spits whatever it is he's brought up from his chest into the dirt, smears it across the concrete with his boot. 'You'd better come in,' he says.

Depaoli's office is in total contrast to Berry's 'Sanctuary'. It's piled with papers, encrusted with stone dust, utterly chaotic. There are three swivel chairs but they're all broken; one's missing an arm, another has a broken back, the third has no padding left of any kind, just bare metal. There's a desk and some shelving and a couple of side units, salvaged, I think, from a kitchen, but you couldn't say anything was in any way organized. There's a PC, a decrepit IBM so delapidated it's hard to imagine it even functions. The only things that look remotely together are the two framed pictures on the wall, each of which show Depaoli standing by a sculpture in a park somewhere shaking the hand of some slick-looking dignitary (different sculptures, different parks, different dignitaries), and the silver mallet and chisel mounted on a little beechwood plinth inscribed with an inscription thanking M. A. M. Depaoli for his long and faithful service to the American Union of Granite Cutters. Oh, and a Mr Coffee machine, which hovers along with some cups on a tray above the mound of catalogues and booklets and directories piled on a two-drawer metal filing cabinet standing over by the wall, and which has the air of being kept in working order less through maintenance than through continual use. Depaoli goes across to it now, fills it with water from a two-gallon jug and switches it on. Reluctantly it starts to gurgle, and coffee fumes begin to displace the dry stink of stone dust from the air.

'You and Jack were good friends then?' I ask.

Depaoli tilts his head from side to side, modestly.

'What makes you think so?'

'Until I mentioned his name I thought you were going to string me up from your crane for interrupting you. Now you're making me coffee.' I don't drink coffee, but I'm hardly going to tell him that, not now I've got on his good side.

He sniffs dismissively. 'Well, you know, I couldn't hold anyone related to Jack responsible for the plain dumbness of their actions. You know, he shot a cap chisel through my hat one time, damn near killed me. And that was the least of what he did. He was five parts insane to two normal, your Jack Reever.' I look shocked and Depaoli laughs. 'Hey,' he says. 'I'm joking. He was a stonemason! They're like chefs! All crazy crazy crazy. It's not a normal job. You have to be fucked up in the head to even want to do it in the first place. You want the truth about your father, well I tell you. He fitted right in.'

Fair enough. 'Was he any good?'

'You mean at carving? He was competent. I don't think he'd carved so much stone when he came to me, but he'd carved wood a lot and that helps, you know, in working with a grain.'

I tense at this. Whenever Jack talked to me about the grain in wood he'd compare it to a woman. One time I remember he'd decided that a group of us were going to spend the weekend making peace pipes like the American Indians used to smoke, though typically Jack had a whole political line about how the Indians never actually called them that – it was English settlers getting the wrong end of the stick and giving what was basically sitting round the fire and chilling out more significance than it deserved.

Anyway, there we were one drab January day sitting round in the living room with these bits of soapstone he'd got from somewhere to make the bowls and and a stick of white ash apiece for the stem. Making a pipe was the perfect thing for the apprentice sculptor, apparently, because not only were you working in wood and stone, the two primary carving materials, but you were also combining the two together in a single finished object – and as any craftsman knew, the combining of different materials was the biggest challenge of all.

That's how he used to talk, Jack, lots of history and deep encouragement, but needless to say I didn't get as far as combining any materials. I was having problems enough dealing with one. The first task we were set was to mark out the centre of the ash stick and then burn a hole all the way down through it using some barbecue skewers that Jack had purloined from the cutlery drawer in the kitchen. Having wrapped their ends around with old scraps of cloth to protect our hands, we had to heat the skewers in the fire until they glowed red hot, then poke them at the wood. It was a task that required a fair degree of patience and concentration if you wanted to get anywhere and not get burned yourself.

Patience and concentration, they were not my closest friends. I stabbed and pushed, pushed and stabbed, burned the carpet, burned the table, burned my hand, but I couldn't get my hole to progress more than the slightest bit. Finally, after moaning that I had a shitty bit of knotty wood, that my skewer wasn't sharp enough, that I didn't want a stupid pipe, Jack took my pipe stem from me and started showing me how. Which would've been fine if he hadn't decided to give me a lecture too, to use me as an example in front of all the other kids. 'This is ash, Ash. It's a tough wood to carve – just like you, you blockhead. It doesn't like doing what it's told. But that doesn't mean you can get all frustrated, lose your temper, force yourself upon it. First rule of carving, kiddo' – he always called me kiddo when he was patronizing me – 'you cannot rape your material. You have to take it with love, you have to coax it, find the grain, you have to seduce it like a woman, and if you get it right it will love you in return.' Jesus. None of us could have been more than eight.

Back to Depaoli. 'Stone has a grain?'

'It's organic material. Of course it does. The way it's deposited, the way it cools – these things mean it will cut in one direction better than another. That every piece will be unique. Take granite. Granite has three separate grains.'

'It does?'

'Sure. First you've got the rift, or what quarrymen call the easyway.' He draws a line across his coffee cup with one badly scarred finger, one of three left on his hand. 'That's the line down which the stone will split most readily, and it's usually the same as the direction the molten magma flowed when it first formed the deposit. You can pick it up by dumping a pail of water over the piece you're planning to carve and seeing how it dries, because the easyway will suck some of the liquid in before it gets a chance to evaporate. You've heard of those magic statues in India, drinking milk? Exact same principle at work.' He draws another line, perpendicular to the first. 'Next you've got the grain they call the grain, and that's your sheeting joints. Those tend to come from all the metal crystals aligning due to the magnetic crystals in the earth.'

'I didn't know there was any metal in granite.'

Depaoli gets up, refills my cup. To my surprise, I've already drunk most of it. 'There's lots. Mainly uranium.'

'Uranium?' At the mention of the word I get a watery sensation in my bowels. Either it's the coffee I've been drinking or it's the discovery that Jack took his anti-nuclear obsession with him when he fled across the sea.

'That's right. For some reason granite has a higher proportion of it than other stones. Four parts per million, or thereabouts. Build a granite basement in your house, you'll give your family more radiation dosage than putting them to work in the local nuclear power plant. It's the radon gas. The radon gas decays from radium which decays from the uranium, see, and they'll breathe it in. It gets into the water too. Lots of the drinking water here has large quantities of radium dissolved in it. And in Europe – that's why spas were spas, because people used to think that the radiation in the water was good for you. They still swear by it in Russia.'

'Yeah, well, look at Russia,' I say, keen to finish up the science lesson. 'Have you got anything that Jack carved while he was here?'

Depaoli looks at me for a long time, his giant eyebrows combing the air for insects to feed into his bulging, hyperthyroidic eyes. Then he sighs, looks at his watch, changes his cap for a cleanish one, picks up his keys. 'Sure,' he says. 'Come with me.'

Battered hands hanging off the steering wheel like two drying lumps of clay, Depaoli drives us north-east through Graniteburg in his pickup. Soon enough the road shakes itself free of the town and slithers upwards to where a small hill cleared of the ubiquitous tall pines and capped instead by a green open meadow of lush, manicured grass juts out of the mountainside. As we roll over the hill's smooth crest a parking lot hoves into view, bordered by a neat yew hedge, at which point the clay lumps come to life and steer the truck into an empty parking space.

'We're here,' he says, as the engine dies.

'Where's here?'

'Cemetery.'

He gets out and I follow him down the path towards a gate set into the centre of the hedge. It stands ajar, and we walk straight through. But what I see on the other side makes me stand and stare.

'Whoa,' I say. 'Does not compute.'

Depaoli pulls out a leather tobacco pouch, starts rolling up a cigarette. 'Sometimes I forget that it's a little unique.'

Cluttering the slope as it curves away into the valley are dozens of graves with barely a regular tombstone among them. Instead there are these . . . consumer monuments, dozens of them, littering the hillside like cloud-carved advertisements. There's a half-scale stone Mercedes hovering on a plinth. There's a marble speedboat plunging through a combed moustache of glittering mica waves. There's a camera, a golf club, a television. A giant die a metre wide balances on its corner, marking a salesman's final resting place. There are houses, aeroplanes. There's a lustrous Ferrari in what Depaoli tells me is a type of granite known as Nubian Black, imported from Africa. There's a four-foot hotdog in Dakota Mahogony from Dakota (for the bun) and Winneway Pink from Quebec (for the sausage). There's an Airstream trailer. A Harley Davidson. A dollar bill. A microphone. A popcorn bucket. A faithful dog. A pipe.

'Did Jack do any of these?' I ask, slightly staggered at the prospect. I mean – it hardly seems his kind of scene.

Depaoli tilts his head, blows smoke. From the side his eyes are like halved ping-pong balls. Comedy eyes, staring straight ahead. And how do eyebrows *get* like that? 'He put in time on some of them. But this kind of work he really hated. He thought it was crazy nonsense, for the most part. Spent half his time complaining about it. Said it was a sign of the nation's moral decay.'

'And what do you think?'

Depaoli shrugs. 'If it's what people want . . .'

'Which ones were his?'

'Oh I don't know . . . I think he did the lettering on that one there, the bushing on that one, maybe.'

'Is that it? Isn't there anything here that was completely his?'

'We're getting there,' he says. 'No hurry, right?'

We wander on, past poker chips and monster trucks, until we turn into a secluded, hedged-in area. Two lines of memorials lead away to where the grass stops and, behind a tidy fence, the trees and wilderness begin. To our left is a little football on a plinth, the grave of a thirteen-year-old boy; next to it a two-foot biplane soars above a granite cloud, and next to that a baseball player stands frozen halfway through a strike. 'That's by Ray Cody,' Depaoli says, indicating the football with his boot, 'another guy who used to work for me. I think it's very beautiful. Jack did too. Pretty much the only thing we ever managed to agree on.'

'What about the biplane and the batter?' I ask. 'Who did them?'

'Those are mine,' he says, turning half away and coughing quietly into his fist.

I kneel down by the biplane to get a better look. Struts, propellor, wings – it's all there, and so delicate it might've been made from polystyrene rather than volcanic rock.

'It's phenomenal,' I tell him, meaning it, but Depaoli pretends not to hear; he's already moved over to the line of sculptures opposite and is inspecting the largest of them, a giant granite teddy bear.

'This is one of Jack's,' he says.

I get up, knees damp from the grass, and go to join him. 'My God, it's huge.' It really is immense. It's got to be six feet from ground to ear. I've no idea what it must weigh. Strangely though, like the biplane, it looks like you could almost pick it up and carry it away. The metal vase of wilting violets set between the base emphasizes the effect, but mostly you have to put it down to Jack's ability as a mason. I don't know if it's the weightlessness, or the size, or the angle of the curves, or the pale, pale shade of grey, but one way or another it reminds me of the orca cast we'd all made together, in Cornwall, on the beach.

'Wow,' I say, because it's the only thing that seems appropriate.

'Yeah. He liked to overreach himself.'

'You don't like it?'

'It looks okay. But what I really think? It's too forced, too metric. Worst of all, it orients against the grain. Remember what I told you about the easyway? Here he's aligned it vertically, so he could work more easily up and down the sides. But this means that the grain is open to the water. Another ten years and it'll start to rot the stone.'

The discovery that Jack made the same mistake with this that he took such pains to lecture me about gives me an unmistakable twinge of pleasure. Ha. Serves him right. I take a few steps back to take a photograph, get myself a souvenir of this little moment, but it seems my camera has decided to stop working – I've had the screen on since we got to graveyard and I think it's drained the battery of all its juice. So instead I wander up to read the inscription.

'She was only three,' I say.

'Uh huh. Jack knew her. Her folks ran the boarding house where he put up when he first came here to Graniteburg; she was born the summer he arrived, if I remember right.'

'How'd she die?'

'Drowned in a splash pool they had set up in the back yard for her to play in. Jack had moved out by then, got his own place just outside of town, but he was real upset. It was very sad. He wouldn't let the parents pay him for the work he did, not even for the stone – he guilt-tripped the guys up at the quarry until they gave him it for next to nothing.'

'That was kind,' I say, ashamed now of my little flush of *schadenfreude*.

'I won't lie to you. Jack could be a real pain in the ass. But he'd stop at nothing when he thought it really mattered.' Depaoli's eyes flick around uncomfortably. He sniffs, pinches out his cigarette, drops the nub in the pouch front of his overalls.

'She must be squashed flat, lying underneath that thing.' It's beginning to seem a little macabre to me, that Jack ran away from me, life, the commune, Stasie, to spend so much time with dead things. I'm beginning to wonder if I got the wrong idea about the whale, always thinking of it as some kind of perfect symbol of how wondrous my family could have been if only it had stayed together. Perhaps it wasn't that at all – perhaps it was an omen of decay, of death; perhaps it signalled the arrival in Jack's life of a negative, depressive force that was going to carry him away from us to work here, entombing people in this cemetery, leaving nothing in his place but a hollow set of memories.

'She's not under it. She's inside of it.'

'*Inside* it?'

'If you could turn it over, you'd see there's a big cavity in the base. The body's in there, in its casket. It's not a headstone, it's a mausoleum. He did another like that too. Commissioned by a rich couple from New York City whose baby miscarried. It was conceived here while they here vacationing so they wanted it buried here as well. Somehow Jack convinced them to let him do this piece for them. Technically it's very good. Better than the bear, though on a much smaller scale. But I can't say I like it, and nor do a lot of folks. Some have even said it should be shifted out the cemetery, relocated somewhere else. But it's still here, yet.'

'Where is it?'

'There, the small one, right at the end. You go look if you like. But if you don't mind I'll just wait for you here.'

I set off across the grass in the direction of the grave. It's by the fence that divides the cemetery from the forest and the grass is longer here; little plastic-looking droplets from the rain that fell last night are still scattered among the wide green blades. From ten metres away it looks like a plain white plinth, squat and square, the kind of modernist grave marker you might find anywhere. At five metres I'm thinking of my shoes; their thin canvas is already saturated. I'm about three metres from the plot when I see, finally, what it is that Jack has carved.

It's a foetus. Life-sized, lifeless and anatomically, absolutely correct. The detail's extraordinary. The tiny little fists, the gently puckered lips, the sleeping eyelids – it's as accurate as a waxwork. It's done in marble, alabaster white, and the surface has that extraordinary smoothness and polish that the best Greek statues have, a hand-touched translucence that glows like skin. But what's most extraordinary of all is that this is not a foetus in relief. It's a foetus in negative, set into the top of the plinth like a scalloped birdbath and brimming full of rainwater. It's so beautiful it makes me gasp. Look, it's saying, I can't carve the child you lost, it's beyond my ability, my art. All I can do is carve the space the death left in your life, all I can do is take a cast.

You fucking arsehole. How could you feel like this for someone you didn't even know? What about the hole you carved in me?

We're back by the statue of the stonemason, waiting for the lights.

'How do I get to Jack's old cabin?' I want to know.

'It's over on the other side of town. Off the quarry road.'

'Where exactly?'

'Well, like I say, you go up the quarry road and once you're out of town take, I think it's the first turning on the right, and it's down that way a mile or two. By the river. In the valley. Sort of on its own. There's nothing much down that way. Never has been, 'cept a few summer properties. In the winter it's no good.'

'So who lives there now?'

Depaoli shakes his head. 'Nobody.'

'It's abandoned?'

'Just some kook.'

'What sort of kook?' The pickup jolts over a pothole as I say this, making the word come out funny. I reckon Depaoli must have taken the tremor in my voice for fear, because straightaway he tries to wind me up.

'A kook, a crazy. One of those survivalist types. Doesn't come into town much. Doesn't mix. Uses drugs, most probably. And paranoid. Nearly landed himself in jail a couple of years back, when he opened fire on a couple of kids.'

'Opened fire?'

'Yeah. Machine gun.'

'Weren't they hurt?'

'Don't think so. Just scared half to death. So you don't want to go creeping up on Cox Macro. Nope. That's definitely something I would not advise.' And then he swings the truck over to the verge about fifty metres from the lights and chugs to a halt. 'Mind if I just drop you here?' he says. 'I've got to go down pick up something from the store.'

'No problem,' I say, and climb out onto the kerb. 'And thank you.' But it's too late for thanks – he's already pulled away.

Cox Macro

The road crests a rise then begins to descend, carrying me deep into a valley dark with tall pines. It's getting late in the day now and the sun is low in the sky; as it flashes into my eyes between the occasional gaps in the trees I start feeling like Deckard in the closing sequence of *Blade Runner*, or Logan in *Logan's Run*.

I always loved *Logan's Run*. It was one of the first TV series I got into after I made the move from Cornwall to Nottingham. Janet and Matthew had a bedroom all prepared. It had wallpaper, grey with thin red and black zigzags, widely spaced. A laquered pine-frame bed with a navy-blue duvet. A pine chest of drawers, pine desk, pine chair, pine wardrobe. And a portable TV. And it was all for me. I'd never even had my own room before, let alone my own TV.

There was a set at the commune, but it was black and white and only used for news and the occasional film or documentary. Everything else was strictly regulated. Even the news was regarded with suspicion – it was watched without guilt only when there was likely to be coverage of a protest march that one of us had been on. Way I remember it, that happened quite a lot – we seemed to spend a great deal of time making CND banners and piling in the bus for a week-long road trip to Windscale or Dungeness or Greenham Common. Mostly it would be combined with a visit to one or other of the free festivals, Stonehenge or Mayfly or Deeply Vale or Glastonbury. We wouldn't go anywhere you had to pay, not unless Stasie was playing, which she often was. It was that whole folk scene. It was fun for us kids – we were left to charge around and do pretty much whatever we wanted. But it's no good in the long run. It leaves you with a false sense of the world, of what it's really like.

And when I got to Nottingham I got given a different kind of freedom. I couldn't go anywhere beyond the corner shop unsupervised but I could watch TV to my heart's content. I think it was part of Janet and Matthew's plan to reprogramme me. And I think it worked. Within a few months I was a total addict. To reruns of US sci-fi serials for the most part: *Project UFO*, *The Invisible Man* with David McCallum, *Knight Rider*, *The Incredible Hulk* with Bill Bixby and Lou Ferrigno, *Logan's Run*.

Logan's Run. What I can remember of it now is mainly just image fragments, some from the film, some from the TV series, mixed up and indistinguishable. Scenes from life in the City of Domes. People in Ku Klux Klan-type robes performing the mysterious ritual of Carousel, which 'reincarnates' people on their thirtieth birthdays. The writhing blue bodies in the Love Shop. Logan's expression when he first makes his escape. The face of Jessica, the girl he takes with him, and the detail of that rosy-pink toga-party dress she wears. The two of them emerging from the trees to speak to the old man living among the ruins of the Library of Congress. Their mollusc-like solar-powered car, cruising along yet another country road that had managed to survive nuclear attack. Various snapshots of a post-apocalyptic America. Jessica touching the old man's wrinkles, amazed that this is what happens to ancient skin. Logan shouting: 'There is no Renewal! Carousel is a lie!'

I think I was probaby more into the TV series than the film. The film has this dumb ending where they go back to the city and Logan trashes the evil computer that runs the place by presenting it with a supposedly unfathomable contradiction, but it was so much better in the series, where Logan and Jessica and their android, Rem, just escaped and went on searching and searching for Sanctuary, for ever if need be. That was where the romance was, in always searching, always moving on. It's an Eden story, for god's sake. Once expelled you can't go back. There is no revolution. That's just dumb.

It's dusk by the time I find the cabin. It has warping shingles and rotten window frames and the roof sags calamitously at the south-eastern end, where a few threads of ragged smoke noodle upwards from a broken chimney pot. It looks like the house of the old woman who lived in a shoe.

A wire cage full of giant brown dogs explodes in a bark-bomb as my car draws up. I park behind the army jeep that's sitting in the middle of weed-choked drive and sit waiting for a minute or two, reminding myself that I grew up around dogs and they're one of the few things of which I'm not actively afraid. Then I get out and walk up to the grey front door, trying not to flinch as an Alsatian, two Dobermanns and an Irish Wolfhound slam themselves against the curtain of wire mesh that's the only thing currently keeping the flesh in contact with my limbs.

Carefully pushing my hand through the rent in the flyscreen, I knock on the door. Once, twice, three times. I'm scared again, suddenly. Any moment I'm half expecting to be shot. Over to my right a light flickers off. I knock again, this time louder. Then I call out, 'Mr Macro? Hello? Anybody home?' No answer. I pull on the screen door and it opens with one of those classically eerie metal-on-plastic screen-door-type creaks. I knock really loud.

Nothing happens. The dogs bark some more.

And then there's a voice, snarling from somewhere inside.

'What da ya want?'

What do I want? 'Er, hello? Is that Mr Macro?'

'Who wants to know?'

'My name is Cooper, and I'm Jack Reever's son . . .'

'Jack Reever's son? Are you serious? *Jack Reever's son*?'

There's silence, for a moment. Then, softly: 'Shit me up!'

Pause. Then the door opens just wide enough for me to get a glimpse of one half of a piratical-looking figure peering out at me from a single, suspicious eye.

'Well, what in hell're ya doin', Jack Reever's son, creeping roun' my patch in the middle of the night? Jack send you, did he?'

'No, Jack Reever didn't send me. Jack's dead.'

'Jack's dead? Far out! Who killed him?'

'Er, nobody killed him – or maybe they did, I don't know. That's what I'm trying to find out.'

Macro stares at me a moment with his yellow orb, then nods to himself. 'Jesus. This is too weird. You'd better come in.'

So much for Depaoli's warning, then.

Macro takes me inside and offers me a drink. Jack Daniel's is all there is on offer. I don't like spirits much, especially neat, but as with Depaoli and the coffee I judge it politic to accept. The room is very humid, smells of wet escalator and has a correspondingly precipitous slope to its warped wooden floor. In the centre is a table, its legs sawn off to counteract the slope, its surface lost beneath a glacier of damp papers, empty bottles, ashtrays, pieces of machinery, crumpled items of unwashed clothing cardboard-stiff with sweat, two bongs deeply stained with use, a solitary shoe and several bracelet-like steel hoops crammed tight with keys. Overhead a single, naked bulb, linked to a wall socket like an astronaut to his capsule by a long, looping piece of cord, farts light across panels of plasterboard so damp and decayed they resemble giant strips of soiled bandage. From inside the yawning sags straw and other dried organic matter slowly drips. This, it seems, is bedding – in the silence I can hear tiny squeaks and trace the pitter-pat of busy feet.

This room – I think it's supposed to be a kitchen. You can tell it's a kitchen because various articles of kitchen-type furniture are ranged around the walls. There, however, the resemblance ends. Each item is slathered in dark whorls of dirt and filth, and they look more like a collection of skid-row drunks than anything to do with food preparation. They include: a rotting chipboard sideboard; some sort of squat, industrial-type fridge; an oven so textured with spills and stains it looks like some kind of giant root ball; an ancient porcelain sink encrusted with crockery and utensils that together have staked out and occupied an extreme position on the hygiene spectrum and don't look like being evicted from it any time soon; and a 1950s Triumph motorbike which for no apparent reason stands propped against the only vacant stretch of wall. All the paintwork, everywhere, is grey, except for where it's black, which I suppose is the fault of the stove – presumably it has been haemorrhaging smoke like that for some time, which would also go some way to explain why there was so little of it managing to make its way up out of the chimney in spite of the size of the fire blazing away merrily inside.

The stove itself is perhaps the most bizarre object in here (which is saying quite a lot). It's the size and shape of a small jet engine, is rusted an even brown and belts out so much heat it's a miracle the cabin hasn't long since been incinerated. As a boy I once saw an old-fashioned corn drier on one of the farms around the commune and it had a furnace just like this, except that one burned oil. I think that's what this is, an adapted drier furnace. Except that no drier furnace I've ever seen was decorated with dials and lights and buttons and radiation-warning labels and had a big sign welded to its top, a sign cut from a sheet of metal with an oxyacetylene torch, a sign saying 'Nuclear Reactor'. I'm about to comment on it when Macro speaks.

'Apologies for not opening the door to you a little sooner but you can't be too careful, living out here like I do. There's some weird folks about.'

I take in my host: the frayed patch he wears over one eye, the stubborn blooms of decay on his four upper teeth, the cloudy skin and the blood-red lightning crackling across the white of his one good eye, the semi-dreadlocked wad of rot-coloured hair.

'Get many intruders, do you?'

'One or two.'

'Well, I'm glad you've given up greeting them with that.' I nod at the antique Gatling gun glinting dully on its tripod in the doorway of the adjacent room.

Macro flushes. 'Who told you 'bout that?'

'It's common gossip, up in town.'

Somewhat disgruntled, Macro shuffles over to one of the kitchen drawers and starts rootling around. 'Well that was years ago. And I fired well above their heads. It was just a warning – they were messing with my dogs.' He nods towards the weapon in the doorway. 'Anyway, that one's just for show. It doesn't work.' He leers a Shane MacGowan leer, moonstruck and snaggle-toothed. 'Though it might, if I put the firing pin back in.'

That's when I realize he's holding something spindly and skeletal. It's an old army revolver, both wooden grips missing from its butt. 'You're not Jack Reever's son,' he says, cocking the gun and pointing it in my direction. 'Jack Reever's son wasn't called Cooper. Jack told me what he'd named his boy was Ash.'

Ever stared down the barrel of a gun held by a maniac and blurted out the story of your life only to have him shoot you? You don't blink, you don't breathe, you don't think. Nothing happens inside of you, nothing at all. It's like your brain's practising for what happens next, giving you a taste of the eternity of nothing that's to come. To all intents and purposes you're already dead, just an empty shell hanging in the air, waiting for gravity to bring you down to earth and your final resting place in one smooth and fluid final slump. And then, when the smile levels out and the hand tendons tense and the hammer smacks forward and clacks on an empty chamber, then something in you does die, in a way. That part of you that crossed into the grave just then, that part doesn't come back. While the diaphragm of your being twangs back into place, howling with the feedback thankfulness of still being alive, the centre of the drum can't help but tear a little, bleed a few particles over onto the other side. It's not much to look at, barely more than a scratch. But you know it's going to be there for ever now, eating away at the fabric around it, working itself wider and wider until one day, inevitably, the power of its suction becomes just too great and all that you are abruptly tumbles in.

'Good answer,' Macro says, before tossing the gun on the table and picking up the nearest of the manky glass flasks. 'Would you like a bong? It's good shit. I grow it myself.' He fits his pulpy lips round the mouthpiece and draws air through the dank liquid that's been sweating quietly away inside.

I can't think of what to say. I'm still in shock, I think, at the simple fact of being alive.

'Don't you want to wash it out first?' is all I can come up with.

'Wash it out? What, are you *crazy*? It can take months to work up a healthy bong water like this. You don't just throw it away. Damn, I've even thought about bottling it and selling it, it's that good.'

'I wouldn't've thought there'd be all that much demand.'

'You'd be surprised. People'll go a good ways out of their way to get hold of quality bong water. But I don't produce enough. Wanna make a successful business out of anything, you gotta shift in bulk. Otherwise there's just no point.'

He digs around in the table mess and unearths a large ziplock bag half filled with dangerous-looking weed that, once exposed to the air, takes about 2.6 seconds to stink up the room. Heartily sucking up lungfuls of the perfume, he works up a clump of it in his palm until it's broken down into a herby-looking powder of small, even particles; these he packs into the bong's dinky metal bowl. I watch him in silence, again catching the quiet clatter of rodent activity. This time the sounds come from the walls. Whatever tribe of creatures is living in there, it's got the whole house fretted with its nests and pathways. The smells, the sounds, the company . . . it's all painfullly reminiscent of my childhood and suddenly it seems like Jack could be sitting here, right here in this kitchen, right here in this chair.

It's nothing, it's the Jack Daniel's that's all, this tingling in my nerves, this warmth in my belly. It's not the spirit of Jack aerosolling into the room, teasingly trying to occupying my actual physical space. It's just that after spending years and years avoiding it I've finally found myself back in his element, his culture, his scene. Everything he ever wanted is right here. Booze, weed, freedom, stuff to carve, motorbikes, guns, psychotic friends. Is this what my trip of discovery is going to uncover? A progression of increasingly useless stoner activities in a series of increasingly desolate hide-outs laid out like cowpats across the USA? And at the end of it, what? Some burnt-out freak whose only reason for not putting a letter or note in with the coffee canister was because he needed the paper to roll his next joint? If that's what I'm in for, I might as well turn round and go home. If that's my heritage, I don't want to know.

'Over to you.' Macro has taken a hit and disappeared behind a curling blue djinn of smoke. An arm extends towards me out of the haze, holding what looks like Aladdin's lamp.

'Er, yeah. I think I'll pass. I don't smoke.' I point to my chest. 'Weak lungs.'

'This won't hurt you man, it's medicine. Perfect for clearing up a touch of asthma. It's not like that shit you buy in the city. I grow this myself.'

'Thanks but no thanks.'

The haze clears and I see that Macro's eye, previously a soggy, puppyish brown, has been transformed into a oil-painted miniature: black sun setting over the apocalypse.

'Your loss.'

'I'm sure.' I wait for him to set the bong back down on the table. 'So you didn't send the ashes then?'

'Who? Me? No friend, not me. I mean, I haven't seen Jack for close on, hell, must be pushing fifteen years now. Not since he left Graniteburg and struck out West.'

He says this like we're in the late nineteenth century, not the early twenty-first. Disappointed to actually hear it even though I knew it was coming, I look through into the next room, beyond the machine gun, to where a dusty hi-fi pokes up from a small pool of scattered LPs. I'm taking bets with myself that there's some Crosby Stills & Nash swimming in there, a couple of Pink Floyds, a shoal of Grateful Dead. Maybe even some Cat Stevens or Steve Hillage, furtling along at the bottom like tired carpet sharks.

'And you've no idea who did?'

'You mean you don't know?'

Was more proof ever needed that marijuana rots the brain? I want to grab this guy by the worn tassels of his stained suede jerkin and scream in his face to wake-the-fuck-up. How stoned is he? Has he even been listening to one word I've said?

But I surprise myself. Instead of firing the smart bombs of fury I act against instinct, ease back on the joystick, cancel turbo-thrust. If he can pretend to be Zen, so can I. 'No, I don't know. That's what I'm trying to find out. That's why I came here, you see? To find out.'

'Shit man, I wish I could be of assistance. But, as I say, it's a long while since I saw hide or hair of your old man. You know, like *anything* could have happened in that time. The mind boggles.'

'But you knew about me. Jack told you he had a son.'

'Yeah, he told me.'

'So he must have told you he ran out on my mother and me?'

Macro shrugs, embarrassed.

'He did mention it, one time.'

'What time?'

Macro gives me a look, surprised I think by my eagerness for information. He's not the only one. 'One time when this little blonde chicklet showed up looking for him.'

Shannon. 'She's the one he cheated on my mother with,' I say thickly.

'Yeah, well, I had it down as something like that. Anyhow, she showed up and he wouldn't give her the time of day. There was a big scene and then she took off and afterwards I asked him what that was all about and he said she was the reason he left England. And that was that. Never told me the specifics, and I never asked.'

Macro guesses that I might want another drink so he reaches for the bottle and pours me one. But my hand is shaking as I lift it to my mouth and I spill some of the whisky on my jeans. I down what's left and hold out the empty glass for a refill.

'And how come you knew about the fact of my existence but Max Depaoli didn't?' I ask, wanting to change the subject. 'I got the impression that he and Jack were pretty close.'

'Depaoli? You've been talking to that motherfucker?'

'Yeah. He's the one who told me how to find you.'

'And about my history with machine guns, no doubt. And he told you he and Jack were close?'

I nod, even though it's not quite true.

'Jesus. Some people have no shame.'

'What d'you mean?'

'Depaoli hated Jack! He was the one who got Jack kicked out of Graniteburg!'

'What?'

Macro unscrews the bowl off of his bong spout, starts cleaning it. 'He was the union rep at the time. The A. U. G. C. – the American Union of Granite Cutters.'

'I saw some sort of award thing from them on Depaoli's desk, a metal mallet and chisel on a plinth.'

'That sounds like one of theirs. Though I shouldn't think more'n five people in the whole damn organization know what to do with a tool that's not pneumatic.' Grunting approvingly at this observation, Macro repacks his bong with weed and takes another hit. 'Depaoli was jealous, was the truth of it. Jack was just as talented as he was with a chisel, maybe more so, and he was real imaginative too. He came here as an apprentice, but within a couple of years he'd already moved out from beneath the master's shadow. His name was getting around and clients were starting to ask for him specifically to work on their memorials. But instead of doing what he should've done, which was quit and set up on his own, he started to slack off in the shop, bullshitting Depaoli, putting most of his energy into carving his own stuff after work.'

'And how come you know all this? Where do you fit in?'

'Because around that time I came to work for Max as well. I filled in the gofer slot that Jack vacated when he'd learned enough to start carving stone full-time.'

'Another refugee from God's Own Rock?'

'Not quite.'

I don't enquire further. 'And you still carve?'

'Nah. Gave all that up years ago. Had some problems with the ligaments in my hand from all the vibration so I started dealing weed to pay the med bills, then by the time they'd fixed me up I'd lost the taste for it. The carving, that is. Not the weed, more's the pity.' Another loud guffaw. 'Anyhow, where were we? Oh yeah, Max and Jack. Well, Depaoli couldn't stomach Jack's success, was the essence of it. And that was partly my fault. Reason I met Jack in the first place was I was writing a little at the time – pieces for art journals, mainly, one or two things for *The Voice*. I came up here to Graniteburg looking for a story, got pointed in Jack's direction, decided he was just the kind of subject I was looking for – this rolling-stone kind of an artist from the Pacific Northwest who'd just spent ten years getting back to nature in remotest Cornwall and was all fired up with these big ideas about his art – and so I did an interview. It got published in one of the journals. I don't remember which.'

'Have you got a copy?'

'Somewhere or other. I'll have to try and dig it out. But yeah – so this interview, well it made quite an impression and raised Jack's profile a few inches above the parapet, and this really got to Max. Here came this slacker, seemingly coasting along, and not only was he carving better tombstones he looked like becoming a big noise in the art world too. Depaoli looked through the union rules, found some piece of crap that forbid union members from carving what they call "black markers" – cut-price headstones – out of official hours and warned Jack that if he didn't quit working on his artworks in the evening he'd get him closed down. Jack didn't stop so Max brought the union down on his head, revoked his carving licence.'

'Couldn't he just carry on regardless?'

'Not unless he paid the six-thousand-dollar fine he'd landed, he couldn't. And it was no good trying to do it in secret – in Graniteburg you can't so much as look at a chisel without the whole town gets to know.'

I'm not sure what to make of all this. I don't feel like Macro's telling me anything other than the truth but then I thought the same about Depaoli. Maybe I'm just gullible. Or maybe they both just believe their own version of events. 'So what did he do?'

'What else could he do? He left, eventually. He didn't have any choice. He packed up his stuff and loaded it into his truck, arranged for this big lump of granite he bought to be sent on by rail – and that was a story in itself: he'd spent months selecting the damn thing, been up to the quarry and shown them exactly the piece he wanted cut, and he'd got so attached to it he couldn't leave it, said one day he was going to use it to carve his masterpiece. Huge thing, eight foot by six on the sides at least, maybe four feet deep, and he was going to load it in the back of his pickup until I pointed out that he'd wreck the suspension before he'd gone three hundred miles let alone three thousand, that it'd cost him more in repairs than it would in shipping. So in the end we took it to the depot and left it there and he drove off into the sunset with just a bag of clothes and a bag of tools and the puppy I gave him riding shotgun.'

As if they understand the dogs in the pen outside fire off a fresh round of high-decibel howls and barks and Macro has to go over to the window, open it, lean out and yell at them to quieten down.

'Nice little mutt, it was. Irish Wolfhound-Alsatian cross, so he probably grew into a nice big mutt eventually. I figured it would do Jack good to have another creature to take responsibility for, seeing as how that was the thing he seemed most keen on avoiding. And it's easier with an animal than a human. Animals are born with souls. Us human beings, we have to build them for ourselves. But Jack took to him right away. Thoth, he named him.'

'Strange name for a dog.'

'Well, you know, Jack was a pretty strange guy,' Macro laughs. 'Thoth was his favourite god – he was the original god of alchemy and Jack was really into all of that. Same as Hermes, basically – you know, hermetic arts and all that stuff, but you can't call a dog Hermes. There's just no way. Leastways not an Irish Wolfhound-Alsatian cross. You know, Jack talked quite a bit about alchemy in that interview – if you hold on a minute I'll go upstairs and have a look-see if I can find it.'

Macro gets up and sways out past the Gatling gun and pretty soon I hear him banging around on the floor above, causing particles of mouse paraphernalia to come cascading out the ceiling and down onto my head. While he's gone I try to clear the detritus from a corner of the table, but when he reappears carrying an untidy stack of papers and magazines he dumps it with much theatre not in the space I've made but on top of an already precarious pile of junk. From the top of the stack he pulls a pale, lemony-coloured booklet, about twenty centimetres square, and waves it in my face. A large radiation symbol has been embossed into the cover between Jack's name and the title: *Frivolous Use*. The colour of the paper's quite unusual – slightly artificial-looking. It reminds me of something, but I can't think what.

'I'd forgotten all about this. Jack sent it to me from Seattle. It's the catalogue from a show he had out there, a couple years after I last saw him. And you've got to check this out, it's just too cool. Watch.' He gets up and goes over to the chipped plastic light switch, one of those old ones that's shaped like a tit, and flips it off. The room goes dark, and a moment or two later I notice that the catalogue has begun to glow.

'Awesome,' I say. Now I remember what that colour reminds me of. When I moved in with Matthew and Janet they got me some glow stars to put up in my bedroom, and it's always that strange slightly lilacy/lemony colour, that paper that glows in the dark. I peeled them off and stuck them all over the ceiling and the walls, trying my best to make them correspond to the constellations the way Jack had taught them to me in Cornwall, on cloudless nights when he was up late working and I'd gone out to the barn to look for him when for whatever reason – damp, cold, scuttling mice, one of the other kids being mean to me – I couldn't sleep. We'd sit on the cliff or, if it wasn't too windy, go and lay down on the beach, and he'd teach me what had been written in the skies by the Phoenicians, the Egyptians, the Greeks.

You couldn't see the real stars in Nottingham, of course, on account of all the streetlights, so night after night I lay awake in my own mini Planetarium in Nottingham, thinking of Jack and trying to find the patterns again. In the beginning it made me feel sad and alone and sometimes I'd even cry, but after a while I started to forget the constellations Jack had taught me and prefer the ones I'd made myself.

Taking the catalogue from Macro, I flip past an introductory essay to a series of photographs of what look like more or less everyday objects, mounted in museum-style display cabinets.

'These are the artworks?'

'Guess so.'

'No sculptures?'

Macro shrugs. 'Maybe he didn't have anything ready. Granite carving can take an age, if you want to get it right.'

I look more closely at the first of the objects – a large silver spoon. 'The Self-Heating Soupspoon™', the caption says. 'Made of radioactive material recycled from discarded household smoke detectors, the Self-Heating Soupspoon has an americium-coated bowl, specially designed to keep your soup warm while you transfer it from the dish to your lips. Perfect for colder climates.'

'Oh.'

'Not quite what they seem, huh?'

'Not quite.'

The next picture shows what I thought was some kind of corset or truss, but reading the caption I realize the main event is a small and elaborate spun-wire brooch, shown on the next page in close-up. 'The High Dose™ Jewelry Collection. Reworked by unemployed goldsmiths, each individually commissioned brooch is painstakingly created out of thorium-impregnated steel wool sourced from camping-lantern mantles. Comes with complimentary lead protective blouse, tailored to fit beneath the wearer's regular evening wear.'

'I take it this is a joke.'

Macro leans over and refills my glass. Unlike before, this now seems like a good idea. 'If there's one thing your old man understood better than anyone, young Cooper, is that there's nothing in life more serious than a really good joke.'

Next up are two pairs of starched, free-standing keks. 'His and Hers Mutation Underwear. Hers is a girdle with deuterium buttons sewn in position over the ovaries, His a comfortable radium codpiece designed both to support and enhance. Tailored from highest-quality American cotton saturated with discarded medical isotopes, these garments don't only look good, they offer a once-in-a-lifetime opportunity to get a jump on evolution.'

'Jesus.'

Macro cackles, takes the catalogue from me and flicks through it to the centre spread, where a crude cartoon shows missiles bursting through the stratosphere and raining down on the former

USSR. 'This was one of my favourites, this one. The Arthead Project. It's a proposal for what to do with a fleet of decommissioned ICBMs. Which is, replace all the warheads with sculptures. That way an advance to DEFCON1 results not in mutual annihilation but in a peace statement being dropped right across enemy territory, totally disorienting your opponent.'

'That's completely insane.'

'Yeah, well, those were more innocent times. Changing the world still seemed possible then. And anyway, it wasn't just anti-war. You could also launch artheads in response to an atomic disaster, Chernobyl, something like that. While the firemen are in there risking their lives to spray a concrete blanket over the melting-down core, missiles could be used to deploy artist-designed warning markers across the contaminated area. Multiple warhead designs would be best: you could fit eight or ten sculptures inside each one and float them down in formation, on parachutes. And because the communication is symbolic you transcend language. With a crack team of highly trained masons standing by round the clock, you could deliver any message you wanted anywhere in the world within a matter of hours. The system could even be funded by using it to deliver cool commercials during times of peace.'

This catalogue – this catalogue is weird. I don't remember Jack having such a dark sense of humour. Most of the time I remember him as being pretty serious and dour. When we spoke it was generally about him trying to instill some principle or ideal in me, which though it no doubt sounded all very worthy and highfalutin at the time would prove almost wholly useless – or even actively counterproductive – in helping me negotiate any problems I might happen to face out in the real world (meaning any place beyond the boundaries of the commune, pretty much). But of course at the time I didn't think that the problems I was having were caused by his advice – I thought they were down to me, that I wasn't good enough or pure enough or whatever to follow through his programme the way he wanted. And I swallowed everything he said, thinking – like you do – that he had all the answers, that everything he said was right. Where this really got me into difficulties was school.

Like all the other adults in the commune, Jack and Stasie didn't really think too highly of school, regarding it as an institution designed to stunt our imaginations and turn us into uncomplaining little automata, primed to spend our lives producing and consuming for the system. This was an attitude with which us kids wholeheartedly concurred, our thinking on the subject underpinned primarily by the lyrics of David Bowie's 'Kooks' and the proto-existential philosophies weaved into the fabric of Jack's stories of how he'd run away from home aged sixteen to go and work as a cowboy on a giant ranch in Nebraska.

We loved these stories. How could we resist? Tales of breaking horses and cutting out cattle, tales of adventure out on the range beneath endless, open skies, stories populated with colourful down-home characters and rich with tips on how to lasso and make a fire and treat snakebite and the best way to make 'cowboy coffee', which was in fact just the same as normal coffee except that you boiled up the water and grinds on an open fire then filtered the mix through a neckerchief before pouring it into a cup, a routine that Jack repeated without fail every morning of every camping trip we ever went on. Alongside the fantasies we spun out of this already rich source material school didn't stand much chance.

As the commune kids went I was relatively quiet but still I was constantly in trouble. Before I even got to school I had a reputation, forged for me by Jake and Max, who though only a couple of years older were already smoking, skipping classes and swearing at the teachers. With them as an example I was going to go bad, it was inevitable, and the teachers knew and hovered like buzzards, fascinated by the inevitability of my fall. The moment something happened – as of course it did – the reaction was immediate, excessive and extraordinarily shrill.

But it doesn't take children long to learn that overreaction is an expression of powerlessness. The teacher that taught me this particular lesson was called Miss Banner, and she didn't teach me all by herself. She had some help from Jack.

Miss Banner was my form teacher, and from day one in her class she and I had a problem with one another, a consequence of my betting Adrian Moffat that he couldn't eat three pieces of chalk (a bet he won, just prior to throwing up). And the litany of misdemeanours went on on a pretty much weekly basis until she discovered I'd been drawing in all the library books I could get my hands on. I don't know why, particularly – I've just always had a thing about scribbling in whatever book I'm reading, it's just something I like to do, like the letter I wrote to Liz in *Urne Buriall*. But Miss Banner was one of those who regard books as sacred objects, to be looked after and maintained in prime condition at all costs. And my actions were, for her, the final straw.

When she found out she threw me out the class and made me stand for the whole morning in the corridor, then when lunchtime came she hauled me out to where her puce Austin 1800 was sitting rusting in the car park and drove me home to the accompaniment of a lecture on how, as no punishment seemed to have the slightest effect on me and the headmaster wouldn't do anything about my behaviour, she had no choice but to take matters directly to my parents.

If I'd been a few years older I'd probably've done whatever Miss Banner said, and willingly. She was young and reasonably pretty, and she had these incredible breasts that danced free of any bra inside one or other of the extensive assortment of fashionably tight tops and T-shirts she owned. But I was still too young to find breasts anything other than oppressive and so I sat rigid in the passenger seat, the weaved vinyl of the seatbelt chafing at my neck, waiting for Armageddon to be visited upon me in the figure of my father. There was no escape. I could try to lie to Miss Banner (and I did, though she wasn't buying it). I could lie to my mother. But I couldn't lie to Jack. He was the one person who inspired complete honesty in me. I couldn't lie to someone who was so firmly committed to searching for truth and authenticity, even if he was my dad. Not aged eight I couldn't anyway. Quite a few years had to pass before I learnt that these are the easiest people of all to lie to. Anyone with an ounce of nous does it as a matter of course.

So we jolted down the track that led to the old farmhouse where we lived, Miss Banner managing to slam the Austin's suspension into the deepest section of each and every one of the potholes on the way. When we got there it just so happened that Dad and Tom were out in the yard, cutting wood. Miss Banner stopped the car, ordered me out and hauled me over to where the two men were standing trying to straightface their amusement at what was happening.

'I'm looking for this young man's father,' Miss Banner said, addressing Jack.

'That'll be him,' said Jack, pointing to Tom.

Tom smirked, unable to suppress a giggle.

'Is that right? Are you Mr Reever?'

'That'll be me,' he sniggered dutifully.

Miss Banner looked from Tom to Jack and back again. She wasn't sure, you could tell, and the doubt had taken a lot of the wind out her sails.

'I'm afraid to have to tell you,' she said, trying to keep momentum, 'that Ash has defaced twenty-three of the school's library books, twenty-three that we've found, at least. And I'm afraid they're going to have to be paid for, and replaced.'

'Oh,' said Tom, sounding a bit more serious now.

'Let's see then,' said Jack.

Sticking out her arm, Miss Banner presented him with the two books she'd brought with her as evidence. Jack took them and had a flick through, showing one or two of the choicer illustrations to Tom.

'I reckon that one's pretty good.'

'Shows a definite artistic talent.'

'You can tell he's your son, alright.'

But Miss Banner didn't like this banter one little bit. 'I think you might take this a little more seriously,' she said. 'Defacing school property is a serious offence.'

'No it's not,' said Jack. 'Let's be honest here.'

'What did you say?'

'I said no, it's not. The real offence is you hauling Ash all the way out here and trying to criminalize what's actually a perfectly healthy creative instinct. You should be encouraging his drawing talent, not stifling it. I've never been able to get him to draw a damn thing but here he is now, turning out what are some very adequate sketches, even if, anatomically, they're – er – not quite correct. What you should be doing is giving him extra tuition in art.'

During this little speech Miss Banner began to squeeze my fingers so hard I thought the bones were going to crack. 'Look. I don't know who you are, but will you stay out of this, please? I'm only interested in dealing with the boy's father.'

'Yeah, well, you're in our place now, and all the men here are his father. That's how we like to do things. And I'd thank you for having some respect.'

'Well, respect is earned, Mr Whoever-you-are, and if you want to earn mine you can start by paying me the money for these books. It'll be £47, if you please.'

'Well, we don't have that kind of money. And even if we did, we wouldn't pay it.'

'Well, you'd better come up with some other solution, because I'm not leaving until you do.'

Miss Banner had guts, I'll give her that. At least least six inches shy of Jack's six feet she still stared him down with all the force that a junior-school teacher can muster. Jack, of course, wasn't easily intimidated and stared right back. They stood like that for several seconds, Jack in his overalls, Miss Banner looking unusually prissy in a white blouse and wool skirt, like Kong versus Godzilla. And as the ground between them shook the realization was slowly dawning on me that I was now forgotten in all this and therefore might just get away with it.

After a good minute of total silence Miss Banner was the first to blink, and she turned and marched back to her Austin and clanked away off up the drive, that being pretty much her only option. Jack gave me a bollocking, of course, when the car had finally disappeared. But it wasn't anything like I'd feared and it didn't matter anyway – he could have made me sleep out in the barn for a week and it wouldn't have dented the pride I carried away with me from that minute spent watching him confront my teacher, solid as a rock, indubitable in his faith in me, prepared to stand up before the world and say to anyone who might care to doubt it that there was no bond stronger than the one that existed between him and his only son. You rarely heard this kind of emotion expressed within the commune, where family ties were regarded with suspicion, and it was something I think I must have longed for without quite realizing it. And now here it was, set right before me clear and uncontaminated. It was gold, for sure, which is probably why I remember it.

And the strange thing is that though this popped into my head as an example of Jack's firmness of purpose, his purity, now I remember it again it seems to me that actually it was pretty funny, that it worked out the way it did because Jack and Tom were larking about. So I guess Jack did have a sense of humour. Maybe I was just too young to understand it then.

By the time I leave Macro's place I'm floating. Not with happiness or euphoria or anything; it's just that I can no longer feel my feet. Macro escorts me outside to the Honda, orders the dogs to shut it and hands me the catalogue and a worn and water-damaged copy of the *Art Forum* issue in which his interview was published. He gives me three other things as well: a newspaper clipping about the opening of the 'Frivolous Use' show from the *Seattle Times*, a copy of a book he says once belonged to my father – though it's not so much a book as the remains of one, a thick wad of pages wrapped in newspaper and held together with a rubber band hefty enough to power a small crossbow – and what's left of the second bottle of bourbon we've got into. 'You're gonna need that,' he says, 'if you're going after Jack.'

I get behind the wheel, reach for the ignition. The engine starts and the vehicle feels miraculous beneath me. I roll backwards until the rear bumper embeds in the steep grass bank opposite the drive.

Standing sepia in the headlights, Macro gives me a double thumbs up.

'Take it easy, Coops my boy. Don't forget to keep in touch!'

I wind the window down and stick my head out, wave, rev up a cloud of silvery smog. 'Thanks Cox. All the best!' A near-stall, a wheelspin, a bout of sudden and hysterical laughter and a glimpse in the rear-view mirror of Macro shaking his head, and then I'm off.

In what it turns out is the wrong direction. Some time goes by before I realize this. Instead of concentrating on the road I've been thinking about the *Seattle Times* article. We'd found it folded inside the back cover of the catalogue, bone dry and powdery with age. As carefully as I could – which wasn't very carefully at all, given how clumsy-drunk I was – I took it out and eased it open on the table. 'Art riot in Fremont,' the sub-head read.

> Traffic came to a standstill in the Fremont area of Seattle yesterday, when anti-nuclear protestors held an impromptu sit-in in streets around the Electroworks art gallery. The source of the controversy was a show by local artist Jack Reever entitled 'Frivolous Use', several of whose exhibits are allegedly constructed from nuclear waste. Which would be controversial anywhere, but in a self-declared 'Nuclear-Free Zone' like Fremont? You could say it's guaranteed to rub folks up the wrong way. In the face of mounting criticism from local activists, who want the show closed and Reever banned from the city, the artist has been defiant. Yesterday he caused further outrage when during an interview on KUOW-FM he said of his opponents: 'These people are morons. Not only is the nuclear content in the artworks minuscule, not only is it almost entirely harmless, but you can buy it in any neighborhood junk store. They should be thanking me for bringing the matter to their attention, not trying to shut me down.' The artist, born locally in King County but resident in Great Britain and Vermont for much of the last fifteen years, said it was 'weirdly reassuring' to return after such a long break to Washington State only to discover that 'the idiot quotient is much

the same.' The show was due to open today, but with that kind of attitude we don't imagine too many Seattleites will be rushing to see it. Especially if they're likely to get a case of cancer along with their weekend culture dose.

I read this out loud to Cox, who found it side-splittingly hilarious. 'Shit! You know, I never knew that was even in there! Good old Jack! I always wondered why he never wrote a note to say hi or anything when he sent me that catalogue. I guess that was his note. And don't you know, I never even saw it.'

'He certainly never lost his taste for a good row,' I observed.

'Too right. Best thing about him. So. I guess you'll be headed to Seattle, then. Seems like the logical place to start looking for the guy.'

But I was less enthusiastic. 'I don't know. I mean . . . Seattle. That's all the way on the other side of the country. And even if I find out who sent the ashes, I'm beginning to seriously doubt that'll help me get me back my job . . .'

'Your job? What's that got to do with anything?'

I explained.

'You mean to say you're only here to save your job? You've got to be kidding me. Is that really all you care about?'

'Well, you know, that was the initial reason . . .' I said, feeling the heat rise to my cheeks.

'So you're going to abandon Jack like he abandoned you? Fuck, Cooper. I thought you were bigger than that.'

'Yeah, no, I am, but I mean I've also only got a two-week visa and it's such a long way to go . . .'

'What you say? Your *visa*?' Cox jumped to his feet and thumped his fist down on the top of the refrigerator with his fist. 'Fuck *that*, man! Jesus, Cooper, you're on a *mission* here. *Fuck* bureaucracy. What's got into you? Of course you've gotta go to Seattle. You've gotta go to Seattle and find out what happened to your dad. These are your *roots* we're talking about here. This is your heritage, your *history*. *Who you are*. Any fat-arse immigration official who wants to argue with that, well, fuck him!'

He was right, of course. I had no choice but to do what he said. For once in my life I had to seize the situation, take charge. I could feel words like fate and destiny beginning to form themselves upon my palate. I silently sounded my name to myself . . . it seemed like it already had a new and fulsome weight. And so with the fire thus rekindled in my heart I stood with Cox and we drank to this new leg of my mission.

Then I said goodbye and got in my car and drove off in the wrong direction. And now I'm lost in the woods, drunk as a skunk, feeling paranoid and filled with doubt and already beginning to lose heart.

I'm not going to let fear overtake me. I'm not going to turn back and ask Macro for directions. I've got a map. All I need's a bit of grit and determination. All I need is to stop worrying, and exhilarate. Exhilarate, accelerate, accelerate up this hill, pedal to the metal, no one's around, let's go for it. It's only a Honda for God's sake, it's not like the damn thing can go very fast . . .

Which is precisely the moment that the road swerves greyly away to the left and I'm too slow to follow and now there are no trees and the moon's right there in front of me, foreshortened and massive, a hole punched in the sky. The wheels strike the verge and for a moment I'm weightless, in perfect harmony with my vehicle, travelling sideways through space. Then with shocking suddenness we're real again and rolling and for some unmeasurable stretch of time everything's in total chaos and then just as suddenly everything is perfectly silent and still.

Told you I had toxoplasmosis.

The thing that stuns me most is that I land right side up. I have a brief flash of panic when I can't open the door, but I calm down when I work out that's because it's locked. I open it, get out, walk around in a figure of eight. My ribs hurt, but apart from that I think I'm basically okay. I'm not so sure about the car. There's a dent in the roof, one brake light is smashed, the right wing is caved in, the bodywork is badly scratched. There's quite a bit of mud and grass embedded in around the door sills, and the rear bumper's been ripped clean off. I get back in, turn the key. Drive forward, drive back, turn the wheel, drive round in a circle, first this way, then that. Seems alright.

I get out again and look around. I'm on an open patch of grass beneath an upturned sugarbowl of stars. Christ. In England you never see stars like this, not anymore – too much light pollution. In the bright moonlight I can see the skid marks I made in the earth. What I thought was a distant ridge of trees is in fact a hedge. Suddenly I realize where I am. I'm at the cemetery.

I leave the car and walk over to the gate. It's locked, but it's easy enough to climb over. Once inside I wander down the slope among the tombs and mausoleums. The marbles and granites have turned blue in the pale, polarized glow. They look fragile and thin, like they've been blown from liquid eggshell. The football in the children's section looks like you could kick it. The biplane looks like any moment it could soar into the sky.

The teddy bear wants me to go up and hug it, so I do. Then I clamber up onto its head and try to find the constellations Jack taught me, years ago. Cassiopeia, Cygnus, Auriga, Lynx. Ethiopians, Phoenicians, Poles, Greeks . . . human history scratched out across the night. A satellite slips between the outstretched arms of Perseus and I think of my job back in England, of nuclear missile defence. What new constellations will be formed when that giant armoury has been clipped round the earth, its turrets all facing in? What new pictures will it pin up in the heavens, this new network of steel and plutonium and silent laser light? Jack would've hated it, of course; he would've thought it was the worst of all possible things. Maybe that's why I love it so much. Sweet revenge. Maybe he told someone to send me the ashes deliberately, knowing it would cost me my job. A final parental gesture, a last piece of advice. No, that's ludicrous. He couldn't've known about the anthrax effect. Unless it was him sending the hoaxes around the US of course. Now there's a thought. I wouldn't put it past him. That'd be a thing to find lying at the bottom of all this.

I can't take the car back to the hire centre. They'll nail me to the floor for what I've done. I'll just keep it till I don't need it any more, then dump it and report it stolen or something. I'll drive the Honda to Seattle. See America. Road trip.

America

New York, Pennsylvania, Ohio, Indiana, Illinois, Iowa, Nebraska, Wyoming, Idaho, Washington. The road trip wasn't quite what I expected. It took me six solid days, not the three I'd thought it would. And there were no crazy adventures or B-movie detours off into the unknown. All I did was sit on various highways, hour after hour, for several days.

My main impression was one of *stuff*. So much stuff, everywhere. Houses, shops, roads, cars, buildings and infrastructures of every kind, neverending. And flags, of course, flags and flags and flags, just like back in Boston, hanging from windows, draped on car bonnets, painted on walls, fluttering on poles, little red, white and blue blisters on the skin of a country whose immune system is under threat.

This idea quickly took hold of me and now when I looked at the map the roads seemed like arteries, the rivers like veins, the great lakes some kind of liver/kidney/heart combo shunting a billion little car-based corpuscles around a body bloated and cancerous. It frightened me. How could all these people, all these businesses and franchises, how could they all *carry on*? I mean, what fuelled them, what powered them, what fed them? Where did it all come from? The more I thought about it the more it seemed impossible to me that so many things, so many places could even exist. I began to feel suffocated, to find myself almost continually short of breath, and it didn't help matters when the Honda's air conditioner broke down and started producing so much condensation that I had to either sit with a cut-off water drum jammed down by my feet to catch the constant stream of drips, stopping every hour or so to bail it out the window, or switch the unit off. But if I did that, then pretty soon I *really* couldn't breathe, and I was getting through my small stock of inhalers fast enough as it was.

These small dramas inside the car contrasted strongly with what was going on outside. Everywhere I went I had a feeling I'd been there already. It was all known and mapped and franchised, devoid of surprises, totally. Even in the open spaces of Nebraska and Wyoming, even driving through Yellowstone, everything was laid out for me. Organized. Once I'd decided where it was I was going I didn't really need to think. Just point the car and press the pedal and stop off at a Burger King or Taco Bell every now and then to get something to eat.

As I switched from highway to gas station to motel to fast-food restaurant and back to highway I quickly lost any sense that I could just turn off the road and stop. In this huge network of choice I had none. I wasn't driving the Honda, the Honda was driving me. Even the air began to feel manufactured and the effort I was making to pump it in and out of my lungs was the work I owed it to keep my place as a component in this vast machine. The exhilaration I'd felt back in the Graniteburg cemetery, when I'd made the decision to run out on the car-hire company, had long ago abandoned me. I began to feel empty, insubstantial, utterly irrelevant. I looked at my surroundings and could summon no adequate response. It became a huge feat of concentration even to keep my mind on the road ahead. I stopped joking to myself about toxoplasmosis and began to wonder quite seriously if I might actually have it or something like it. On day four, it must've been somewhere outside of Des Moines, I seemed to float free of myself altogether. I lost all sense of who I was, what I was experiencing or where I was going. I must've still been functioning on some kind of level because I continued to drive and eat and bail out the water drum. But I don't remember any of it.

When I finally came to I was travelling on a narrow highway bordered on both sides by a giant field of perfect, swaying corn. Visually it was very intense, like the whole world had been split into two planes: one yellow, one blue. Other than the Honda there were no cars on the road so I slowed to a crawl while I tried to work out where on earth I was. And then, on my left, I passed a large wooden sign.

Genethics Late Harvest Corn™

The crop you have been viewing has been proudly brought to you by Genethics Inc.

Genethics – filling the breadbasket of America

(This crop has been genetically improved. All persons found tampering or attempting to tamper with it will be served in accordance with Federal Law.)

My first thoughts were of Jack. I knew so clearly what, in my place, he would've done it was like he was sitting right here in my seat again, simultaneously occupying the exact same physical space. On seeing the sign he'd've pulled directly over onto the side of the road, stopped the car, got out, walked ten yards into the field and taken a piss on the wheat. And if Stasie had been with him she'd've laughed, ranted for a while about how nothing was sacred and how there wasn't anything left that wasn't artificial, and then lit up a joint. While she smoked it she'd have burbled on for ten or fifteen minutes more about how terrible it all was, how shit everything had become, then she'd suddenly switch and become morose and withdrawn and irritable for the remainder of the journey.

When I saw the sign I felt both of these reactions echo round inside me, searching for expression. I even shook my head and let out a sort of sighing laugh like my father would've done. And that's when it struck me. Since leaving Graniteburg I'd been seeing everything through his eyes, from his point of view, almost like it *had* been his ghost I'd felt step into my space in Cox Macro's kitchen that night. And now I did stop the car and pull over and take a moment to gather my thoughts. It was so odd, I can't describe it . . . it was like being possessed. I actively had the feeling of trying to squeeze him out from inside my head. Looking at the sign really helped – in fact I think that the sign was the trigger for me to come back into myself. Because my reaction to it was 100 per cent different from what Jack's and Stasie's would've been.

What the sign made *me* feel, you see, was safe.

The next time I saw a town I left the highway, took a break and started going through the things Cox had given me. The first thing was his interview, which wasn't as enlightening as I'd hoped. Mainly it dealt with stuff I already knew about Jack's background as a sculptor, stuff that was in circulation at the commune. Anyway, here's the text; you can judge for yourself.

The Atomic Alchemist

Concluding our series on the contemporary American craftsman-artist, this month we meet up with the sculptor Jack Reever. Seattle-born Reever left home as a teen and worked as a cowboy in Nebraska before attending the Northwestern College of United Arts. After completing his course he apprenticed to Cascade artist Mike Talus, then traveled to Europe and the UK where he lived for over ten years and was active in the Campaign for Nuclear Disarmament. He returned to the US in the early 1980s, specifically to Graniteburg, Vermont, where his highly original tombstones, strange visions in marble and granite, have made enough noise in the normally very conservative and traditional memorials industry for his name to come to the attention of us here at Art Forum. *So we sent* ***Cox Macro*** *to catch up with him in his cabin in the woods . . .*

CM: When you first came to Graniteburg you apprenticed with Max Depaoli, who's well known for his civic memorials. But since you learned to carve stone you've concentrated on individual tombstones, mausoleums and shrines, a market which went over almost entirely to mass production long ago. At best it's regarded as journeyman work. Why, as someone who sees themselves more as an authentic, Romantic-style artist than a craftsman, did you choose this area to go into?

JR: Okay, well first off, let me start by saying that for me craftsmanship is 99 per cent of art and that I don't see a conflict between great art and commissioned work – I mean, 99 per cent of all the art that was produced during the Italian Renaissance was done on commission, and it didn't do Michelangelo any harm. And second, if something traditional has been replaced by mass production, well then, right there's the best reason of any to revisit it as an artisan, try and recreate it. Because you can guarantee that mass production will have killed it stone dead, if you'll excuse the pun. And then thirdly, I'm a sculptor, and it's hard to look at the history of this art form and not see a deep connection between stone carving and the remembrance of the past. Sometimes it almost seems to me as if preserving the memory of what's gone is why sculpture was invented, when you think back to all the busts and statues and obelisks and so on that human beings have erected to the memory of themselves and each other over the centuries. The latest studies suggest that's why Stonehenge was built – it was at a point in history when climate change was causing the disappearance of the larger mammals from the area that's now the British Isles and people were forced to turn away from hunting, which had been their primary source of food, and start farming instead. Farming involves much more work than hunting, of course, it's like a seven-day activity instead of something you go out and do a couple of days a month. And so they were angry, and scared, and felt the moon goddess – who'd ruled the hunting cycle, because hunting mammals is best done by full moon, at night – had deserted them. And so their priests built them Stonehenge, which is actually designed kind of like a theater, to show how the sun, which now ruled the lives of the populace much more than the moon did, actually followed the patterns the moon made in the sky and in a certain sense was therefore subservient to it in the celestial pantheon. So this monument provided people with a very strong link with what had gone before at the same time as giving them reassurance about the future. And that's what sculpture does.

CM: But what about more personally? Would you say you've always had an attraction to death?

JR: Well, maybe not to death – I'm not one of these gothic types, hanging out in graveyards all dressed in black. But I guess some kind of interest in burial as a ritual has always been there. I had a kind of religious background, growing up, and I can remember carving little tombstones for pet kittens or hamsters that had died, that sort of thing. And maybe more interestingly I would often create imaginary archeological artifacts and hide them somewhere and never tell anybody about them. I grew up during that big wave of post-World War II family-house building, and there was always discarded construction material in our neighborhood, in the ditches and on the vacant lots and stuff, and bricks were easy to come by. And a lot of different kinds of bricks, almost all fired clay. Very difficult to carve, very fragile; trying to carve figures you'd always break 'em at the waist or else you'd break off the head at the neck. But I'd carve these little figures like little magic dolls or something, and I would take them on my bicycle about a quarter or a half a mile to where this housing development I lived in became a steep bluff, an embankment, oh, it seemed huge then, though I should think it was only about a hundred or a hundred and fifty feet high, that's all. And down at the bottom there was an old railroad track there and then beyond that Puget Sound, which is saltwater. Course I loved beachcombing, you can't keep kids away from anything neat like that. But I mean, I can remember I would carve one of these little things, maybe after three or four tries I would get one that hadn't broken yet, and then I'd take a garden trowel from the garden supply of tools in the back yard and I'd get on my bicycle and bicycle over to the top of the bluff. And when I got there I'd get off and walk down this long precarious trail until I reached the railroad tracks where I'd dig this hole as deep as I could reach into this huge clay bank. Then I'd slide my little figurine in and carefully pat all the dirt back in and leave no trace of it, and never tell a soul. So that's an example.

CM: That's great, that's a great example. So maybe . . .

JR: [interrupting] So this would be something for you to remember – should you ever become an archeologist or marry one or anything: don't take anything you find at face value! It may not be tangible proof of a civilization as yet undiscovered. It could merely be proof of a seven-year-old with an artist's soul.

CM: [laughing] So who would you say were your influences?

JR: That's a tough question to answer, there are just so many. Someone, John Lennon or someone like that, once said that your influences are whatever turns you on and I'd pretty much agree with that. But in terms of my general approach and methodology as an artist I guess the guys who had the biggest impact on me were the ones I did my apprenticeship with out on Blakely Island in the early 60s. Mike Talus and Arthur Nutsch and the other guys who were out there, they were part of what was known as the Cascade School, which basically started with a couple of artists coming back to the States after real terrible experiences in World War I and thinking, 'Fuck it, you know, human nature and culture is totally fucked; I'm gonna get into the beauty and the secrets of the natural world.' And some of the people who'd kind of inherited that tradition and would end up linking it to the more intellectual side of the hippy community were living on Blakely, which was a two- or three-hour drive north of Seattle and then a ferry ride. And it was idyllic: small island, heavily wooded, tiny population – mostly artists – and no electricity or telephones. Most of the people there were in their mid to late thirties and here was I, about eighteen years old, turning up to help Mike on a couple of commissions more as a favor on his part to my art teacher back in the city than anything else. So I was pretty impressionable, but also I was keen to learn.

CM: What was it like?

JR: Like? Well, like I say, it was pretty idyllic. Mike and his wife lived on an old farm, small, thirty acres of cleared space surrounded by trees in sort of the central portion of the island. A typical set-up for a lot of artists in the western United States at that time, and what was also fairly typical was that the barn had been converted into a studio. It had a little wood-burning stove, it wasn't fancy at all, but it was watertight. And about a hundred yards distant from that was an old-fashioned two-story saltbox house, that is, a house with two storys at the front and one at the back and a gable roof that extends down over the rear. And it looks like a saltbox, hence the name. This one had no insulation, one wood stove, no electricity and a well that was a bucket on a rope. And the deal was I was to assist on the commissions and help out cutting firewood and doing chores and in return I received a small stipend, I could live in the saltbox house for free and I'd get a certain amount of access to Mike's tools and expertise. Perfect.

CM: And what sort of stuff were you learning?

JR: Oh, wood carving, mostly. I mean, at its worst the Cascade School was into weathered driftwood and real artsy-craftsy nature stuff, the kind of thing that ballooned into New Age kitsch. But at its best, like out on Blakely, you had artists – and I'm going to stick to the sculptors here – like Mike and Arthur who took an enormous pride in the careful selection and seasoning of the woods they used. At the time, like I say, I was right out of art school; when I went to do a carving I chose whatever I could pick up and use and worked on that. But here were these guys discussing the merits of trees that were still growing! And when they thought a tree was ready – cedar and ash and juniper were the real popular ones; ash especially is just beautiful stuff to carve – well they'd go out and cut it down and peel off the bark and season it and then wrap it in plastic and wait maybe five years before they'd start to carve it, though all that while they'd occasionally come back to it, unwrap it, consider what it might become, maybe carve a little sliver or two off. You know, just to get the feel of the wood.

So, I mean, these guys were serious, and that was the key, that meant a lot to me. I definitely didn't have any inclination towards commercial art or commercial applications; for me sculpture was the next best thing to a religious vocation, an expression of the soul. And these guys were the same – romantics, I guess. And the main thing they taught me, other than good wood-carving techniques, was respect for your material. So this is where I learned that when you're doing a carving the material, in this case the wood, it tells you what it will and won't accept. You have to take it with love, you have to seduce it, and it in turn will seduce you. The whole aim is let your artistic vision and skill be catalyzed by the understanding of the material that you gain as you work with it and so seamlessly blend your artwork with what that piece of stone or wood wishes to become.

CM: Sounds pretty fundamental.

JR: Oh yeah. Because it doesn't just apply to decorative carving but to all the plastic arts. Take architecture. Whatever you want to say about the society of the Maya or the ancient Egyptians, there's absolutely no doubt that these people understood stone like nobody before or since. The Maya had no metal tools and yet if you go to one of their temples, say at Chichén Itzá or Palenque, and look along any step that hasn't been too worn away by the ravages of time, you'll see it's as true as any course of brickwork you'll find in any modern city. The only way to do that is by being so in touch with a material that you know everything there is to know about its grains and faults and tendencies. I mean it's scary how good these guys were. And I have a theory about this which goes to explain how it is that civilizations so distant in space and time as the Eygptians and the Maya could come up with such similar designs for their pyramids although we have to assume that there was no communication between them. And it's because the design is within the material: the stone itself encourages such stepped pyramids. It's the simplest shape available that's afforded by the stone. I've seen photographs of a mountain on the south-east coast of Iceland which has eroded along its faults and fissures into almost a precise reproduction of the Kukulcán pyramid at Chichén Itzá. And the Maya had to exploit the same tendencies in the rock that the geomorphological forces exploited. There was no other way. And if you do that there's an 80 per cent chance – if you're trying to build an impressive structure – that a stepped pyramid's what you're going to end up with. And to prove just how well these people understood the materials they were carving, not only does the Kukulcán pyramid actually encase an earlier, smaller one and not only does its design incorporate the huge complexities of the Mayan calendar but the dimensions of the treads and risers of the steps are designed so that an echo which bounces off them imitates the descending chirp of the call of the quetzal, the sacred bird featured in the pyramid's carvings! I mean, these guys made history's first sound recording out of stone! That's true obsession, true technique. And it's my contention that we've got nothing in our culture to compare with that, except maybe the way we know how to exploit the reactive properties of uranium and plutonium. And as a sculptor I wanted as near as I could to approach this kind of sensitivity in my work and part of that was developing a belief that all materials have their appropriate uses.

CM: How do you mean?

JR: Well, if I wanted to carve a rose, I wouldn't choose a hard, glassy material like obsidian or something, because it wouldn't be true to the nature of the material; the material is not 'rose-like.' I mean, there are reasons you might want to make an obsidian rose, the result might be quite spectacular, but it would be dominated by the contrast in the materials and the spectacle of the thing and therefore ultimately quite shallow as a piece. So I'd probably turn to a metal, a gold or a silver, something with which I could fashion very fine leaves and the texture of petals. And I see that as being a relatively unbroken chain of human approach to material use since way prehistorical times. Taken this way, sculpture is a way to discover the essence of materials, not in the sense of Platonic essences, which are so abstract and metaphysical they amount to little more than pointless generalizations, but in the sense of discovering the personality of a material, which means working with it to discover the processes that brought it into being and which link it to other materials that share certain of its properties. In this sense sculpture's got a great deal in common with the practice of alchemy.

CM: Now there's a word.

JR: And one that's very misunderstood.

CM: What would be the correct usage of that term, then, to your way of thinking?

JR: Well, that's not a simple question to answer. Alchemy's not one thing, it's many things – which means it's its own history, more or less, not any set of a priori principles. It starts back with the ancient Egyptians and the magician-god Thoth. Thoth was the scribe of the gods, the god of knowledge and justice, inventor of mathematics, astronomy, engineering, controller of the moon and master of magic. When the sun-god Osiris was murdered and his wife Isis, the moon-goddess, needed to bring him back to life long enough for him to get her pregnant it was Thoth who taught her the necessary spells. And when Isis's son Horus was born it was from Thoth she got the runes and charms needed to protect him from the evil designs of Seth, Osiris's usurping rival.

Anyway, like I say, this Thoth, who the Greeks renamed Hermes, he was the one who gave the Egyptians the gift of alchemy, which to them wasn't just about transforming lead into gold like we think about it but about any kind of transformative process. So if you added yeast to bread, changed it from this indigestible flat slab into this beautiful delicious fluffy thing that was your staple foodstuff, then that was alchemy. If you took some water and fermented it with hops and yeast and made it into beer, that was alchemy too, not just because it magically made you drunk but because the alcohol killed the harmful bacteria and made water much safer to drink; you didn't get ill from it like you did before. The same if you extracted a dye from a plant or animal for dying skin or clothes – some of these extractions were extremely complex processes, effectively magic spells, but if you followed them exactly, they'd allow you to take a couple of bushelfuls of whatever raw material it was you were starting from and end up with a saucer of intense, unadulterated color that would stain indelibly whatever it came into contact with and remain untarnished over time. And in a world of constant decay and change, that was pretty magical.

Naturally enough such transforming processes were also thought of as purifying – literally a gift from the gods. Bread is the obvious example – by adding yeast and baking you could transform indigestible dough into a staple food. Manna from heaven. The dye thing was more symbolic, partly because it was so difficult to produce and partly because its effects were visual rather than visceral. The royal purple that the ancient Egyptians wore, and I think the Mesopotamian Basin People before them, was extracted from a particular gland in a small shellfish that's found in the Mediterranean, a little bivalve. If you catch a couple of thousand of these bivalves and remove their little gall bladders and then bleach them and dry them and grind them and add alcohol to them and leach that out and then evaporate off the leach you finally end up with this beautiful purple dye that was reserved for royalty. Royal purple – the British royal family still uses it today.

And in fact there was a connection there, because it now seems – due to traces of Cornish tin that archeologists have found in Egyptian metal tools and jewelry – that the Egyptians and the Phoenicians had trading routes with Cornwall, and that one of the things that they exchanged for the tin they took was the knowledge of how to make woad, the blue dye the ancient Britons liked to decorate their bodies with. An extremely complicated series of steps is required to extract that dye from the parent plant – so complicated in fact that the exact techniques that were used have been lost today, though we know it's at least a three-step separation and fermentation process – and so it was extremely unlikely the ancient Britons stumbled on it by accident. They just weren't all that advanced. And before you say, well, look at Stonehenge, I have to tell you that it's very likely the astronomical and technical knowledge needed to build that monument came from foreign parts as well.

And so woad extraction can be considered alchemical knowledge, part of an alchemical process. There would have been a ritual surrounding it, just as there was with the use of the dye as body paint, and that ritual would have had psychically transformative properties as well as physical ones. And over the centuries – over the millennia – these techniques got divorced from the original alchemical practices and passed out into the religious community and the metallurgical community and the painting community and the sculpting community and also of course into general use, because you have to remember that all these practices weren't strictly separated from one another as they often are today. Alchemists were also searching for the secret of eternal youth and health, and so were often physicians – Paracelsus being the famous example – or pharmacists, or wool-dyers, or philosophers, or soothsayers, or astrologers or all these things at once.

CM: But a lot of these people were charlatans, con men.

JR: Sure, and that's part of the reason that during the Dark Ages and much of the medieval period the practice of alchemy was forbidden. The church opposed it as a black and satanic art, one that put forward a banned interpretation of the meaning of Christ and the Holy Trinity, and kings and rulers tended to suppress it because they feared that anyone able to manufacture unlimited amounts of gold and silver would quickly become a major challenge to their reign.

But around the time of the Italian Renaissance much of the genuine knowledge contained in alchemy started coming to the surface, mainly because metals were growing in economic importance and alchemy seemed to contain the secrets of how they had been formed and how they could be purified. The process of production of metals was thought to be be akin to that of fermentation, used in the exploitation of those most ancient of alchemical practices: brewing, baking and dying. Because these processes were found in organic matter the active principle involved was often referred to as the 'vegetative principle', and it was to this principle that Sir Isaac Newton later looked when he was searching for a basis for his theory of gravity. Many alchemists, Newton included, thought that the ancients had possessed an almost perfect knowledge of the world and its processes that was later lost, and that these secrets lay concealed in the infamous crab formula of Zosimos or the words of the *Tabula Smaragdina*, the emerald tablet of Hermes Trismegistus, a series of ten instructions carved into a crystal plate. This was sort of the Ten Commandments of the alchemists, and though it turns out the thing was a fake, manufactured by the Gnostics in the second century CE when they were trying to convince everyone that their alchemically informed version of Christianity was better than what eventually became the orthodox one, for a long time it was incredibly important.

As a consequence of their theories of the actions of God, the process of the fall and the creation of the seven base metals the Hermeticists believed that it was within the power of man, indeed, that it was man's purpose on earth, to try to reconstitute the original sophic elements and so heal the universe – an idea which also crops up in the tradition of Jewish Cabala. By taking base metals and 'purifying' them, they believed they could 'transmute' them up the ladder of metallic purity towards the purest of naturally occuring minerals, silver and gold. By purifying gold itself they believed it might be possible to return it to its superfine original state, which would be equivalent to recreating a tiny sliver of one of the active principles of God's original plan for the creation. The powers of such a substance – known by many names, the most common of which was the *lapis philosophorum*, the philosopher's stone – would be immense. Just as the theory of the creation of ores described, under the right conditions it would be able to transmute base metals into gold and transmute gold into more of the *lapis* itself. It would also be able to heal all manner of diseases and, indeed, to help to heal the entire creation, to return it to the original form of God's plan. And if you think there are parallels here with the hype that's talked about the benefits of nuclear power and the manufacture of plutonium, then all I can say is you're not the only one.

So that's alchemy, more or less, and it was one of the things I was interested in.

CM: You say you see parallels between alchemy and atomics. Do these connections also operate in your work?

JR: I guess you could say that. I mean, the whole nuclear thing is part of why I came here to carve granite in the first place.

CM: Can you say a bit more about that?

JR: It's kind of complicated, but I'll try. I mean, as you know, I was pretty interested in nuclear stuff. Part of that was that, like a lot of artists, I'm pretty anti-nuclear; I guess that's the Cascade influence right there for sure. And when I got to England I fell in love and got into the whole hippy thing and ended up setting up in a commune with some other artists I met down in Cornwall, kind of like a mini Blakely – I guess I was trying to reproduce the conditions of the place where up till then I'd been the happiest, set up kind of a substitute family – a substitute for my own, real-life family that is, who I'd never gotten along with from the outset. And being part of CND just went along with all of that.

But one of the things about protest is that if you take it seriously, which I did, you're beholden to educate yourself about the issue in question. And so I started to read up on nuclear science. And two things soon struck me. One was to do with how similar the knowledge structure of nuclear science is, or at least was, in the early days of the nuclear age at the beginning of the century, to that proposed by alchemy. This is no accident of course – it was John Dalton in the early 1900s who did the first real work in separating out fact from alchemical myth and magic and drew up the first proper table of the elements. Then, when Bequerel and Curie and Rutherford and Bohr come along to show us how each of the ninety or so chemical elements that made up the Periodic Table were themselves made up of simpler elements, of protons and neutrons, just two units which when combined would always capture an appropriate number of electrons and hey presto, the atom – which makes up all matter, absolutely – it's still all looking surprisingly alchemical.

The picture gets a little more complicated later, when the move into the subatomic realm gets underway. But you don't need subatomic physics to build a reactor to make plutonium. When they built the Chicago Pile these guys were doing Newtonian physics with atoms. It was all they needed to know.

But of course you can't do the science without producing all the shitty by-products, which brings us neatly round to the second thing that struck me about nuclear science, which is that its pursual [*sic*] is inseparable from the practice of burial. As well as doing a bit of work on the study of the more theoretical end of things I'd also been reading another bunch of articles about the long-term storage of nuclear waste, about how some of this stuff was going to need to be stored for tens or even hundreds of thousands of years before it had decayed away enough for it to be safely reintegrated into the environment. And it turned out that granite batholiths, because of their strength and stability and low water permeability, were amongst the most favored storage sites. Canada and Sweden both had projects for granite depositorys underway and though in the US the powers that be were looking as much to basalt and giant salt deposits as granite itself, they had done viability studies on the Graniteburg deposit and had already built nuclear command and control centers like the one at Cheyenne Mountain deep inside huge granite formations because these were the only things that could survive what amounted to a direct hit by a nuclear weapon. And in my artist's way I had this flash of what we like to call inspiration but may just be an attack of stomach gas, and I thought, hey, wait a minute, there's a connection here. Because the fact was, building these depositories, these mausoleums of waste, was turning out to be a lot more complicated than anyone had thought. Even with granite you couldn't be sure the stuff inside would be safe for a hundred thousand years. I mean, that's like a proper geological timescale, way beyond the human scale of things, way, way beyond the range of what's predictable.

The problems were proving so huge in fact that, despite billions of dollars spent in feasbility studies and planning, the US had not managed to construct a single waste depository. They had no back-end, in the terminology. What they had was all this high-grade waste sitting around in ponds and tanks designed to store it temporarily and nowhere to put it. I mean, we're talking for getting on to a hundred thousand tonnes of this stuff that's so toxic the tiniest particle of it can kill you. And no one was talking about it. It was weapons proliferation that was getting all the attention, our ability to blow up the planet overnight. What was getting overlooked was that even if we didn't blow it up we were already well on our way to poisoning it irreversibly, given all this stuff we had just lying around the place.

And it seemed to me that right here was one big internal contradiction in the nuclear industry's future plans for itself. And I thought, hey, maybe if I apply my art at this precise juncture then I can bring people's attention to it and somehow split it open. Not that I had any idea how I might go about doing that, precisely, but still it seemed to me that perhaps here was a chance to really change things. I mean, here I was doing all this carving on the one hand and all this protesting on the other, and it seemed to me what I really should be doing was trying to combine the two. And apart from anything else I was starting to realize that when confronted with the true size and scale of the nuclear industry my little wood carvings, authentic and beautiful and in praise of the natural world though they may have been, they weren't going to make any difference to anything. I mean, forget about David and Goliath, this was like going up against an interstellar battlecruiser armed only with a peashooter and even in the movies they won't let you get away with that. [Laughs]

CM: So you think that art should make a difference?

JR: Oh yeah. And that's not just an artist's narcissism speaking there, it also goes back to that alchemical ideal.

CM: And that's why you left Cornwall and returned to the US, to study granite carving?

JR: Yeah, pretty much. I mean, things weren't working out for me there in any case; I had visa problems and personal problems and all the rest, and everything was pointing to it being about time to move on. And so I thought, well, you know, I'll high-tail it to Vermont, the site of one of the biggest granite motherlodes in all the world, apprentice myself to a master stonemason and set about learning how to carve this king of stones.

CM: So you do have ambitions beyond carving tombstones for rich New Yorkers?

JR: Heh – guess I've given myself away a little, huh? You're a better interviewer than you look.

CM: Thanks – I'll try and take that as a compliment.

'Personal problems.' Right. So that's what me and Stasie were, were we? 'Personal problems.' What a wanker. What a cunt. How dare he mention his time in Cornwall like that and not even mention us? How could he do that? How could he use the experience as capital in an interview and treat it so partially? The first time I get to this bit it makes me so furious I can't read on, can't even get through the lunch I'm eating in whatever place it is I'm eating in. I end up pushing my plate away then leaving the restaurant and driving in a red funk for the remainder of the afternoon, hardly registering the road through the glaze of my own anger until I notice it's getting dark and I need a piss and a motel for the night, a motel with a TV and a liquor store nearby so I can sit and drink and watch the screen and study it for clues as to why Jack Reever seems to have found it so hard, after he ran away, to acknowledge the fact of my existence.

I remember my father's interest in alchemy all right, and it wasn't as highfalutin as Cox's interview makes it sound. I think it must have been making the cast of the whale that inspired him, because right after that – the very next day, in fact, after he gave that bulla to Moon – he requisitioned a disused section at one end of the barn where he and Tom had their studio for a new project. It was an old cattle stall or something, dark and dank and musty, but he swept it out, dangled a light down from the beams on a strand of dusty flex and rigged up a workbench out of a salvaged railway sleeper.

The workshop was for metalwork, supposedly, but Jack couldn't go and pay for a weight of measured gold or silver to work like anybody else; he had to make the stuff himself. Following a design they'd found in some old book or other, he and Tom built themselves a small blast furnace against the back wall of the barn. It sounds impressive but it wasn't; just a four-foot high box of house-bricks built around a concrete hopper that fed down to a vent from which the melted slag could flow. Set a little higher up were two other vents, but these were input vents, designed to take the nozzles of two giant pairs of blacksmith's bellows which had to be pumped in rhythmic sequence (guess whose job this was) to provide a continual feed of oxygen to the carefully layered stack of ore and charcoal blazing away inside and get it up to smelting temperature.

Once we had the furnace the next thing we needed was some ore. Gold mines aren't the kind of thing you find yourself tripping over every day, but it turned out that there was one in Wales, just to the north of the Brecon Beacons, about six hours' drive away (meaning four hours' drive away in any vehicle other than Jack and Stasie's van). As a general rule, commune road trips were greeted with less than 100 per cent enthusiasm by the younger members of the team, owing to the general level of discomfort, disorientation and disaster they involved. But a mission to find gold? That was different. If nothing else it had to be an improvement on yet another weekend spent camped outside the gates of Hinkley Point.

So early one Saturday morning around 5 a.m. we set off towards the M5 full of dreams of riches and grand designs, Jack at the wheel, Tom riding shotgun, and Max, Moon, Jake and me bedded down on the assortment of manky blankets and smelly sleeping bags that were stored for such occasions under one of the bench seats in the back. Tom woke us up as we were crossing the Severn Bridge (the old one) so that we could get a look at the giant suspension span, which in those days was still regarded as pretty grand even by such supposed enemies of progress as the commune members, and from then on as I remember a combination of dead-leggings and farting competitions kept us pretty much occupied at least far as Abergavenny, where we stopped for a fry-up in a roadside caff.

We arrived at Dolaucothi gold mine around midday, but I don't think it was quite what my father had had in mind. The valley may have been mined for gold since pre-Roman times (as he'd kept telling us on the way) but now it was a National Trust property and the site was all fenced off. Jack was furious. He'd been hoping to find a wild, abandoned place, full of overgrown pits and half-collapsed tunnels that we could explore for a few hours in search of seams of metal which he and Tom could then attack with the pickaxes they'd brought. But there was none of that.

Since we'd come all that way we took the guided tour, which was interesting enough – though Jack did his best to ruin it by contradicting the tour guide every time the poor bloke opened his mouth – but there was clearly no way we were coming away from the place with a few sacks of ore like he'd intended. Not, that is, until he and Tom conceived the thrilling plan of parking up down some side road until after dark, then sneaking in under the fence to steal some of the sample rocks piled inside one of the old-fashioned wooden mining wagons we'd seen that day and which the guide had said were indeed ore-bearing and taken from one of the few workable seams left on the site.

This wasn't as difficult as it might sound. I don't think anyone at the National Trust had ever considered the possibility that someone would be insane enough to try and pinch this stuff. There was no night watchman and the fences were designed more to deter casual vandals and walkers from straying from the valley's hiking paths rather than a thief of purpose and intent. Plus ore is rock, and rock is heavy, and if some crazy person was intent on carting it off in hessian potato sacks in the middle of the night then good luck to him, was probably the attitude. How were they supposed to know the crazy person in question happened to be Jack?

So there we were, the six of us, sneaking our way through the woods towards the fence. In keeping with our lunatic intention the moon was high and full and flooding the forest with narrow-spectrum light, blank and polarized. All around us the profiles of the trees were picked out with extraordinary clarity while their trunks were absolutely black and devoid of any detail, gaps in the gauzy fabric of the night.

With Max and Moon posted as lookouts, Jake and me helped

scrape a channel beneath the fence then hauled up the mesh while the two adults (did I say adults?) scrambled underneath. Once they were through we watched them make their way commando-style towards the little railhead and the series of dark parallelograms which contained the prize.

Throughout the whole operation my heart was in my mouth. I remember being scared, completely scared, thinking that we were going to get caught and go to jail for ever, but even more strongly I remember hating Jack, hating him for being my father, hating him for the way he was treating me. I was still sulking about the bulla thing and now he'd gone and made my pain and jealousy even more acute by giving Moon what I perceived to be the cushty job of lookout while I was ordered to get face down in the dirt and start digging like a rabbit.

I wished we hadn't come; I wanted to cry and go home to the safety of Stasie and my bed. But Jake was there waiting with me by the fence and he didn't seem to be scared at all. Quite the opposite – he was angry at not being allowed to go through into the compound with the men. He was swearing and complaining and saying that they were stupid, they could carry so much more if they'd let him go in with them. I said nothing, just told him to keep his voice down, to which he responded that there was no reason, there was no one here, it was all completely fine. Then he started crawling underneath the fence.

I tried to hold him back and he threw me off, told me he was going, that he wasn't going to miss out. Miss out on what? Jack and Tom had already filled their bags and were staggering back under their weight, but Jake was still determined to run and join them – I think he had this idea that gold nuggets like we'd seen in the museum were lying around out there for the taking. Of course all they did when he got there was hiss at him to stop pissing around and get back and hold the fence like he'd been told. But just as he was on the turn, just as his shoes gripped the ground and propelled him back in my direction, I heard a shout come from the direction of the road, a single word that threw me into a total panic.

'Police!'

Immediately I dropped the wire and started running in the direction of the voice – slightly bizarrely, given that that was where the police – if police there were – would be. But fear had overtaken me, and the more I ran the more frightened I became. The trees were no longer elements in a fragile light sculpture like they'd been on our way in; now they weren't separate entities at all but the fronds and radicles of one single gigantic plant, a gigantic spongy network of breathing being. I could hear my name being called out behind me but it was of no consequence; my sole thought was not to be caught, not to go to jail.

I ran until I tripped. I'd been following the natural path we'd filed along on the way in, a deer path or something, one which was relatively easy to make out even in the moonlight. But what I couldn't see were any obstacles lying at the level of my flitting feet, and soon enough I encountered one – an exposed root or a fallen branch – and I caught my toe and down I went.

I landed with a thump and rolled off the path and into the undergrowth, hurt but not too hurt and sobered by the impact. I'd fallen into a kind of natural hollow, dusty with leaves and twigs but otherwise quite hospitable, and I was just lying there half feeling sorry for myself and half congratulating myself on my skill at managing not only to roll with my fall in a reasonably agile manner but also to end up in such a good hiding place when I spotted something familiar-looking, lying white and bright in the middle of the path about four feet from where I lay.

It was the bulla. Quickly I reached out and snatched it up and examined it – the thong was still attached but the knot had come undone. It must have worked itself loose without Moon realizing and fallen from his neck when he and Max were sent off to their post. I couldn't believe it – it was like a gift from God. There was no question in my mind of returning it – I'd always regarded it as rightfully mine and now fate had delivered it into my hands I wasn't going to give it back. So wrapping the thong around it, I shoved it in my pocket just as the others came hurrying down the path.

It had all been a joke, of course. There were no police, no night watchmen, no threats of any kind – all that had happened was that Moon and Max had got bored waiting and wound each other up into spooking us by raising a false alarm. When we finally emerged from the woods they were almost incapable with glee at our worried expressions and as Jack and Tom weren't particularly angry at them, having managed to achieve their objective before they started crying wolf, the joke lasted for quite some time. Or until we were half an hour or so away from Dolaucothi anyway, at which point Moon discovered his missing totem.

He was really quite upset. But despite lots of sympathy all round – and I did a fantastic job of faking it – there was no question of our going back to look for it, certainly not when everyone had only just got over having the threat of being rumbled by the authorities so present in their minds. So that was that, and now the bulla was mine. My precious.

But my satisfaction was quite short-lived. Now that I had it what could I do with it? I couldn't carry it around for luck, like Moon had done – if anyone saw me with it, my thievery would be discovered. So I kept it hidden in a secret place I had, behind a loose piece of skirting in my corner of our bedroom, and only took it out occasionally, at night, to gaze at it, to test its smoothness against my equally smooth skin, and to experience thrills of ownership and pangs of guilt in pretty much equal measure.

What I couldn't shake was the awareness that possession of this object wasn't making me bigger in my father's eyes, which was the thing I really craved. If anything I felt even smaller and more paltry than before – and also tainted by my immoral deed. By not returning the bulla to Moon, rather than banish the threat of his usurpation I'd made him seem more princely and honourable and therefore more worthy of my father's love than I was myself, and in the end unable to work through this conundrum I set about trying to forget I even had the thing, telling myself that I was going to wait till Moon's birthday and then I was going to return it whenever it forced itself into my mind.

I don't really remember how it all panned out. I think we were all pretty much preoccupied around that time with trying to smelt the ore, and that kind of dominates my memories of the time – mainly because it was such fucking hard work. First the rocks had to be placed in an old iron bath and bashed with heavy wooden stakes with squares of lead sheeting bent around their ends. When they were crushed up into tiny fragments these had to be washed, then crushed again, then washed, then crushed, then washed still more.

Setting and tending the fire was just as tough. Jack bought a truckload of charcoal from a local farmer and we had to hump bags and bags of the stuff from the road down to the barn. Then when the furnace was lit it had to be continually pumped with bellows to keep it as hot as possible. As the charcoal inside burned away the ore new layers of both had to be added in on top, and all the time the bellows needed to be kept pumping. Looking back on it now, this really wasn't something kids should've been involved in. Apart from the heat and the danger of the thing exploding the fumes coming out were dioxin-rich to say the least, and since I was the one who seemed to spend most time on bellows duty I breathed a fair old quantity of them in. I wouldn't be surprised if all the smelting we did that summer was the trigger for the asthma I've suffered from pretty much ever since. Fucking Jack. The whole thing was just completely irresponsible.

When, after several hours of baking-hot work, the guts of the furnace had been transformed from a simple fire into a white-hot jewel of molten slag, Jack would tap the vent at the base with an iron bar and let the innards pour forth down a hardened clay channel into the bowl-like forehearth, where it stood for a few short minutes to allow any slaggy residues and impurities to rise up and form a crust upon the surface. After this the hearth was itself tapped off, at which point the theory was that any pure-ish metal that lay beneath could flow down into a series of shaped cupelling hearths where it would cool and harden into finger-sized ingots.

But of course this didn't happen. Despite multiple attempts we never got more than the faintest trickle of metal out of the thing. Jack claimed himself extremely satisfied and took the scrapings off into his workshop where he fashioned a few six-inch lengths of wire and a couple of golden pins, but without heaps of bullion piling up against the wall of the barn the rest of us soon lost all interest and were no longer available to be inveigled into helping. All in all the impression I took away from the whole saga was that my father was a bit of a maniac and – worse than that – a failure. Especially when he wouldn't leave the furnace alone, kept firing it and fiddling with it for weeks after. All the rest of us could see what a useless idea it was. But something about it had really got to him.

But here's a thing. That old book that I said that Jack and Tom were using? I think it was the same one that Cox gave me along with the catalogue and the interview, the one without a cover.

DE LA PIRO-
TECHNIA.

LIBRI. X. DOVE AMPIAMEN
te ſi tratta non ſolo di ogni ſorte & di-
uerſita di Miniere, ma anchora quan
to ſi ricerca intorno à la prattica di
quelle coſe di quel che ſi appartiene
a l'arte de la fuſione ouer gitto de me
talli come d'ogni altra coſa ſimile à
queſta. Compoſti per il. S. Vanoc-
cio Biringuccio Senneſe.

Con Priuilegio Apoſtolico & de la
Ceſarea Maeſta & del Illuſtriſ. Sena
to Veneto. M D XL.

This is the frontispiece, which I certainly remember. *De la Pirotechnia*. So that's what it was called. It turns out to be a treatise on metals and metallurgy, and according to the introduction the guy who wrote it was born in Siena in 1480. Vannoccio Biringuccio he was called. Dad was an architect and 'superintendent of streets', Mum was . . . the introduction doesn't have a lot to say about Mum, so I can't tell you anything there. Around the turn of the century young Vannoccio left home and travelled around a lot in Germany and Northern Italy, gathering metal-working knowledge on behalf of his lord and patron, Pandolfo Petrucci. And he learned enough that when he returned to Siena around 1510 Pandolfo put him in charge of the local iron mines.

He obviously made a fair fist of it because when Pandolfo died his son, Borghese, gave Biringuccio a post in the armoury. Things looked pretty good, so good that Vannoccio decided to join Borghese and Francesco Castori, the head of the mint, in a major scam to debase the alloy used to produce the local coinage and embezzle the proceeds. But when a popular uprising ousted the ruling family from its seat of power Biringuccio had to flee the Sienese dominion along with most of his aristo friends and go back on the road.

Still, the bad times didn't last – seven years later, in 1523, when Pope Clement VII got the Petrucci family reinstated to their former position, Biringuccio got his old job back. A year later he scored himself a monopoly on the local production of saltpetre and would soon have been rich if it hadn't been for another uprising against the Petrucci in 1526. The Sienese people were so happy at having kicked out their oppressors for a second time that for a while they used the date as a year zero for their public books. Biringuccio, fortunately for him, was in Florence at the time so he didn't get put to the sword. But his property was confiscated and he was declared a rebel and consequently banished.

Not one to side with the oppressed masses, Biringuccio threw his weight behind an armed assault on the city of his birth. When that failed he carved out a living casting cannons for Italian aristocrats. He had to wait for another seven years for peace to descend again on Siena; when it did he managed to pull in some old favours and sort himself out with a senatorship. Back in the driving seat, he expanded his cannon-making business to encompass the building of fortresses. He turned out to be pretty good at that – so good, in fact, that in 1538 he was invited to Rome to become the Director of Papal Munitions, the Pope's armourer, in other words. Unfortunately he didn't get too much time to enjoy his new position because a year later he was dead. Stress, probably. He left behind the manuscript of *De la Pirotechnia*, unrevised, uncorrected but complete. It was published the following year.

It's an amazing book. In the evenings as I cross America I read it in the mass-produced rooms of the various motels and Travelodges I stop in for the night. By day, as I drive beneath the untold miles of telephone cable and powerline that net the air above me, it occupies my thoughts. Chapter by chapter Biringuccio tells you how to find metal ores, how to mine them, how to smelt and assay your findings, and then how to turn them into everything from wire and plate to guns and coins. He tells you how to manufacture bellows, crucibles, kilns and moulds, how to make a mirror, how to cast a bell, how to make lead shot and gunpowder, even how to make fireworks. It's hard to believe, but no one had ever written all this stuff down before. No one had gathered all this knowledge together and laid it out like this, in an open and accessible manner. Most of the information that existed was heuristic, tainted with liberal doses of alchemy and mysticism and known only to the trades – passed down from father to son and master to apprentice, and not shared between guilds or disciplines. Before the *Pirotechnia* came along nobody had a proper overview of the metallurgical processes that underpinned the wealth and power of the Italian city-states which sprang into existence during the Renaissance. And then – bang – there it was. Everything's in it. It's a blueprint for the industrial revolution. The America I'm driving through, this network of franchised mass production bubbling like a foam around the mineheads of metals, DNA and, above all, oil – this is the world of extruded exploitation envisaged in Biringuccio's book. He saw this possibility; his was a vision of a capitalized economic civilization far beyond the confines of that still semi-feudal society the vast majority of his contemporaries inhabited. He's the Machiavelli of economics, if you like. Or maybe the Galileo.

Which is why it's a bit weird that my father, self-styled alchemist, reactionary, rejector of all things tainted by consumerism and capital that he was, spent so much time with him. The Jack I knew, he would've regarded this work – at best – as the product of an evil genius. Apart from anything else, Biringuccio *hated* alchemy. He called it 'sophistic, violent and unnatural'. He said it was pursued only by 'criminals and practisers of fraud', that it was 'founded only on appearance and show', that it contained only 'vice, fraud, loss, fear and shameful infamy'. Biringuccio is absolutely not a mystic – he's the true predecessor of John Dalton and the scientific rationalists. And in the *Pirotechnia* he's bent upon wresting the techniques of separating, purifying and recombining elements fundamental to all metallurgy away from those who'd muddled them with the transmutation of metals and the purification of the soul, and handing them over to the rational empiricists. Alchemy was less the foundation Biringuccio wanted to build on than the ladder he wanted to kick away.

Was Jack making the same kind of transformation? Did he hate Biringuccio, or did he love him? I don't know. I just can't tell.

Dr Metzger

I get off the interstate at one of the signs saying 'Downtown' and drive around randomly looking for a place to stay, wondering why everything seems so peculiarly familiar, until I remember that I built and ran this place myself about eighteen months ago: Seattle looks exactly like the last game of *SimCity* I played. In the end I go for a Ramada on Fifth, next to the monorail (always popular with hotels), at the end of the avenue of US flags. I go in, take a room, have a shower, unpack. When I find my camera I realize that I've driven all the way from Graniteburg without it having occurred to me to take a single photograph, which puts me in a bad mood straightaway.

I take my mood out on the waitress in the drab little restaurant, who I manage to upset with rudeness in the course of ordering a Coke, a burger and a salad bar. By the time the burger comes I've got a stomachache but I eat it anyway. While I eat I finish reading the *Pirotechnia*. I've only got a couple of dozen pages to go, but by now all of the last few latent scraps of glue and string that have been binding the book together have finally given out and I'm turning the sheets of paper one by one, as if I'm reading the thing in manuscript. When I reach the final page – which is quite an odd final page, given that after all this talk of metals and mirrors and furnaces and cannons Biringuccio has signed off with a brief but hokey monograph on the 'fires of Love', which he claims burn more deeply in him than the fires of economics (a claim which, page for page, is patently false) – I turn it over and add the two final, blank sheets to the completed pile only to discover, scrawled in Jack's childlike handwriting across what would have once been the inside back cover, a name and a phone number.

Dr Philip Metzger

206–555–5432

When I see this I forget about my stomachache. Packing up my things I leave the Ramada and walk a couple of blocks down the street to an internet café I drove past earlier. A quick websearch (and by the way, don't think I haven't already tried using the web to track down Jack – I have, several times. Nada) and I get my quarry in my sights: *Dr Philip Metzger, Lecturer in Applied Nuclear Physics, University of Washington*. There's even a photo of him, a blurry digi headshot, though it looks a little weird, like whichever software package last got used to handle it misprocessed the ratio between the X and Y axes and squashed all his features a little in the horizontal plane, making him end up looking like some sort of dwarf.

The website also provides a contact number for his office, a different number from the one Jack had written down, which I assume is out of date.

Next morning, after breakfast, I call the number from my room.

'I'd like to speak to Dr Metzger, please.'

'Dr Metzger's not available right now.' It's a woman's voice, twiny and metallic.

'When will he be back?'

'Who's this calling, please?'

'Erm, it's kind of a personal call. Is there any chance of making an appointment?'

'Not until I have your name.'

'Can you just tell him it's about Jack Reever?'

'And may I ask what it's concerning, Mr Reever?'

'No, I'm not . . . could you just tell him I'm Jack Reever's son? And that I'm only in town for a couple of days, but my father died recently and I'd really like the chance . . .'

'If you'd hold for a moment, please.'

It's an order rather than a request and before I can reply I've been deposited in the middle of 'Horse with No Name' by America, which for some unfathomable reason the University of Washington seems to have decided is the ideal choice of muzak to pipe down the line to those they're holding in call-limbo.

A minute passes. Two. The song jangles, fades, then loops. The lyrics begin to seem enormously appropriate and apt. Another minute. Another. The lyrics, I realize, are utterly nonsensical and ludicrous.

I'm about to go through the desert one more time when the song cuts out and I'm bounced out of purgatory and confronted with a judgement.

'Dr Metzger will see you this afternoon at 4.15.'

'He will?'

'If that's not convenient . . .'

'No, that's fine, it's perfect. I can make it.' I ask her for directions and tersely and efficiently she gives them to me. Grabbing the complimentary Ramada biro and notepaper I scribble them down as best I can, which isn't altogether accurately considering how halfway through I'm distracted by the thought that when I write fast my handwriting is unnervingly similar to Jack's. A fact I find unsettling, to say the least. This specific revulsion I honed and burnished during my teens, but even now I still hate the idea that any part of me was also a part of him.

Despite the haphazard note-making I find the place okay. I park the Honda (which after my barrel roll in Graniteburg plus six days of solid driving looks like something out of *Sega Rally*) and negotiate a labyrinth of campus buildings until I locate the steely voiced secretary a minute ahead of time. To punish me for not being early she keeps me sitting on a low foam sofa thumbing through a copy of *Nuclear News* until 4.28, when she gets up and leads me through into the doctor's office. Which is the point at which I realize that there was nothing wrong with the image-processing software after all. Dr Metzger looks like a dwarf in the photo on the website because . . . well, because Dr Metzger *is* a dwarf.

Without moving out from behind his desk, a normal-sized desk behind which he's perched on a chair that's legwise somewhere in between a normal chair and a barstool, Metzger offers me a choice of either of two burgundy-leather bucket seats. These are sufficiently close to the floor to compensate for the difference in our heights, and when I've slotted my arse down into one of them (the right-hand one) I find myself in the slightly unsettling position of having Metzger glaring down at me.

Feeling at a disadvantage, I gabble out my lines: thanks for seeing me at such short notice, I am indeed Jack Reever's son, we were estranged, I'm trying to find out how he died and who sent his ashes to me, I got your name from some papers that recently came into my possession.

'I can see how that would happen,' says Dr Metzger after I explain how the ashes lost me my security clearance on the base. He has a little wooden box to help him get on and off his chair; he has one wheeled ladder next to his shelves; he has another beside his filing cabinet.

'And so I'm trying to find out who sent the package to me, because maybe it'll help me get my job back,' I say, trying to keep my mind on the matter in hand and away from Dr Metzger's range of restricted-height lifestyle accessories.

Dr Metzger chuckles. 'Quite a mess you're in, isn't it?'

I spread my hands and raise my eyebrows in a transcultural expression of helplessness and defeat.

'Well I can't be of too much assistance to you, I'm afraid. Until you told me I had no idea that Jack had passed away. And I definitely didn't send those ashes. I'm not blessed with the world's greatest memory, but it's hardly the kind of thing one is likely to forget.'

I wonder – is he talking like this for my benefit, because I'm English, or is his studied turn of phrase part of a more general styling? He certainly is very dapper, what with his tailored three-piece suit, silk pocket handkerchief and floral tie. Maybe elaborate manners are one of the ways in which he compensates for his lack of height.

'But you did know Jack?' I ask.

'Oh yes,' he says. 'Very well. He took my course.'

'Course?'

Metzger pulls a thick brochure from one of the drawers in his desk, flips through it, marks something with a fountain pen he produces from his inside jacket pocket, then turns it round and shoves it – open – across the leather inlay in my direction. I lean forward and take it. The page displayed lists a selection of part-time courses and study programmes one of which – *Introduction to Nuclear Physics* – has been starred with blue ink.

'It's one of the ones I teach,' the good doctor says.

'And my father took this course?'

'That's right. He was among the more unusual of my students.'

'Why unusual?'

Dr Metzger emits a breathy sound, half a cough and half a laugh. 'Many reasons, I'd say. But the main one? Probably his somewhat unhealthy obsession with Fiestaware.'

'Fiestaware?' I say.

At the question the doctor's eyes grow bright and shiny with enthusiasm, like a labrador's. Straightaway he slides off his chair and toddles over to a low sideboard-style cupboard over to my right. His genial attitude combines with his tiny size to make me think of one of J. F. Sebastian's house replicants in *Blade Runner*. But that's better than what would be happening if Miles were here. If Miles were here, he'd be wanting to ask Metzger if he knew how to get hold of a mithrail tunic. Metzger's so keen to help that he'd probably have started looking for one too.

When he speaks the words positively gambol from his mouth. 'Before the nuclear age the only real use for uranium was as a dye,' he says. 'The Romans used it to colour pottery. The Amerindians used it for making warpaint. In medieval Europe it was used to tint stained glass – up to five colours can be got from it, by varying its concentration. During the 1930s Homer Laughlin China of West Virginia used it to create the Mango Red colourway in their Fiestaware range of household crockery.'

He opens the door and takes out a package double-wrapped with plastic bags and rubber bands, then a hefty metal box with what looks like an old-fashioned radio microphone attached to it by a length of black rubber hose. He sets both these things down on the floor then depresses a black switch on the box's handle.

Immediately the box begins to emit a low, electrostatic crackle. 'This is a Geiger counter,' he says. 'You used one before?' I shake my head. 'What you can hear is background radiation, though it's probably a bit above normal because of trace elements in the concrete floor.' Next he unwraps the package, which contains two china plates an even orange in colour. 'Fiestaware,' he says, passing one to me. I give it a suspicious look. 'It's all right, it won't bite. You'd need to walk around with it strapped to your chest for a week or two for it to do you any real harm.'

I take it and examine it. It looks pretty ordinary. But then Metzger picks up the microphone bit of the counter and places it against his plate and the needle leaps like a windscreen wiper and the intermittant clicks and crackles zip upwards in intensity until they've blended into an undifferentiated sonic blur. 'Impressive, don't you think? I always do this little demonstration for my incoming students. It seems to get the point across.'

'The point?'

'That radiation's quite ordinary and natural. Let me give you some examples. The cosmic rays that you absorb during a single transatlantic flight are equivalent in radiation dose to one chest x-ray. Smoke a cigarette, you'll leave traces of the radionuclide polonium-210 in your lungs. Spend the night in the same bed with your wife, you're bathing in the ß-particles emitted by the potassium-40 present in her blood. Wear glasses, you'll absorb about 120 millirems a year – approximately the same amount as workers in the nuclear industry – because the lenses contain equal amounts of uranium and thorium. Thorium is used to make the pages of magazines look whiter and feel smoother. Read a magazine, you're getting about the same amount of radiation as you would watching television. Have too many medical x-rays, they might save your life – but they might also kill you, like they do fifteen thousand US citizens every year.' He stops, leans forward, inserts his fingers in the corner of his mouth and pulls back his lips to reveal his teeth. They are frighteningly even and too big for his head. It must be an American thing, this – I've noticed it around. Wanting to enhance and flaunt any personal attributes connected with consumption. Butts, bellies, fridges, engines, teeth. It's the same deal, right across the board. 'Even in teeth,' Metzger continues, mouth restored to normal. 'Uranium is still used to make dentures glow whiter, and each tooth you swap for a false one will deliver you about 0.07 millirems per annum. And between 1945 and 1980, the year when the international ban on atmospheric nuclear testing was finally enforced, a great deal of strontium-90 was released into the environment. The weather system spread it all around the planet and a high proportion of it ended up being deposited in the skeletal structure of growing children on the milk vector. Strontium has a very high affinity for calcium, you see.'

But I don't want Metzger's scary stories about radiation contamination. 'So? The human race is hardly in danger of extinction, is it?'

Metzger nods, smiling and blinking like an idiot. 'Well you see precisely *because* radiation's everywhere and in everything,' he says, not in the least fazed by my pugnacious comments, 'all living beings on this planet have evolved to tolerate a certain amount of it. In some places that level of toleration can really be quite high.' He proceeds to tell me about the Morro de Ferro thorium deposit in Brazil, where there are plants that have absorbed so much radiation from the soil that they can take x-ray photos of themselves, and the natural nuclear reactor in Gabon, where several eons ago enough water seeped into a particularly large deposit of uranium-235 to moderate the neutrons flying around inside and start a chain reaction that simmered for about two hundred thousand years before finally burning out.

'My point exactly,' I say, grinning with pleasure at these new science factoids and thinking that I can't wait to pass them on to Miles. 'As usual everyone's getting worked up over nothing.'

Metzger clambers back into his chair and I pick up the Fiestaware plate and turn it over, as if by touching it, sniffing it, holding it I can learn something about Jack's intention.

'What did you mean, "obsessed"? Was he collecting it or something?'

'Oh yes, just that. And quite a lot.'

'Why? What for?'

Metzger holds his hands outwards and palm upwards in an elaborate shrug. Because of his size, the expression looks somehow comic, even faked. 'He wanted it for his artworks, or so he said. It was never completely clear to me.'

'His artworks?'

'Cooper, I never had another student like your father, before or since. The first day of class I always go around asking everyone why they've signed up, what they're hoping to get out of it. Most of the mature students I get work for the DoE in some capacity and need the qualification for advancement in their job. But your father – I'll never forget it and nor will anybody else. He said he was trying to make sculptures from nuclear waste and wanted to make sure his working practices were safe!' Metzger heaves with laughter at the pure hilarity of the memory. 'I thought he was making fun of me at first, but he wasn't, he was 100 per cent sincere. When I asked him how he planned to get hold of this kind of material he said he'd been calling up power plants around the country, asking if they could spare him any. "And could they?" I asked him. "No," he said. "They think I'm either a crazy person or a terrorist!" And he looked so sad, like he couldn't understand why he was being so misunderstood! My God, it was the funniest thing I've ever seen, that expression of his. Jack Lemmon had nothing to touch it.'

'I saw a catalogue from an art show he did. It had all these drawings for artworks using stuff from smoke detectors, camping lanterns . . .'

'Oh yes. Americium and thorium. That's right.'

'So it was you who put him on to all of that?'

'Correct. I told him it didn't matter if the power plants he was ringing up weren't cooperating, he didn't really need their help. There was plenty of material just lying around the place if you know where to look for it. But it was Fiestaware that really captured his imagination. So he started collecting it. I should think he must've trawled every thrift store between here and California, the amount he laid his hands on. And I didn't know a thing about it until one day he showed up here with a 35-mm film canister filled with uranium trioxide.'

'Where'd he get it?'

'From the Fiestaware of course! He'd been crushing it up and bathing it in hydrochloric acid to break down the glaze! And the sample he brought me was certainly pure. It tipped my Geiger counter right off the scale and gave him a nasty radiation burn as well – like a fool he'd carried the damn thing over here in his breast pocket. When he unbuttoned his shirt he had a bright red welt right here, right over his heart, about the size and shape of my hand.' He raises his eyebrows and holds his palm towards me, to demonstrate.

'Jesus.' Metzger's hand is pretty small, but still.

'Quite. So the first thing I did was drop those canisters inside a lead box and give him a good talking to. Art for art's sake and all of that, but there was no point in him doing it if he wasn't going to be careful – I was a bit disappointed, I have to say, that he hadn't learned a bit more from the course, considering how he'd been a pretty conscientious student. So I helped him get hold of a suit and a glove box and a dosimeter and various other pieces of standard equipment, and reiterated the basic guidelines on how to handle this kind of material.'

'You didn't try to stop him?'

For the first time since I've been in his presence Metzger's expression flattens out, wiped of joviality. 'I don't know how well you remember your father, Cooper, but my impression was of a man who, when he put his mind to something, was almost impossible to stop. I felt I could either help him out or let him go it alone. Of the two courses, I judged the former to be the least irresponsible.'

This seems fair enough. 'So what happened next?'

'Jack went away and I heard nothing for a while; the course was finished up by then. Then, after maybe a month had passed, I received a letter. He said he'd been working very hard, taking care to follow all my instructions, and was getting on very well. He'd got himself a Geiger counter – made up from a kit they sell in

Radio Shack – and he was getting his dosimeters developed at the address I'd given him, so he was sure he wasn't exposing himself or spreading contamination about the place. He'd collected a much larger sample than he'd had before, had it safely installed in a lead-lined container, and now he wanted to get it analysed and certified so that he had some record of exactly what it was before he went about incorporating it in a sculpture. And he wanted to know if I could do that for him.

'Well I couldn't, of course. I don't have the facilities – and even if I did, there's a whole range of rules and regulations governing that kind of thing. You can't just go ahead and handle these kind of materials, not without the proper authority, not if you're in an official position. So I wrote back to him recommending that he visit the State Office of Radiation Control, the same place that was developing his dosimeters. A few days later another letter arrived saying that's what he was going to do.'

For a second time Metzger slides down from his chair, though this time it's to head over to his bookshelves. Manoeuvring the wheeled ladder into position, he climbs up and retrieves a box file from its slot on the fifth shelf up, placing it on the platform at the apex of the steps before climbing down again. I understand that it would be impolite for me to offer to help, so I wait and watch while he performs this careful callisthenic: hands on ladder, left foot down one step, right foot down to join it, hands off ladder, box file down one step, hands on ladder, left foot down one step, etc – it's like watching an Ewok trying to clamber out of a disabled walker. The best bit's when he stands on tiptoe to cantilever the box file up onto his desk before hauling himself back into his chair. Metzger's a man who clearly decided some time ago that he wasn't going to be intimidated by a world that happened not to be organized to suit his size. I wonder if that's why he became a nuclear physicist, because the subject represents some kind of victory of scale, the ultimate triumph over the very large by the very small.

Back in his chair he pulls the file towards him, flips the lid and works his blunt fingers beneath the spring-loaded metal bar, then he lifts out a wad of papers and starts leafing through them, paring back the individual sheets like a teller counting banknotes. When he finds what he's looking for he removes the papers already counted and places them in a careful pile face down on the desk.

'This is the next letter I had from Jack,' he says, addressing the sheets he's holding in front of him. 'I think you might be interested to hear what it has to say. I'll read it out. First though, some refreshments.' Picking up his phone he buzzes his secretary to bring us through some coffee. Then he clears his throat, puts on the reading glasses that hitherto have been hanging round his neck and, in that peculiar buzzy and flattened voice of his, starts to speak.

Dear Phil, he says the letter says. *So I took your advice and divided out my sample and took a piece of it over to the State Office of Radiation Control like you said. I found it without too much trouble and convinced the parking guy to let me in the parking lot which he really didn't want to. And I could kind of see his point – sitting there among all the sedans and coupes and limousines my beat-up old pickup looked like a fungus at a flower show.*

Once I'd gotten parked up I headed out across the blacktop toward the entrance, following all the cute little signs and sliding up the cool wheelchair ramps. At the door there was no bell so I went straight on into the small, low-ceilinged lobby. What a place, man! Those green walls, whoever thought of that? Truly unwelcoming and drab. That there was no one at the reception desk made it worse, and I think I'd've turned round and walked right out of there again if it hadn't been for this big old goldfish swimming around in a tank so murky and green that it was a pretty much exact match for the décor.

I was a little early but the time for my appointment was drawing close so I waited around for a while, pacing to and fro, hoping that somebody would materialize and point me in the right direction. Then, after five or ten minutes had passed, I began noticing something a little out of the ordinary. The goldfish in the tank up on the counter? It seemed to be following my movements back and forth across the room.

I made a couple of sudden changes of direction, trying to confuse it, but sure enough the damn thing was tracking me. 'Hmm,' I thought. 'A homing carp.' Thinking that this is some extraordinary animal I decided

I'd better go over, get acquainted. But squatting down and putting my nose to the glass to say hi I discovered something really *bizarre. This fish didn't have any eyes!*

Just then there's a knock on the door and the doctor's secretary comes in carrying the tray of coffee. Metzger pauses the reading while she hands us each a cup.

'Where was I?' he says when she's done. 'Oh, that's right. The fish. I don't know what I think about that. I assume it's just one of Jack's jokes. I've been to this place myself often enough and I've never seen a goldfish. Still, you never know. Stranger things have happened. Anyway, let's go on.'

This fish didn't have any eyes! Where they should have been there were two empty sockets with a kind of half-bubble miniscus of transparent membrane grown back across them and no eyeballs at all. But get this; now I was looking at it the fish started swimming along one side of the glass until it bumped its nose at the corner, then did a right turn of ninety degrees and swam along the next side till it bumped its nose at the next and so on and so forth. Started acting all blind, in other words, like it was giving out that it had never been watching me in the first place. But as soon as I stepped a few paces back and started moving around, it went back to tracking me like before. How Zen is that? What must it be like to be this fish, stone-blind but so in tune with its surroundings that it knows exactly what's going on all over this lobby? This must truly be the Buddha of all fish. Leastways, that's what I thought.

Anyhow, just at this point the fish moved away a couple of inches to its left and stopped. And when I turned around to follow its (non)gaze what should I find but this woman standing there, who must've snuck up behind me without my realizing. 'Can I help you?' she says, sounding all official even though she's dressed in running shoes and chinos and a striped polo jersey and has her blonde hair done up in a braid like she's just been out for a run. 'Hey,' I say, a little embarrassed at not noticing her earlier. 'You know that your fish is blind?' 'Is it?' she says. 'No, I didn't know that.' Sounded like she didn't care too much either. Am I here to see anyone in particular, is all she wants to know. I dig down into my Carhartts, pull out the scrap of paper with the details of my appointment with Ms P. Flamel written on it and hand it over. 'It's for a gamma scan,' I explain, holding up my sample box. She could have been any age from early twenties to late forties almost. It's hard to tell. 'Well, it's your lucky day,' she says, but making it sound like in fact it's my unluckiest ever. 'I'm Ms Flamel. If you'd follow me . . . ?'

Well whaddaya know. So we go through a door and down a long corridor past dozens of identical clerical cubicles, some with people working away at computers inside them, some completely empty and quiet. Left and right we go, up and down, and soon I'm totally disoriented and beginning to totally identify with my friend the Zen master goldfish. And then Ms Flamel opens a door and ushers me into a room full of desks and suits and noise and bustle.

Snagging a couple of male colleagues on her way through the chaos, she leads us all into a side office where everyone sits down while I give them the spiel, show them a couple of drawings, then pull out my sample and put it on the desk. One of them puts on some protective gloves, brings over a Geiger counter, flips open the box, holds the counter over the smaller container inside. The needle pegs as I knew it would and they all give each other this look, like they've learned it in technocrat training school or something. Then Ms P. Flamel thanks me kindly and asks me to call back in a week. And I'm escorted out, leaving my sample in their clutches.

Seven days later back I come. This time there's a receptionist and she calls Ms P. Flamel for me, and while I wait I say hi to the fish and sprinkle its tank with a few crumbs of bagel that I'd saved up specially from my breakfast for the purpose. Ms P. Flamel comes out to get me, and this time she's dressed in a worsted grey trouser suit, a pretty pricy number by the look of it, and takes me through. But we don't go into the office we went into before, no sir, not this time. This time we go into one of those clerical chambers off the first long corridor. And it's in here that she tells me straight out that her agency no longer accepts 'walk-ins' and I'll have to get my analysis done somewhere else.

'Oh, okay,' I say, trying to contain a disappointment verging on fury – I mean, this whole performance has now wasted a couple of days of my time. 'Well,' I ask, 'would you mind letting me have my sample back?' At which point Ms P. Flamel, with all the emotion of a bucketful of plaster of Paris, tells me she's sorry, but it's been mislaid. 'Mislaid!?!' I say, perhaps overcompensating a bit in the other direction for her total lack

of affect. 'Am I hearing this right? What do you mean, mislaid? Weeks – no, months – of work went into that! Not to mention that that stuff is radioactive! You should know better than to just leave it lying around!'

'There's no need to raise your voice, Mr Reever,' is what she says.

I was about to protest that I hadn't been raising my voice when I realized she was playing one of those female games on me, the ones I always lose, and so straightaway I stopped myself. I mean, I haven't been married for nothing, right? Exerting what I might say was an almost superhuman level of self-control, I asked her instead where I might get another scan done. 'We don't carry that kind of information,' she said. Well, you know, I should have seen that coming. And thinking that was me done, I turned to go. Which is the point at which she got out her heavy artillery.

'Mr Reever,' she said very, very quietly, in a voice that made my blood freeze, 'if you're thinking of processing any more uranium glaze then there's a couple of things you might like to know.' 'Oh, yes?' I asked, choking back an urge to commit physical violence. 'And what might those be?'

She turned to a blue loose-leaf file that just happened to be lying on the otherwise empty desk and flipped it open. I found out later what this official-looking document was – it was the Washington State Statutes and Rules, Volume XIX: Radiation Protection. Hardly a bestseller, then. No doubt you've come across it somewhere, but I certainly hadn't.

With a sinking feeling in my heart I watched her tiny fingers with their neatly pared nails as she laid the volume flat on the desk and flipped it open. And lo, the relevant regulations had already been marked out, something of a weird coincidence I'm sure you'll agree. She asked me how much Fiestaware I owned and I said, in a helpful manner that sounded just as facetious as I could possibly make it, that I had maybe three or four hundred poundsworth of the stuff. So she read out the bit that says that possession of exempt material is limited to fifteen pounds at any one time and no more than a total of one hundred and fifty pounds in any particular calendar year.

According to what the Statute said, the only way I was going to continue to be able to work with Fiestaware was if I chucked most of what I'd collected away and stored the remainer in appropriately labelled bags. I asked what the appropriate label was and get this: the appropriate label is 'Exempt Source Material: No Label Required.' Needless to say,

Ms P. Flamel didn't even give up a hint of a smile at this piece of bureaucratic insanity, though I for one thought it was goddamn hilarious. 'You've got to be kidding me?' I said.

'No, I am not kidding, Mr Reever,' was her answer. 'In addition to that you will have to wear a personal dosimeter at all times while you are working with said Exempt Source Material and file quarterly reports on your exposure to radiation.' I would have liked to point out here that this I was already doing, thank you very much, but she didn't pause for breath before going on to tell me that even were I to do all that I'd still only be allowed to break the Fiestaware into pieces and no more. Any attempt to separate the glaze from its underlying base would be construed as 'mining and milling of radioactive source material,' for which, apparently, I needed some sort of a license.

'And how much is this license?' I asked, by now pretty much convinced I was actually dreaming this whole scene. 'Well,' she mused – oh she was really enjoying this now, I can promise you, despite the complete lack of any outward sign to indicate it – 'there's a one-time application fee of $27,000, and several additional charges. These include Licensing: $165,000, Inspection: $90,000 and Miscellaneous: $10,885, each of which is payable annually. And then you'll need to install double hurricane fences on your premises and employ a full-time security team, as well as bringing your buildings and storage facilities up to the appropriate safety standards. Oh yes, and you'll also need some guard dogs.'

'Well I've got one of those,' I said, thinking of Thoth. 'Pets don't count,' she shot back, quick as a bullet. And that was that, really, except for when I told her I'd think about it and she told me back I could think all I liked, but in the end I still wouldn't have any choice.

Well, you know Phil, it's like Biringuccio has it in the old Pirotechnia –

'The *Pirotechnia*?' I interrupt.

'Oh yes,' says Metzger, looking up. 'It's a book on metallurgy, Italian, sixteenth-century. Jack was always quoting from it. He bought me a copy as a goodbye present when we finished up the course – I'd show you but I don't have it here. It's rather obscure, but very interesting.' Then, without pausing to see if I have any further questions (I don't), he continues with the letter.

– when he says that you can have a good keen nose for sniffing out

gold, you can work hard day and night at your mining, you can be all round as lucky as you like with making your strike, but at the end of the day unless you're already rich to begin with you've got squat all chance of striking it big. It's the way of the world, I guess, giant shitball that it is.

So I've done the only thing I can do. I've divided up my stock of unseparated Fiestaware into bags like I've been told, marked them with the 'No Label' labels, and dumped them with the few friends I still have left who're speaking to me, asking them to keep the stash out the way some place safe where the cat won't curl up and go to sleep on it.

Don't think, though, that I'm giving up. No way – some dumb book of rules has never stopped me before and it won't stop me now. I've decided to try a different tack, is all. I've heard about this big repository they're building over at Salt Mountain in Nevada, and since I figure they're basically trying to do the same thing as I am only on a slightly different scale (and with a reasonable budget), I'm thinking of heading down there. See if I can't convince them to give me some work. It's a long shot I know, but there might be a freethinker in amongst the pencilheads who can see the benefits of having an artist on board.

I must be crazy. Though I guess you already knew that, Phil, though you're too damn polite ever to have mentioned it. Making it doubly incredible that you've gone so far out of your way to help me, which help I can never repay. What I can do, though, is do like Picasso did when he couldn't make good yet another of his many bar tabs and make you a gift of the enclosed picture. It's a study for a piece I've just started working on and hope, one day, to complete. When it's finally finished you can be sure you'll be top of the list for the private view – though right now that could be some time away, so don't hold your breath.

Till then, good buddy, you take good care.

Yours faithfully and all that jazz,

Jack Reever, Artist

Metzger folds the letter and uses it to indicate a framed picture on the wall; one of a number of mounted certificates and photographs of the Doctor in the company of various people I assume are well-known academics or politicians (and one of whom, I now realize with a jolt, is Bill Clinton), I hadn't noticed it before. 'That's the picture,' he says. 'A little macabre perhaps, but I like it.'

I get up from my chair and go and take a closer look. It's a small sketch of a skull – a horse's skull, I think, done with pen and ink and coloured in with watercolours. It's much more sober and restrained than any of the stuff I saw in Macro's catalogue, but it doesn't look much like a sculpture. In the corner, in Jack's looping, untidy writing, are the words: *Study for 'The Herm'*.

'What's a herm?'

'Ah, yes. Very interesting. At the time I did consult the encyclopedia in order to get some kind of clue as to what it might all mean, seeing as how Jack didn't provide any explanation. But the only reference I could find was to a road or property marker used in ancient Greece, the name being derived from the god Hermes, the god of travel and communication, which didn't seem to make much sense. That's about as far as I got, I'm afraid.' Metzger smiles brightly, clearly happy to abide by the conclusion he'd no doubt reached a long long time ago that art was not his thing, that he was never going to understand it, that it would no doubt be better for all concerned if he just let it be.

The Herm, huh? I wonder if this was the 'masterpiece' that Jack was intending to carve from that giant block of stone he took with him when he high-tailed it out of Graniteburg. It strikes me that if this object in fact exists, it might somehow be the key to everything. If I can find it – and let's face it, a two-tonne hunk of stone is probably easier to trace than a dead man – maybe the secret of what happened to Jack and who sent the ashes won't be far behind. And where do you find art, if not in a gallery?

==> next stop = the Electroworks. Q. E. D.

Patrick Belin

Patrick Belin's place isn't easy to locate. Fremont is the old industrial quarter, down by the docks, but I manage to take a wrong turning off the expressway and end up trapped in this absurd one-way system it takes me forty minutes to negotiate. Then when I do get there it's like driving onto a *Mad Max* set. It's all a maze of battered warehouses and machinery-filled lots until suddenly you realize there's a new layer of tarmac beneath your tyres and the signposts are all standing straight and what was once a wharf has been revamped into a marina, the warehouses and depots now filled with cafés and expensive flats. Regeneration. It's the same deal the whole world over.

Sunning itself behind an impressive curtainwall of glass, the Electroworks could almost be round the corner from Miles's flat. Inside I can see five or six people clambering about on a tower of scaffolding, putting up – or taking down – a large piece of installation art, a giant robot of some kind. I park the Honda and go inside, ask one of the technicians if she knows where I can find Patrick Belin.

'Pat?' She points up to a silvery catwalk that runs around the walls about fifteen feet above our heads. 'Studio Three.' As I turn to go she touches me on the shoulder. 'Does he know you're coming?'

'I doubt it.'

'Then watch out.'

She doesn't tell me why, just smirks and goes back to roping a piece of robot to a hoist. This is the second time I've been given a mysterious warning about one of Jack's old friends and I'm already tiring of it, so I curl my lip to her back and cling-clang my way up the steel stairway and onto the catwalk.

The building smells metallic; despite the sandblasted surfaces and trendy interior refit the taint of thousands of gallons of industrial chemicals still lingers in the air. There's other smells as well – coffee, for example, and varnish too. Or maybe it's glue. And tobacco. There's a definite strong smell of tobacco. Which gets stronger and more definite as I approach Studio Three.

The door's closed but set into it at about eye-height is a slidy wooden panel with 'Keep Closed' scrawled on it in marker pen. I slide it back; behind it a little pane of wire-reinforced glass lets onto the room. Bending a little and shielding my eyes from the glare of the corridor lights I take a squint inside.

Studio Three is much bigger than I'd expected. I think it must extend partway into the building next-door. Twenty-five, maybe thirty feet high, it's shoe-box shaped except where there's a stubby concrete mezzanine wedged into the far end, accessible via a narrow metal ladder bolted to the left-hand wall. Next to this ladder the wall is shelved, and these shelves are filled for the most part with neatly arranged and colour-coordinated plastic Curver storage boxes containing what look like electrical components, though from this angle it's difficult to tell. On the lower tiers there are some bigger items, aqua-screened oscilloscopes and circuit-boards and so on. But this is nothing to compare with what's sitting wedged into the shadow of the mezzanine.

At first it's hard to make out what they are. There's six or seven of them, divided into two groups with a gap running between them. They vary in size, the smallest being just under a metre tall, the largest just over two. Their resin plinths, copper coils and metal globes make them look a bit art deco, like they've been salvaged off the set of an old *Flash Gordon* episode. What I think they are is Tesla coils; Tesla coils and Van de Graaff machines. From the intense humming sound that's coming from the room, audible even on this side of the door, I'd say that most of them are currently switched on.

Moving from machine to machine, connecting and disconnecting wires, checking power supplies, messing with various things, is a chubby, hairy man with a turd of a cigar stub cleated into the corner of his mouth. After a minute or two Belin – and it's surely him – emerges from the gloom and comes out into the middle of the room where, strangest of all, a sort of giant stretched canvas lies propped above a large, low aluminium bath. This bath is about three metres by two, maybe six or eight inches high at the side, and beside it there's a small set of folding metal steps, the same kind I've got back home for doing DIY.

What he does next is completely unexpected. Climbing up the metal steps, he stands like he's going to try to dive through the canvas and into the bath. But he doesn't dive. What he does instead is unzip his fly, take out his prick – which bears a striking resemblance to his cigar – and start to piss. Left to right, up and down, he urinates liberally across the canvas like a little boy peeing his name into the snow. Maybe that's exactly what he's doing, writing his name. I can't tell.

When he's finished Belin gets down from the steps and lifts the canvas vertical. It turns out to have a pair of feet built into the frame I hadn't seen before, feet equipped with coasters, which allow the upright piss painting to be wheeled across the room and into a gap between the Tesla coils, where he positions it very carefully according to a set of marks made with masking tape upon the floor. Next he ascends the ladder to the mezzanine and a bank of grey control panels, featureless save for a series of hefty power switches, dials and warning lights. He throws each switch in turn, checks a couple of the dials, jots a note onto a clipboard, then hurries back down the ladder to fetch a large rubber welding helmet down from off the shelves. Without removing his cigar, he puts this on, then he turns to face the array of coils and generators. Minutes pass. Just as I'm about to give up and knock several arcs of frozen light split the space between the two groups of machines and everything goes white.

For what seems like an extreme length of time I can't see anything at all. This, presumably, is what the girl was warning me about. While I wait for my vision to return the smell of burning ozone drifts up at me from beneath the studio door. For some reason I find this vaguely reassuring.

Eventually my retinas begin to recover from the shock. Straight ahead I'm still seeing a big white disk but after a bit of blinking and rubbing it strobes green and purple then begins to shrink, so I suppose I haven't quite gone blind. I discover that if I tilt my head back about sixty-five degrees to the vertical and sharply to the side I can see almost normally.

I locate the door and knock.

'What?' yells the voice inside.

I turn the handle, enter. The disk prevents me from seeing Belin's face, but I can see his crotch so I speak to that instead. After all, I'm already quite familiar with its contents.

'Patrick Belin?'

'Who wants him?' If an electric fence could talk it would have a voice like this.

'You don't know me but . . .'

'Fuck off, I'm busy.' The legs turn and walk away, leaving me with an image of two dusty buttocks.

'It's about Jack Reever.'

'What d'you say?' The legs stop, but don't turn back. The disk shrinks a little more, floats around a bit, pulses from green through blue to pink. 'Jack Reever?'

'My name's Cooper James. I'm his son.'

Belin's steel-toecapped work boots stomp over to my right, where they greet the wheeled splay of a swivel chair's stalk. A brief flirtation is quickly followed by a violent parting, and the chair spins speedily across the concrete floor in my direction. Thanks to a sudden movement of the disk, now a brutal red in hue, I misjudge its movement and allow the seat's hard metal edge to catch me painfully just above the knees.

'Sit.'

I do as I'm told. The after-images have slid up and to the right and I can now see Belin's face: the full goatee sprouting muff-like around the chubby, amphibious lips, the eyes like bullet holes in safety glass, the sweaty gypsy mop.

In a studied fit of artistic pique Belin ditches his cigar stub in a wastebin, retrieves a small but perfectly formed aluminium tube from his front pocket, pulls out the plastic stopper with his teeth, spits that too towards the bin (and misses), tips out a fresh cigar, crumples the tube pseudo-powerfully in one hand while biting off the sealed end of the cigar with a set of suspiciously un-nicotine-stained teeth, spits that towards the bin (and hits), follows it with the compacted tube, then finally produces a brass Zippo from his pocket and like an idiot puts it to his stogie. I say like an idiot because even I – who doesn't smoke, has never smoked, has no desire to ever smoke on account of how it's such a putrid Morlock habit – even I know that lighting a quality cigar with a petrol lighter is a sacrilege, on account of how the heavy perfume of the petrol gets into the weed and taints it. You should use a long, specially seasoned cigar match or, ideally, a gas lighter. (I learned all this from a TV documentary I once saw on Cuba by the way, in case you're wondering.)

I don't mention any aspect of my accidental aficionado knowledge to Belin, because I don't think he'd appreciate it. But knowing what I know as I watch him act like he's acting seriously lowers my opinion of him, though not as much as watching him piss all over his canvas did. And not nearly as much as what he does now, which is bend close, put both hands on the arms of my swivel chair and blow smoke in my face.

'Where's the money, Cooper?'

My vision has cleared completely, almost. I can quite clearly see the coin-sized ember at the end of my interrogator's cigar. Not that I need to see it. As it's dotting around about an inch from the end of my nose, even if I had gone blind I'd still be perfectly well aware that it was there.

'I'd really rather you moved that thing away, if you don't mind.'

'WHERE'S MY FUCKING MONEY?'

'What money? I've no idea what you're talking about!' Notice here, if you please, the fine job I'm doing of exercising self-restraint.

'THE TEN THOUSAND BUCKS YOUR FATHER OWES ME! WHERE IS IT?'

There isn't much point, it seems, in trying to be polite. 'How about – I've no fucking idea!!?'

'WHY THE FUCK NOT?'

'BECAUSE MY FATHER'S FUCKING DEAD, YOU FUCKING ARSEHOLE.'

Pause.

Belin retreats a bit and takes a puff or two on his cigar while he considers this.

Finally he speaks. What he says is this.

'Well that's just fucking typical.'

Which pretty much rules him out as a possible ashes-sender and rounds down the number of names left on my list of suspects to a nice neat nought.

We're in Belin's office, a tidy environment next door to the electrical lab and walled not with shelves but with fitted Hon filing cabinets. I've been showing Belin the catalogue I got off Cox, in order to get him to open up. It's a bit like playing an adventure game, this quest I'm on. Explore the town until you've found the sextant, the hauser and the flick knife, give them to the old sailor drinking in the corner of the Tipsy Parrot and in exchange he'll get you passage as a stowaway on his ship, which is the only way (save from hacking the program and equipping yourself with a motorboat, which Miles and I did in fact do with one particularly frustrating Commodore 64 game) you can cross the ocean to the island where sleeps the beautiful princess. Etc.

'So you've known Jack a long time, then?' I prod. 'From back before he went to Europe?'

'Er, yeah, you could say that,' Belin huffs. 'Jack and I go way back. He ever tell you anything about Blakely Island?'

'Of course.'

'Well, that's where we met. My old man was one of the artists living there. Jack and me, we hung out together all the time, learning how to carve. We were like brothers, more or less.'

I don't need to raise my eyebrows – they do it of their own accord.

'You don't believe me?'

'The way you've been talking about him in the last few minutes, it doesn't seem like you and he were friends.'

'Yeah, well, we're not any more, are we? Not since he ran out on me. What I didn't realize at the time was how much Jack had changed.'

'In what way changed?'

'If I had to reduce to it a single thing I'd say he'd become . . . *obsessive*. He was always focused, Jack, he always got 100 per cent absorbed in whatever he was doing. And I'd always been impressed by that, especially when we were young sculptors starting out.' He's standing at the window, looking out towards the bay, trying to pick a splinter or a line of dirt from beneath one of his fingernails. 'But when he showed up here after he'd been in Graniteburg he was drinking a lot, which is something he never did on Blakely. Here was I trying to get the show up and running – which was a fucking headache all its own – and he was disappearing off for days at a time on these drinking junkets. I mean, to me it just seemed totally irresponsible. But maybe he was punishing himself.'

It strikes me that Belin doesn't actually believe this, that he's just saying it to make me feel better. I can't decide whether I appreciate this tact or not. So instead I ask him about Metzger and the course Jack was attending.

'He never mentioned any course to me. It's possible.'

'And Salt Mountain, he ever mention that?'

'What, the place down in Nevada? Not that I remember. That where he went?' He tries to say it like he doesn't care.

'That's what I'm trying to find out.'

'It would figure. But like I told you already, Jack disappeared on me. I've no idea what happened to him. One day he was here, the next day he was gone. If you ask me, it's beginning to look like an escape artist was the only kind of artist he really was.'

I've no reason to find this comment hurtful – other than as

things stand it looks pretty close to being the truth – but I do. Belin sees it in my face.

'I'm sorry, but you know, maybe this was Jack's real true self all along, this arrogance,' he says. 'I mean, it's just not *normal* to treat people that way, right? I should've seen the signs, the way he walked about like he was this big-shot genius, throwing out ideas and expecting the rest of us to scurry round and do the best we could to help him realize them. I mean, just look at this place. Jack and me set it up together but guess who ended up doing all the work?'

'You and Jack set this place up?'

'Sure! Our shit was too weird to get shown at any of the stuck-up galleries downtown, so we started up our own. It was what you did. Jack had come back from his travels full of all these big ideas about art and science and stuff, they chimed right in with how I was thinking at the time, and after a few months bitching about how the art scene here was dead on its legs we decided to look for a venue where we could do things the way we wanted. And so we started looking.'

'And this is what you found?'

'Yeah. It was still operational as an electroplating factory back then and Jack, he was working here, same kind of industrial blue-collar job we all did back in those days to pay the rent. He was always coming back with these outrageous stories about what a two-bit outfit it was, how it was forever on the edge of getting closed down, how it broke every safety rule in the book. Then one day one of his no-brain co-workers – and this place employed real scum, let me tell you, drug-addicts, psychos, ex-cons, you name it – one of these losers skipped out on his shift to smoke some crack in his car, out in the parking lot. Being more than averagely sub-normal, he'd taken too big a hit, passed out, dropped the pipe on his trousers and set them alight. Well, thank fuck Jack was the kind of guy who needed to step out for a cigarette every fifteen min-utes; soon as he saw smoke coming from the car he ran on over there and managed to pull the guy out just in time. It was gonna be a while before he'd be seeking female company again if you get my meaning, but he wasn't gonna die. Which he definitely would've done, since only a minute or two after Jack got him out the fire got into a gas line and *boom*.'

'Shit.'

'Shit is right. And anywhere else that'd've been the end of it. Not this place though. The explosion brought all the other monkeys out who straightaway started to panic – not because their colleague and co-worker was in danger for his life but because they had to stash their own supplies of junk before the police turned up and started a general shakedown. So they started running round hiding stuff and with no one left inside to do the safety checks a vat of chemicals overheated and started spraying all over the place. Before anyone knew what was happening another fire was underway, a real fire this time. By some miracle they got it under control before it could do too much damage but this was the third time something like this had happened and the regulators closed them down.

'Then one night after the fire happened Jack and me, we were having a beer together in a bar somewhere and Jack was bringing me up to date on the whole situation and he said to me: "Hey Pat, I know the guys who own this place, I'm in with them, and I reckon it'd make a great gallery and studio space. If we make an offer now, they'd be so keen to have someone take it off their hands we'd get it for a song. It could be exactly what we're looking for."

'And he was right. We borrowed some money – or rather, I borrowed some money on our behalf, Jack's credit rating being so bad he couldn't even get stood a drink – and we bought up the gutted shell and did it out. Half the old industrial equipment was still in here, one end was all fire-damaged, but it was cool. And Jack was so buzzed about staging his show in an old electroplating factory. The two things he was most into at the time were alchemy and atomics, and he figured electroplating fit right into that. "The rearrangement of metals at the molecular level." That was pretty much his catchphrase around that time. Not that he ever managed any such rearrangements personally. But that was the theory.'

'And so that's when you put on Frivolous Use?'

'Not right away. We were in here quite a while first, me, Jack and about three or four other artists who were into the same ethos and needed a lot of room to work. We each took over one of these side spaces as a studio – the one I'm in is the same one I had originally; Jack's was down the hall, the robot people have it now – and got on with making stuff. Or most of us did. Jack though, his space was more like some kind of dumping ground.'

'What for?'

'For all the stuff he was going round collecting – or that the rest of us were going round collecting for him; he had us all at it. Anything we could lay our hands on that might have a trace of radioactivity in it, it was in there. Piles of smoke detectors and cans of radium paint and all sorts of junk like you wouldn't believe.'

'Fiestaware?'

'Oh Jesus yes. Heaps and heaps of it. He was more into that than anything. He could've opened half a dozen kitchenware stores, the amount he had. Crushing it up, sticking it back together – you name it, he was doing it.'

'You mean he made things with it?'

'Oh yeah, and the rest.'

'But I thought the show was only sketches?'

'We just used the sketches for the catalogue. If there'd been just sketches, we wouldn't've had a problem. It was the sculptures caused us all the upset.'

Suddenly I'm all excited. 'Was one of them like an eight-foot long horse's skull, carved out of a big granite block?'

Belin laughs. 'No, 'fraid not. Wish it fucking had been – might've been worth something. I know the piece of stone you're talking about, it's the one Jack brought with him all the way from Graniteburg, right? Yeah, I remember that all right – I had to help go get the fucker from the railroad depot when it arrived. Damn near broke my hoist. No. He never did a thing with that – just kept it lying around, cluttering up the place.'

It seems odd that Metzger didn't mention this – maybe he simply didn't know about it. I'm beginning to realize this is what Jack was like. It wasn't just me and Stasie he compartmentalized – the man compartmentalized every aspect of his life. Each of his friends seems to have been kept in their separate world, mutually unaware of each other's existence. It's almost like he was keeping himself a step back from all of them, watching them, taking from them, appearing to give friendship in return but in truth never becoming emotionally involved. It's freakish behaviour, slightly. Did he act like this intentionally, as part of some kind of strategy? Was he labouring under the illusion that he was some kind of existential genius who shouldn't allow himself to become tainted by the world? Or was it involuntary and he was just the way he was? A kind of autism, almost?

It's impossible to tell.

While Belin's been talking he's gone over to the filing cabinets, riffled through the drawer labelled 'PQR', and pulled the file labelled 'Reever, Jack'. He lays it on the desk and starts leafing through it. It's beginning to seem to me that this is what people really leave behind after they are gone, a series of more or less random pieces of paper in half-forgotten drawers and cardboard boxes. Jack's generation, anyway. All my generation will leave is a fading pattern of electrons in the networks. Electronic ghosts. Which I suppose makes just as much sense if you're looking for an analogue of the soul, a metaphor, a map. It's just that the rate of turnover is so much faster, that's all. Faster and easier and much more efficient. But perhaps that's the kind of thing we like.

'That's one of the sculptures that was in the exhibition,' Belin says, extracting a photograph from among the papers and handing it to me. The picture's of a largish glass fish tank, filled with broken shards of orange crockery, topped off with water and mounted on an aluminium trolley. A big yellow warning light has been fixed to the metal lid along with some kind of pump. At one end a small plastic tap has been let into the glass; it opens into the hopper of a Mr Coffee machine, positioned directly underneath on a special little shelf. The trolley and lid have been decorated with black and yellow WARNING: RADIATION tape. Inside the tank several gaily coloured fish are swimming happily in and out of the caves and tunnels formed by the Fiestaware.

'What the hell is that?

'I think it was supposed to be some kind of homemade atomic powerstation.'

'How's it work?'

'Oh I don't know. Some crazy Reever way or other. There's some notes about it on the other side, if you look.'

I flip the picture and scan the explanation Pritt-Sticked to the back. The piece was called The Mark IV Studio Reactor, and the idea seemed to be that you could plug it into a standard wall socket. This would cause elements in the base to boil the water which would then rise as steam, condense against the lid, and fall back into the tank. In the process, the water gave off hydrogen which was removed from the system by an air pump. Removing the hyrogen converted the water into heavy water, which has a high concentration of deuterium, and at some point (i.e. after about two thousand years, all other things being equal) there'd be enough deuterium to react with the uranium in the plates and (in Jack's dreams) trigger a mild amount of nuclear fission. The whole thing would eventually go critical, the neutron flux produced would trigger the warning light positioned on the top to let you know that the long-awaited event was finally happening, and the faucet would open letting the superheated water run into the hopper of the coffee maker. 'Heat, light and coffee,' the paragraph concludes, 'the basic requirements for any artist's studio.' Right.

I turn back to the picture and try to connect this absurd object to the hippy wood carver I remember. But it's simply not possible. That Jack – he couldn't have made this. Or wouldn't have. Is this the real you, Jack? Was the hippy crap all just a massive pose? A failed experiment? Is that why you ran out on us? Because something made you realize you weren't what you thought you were? Or what you should be? And what made you realize that? Was it Stasie? Was it the commune, our whole scene? Or was it something else?

Then down on the corner of the fish tank, barely visible, I catch sight of something I recognize etched into the glass. It's very small, but it's definitely there. The symbol.

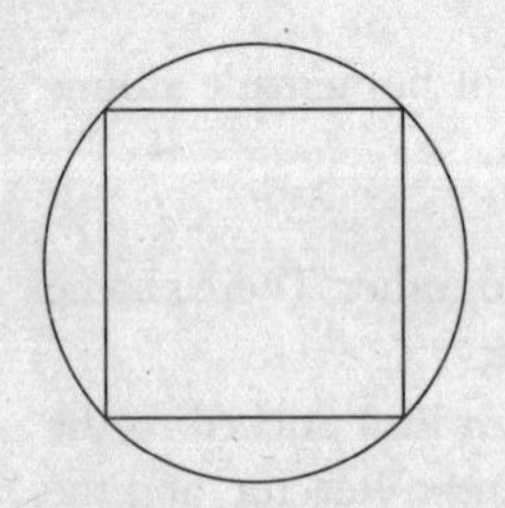

I point it out to Belin, ask him what it's supposed to mean, but he doesn't know. 'Jack was into all that stuff, magic runes and all the rest of it. Never made sense to me.'

Stumped for questions by the total bizarreness of the Studio Reactor, I pull magic item number two from my Cisco Systems backpack: the 'Riots in Fremont' clipping.

Belin sighs, goes over to the water cooler, gurgles liquid into one of those cone-shaped paper cups. 'Somehow the local anti-nuclear lobby got hold of the fact that Jack was working with radioactive materials,' he says. 'It didn't make any difference to those imbeciles that all the stuff he was using he was buying up in garage sales and junk stores; Fremont was a no-nukes zone and that was that. They tried anything they could to stop us going ahead with it. They had a two-day sit-in out here in the street, they superglued the door locks on the building to stop us getting in. They even got to handing out cream pies for people to throw at any members of the public who were foolish enough to try to come and see it.'

'Jack must've been furious.'

'Jack? Furious? He was having a ball! He liked nothing better than a fight – it meant he was the centre of attention. The press were all over him about it. He was on the radio – not just once like it says in your article but lots of times. Even the local cable station came down to gawp at him.'

'So in the end it all turned out okay?'

'No – no way. You'd've thought so, all publicity supposedly being good publicity and all of that, but it worked against us big time. To start with we couldn't shift the protesters who were picketing the place. We even tried a legal challenge but we had no chance – they'd fended off far worse than us. And even if they hadn't been there, no one was coming anyway, as every bit of press we'd had had given out that visitors would be putting their lives on the line from the radiation just by stepping through the door. I mean, that piece you've got there was typical, people believed it. So no. Financially speaking it was a disaster. We had no public, we didn't make a sale.'

'And that's how come he ended up owing you all this money?'

'No.'

'So what was it then? Because he never paid you back on the loan for the Electroworks?'

'Well, yes, but that doesn't really matter, because all that meant was that I effectively owned the place outright, and I made the cash back in the end.'

'Then why?'

'Because about six months after the show we got a call from the State Office of Radiation Control, who said they were conducting an investigation into allegations concerning the storage of unlicensed radioactive material on our premises. Couple of guys came down here, took one look inside Jack's studio, made us evacuate the premises immediately. They posted guards, strung yellow tape up everywhere, called in a Haz-Mat SWAT team all dressed up in those bunny suits they have. These guys sacked up all the stuff Jack had been collecting, all the sculptures, everything and hauled it off for "analysis". Not that anyone expected to see any of it again. Except for Jack, of course, who spent his time yelling at them about his human rights, about how they were a bunch of fascist pigs, about how he'd taken proper precautions and there wasn't any contamination.'

'And was there?'

'Apparently not. In the beginning they were saying that they might be forced to have the entire building razed to the ground. But whatever Jack had been up to in there it turned out he must've been reasonably careful, because after a week they announced the place decontaminated and disappeared, leaving us minus Jack's artworks and plus a bill for the clean-up operation.'

'Ten thousand dollars?'

'Nine-thousand, one hundred and forty-three dollars and twenty-seven cents, if memory serves,' says Belin, reciting the figures with a wounded air. Clearly the information is seared into his cortex.

'What you need to understand,' he says, sifting through his Reever file again and passing me a sheaf of documents pertaining to the decontamination, 'is that he was kind of like a child. A talented child. He hated me for even suggesting that we were going to have to find a way to come up with the money. It was out of the question, he said, to pay those bastards for stealing his art – it was adding insult to injury. It was us who should be suing them, was his way of seeing it. As to how we were supposed to find cash to pay a lawyer when we were still in debt from our previous legal tussle with the anti-nuclear protesters, well, that he didn't have too many suggestions about. He hung around for a week or two, getting drunk and railing at the government, the nuclear authorities, the anti-nuclear lobby and most of all at me, until in the end he wound me up so much I lost my temper and told him to go fuck himself.'

I hold my expression steady, don't permit the merest flicker. 'And did he?'

'I guess so. Because that's when he disappeared. Took his precious granite block with him as well, though how he snuck it out of here without my seeing him I'll never know. Look, Cooper, I know he was your father and all, but as far as I'm concerned he goaded me into saying those things so he'd have an excuse to run out on me instead of sticking around and helping me come up with the cash. He was so fucking full of it – it was his idea that we make a stand, go to prison if we had to. And when I told him I wasn't prepared to sacrifice my freedom for his principles he told me that I should sell off the Electroworks, pay the bill and walk away. That at least he'd be able to respect.'

'But you didn't want to do that either?'

'Why should I? Like I told you, it was me who put all the money and effort into this place, me who put up the investment. I was building something here. I didn't want to throw it all away over a stupid principle.'

'Was it stupid?'

'You tell me. But I didn't see Jack Reever sticking around for long enough to go to jail. And I guess . . .' But he breaks off there, doesn't complete the sentence, just shakes his head sort of hopelessly. There's something in this gesture that reminds me of Miles and I get a flash of Jack running from Belin and his profit-and-loss version of art, except it's not Jack running from Belin it's me running from Miles and his offer of a job. The situations are utterly different but at the same time they're the same, I know they're the same, I can't tell you how I know it but I do. Suddenly I understand what happened here. I can see it. Everything. On the one hand I sympathize with Belin; it's clear that on one level Jack behaved pretty badly. But on the other, what was the point in setting up a gallery outside the system if when it came to the real crunch you didn't sacrifice it to the cause? Belin can dress it up anyway he likes but the fact is he sold out. And my father, that was the one thing he'd never forgive you for.

I'm holding the bills for the decontamination now, I've got them in my hands; there's the figure exactly as Belin recited it, right down to the final cent. I look at it, I try to care, but I don't. Belin's shaking his head again, just watch him shake it, but I feel just like I did that day when Jack turned on Miss Banner. Him, me, together, righteous, facing down the world. It's an awesome feeling. Powerful. It's what you feel like when you have a father you can trust.

But then, as suddenly as it's come, the feeling's gone and Jack is lost to me again and I zone back to the present and the figure of Belin staring out the window at a ship that's slowly manoeuvring into the docks and the realization that it's warm in here and that I need a cup of coffee and that it's time to move along.

Salt Mountain

The town of Jackass Flats sits just off Highway 95, on the site of an old abandoned silver-mining settlement that never got as far as naming itself. But the key fact you need to know about Jackass Flats is that it isn't where it's supposed to be. It's supposed to be twenty miles further east, where the actual section of the planet named Jackass Flats still is. The town itself got moved in 1949, eighteen months before the first atmospheric nuclear test was conducted at Frenchman Flat, which – as you might've gathered – isn't very far away.

You're technically in the new improved Jackass Flats as soon as you turn off the highway and pass the old 'Welcome' sign, metal and rusted and very B-movie, about a hundred metres down the way. But you haven't really *arrived* until you pass the sign just beyond it, the shinier, newer, far more expensive sign, the sign that says: 'Welcome to Salt Mountain!' in a spangly, handwritten font. The sign that says: 'Proud to be the Choice of the US Department of Energy for a Cleaner, Brighter Tomorrow' in copperplate gothic, underneath. It's like the signs outside of Featherbrooks. It's hard to believe that this is the place Jack came hunting for a job.

Even without the sign it would be a weird place. The road curls through album-cover country, rangy desert peppered with cacti and various other spiky-looking plants. To my left a track beaches out just short of three broken old buildings: a farmhouse, a store and a barn. It's like a scene from *Resident Evil* or *Silent Hill*. Unable to resist, I stop and take a look. Inside the house a few scraps of wallpaper adorn the wooden walls and, incredibly, the remains of curtains still hang in one or two of the windows. But that's all that's survived the generations of local teens drinking and groping in here. Clearly there were other buildings once, but they haven't been so lucky – kicking around in the dirt I find large grey rectangles of ash, littered with charred lintels and old and bent nails. House graves. Money trees seem to like these – they grow across them thickly, leaves swollen and rubbery. The ash must be full of nutrients or something.

Gingerly, testing each step before I trust it with my weight, I climb the creaking staircase. At the top a small landing lets into what must've once been three small rooms but is now more nearly one, the room dividers having been more or less demolished. A bird clatters up and out the window when it hears me coming and I pick my way across what's left of the floorboards and blink out in its wake to see what I can see.

What I can see is sagebrush, desert, a ring of distant mountains blue as lakes. There's the Honda, and there's the track I drove down slithering away through the scrub to join the highway. And there, on the hardtop, waiting by the turn-off, is a dull-white pickup truck, windscreen and bull bars sparking with shards of sun.

I get the fear immediately. What's it doing? Waiting for me? I can't see any markings so I don't think it's highway patrol, but maybe they've been baked into invisibility by the brightness of the light. Or maybe it's a local farmer, come to tell me I'm trespassing. Local something . . . local bully boy, probably. Anyway I'm leaving, and right now. I don't want trouble. I've already got enough of that.

But I'm being paranoid. By the time I get back to the road the truck has gone and I see no further sign of it, not during the half-mile drive I have to make before the town begins nor in the town itself, laid out house-deep along the road like some stratified relic of human habitation.

Thinking archaeology, I sift down through the levels. Trailers and tract homes come at me first, cheap breeze-block houses with metal roofs and dusty Chevys parked up out front. One little shopping development, signs all in Spanish. Peeling paint, torn fly-screens, broken chairs on buckling patios, dogs lying in the dust asleep (or dead). A gas station, a non-brand pizzeria. Then more houses, more upmarket, one in eight recently painted, one in ten with a new truck or car out front. Satellite dishes, cheap ones, dusty and austere as desert flowers.

Soon enough the suburb gives way to a low-rent corporate strip. Here are food courts, a Safeway, a Wal-Mart, some place called Nevada Fashions, a used car lot (Jackass Autos), two gun shops (Guns 'n' Gear, Jake's Rifles and Sidearms), a drive-in Burger King, a drive-in Taco Bell, a couple of motels, a coffee shop called Martha's Coffee with a restaurant next door called Martha's Ribs, a single bar (the Smiling Coyote). Everywhere there are flags, though in contrast to further north here there are as many Southern Crosses as Stars and Stripes: draped from windows, from parapets, from bought or makeshift flag poles; pinned to doors and noticeboards and across the inside of car windows; clipped into little shrines and memorial dioramas baking in the sun in people's front windows.

Running down the side of the Smiling Coyote is wide access road, a white polythene banner slung across its width on poles saying 'Wanaput Nation RV Resort and Camping'; on the other side a giant concrete teepee peaks above an irrigated copse of trees surrounded by circled ranks of caravans and Winnebagos. But past the RV park Jackass Flats turns residential once again, though it's richer now, with much less dust and much more foliage. Houses are larger, flasher, tidier; their stoops are of deliberately cracked stone instead of sun-cracked concrete; any dogs I see are pedigree and too expensive to be allowed to lie in the street so are safely corralled in leafy, wire-fenced yards. Then: a second food court, much more upmarket than the first, with a Wendy's, a Starbucks and a few 'authentic down-home' bars and eateries (Carmel's, Chuck's Bar and Grill, the Bagel Place).

Not far past this the houses stop abruptly and there's nothing for a while, just desert again, more stubby, spiny things. Then, suddenly, like the town's paused in its chewing before biting off a final gigantic mouthful, there are these two enormous buildings of steel and glass, one on each side of the road, facing off across their parking lots like duelling bison. In the red corner, the Desert Spring Hotel (a Marriott). In the green, the Dry Beaver Casino (a 'Wanaput Nation Cooperative').

There's no more town after that and less than a mile beyond the hotel the road comes to an end. Or rather it doesn't – it carries straight on, but without the appropriate security clearance you can't drive along it because you've reached the perimeter of the Salt Mountain military reserve. There's a fence here, and a guard post. The fence is new – the mesh is still bright and the razor wire coiled at its apex is cut into rectangular barbs according to the latest design. Far beyond the barrier and the guards, rising out of the desert perhaps five or six miles away, is what looks like the hill in *Close Encounters* where the aliens land. This is Salt Mountain – its western end.

On that side of the fence nothing much seems to be happening. On this side though there's all sorts of shit going on. Most of it is happening in a makeshift encampment of forty or fifty tents, teepees, trailers and trucks struck here in a circle by the side of the road with a few dozen people – hippies and traveller-types – wandering about. Surprise surprise, it's a protest camp.

Salt Mountain is just inside the south-west border of the Nevada Test Site, which is a restricted military area. It's where the nuclear tests were done in the 1940s and 50s, though that's no longer what it's famous for. These days the main point of reference is Groom Lake, aka Dreamland, aka Area 51. Stasie's an Area 51 expert, of course. Her and David Icke.

Clearly this point of view is completely brainless. It might've conceivably been understandable in the 1970s, when half the western hemisphere was whacked out on marijuana and getting an O level in physics was still a mysterious and impressive thing, but these days any prat with an internet connection can get online and pull down decent information on any subject in a matter of seconds. I know the newspapers like to give the impression that the net's full of nonsense and false information, but this is presumably because they're terrified of the general public working out that with a basic understanding of the way search engines function and a bit of common sense they'd have no need any longer for their services.

So I got online courtesy of the cybercafé in Seattle, and this is what I learned. I learned that right now waste storage is the nuclear industry's biggest headache. I learned that most reactor fuel comes in the form of long stainless-steel rods called fuel assemblies, which are filled with pellets of uranium. These are inserted into the reactor core until all the uranium in them has been fissioned, then they're taken out again. Now they're not full of uranium any more, they're full of 'fission by-products', which is a polite name for cesium and tritium and americium and plutonium and all sorts of other unstable and highly radioactive elements that cluster around the top end of the Periodic Table. This stuff is the most highly toxic stuff on the planet, more or less. Just go near it and you'll die. And typically, though we're churning out more and more of it each and every day, we've got nowhere to put it. Meaning that right now most of it's sitting in cooling pools outside the reactors that are producing it, pools originally designed to hold the spent fuel assemblies for about six months, which is how long it takes for the worst of the radioactivity to decay away and make the assemblies safe enough to handle. The idea was that after that the assemblies would be moved and either reprocessed or disposed of in another, as yet unspecified, manner. But mostly that just hasn't happened, and some of these pools have had assemblies lying in them for over twenty years.

The few assemblies that have been moved have generally been

placed inside steel canisters which are then dried out and pumped full of helium before being welded shut with double thickness lids. These canisters are placed inside what they call 'storage casks', basically giant Coke cans with an outer wall of concrete three-quarters of a metre thick and an inner wall that's minimum four centimetres solid steel. Once filled, these casks usually end up sitting in rows outside nuclear facilities for want of any better place to go. You're not allowed to move them anywhere in any case. If you want to shift the contents you have to break open the storage cask, take the canister out again – remembering that this thing is still super-hot and very radioactive – and put it in a special transportation cask, like one of those you've seen shown on the news with trains crashing into it to show how safe it is. Then you can ship it round the country, as long as you've got railways strong enough to take the extraordinary weight and teams of radiation experts capable of monitoring the thing at every stage of its journey to check there's been no leak of any kind, that is.

Of course, there's no point in transporting it unless you've got some place to transport it to. But where? This stuff isn't going to be safe to let back into the environment for around a hundred thousand years, which is the kind of timescale human beings can't even begin to comprehend. Realizing that a hundred thousand's an impossibility, the nuclear industry, sensibly enough, has decided to set its storage target at a mere ten thousand. Ten thousand's doable, apparently. In ten thousand years we'll either have new technologies that can deal with this stuff effectively enough to extract it and repackage it or we'll be in some new dark age – or more likely completely extinct – and no one will care.

Even so, ten thousand years is a long long time to plan ahead. By then the continents themselves will have shifted around quite significantly. So you can't put your dump near anything that looks remotely like a fault line or a potential release valve for a volcano. And you've also got to find a place that's likely to stay really really dry. Water will corrode any metal it comes into contact with, given long enough. It can even trigger a chain reaction if there's enough of it, like in that natural reactor in Africa that Metzger mentioned to me. And once it's got through whatever can you've stored your hot radionuclides inside of, either by corroding it or by encouraging the transuranics inside to melt themselves down, it'll whisk them away to the nearest water table, from there to a river, and then all round the biosphere. Which is not a lengthy process.

So the point about Salt Mountain is that it's about as dry as it gets. As its name suggests it's made largely out of salt, sodium chloride to be exact, part of a massive deposit that was left when the Permian sea evaporated away 225 million years ago. The presence of so much salt means two things: geological stability and the almost total absence of moisture of any kind. The area receives less than twenty centimetres of rain every year, 97 per cent of which is evaporated back into the atmosphere before it can penetrate into the ground. And salt rock's also good because unlike most rocks it's quite plastic. It moves around. If fractures develop, they'll close up again. If you bury something hot in it, it'll melt the salt all around it, which will then pack in tight and encase your buried hot thing very nicely. And if you need to get your hot thing out again? Salt's relatively easy to excavate. There are downsides, naturally, the main one being that salt's pretty corrosive stuff of its own accord, and even without any water around to help it could end up attacking your canisters all by itself. Which would be bad. Still, the powers that be seem to have decided that Salt Mountain's the best option there is. So that's that.

Anyway, once you've got your site you can't just dig a hole, shove in all your transportation casks and cover it up again. You've got to put your waste in a receptacle robust enough to last the distance. This is the modern equivalent of preparing mummies to survive undecayed for thousands of years inside the pyramids, except that it's much, much harder. Consider again: *ten thousand years* at temperatures of thousands of degrees and also, quite possibly, if your mountain collapses in on itself at any stage, hundreds of thousands of tonnes of pressure. And these are your *minimum* requirements. We're talking redundant systems, aluminium alloy heat-conductors, depleted uranium lids, boron panels for stray neutron absorption, plus an overall facility design that's going to be readily communicable and idiotproof to whoever's job it ends up being to get it out the ground and repackage it sometime in the far, far distant future.

The scale of this is so enormous, the cost so mind-bogglingly huge, there's no way you can stand against it. You'd be like an ant trying to face down a juggernaut. How were you going to beat that, Jack? Or had you finally realized that you couldn't? Had you read the *Pirotechnia* and realized that this was the same deal, but five hundred years further down the line? That a global nuclear economy was as inevitable in the wake of Curie and Bohr and Rutherford as the industrial revolution was post the metallurgical discoveries of the Renaissance? Had you finally accepted that? Were you really coming here to see if you could swing a job as part of their design team, help answer questions about how to communicate technical knowledge about the storage facility to future generations (not that I'd've given much for your chances)? Or was that just a joke, a cover story for some new and madcap art scheme?

Well I suppose this is what I'm hoping to find out.

I ask after Jack at the RV resort and the casino, but in both places I'm told to try again tomorrow, during a different shift. Someone suggests that I go down the street to the Salt Cellar, since that's where the DoE officials drink when they're in town, so after checking into one of the town's two cheap motels that's what I do.

Seven o'clock sees me at the bar, ordering an orange juice and asking the barman if anyone who works on the facility's been in. Sure they have, he says. Claude Fioravanti was in here five minutes back – you just missed him. He's gone over to the Marriott to have dinner with some visiting dignitaries. So I down my drink, tell him thank you, jump in the Honda and hurry down the street.

Inside the dining room I get one of the waiters to point Fioravanti out. Four men at a table, white shirts, blue business suits. The taller of the four, the one with a sky-blue tie and lightly oiled black hair, that's the guy I'm looking for.

It doesn't seem like a good idea to just charge up and interrupt so I borrow a piece of paper from reception and scribble out a note. Something tells me that a more circumspect approach than the one I usually employ might be advisable on this occasion, so I write that I'm over from RAF Featherbrooks on a visit and if it wouldn't be too much trouble could I have a quick word? Apart from the naming of the base I keep the note as vague as possible. What I definitely don't do is mention Jack.

The Featherbrooks reference works as exactly as I'd hoped it would. The nuclear industry looks after its own, I know that much, even if it never told me exactly what job I did. Peeping through the window in the dining-room door I can see Fioravanti being handed my message, reading it, wiping his mouth, excusing himself and getting up from his seat.

I check my reflection in one of the lobby's many floor-to-ceiling mirrors. Look at me: a body that stomps the line between chunky and overweight, flat-fronted trousers corrugated with sweat, a once-white cotton T-shirt emblazoned with a large Silicon Graphics logo, limp blond hair just long enough to cover my baby-pink ears, large round plastic-framed glasses that are supposed to be clear but in this light look faintly mauve, and splayed Converse trainers well greyed from dirt and bursting from the strain of carrying all of the above . . . on a good day I've got a hint of Matt Damon in *The Talented Mr Ripley*; on a bad one I'm more Philip Seymour Hoffman in one of his repressed-paedophile roles. Either way I doubt that I'm what Claude Fioravanti's expecting to see.

But it's too late now. Here he is, stepping out into the lobby, clutching his napkin like a throttled dove.

'Mr James?' he says, looking infinitely disappointed as he takes me in. 'How may I help you?'

'Hi, yes, look, I'm really sorry to take up your time like this . . .'

'Don't apologize. What is it you want?'

'Well, to get straight to the point . . .'

'If you would – I'm a little busy.'

'I'm looking for information relating to the whereabouts of a man named Jack Reever. I believe he was located here sometime within the last ten years or so . . .' Exactly why I'm talking like a TV FBI agent I have no idea.

Fioravanti's looks like a man who's just broken a tooth. 'I know when that motherfucker was here,' he says.

Motherfucker, huh? Looks like I'm getting warm. 'And . . . ?'

'Listen, son. I don't know who you are or what your business is. I don't know or care if you really work at Featherbrooks like you say you do. But if you take my advice you'll keep as much distance between yourself and Jack Reever as is humanly possible. The man is a certifiable lunatic.'

I hear the words. I take them in. But you know what? I'm getting a little tired of people telling me my father was psychotic. I'm thinking of instituting a new rule: the only person allowed to be rude about Jack Reever from now on is me. 'At least you remember him,' I say.

'How could I forget? He showed up here completely out of the blue, saying he was an artist, going on about cave painting, telling us we needed him on our team. Like we didn't know what we needed. We knew alright – and it didn't look like him. But he wouldn't take no for an answer, kept coming to my office, stopping me in the parking lot, even came out to my home. After I'd finally made it clear to him that we didn't want him around – and that took some doing, believe me – he posted himself by the gates down the road there, out by where that dumb-ass protest camp is now, and started digging himself a hole.'

'A hole?' Of all the tales of my father's antics I've heard so far on this trip, this is perhaps the most immediately mystifying.

'A hole. When someone demanded to know what he was doing he told them he was building his own spent-fuel depository seeing as how we wouldn't let him work on ours. Then he put up a sign, pasted the plans for his proposal to anything that didn't move in town and started sending us letters inviting us to pay him to take in any waste we couldn't accommodate in Salt Mountain itself.'

'Is it still there?'

'What?'

'The hole?'

'How the fuck am I supposed to know? You think I spend my time hanging out with the morons in that camp?'

'I suppose not.'

'You suppose right.'

'So what happened to Jack?' I have a vision of him digging away late one night at the bottom of a sixty-foot excavation like one of those tunnels characters are always digging in cartoons, and digging and digging and digging until suddenly the roof caves in.

'What d'you think happened? He wouldn't stop when we asked him to so we had to call up the sheriff and get him to throw your Mr Reever in the county jail. You can't have people going round digging holes by the side of the road, especially not just outside of a federal nuclear facility. Plus he was stirring up trouble all over town. See – it wasn't just us thought he was crazy. It was the protesters too. They hated him just as much for the mess he made in their camp down there. He even got the Wanaput all worked up again, and they'd been quiet as mice ever since we'd gotten them a licence so's they could build their damn casino across the street. No one wanted him here, and I mean no one. He got up everyone's nose, upset the status quo . . . this was a nice quiet town till he showed up. I tried to help him, really I did, but the maniac attacked me when I went to visit him in jail, damn near broke my nose. If I'd pressed charges, he'd still be there today, but out of the goodness of my heart I had him tagged as mentally unstable and we got the authorities to ban him from the state.'

'Wasn't that a bit extreme?'

'Extreme? The man was a rabid dog. In any sensible country we'd've been able to have him put to sleep. You can't go kicking up that kind of fuss in places like this. The future energy prospects of the entire US depend on us getting Salt Mountain right. What in hell did he expect?'

'I don't know,' I said. 'Maybe to be consulted. Maybe to get involved. Maybe not to be completely railroaded by such an obvious prick.'

Fioravanti chews the air. He wasn't expecting this. Nor was I, if truth be told. I guess my rule has come into effect a bit sooner than I thought.

'Just who in hell are you, anyway?' he says finally.

'No one,' I say, already beginning to regret my outburst. And before he can have me thrown out of the hotel I turn and run towards the low blaze of evening sunlight that's beyond the lobby, through its exit wall of pillarless plate-glass doors and out into the desert heat.

As I hurry to the Honda, mind a-whirl, something nags at the periphery of my vision. I resist the temptation to turn my head; instead, as I get into the car, I sneak a full-on glance round the corner of the doorframe. I can't be sure, but it looks very like the same white truck that was waiting at the turn-off. There's someone in it too; sitting in the driver's seat, pouring coffee from a flask, the peak of a red baseball cap pulled low over his face, a pair of plastic sunglasses wrapped around his face.

That's all I get. Then I go. But I saw enough to see that there weren't any markings. Whoever he is, he's not highway patrol.

Tracked by two of the CCTV cameras mounted on the fence posts, I leave the Honda and walk in the direction of the encampment. I head straight for it, telling myself there's no point in trying to appear casual or circumspect, but it's also because I think that if I don't go there directly I won't go at all. It's clearer to me now why I didn't come and ask questions down here earlier, when I first arrived. It's because I was scared to, that's why. But I've paid a heavy price for my prevarication – the sun touched the horizon as I was driving here and now the light is fading fast. I'd really rather not be entering the enemy's camp just when it's getting dark.

Still, there's clearly light enough for everyone to have been watching me since the moment I got out the car. Worse – and wordlessly, like it's some kind of emergent hive-mind defence-response – ten yards from the first tent a crowd starts forming, a crowd made up of scary ecoterrorist types my age or younger. One or two jeer at me as I walk by, but I ignore them and focus on a bearded bloke in his late fifties sporting a Burning Man T-shirt and a pair of non-threatening dungarees who's squatting by a smouldering campfire, scraping the contents of a pan into a refuse sack.

I've more or less made it to my destination when a boy runs up. He can't be more than nine or ten but he stands in front of me brazen as you like, folds his arms and blocks my way. His ears are what I notice first; they poke through his mane of hair like wonton in a dish of noodles. One side of his face is clean and glowingly prepubescent, the other is smeared with what looks like rust. His navy-blue polyester running pants are too long for him and splay on the ground around his unshod feet, covering them completely except for a single battered-looking toe. I don't know what colour his inside-out T-shirt is supposed to be but there's no doubt about his eyes, which even in this half-light emit a sharp and painless grey.

'Fuck off,' he says. He's a time machine. My throat tightens, my tongue begins to swell. I can't remember how to breathe. This time it's not an asthma attack, it's a mirror. Little bastard, standing there like my younger self. Let's see how he feels in a few years time when he's been betrayed by all this self-righteous integrity, when he works out that vegetarianism + no responsibilities ≠ world peace. Let's see how he likes it when he ends up a traitor to the cause, when he can't find the purity or commitment that it demands of him, when he works out that he has to leave because he's living a lie, that the people around him weren't telling him the truth, that there are in fact lots of good things in science, in progress, in TV, in technology. That modern life is okay, that it's okay to like the banal, the superficial, the disposable, the inauthentic, the ordinary. That while it's easy to lie around demanding a world with less injustice, less pollution, more humanity, it's a lot less easy to make it happen once you realize that human beings are a very long way from being capable of actually creating it. I mean, this kid, who's going to be there for him? Look at the faces all around him. How many Stasies and Jacks are standing there among them? How many who for all their ethics and principles are capable of keeping even their own lives on some kind of steady track?

I suppose you think I'm being prejudiced. But consider this – consider what I didn't tell Liz that afternoon when we were out with the ashes on the cliff. Consider what actually happened after my father disappeared.

See, we didn't know he'd gone for good, not straightaway. It took a good few months to work that out. During that period Stasie started out upset and ended up completely mental. After the initial period of anger and rage and depression had passed (along with the spice of two suicide attempts) her next thought was to go to America to look for him. The others convinced her not to, but then she started disappearing off herself – taking trips to London which got longer and more frequent, telling the rest of us she was reviving her musical career.

Meanwhile I was having my own little period of madness. The idea that I wasn't going to see my father again was utterly inconceivable to me, and long past the time it was obvious to everybody that my family had irrevocably fallen apart I was going round saying 'when Jack gets back this' and 'when Jack gets back that' like a looping sound file. But no one in the commune said anything, not for ages, and it wasn't until my level of denial started bordering on the psychotic that finally they got worried enough (or annoyed enough) to try and do something about it.

In the end it was Summer and Tom who broke it to me. One day after breakfast they took me through into the living room, sat me down and broke it to me straight: 'Cooper, I don't think Jack's going to be coming back here to live with us.'

'So will I be going to live in America with him, then?' I asked, because that seemed like the logical alternative.

Tom and Stasie exchanged a worried glance. 'I don't think so, chicklet,' Summer said. 'I don't think that's going to happen.'

It took a while, but once it dawned on me that they were right, that this was the situation, I fell into what I suppose was a depression – though no one calls it that when you're ten, or they didn't in the 1970s anyway. My initial reaction was to find someone to blame, and the most likely candidates, it seemed to me, weren't Jack or Stasie or Shannon but me – and God.

I'd never believed in God. We didn't in the commune, at least not in a recognizably Christian way. But quite a lot of God went down at school – proselytized in large part by Miss Banner – and in the crisis of confidence that the sudden absence of both my parents triggered in me I started to think that we were all wrong, that we were all mistaken, that God did exist and that he'd taken it upon himself to punish me for my sins, the list of which was long and subject to continual extension and revision but which always included: daring to disbelieve in his existence; being mean and disruptive in Miss Banner's class; drawing in school library books; and – most of all, at the very top of the first column, every time – stealing the bulla from Moon.

My guilt and paranoia got so bad that I actually found the courage (or more likely got driven by the fear) to take myself off to the staffroom one lunch break, find Miss Banner and apologize for my behaviour over the previous couple of years. She took it with very good grace, steered me off into an empty classroom and said she'd heard I'd been having bad problems at home; was everything okay? That's the point – if there was one; memory seems to manufacture these moments of transition but I'm sure the actual experience of change is far less episodic, far more gradual – it all became very real, suddenly. I burst into tears and threw myself onto the teacher's mercy as only a ten-year-old can. And her response was such that in my own unformed way I realized the pointlessness of my rebellions – mine and the commune's too – and began to accept that the everyday life led by the world at large wasn't so bad or terrible.

I planned to apologize to Moon as well, especially after the obvious success of my apology to Miss Banner. But I never did. Maybe I wasn't scared enough of my friend, maybe I didn't have the courage; but there's a more concrete reason too. Any apology would mean confession of my theft, and confession would mean the return of the object I stole. But when I went to get the bulla from my secret hiding place – and I got that far with my intention, so I wasn't completely a lost cause – the bone and the thong attached to it were gone. I was mystified. Maybe Jake or Max or someone found it and filched it. Or maybe it got hauled off by one of the many mice that lived inside the walls and who, since they were quite capable of eating wood and plastic, would no doubt have snacked quite happily on that thin leather strand. Anyway, I never found out what happened to it and, since it seemed the height of lameness to confess both to stealing *and* to losing the damn thing, Moon never got his apology.

This all happened during Stasie's longest continual absence, about six weeks all told. When she eventually returned it was only to take off again almost immediately, though this time with one difference – this time she took me with her. She'd got a gig playing support with The Mulberries – mainly because she'd started sleeping with the drummer – and for the next three months we travelled all over Europe on a chaotic festival tour. There were parties, drugs. It never stopped. I think Stasie expected the band and crew to sort of collectively parent me like the commune had done, but it didn't work like that. I spent most of the time hanging out with the roadies and the various members of The Mulburries' motley entourage of hippy chicks and groupies, who did useful things like teach me how to play cards, smoke and tell fortunes using tarot cards. With Stasie's help – it was during the tour that she changed my name, by introducing me to everyone as Cooper and insisting that I not respond if anyone called me Ash – they also made me realize that it wasn't God who was to blame for Jack's departure but Jack himself. And they taught me to be angry with him. I think it was the easiest lesson I ever learned.

Weird and disorienting though it was, I have pretty good memories of that period – I was the centre of attention, enough was going on around me to take my mind off things, I didn't have to go to school, and as far as I recall I pretty much enjoyed myself. But it wasn't long before Stasie went completely off the rails. She started taking heroin and when the tour finished and the band returned to England she stayed on in Barcelona, which was where they'd played their final gig. She'd finished with the drummer by that time and had taken up with some loser who called himself Scuffles, don't ask me why. He was a dealer I think, some drugs casualty anyway. He was as thick as shit but what he did know was the site of every hippie hangout on the Costa del Sol and therefore where to score, which was good enough for Stasie. He also knew how to feel me up, which was grim, though he never did anything worse than that. In the way of these things I didn't think too much about it at the time – I'd seen plenty during the tour to make me (I thought) wise beyond my years in the various permutations of human sexuality. But when I hit my early twenties it needed some pretty thorough working through, to say the least.

Anyway, no point dwelling on that now. For a while we moved down the coast, following the heroin, living off Stasie's earnings from the tour, before crossing over into Morocco where we got ripped off for quite a lot of cash almost immediately on arrival in Tangier – part of me wonders if it was a set-up and it was Scuffles who ripped Stasie off. Either way he disappeared soon after, and Stasie and I left the city and travelled down the coast, ending up in the heart of the medina in some little village whose name I never did find out with a bunch of Moroccans who as far as I could tell were fucking my mother in return for providing her with food and drugs.

I liked the Moroccans much more than I liked Scuffles, that was for sure. And there were other advantages too – good food, a continued lack of school, days spent playing football on the beach with the local kids. Maybe the reason I don't tell anyone about it is that it's the kind of childhood lots of people wish they'd had – or think they wish they'd had. What they don't get is how the fear, the uncertainty, it gets into your bones. Or your lungs, in my case. This was the period when my asthma really started coming on, and then my eyesight started going too, really rapidly, though no one actually noticed, not until after what happened next.

The Mulberries' drummer, he'd been worried about Stasie and me disappearing off the way we did. He'd gone back to England, found out she'd got an older brother, told him about the scene we were headed into and basically put the shits up him. My Uncle

Matthew flew down to Spain to look for us and somehow managed to trace us all the way to the village where we were living. One day he just showed up at the house where we were staying, said he'd come to take us home.

Stasie wouldn't leave. She kicked up a massive fuss, refused to let him take me. But take me he did, leaving her with enough money to follow if she wanted, which eventually she did. Eventually.

So now both my parents had abandoned me. This was too much. My whole world, such as it was, had altogether collapsed. My friends, my family, the commune, the culture I'd been brought up in, even my name . . . all gone. Gone. The coping mechanisms I'd previously come up with: denial, my God complex, the seething rage I'd been directing at the figure of my absent father, none of these were any use in helping me comprehend what was happening and so they completely fell away. All I felt was empty, hollow as a drum. It wasn't even that I retreated inside my shell. Of the next two years of my life I remember almost nothing. Experience didn't impinge upon me, or if it did, it didn't imprint. It was like I didn't exist.

Apart from the series of disasters that had just befallen me I think what I found most unsettling was the amount of time I was expected to spend alone. I had my own room, a concept that was entirely new to me, and though Janet and Matthew's house was in a well-populated suburban street it somehow felt more isolated than the farmhouse ever did. The two girls were nice enough but not particularly communicative and I never met the neighbours or anything like that. Janet did her best to make me feel welcome but I could sense the basic unconventionality of the situation never sat happily with her. Matthew was a workaholic and was never home. At school I was thought of as different so I got bullied, then they found I needed glasses, which made it worse. I was pretty unhappy until they bought me a computer, a Sinclair Spectrum. It was love at first sight – there's nothing like code when it comes to male-teen alienation. That little black box, it plugged straight into my head. I could go in there, create and conquer whole worlds. So that's where I went.

I soon became so withdrawn that it began to worry my new

family. Asperger's syndrome had only recently been recognized and Janet, always alert to the latest medical trend, carted me down to London on the train on several occasions to see various specialists and get me diagnosed. I filled in various questionnaires and did lots of tests and talked a lot about my feelings to people I'd never met before. But in the end it seemed I was depressed and introverted rather than actively autistic. Which no one thought greatly surprising, once they found out what I'd been through.

What I didn't know, not that it would have made much difference, was that my mother had come back to London, had a breakdown and been committed to the Maudsley – the psychiatric hospital – suffering from drug-induced psychosis. No one told me this – the story they fed me was that she'd gone to India to become a Buddhist monk (how that was somehow regarded as a more constructive fate I've never quite been able to fathom). Either way I didn't discover the truth till I was studying for my A levels, by which time she'd been discharged and was working in a pub. How did I find out? Because one teatime she just turned up on the doorstep and told me. It was that banal. Maybe she'd been waiting until I was the only one home or maybe it was just (un)lucky chance, but there we were, just the two of us. She sat on the sofa smoking her Bensons while I made us tea, then told me about the mental hospital and her job in the pub and the part-time courses in herbalism and psychotherapy she was taking. There wasn't an apology or anything like that, though she did offer me a room if I wanted it in Granny and Grandad's old house, which she informed me she was moving back into. I told her thanks but no thanks, I was happy enough where I was (though I wasn't). Perhaps it was just as well – there's no way I'd've been able to stick it once she started converting the place into that retreat. I'd moved on too far into a different way of life to ever consider going back, become absolutely conservative. To all intents and purposes I'd swapped sides.

But don't think I didn't rediscover my anger. Of course I did, however much of a contradiction it was for me to simultaneously despise Jack's way of life and the suburban fate he'd consigned me to. Anger, hatred, emptiness, betrayal – paradox is the powder that ignites them not the foam that puts them out. Once I reawoke to my emotions aged sixteen, seventeen, the fury came back with such intensity that by the time Stasie reappeared in Nottingham I'd already been treated for an incipient stomach ulcer. I mean, I've suffered from this shit every day of my entire fucking life, a life which would have been completely, totally different if Jack hadn't upped and left. And each and every one of those days I've banished the thoughts of suicide that without exception are waiting there to ambush me the moment I awake, crawled out from my pit and faced the day – and faced it well, beaten it, turned it into a tool with which to make something of myself. And of all the obstacles I've faced, of all the problems the world's thrown at me, of all the holes I've dug for myself, none has been as paltry or as insignificant or as easily routed around as the pathetic figure presented here by this ignorant, arrogant, snot-nosed kid who doesn't know a shit about anything life's got in store for him. So if he thinks he's going to stand in my way even for a moment, he's got another think coming, the little prick.

'Fuck off yourself,' I say.

He glares at me for a moment, then runs up and kicks me in the shin. The crowd explodes with laughter and applause and the boy backs up a couple of metres, holds his hands above his head like a celebrating footballer and does a little victory dance.

At the sight of this, something in me snaps. Without thinking about it I'm up and at him, shoving hard at his shoulders. Fear floods my chest as some part of my limbic system registers that I've just crossed a line, but I don't stop. The kid's face switches from smiles to shock as he stumbles backwards, and as I shove him a second time I feel my fear thrill down my arms, leave my body and enter his. It's a total buzz.

'You little shit, you fucking little shit, who the fuck do you think you are, you think you can do that kind of thing to me . . . ?'

The second shove proves harder than I'd reckoned and the boy trips and falls. He hits the ground and arches up and over, starts writhing, crying. Shit, I think, shit I've hurt him, and I reach a hand out to him and drop to one knee to check if he's okay. But then the writhing and the crying stop and he flips back viper-like and spits an oyster right into my face.

It smacks onto the right-hand lens of my glasses and hangs there, clouding the world from view. For a moment we're both frozen, amazed by the accuracy of his strike. But then the crowd erupts and he starts scrabbling away.

He's half on his feet already by the time I grab him. The anger's back, it's taken over, it's dictating the actions of my hands. It's told one to get hold of this boy's T-shirt and it's told the other, the one that only a second earlier was reaching out to help him from the dirt, to clench and make a fist. And it's so busy doing this, so fixated, that it doesn't see the danger coming until it pops up right in front of me and strikes me hard and smart on the side of my face with a clenched fist of its very own.

Now it's me down in the dirt, holding my jaw, gasping through the pain. The difference is that I'm not faking it.

'Ow! Ow!' I'm saying. My assailant comes forward, chest heaving, tendons springing from out of nowhere to mesh his arms like some kind of exoskeleton. All around it's getting darker because the crowd has started closing in. Oh shit, is what I'm thinking, you've really gone and done it this time Cooper, now you're really fucked. 'I'm sorry – I'm sorry, okay . . . don't fucking hit me! I'm just . . . I'm sorry, okay?'

Pathetic. If I was them I'd lynch me.

'You pick a fight with my brother you pick a fight with me.'

'Yes, yes I know I'm massively sorry I don't know what I was thinking . . .'

The effect of this apology is to trigger a well-aimed kick directly at my ribs.

Ouf.

'No, please don't, no, not – '

Another kick, intended for my groin but connecting with my hip, finishes my sentence for me.

'I'm looking for Jack Reever,' I shout, 'does anyone know Jack Reever?' But it's useless. Kicks start jabbing in from all around as the other members of the crowd decide that now's a good time to join the fun. 'Jack Reever!' I shout as their boots pummel heavily into my buttocks and back. I curl into a ball, clasp my hands over my head. 'Jack Reever Jack Reever Jack Reever!' I yell into my chest as someone's foot smacks square across my neck.

And then a voice – a human voice – registers above the jackal frenzy, ordering them to let me be. It's apparently a voice with some authority because instantly the kicks subside. Its owner cleaves his way through the little cell of bodies, bringing with him air and sky and calm.

'Get up.'

I twist my head, venture a peek from out behind the barricade I've made of my arms. It's the bearded guy in the dungarees, the one I'd originally been headed for before I got distracted into getting myself beaten up.

'What d'you want from us?' he asks, once I've got back up on my feet.

For a minute or two I'm too busy checking for broken bones and trying to clean the dust and sputum from my glasses to answer him.

'Well?'

'I'm looking for someone who can give me information on Jack Reever,' I pant. 'I heard he spent some time here. Digging holes.'

Dungarees gives me this look like I know something I shouldn't. 'And what are you to him?'

'I'm his son,' I say.

He stares at me a moment longer and, glasses once more operational and back up on my face, I return his stare. Then he nods. 'Alright,' he says. 'You'd better come with me.'

The tent is old, army surplus, probably the same damn tent the blokes on the other side of the fence used for field training. Though they wouldn't have filled it with tie-dye and incense, not unless it dates from Vietnam, which I suppose it might do. Anything's possible.

It's just me and Dungarees now, me and Dungarees and the boy who started everything, who's sitting in the corner lighting tea-candles and who turns out to be Dungarees's youngest son. The three of us, we've made our peace and Dungarees has given me some painkillers and a cold compress for my jaw, and he's been telling me how Jack and he and about twenty others came down here and set this camp up soon after work began on the storage facility. I ask him when that was and he says right after the show Jack did in Seattle.

'You mean Frivolous Use?'

'That's the one.'

'But Jack went to war with the protest movement in Seattle after that show went up.'

'Why? Because they superglued his locks?'

'That's what the papers said.'

'Right. The papers. So it must be true.'

'I spoke to his partner at the Electroworks, Patrick Belin. That's what happened.'

'I know that's what happened.' Dungarees takes out a packet of tobacco from his pouch, starts to roll himself a cigarette. His nails are split and brittle, and the tight skin of his hands is flecked with scars and moles. On the second knuckle of his right-hand index finger a large wart squats, bug-like. 'It was me that did the supergluing.'

'You? I thought you told me you were friends.'

'Don't you get it? He *asked* me to do it. It was planned. We cooked the whole thing up between us.' He chuckles at the memory. 'He tipped me off about the show, I organized the protest, came down with a couple of buddies the night before, fixed the locks like we'd agreed . . . and it worked just like we thought it would. The press picked it up and the show was big news. It would never've got on the radar screen without it. The press wouldn't've given a flying fuck any other way. They're not interested in what people think – conflict's what they're after. Bullshit controversy that covers up the real truth of everything.'

'And no one told Belin?' I ask, ignoring the standard-issue nonsense.

'Of course no one told him. You've met the guy. That broomstick he's got rammed up his backside? It's not a recent acquisition.'

I consider all this for a few seconds, and conclude that I'm not surprised at any of it.

'So then you came down here together?'

'Jack came first. He'd picked up on what was happening on account of his interest in the waste issue – this was at a time, remember, when everyone else had tunnel vision on reactors and plutonium. They were doing their best to keep the whole project under wraps, at least until work got underway. All the politicians have long since been in the pocket of the industry, the local Wanaput were bought off with a lump of cash and a bunch of gambling licences . . . no one was doing anything to try and stop it. Jack called me up, told me what was going down, said did I want to help him start a camp. I was looking to get out of the city, get my teeth into something new, I said sure. I put the word around, a bunch of other people came to join us – been here ever since. See, the way we see it, this place is the Achilles' heel of the industry. They can't dump their waste; sooner or later it's gonna become politically unacceptable for them to carry on producing it. That was Jack's theory, anyway, and even after all these years I still think it's right.'

'Otherwise you wouldn't be here.'

'You got it.'

'He ever mention anything to you about applying for a job? Before you came to join him?'

'Where? At the Mountain?'

I nod. Dungarees laughs.

'Doing what, exactly?'

'I don't know. Concept design, maybe?'

He shakes his head. 'Jack would never've gone to work for those shitbags. Apart from anything else he'd never've passed the first security vet they put him through. And anyway he gave up art when he left Seattle.'

'But I heard he was working on some kind of big granite carving. What happened to that?'

'Oh yeah, that was here alright, fucking useless hunk of stone. Jack got me to help him bring it down here; damn thing wrecked the suspension on one of my best vehicles. We had to sneak it out the Electroworks as well – Belin put new locks in after the gluing incident and was too tight-arsed to change them again when Jack disappeared owing him all that money, and of course Jack had kept a copy of the keys. But after all the trouble he put me to I never saw him work on it. It ended up being used as pirate ships and castles by the kids.'

'So he didn't work on anything at all while he was here?'

Dungarees shrugs. 'Like I told you, Jack wanted to get back to his roots, to direct action. It was the show that did it . . . he'd spent all this time putting it together and then he realized that it wasn't going to make the slightest bit of difference, even with our fancy little media coup. The only carving I ever saw him do was whittle a couple of dry old sticks into snakes and geckos for the children. But that was pretty much it on the art front, apart from some sketches. He had an old horse's skull he'd found lying around that he liked to set up and draw. Must've done a hundred different versions of it. But apart from that . . .'

But I already know about the horse's skull. 'What about this hole he dug? He regarded that as art, presumably?'

But Dungarees is getting bored of this conversation. 'Fuck art. It's bourgeois shite, camouflage for the machine. Jack knew that. He wasn't under any illusions on that front; he'd kicked around too long. Way he saw it, art was always about the past – and he wanted to think about the future. He couldn't see any point to it unless it went some way toward helping future generations deal with the shit we're busy trying to lay on them. He didn't dig the hole because it was art. He did it because he knew it would wind up them inside the fence.'

'And did it?'

'Oh yeah. It gave them just the excuse they needed.'

'For what?'

'To lock him up.'

'They arrested him?' I say, feigning ignorance. I think it's better if Dungarees doesn't know about my chat with Claude Fioravanti. It might contaminate his side of the story.

'Yep. Couldn't do it for demonstrating – state laws don't permit it, though not for much longer if the fascists get their way. But the hole was close enough to the fence for them to be able to call it a security risk, like maybe Jack was going to try and turn it into a tunnel or something – or maybe plant a howitzer in it – and they came down here and took him away. Threw him in the county jail to cool him off then kicked him out the state.'

'And then what happened?'

'Nothing. Some farmer guy he'd befriended up in Atomville showed up here about three months later on his behalf and carted off the granite block, and that was pretty much the last I heard of him till you showed up.'

'What's Atomville?'

'Production facility in the northern desert, backside of the Cascade Mountains. It was built in secret under the Manhattan Project in '43; been churning out product ever since.'

'Product?'

'Plutonium. The old code name for it. Seemed like a step back to me, to go to Atomville; I mean, that's where I was in the sixties. But that time is past. Waste is where protest's at these days. Not warheads.'

'So you didn't stay in touch?'

'Nope. No point. We'd kind of fallen out over the hole, in any case. I always thought it was a bad idea to dig the thing, that it wouldn't do any of us any good. But he was determined. He had some sort of personal beef going on with one of the DoE mucky-mucks that run the operation here I never understood. It's always been my policy to have as little to do with the authorities as possible; way I see it, soon as you open communications with these assholes they see to it you're compromised. No – you've just got to stick to your principles and do what you think is right. There's no middle way.'

'And Jack thought there was?'

'Maybe. Though he probably changed his mind on it after being locked up like that. I daresay that's why he never came back down here after they let him out. Couldn't face being proved wrong,

Jack. Your father was a guy who couldn't find his way to stepping down over anything.'

I nod. 'So they say,' I say.

'They?'

'They. You. His friends. It's the only thing about him you all seem to agree on.'

Before I leave I ask Dungarees if he'll show me the hole Jack dug. He doesn't see the point, he says, for years it's been nothing but a rubbish dump, but I persist and so sighing heavily he gets to his feet and leads me through the little settlement, past trailers and tents warm with throbbing lantern light. Children crowd onto thresholds to gawp at me; women look up from books, fires, conversations, their faces pinched and drawn. From behind me come the sound of footfalls, scuffles, murmurs . . . a small procession is forming in our wake.

Then we're out beyond the camp with nothing in front of us but the desert and the fence and we're walking towards where a row of cacti, the tall, pipe-organ type, are growing this side of what looks like a patch of shadow beyond the reach of the feeble yellow generator light that bleeds out from the tents and trucks. That's the hole. I can smell it.

My guide leads me to the edge of it, shines in a torch. The smell is rotten, stale – not a smell: a stench. The bottom of the pit glints with the hard curves of bottles and cans and the softer slicks of rotting vegetables, plastic bags, discarded clothing. The steep sides are busy with little avalanches of human piss and shit.

'This is it?'

'That too.' Dungarees points to something lying in the sand beyond the corner of the pit, something dark and square. I walk over to get a better look.

It's a sheet of metal, carved into an irregular shape with various small sections cut out of it. I can't make out what it is at first. Then, realizing that it's upside-down, I flip it over, causing total panic in the microcosmos of bugs and beetles living underneath.

It's a sign. The shapes are words, crammed together so they could be cut around more easily, making them a little difficult to read.

'Reever's Waste Repository,' they say.

How does this make me feel? I'll tell you how. It makes me feel like taking a gun, shooting myself in the head, falling forward into the pit. Game over, is how it makes me feel.

Is this what my father has bequeathed to me?

The sign still in my hands, I look up to where Dungarees is standing smoking, looking strangely younger than he did before. His elder son, the one that punched me, has reappeared and stands beside him, watching me, tall and proud as a prince attendant on his father's throne; the younger one, the one I shoved, squats off some way to one side, pretending to ignore me while toggling the on/off switch of a pocket torch that just happens to be angled in my direction. Behind him is the fence and beyond that the truncated cone that is Salt Mountain is glowing gold in the last rays of the setting sun. And what I think is: here, this is our legacy, this is our inheritance – mine, these kids', all children's to come.

Phonecall

I leave the camp and go for dinner at Chuck's Bar and Grill, hoping that a steak sandwich will do something to revive me, but the moment I sit down I'm overcome with a feeling of total listlessness. My body aches from the beating I received; I have bruises all down my arms and legs; the right-hand arm of my glasses is in fact really badly bent and though I get it straight enough to be functional at some point it's going to need replacing. I drink two beers before the food comes and when it does it disgusts me suddenly and I no longer want it. I pick at the fries and order more beer while I try and work out what I'm going to do.

I don't want to go to this place, Atomville. I want to go home. I don't want to think about Jack any more. All it's doing is making me angry and upset. So he left us and spent the rest of his life schlepping around America, making artistic statements that no one gave a shit about, failing to change the world. Who cares? Not me. I wish I'd never come. I mean, if I thought my life felt pointless back in England, it wasn't anything compared to how I feel right now.

Eventually I can't stand it any more – the uneaten food, the empty restaurant, the tediousness of the football game being silently played out on the wall-mounted television – and dumping the contents of my wallet on the table I leave Chuck's Bar and Grill and head back to my motel, which is a small two-storey affair with open-air corridors that let onto a concrete courtyard-cum-driveway, not unlike the motel in *Memento*, if you've seen that film.

Once inside my room I finish off the bottle of Jack Daniel's Cox gave me in front of the TV in an effort to make everything go blank, but it doesn't work so I get out of my clothes and climb into bed. But then I can't sleep – every time I close my eyes the long drive from Vermont replays across the inside of my eyelids like a giant game of *Carmageddon*; either that or some or other memory of my childhood judders into life in glorious Cinescope. I don't know which is worse.

Unable to close my eyes, what I end up doing is watching the lights from passing cars rake across the ceiling. More cars pass than you'd expect, for a town this size. I try to count them, like sheep, and amazingly it works. After I get to fifty-seven I enter into a vaguely trance-like state. At seventy-six my eyelids droop and close. Sometime after one hundred and twenty I stop counting altogether.

Then I'm dreaming of a motel room, a TV on mute, a ringing phone. The phone rings and rings. The ringing is very real. The ringing *is* real. I scrabble for the handset, pick it up. 'What?'

'Cooper? Is that you?'

'Liz!' I sit up, rub my eyes. My head hurts, my mouth tastes all metallic. The room seems smaller than before. Where in fuck's name did I put my fucking glasses?

'Oh. So you do remember me. I kind of thought you wouldn't, considering I've not heard a squeak from you since you left.'

'Wait a minute . . . just wait one minute . . .' I chase a fumble across the bedside table, under the pillow, along the floor beside the bed. Turns out I'm lying on them and now the other arm is bent. Jesus fucking Christ. 'How did you know where I was? How did you find me?'

'Some guy called Claude Fioravanti called the base, checking up on you. After that it was pretty easy. There's only about three places to stay in Jackass Flats. This is the second one I tried.'

So Fioravanti went and checked up on me, did he? I should've guessed he would. 'Couldn't you have thought about the time difference before you called me? You woke me up.'

'I had this crazy idea you'd be pleased to hear from me. The mail we got from Fioravanti said you looked like you might be in trouble.'

'Fioravanti's an arsehole.'

'Okay, well, so I didn't know that. I was worried about you, okay? You took off without saying anything. Are you alright? What's been happening? Where have you been?'

'Looking for Jack, obviously.'

'Did you find him?'

'Not yet.'

'So you're still looking?'

'Yes. No. Dunno.'

What am I going to do, tell her the whole sad story? Tell her how I got the ashes confiscated at customs, how I got drunk and trashed a hire car, how I drove right across the continent on a stupid whim, how I got into (and lost) a fight, how I ended up in the dead end that's Salt Mountain? I'm a big enough loser in her eyes already, thanks very much. The idea was to go off to America and come back with some kind of cool and meaningful tale to tell. Not to end up beached in the desert at the end of a long, sad trail of typically Cooperish misfortunes.

'Well listen,' she says. 'I think I've got a fresh lead for you.'

'Oh yeah? What did you do? Hold a séance?'

'No. I ran a credit search.'

'*What*!? At Featherbrooks?'

'Yes.'

I'm somewhat stunned by this. Liz's clearance might be higher than mine, but it's not all that high. 'How'd you do that? You didn't ask Andrews, did you?'

'I used his password.' She sounds sheepish – as well she should.

'Without telling him?' I ask, incredulous.

'Yes without telling him,' she snaps.

'You could lose your job for that.'

'Thanks. I know.'

I'm almost hysterical with glee. Not because Liz might lose her job, obviously – even I'm not that cynical and craven – but that she'd put it on the line for me. That's really something. 'Wow Liz. That's fucking cool of you.'

'I know that too. Look, do you want me to tell you what I risked my neck to find out or not?'

'Yeah, sure, tell me. Please.'

'Well, according to his banking records a few years ago your father took out a mortgage on a property in Atomville, which is a nuclear dormitory town plumb in the middle of Washington State. It's like the heart of the US atomic-weapons industry. They've been making plutonium there since 1943.'

I don't have the heart to tell her I already know all this. And in any case, it's kind of an anticlimax compared to the discovery that she's broken the rules on my behalf.

'Cooper?' prompts Liz, after a few seconds of silence. 'You still there?'

'Yes,' I say.

'You want to take down the address?'

'Sure.' She gives it to me and I pretend to write it down: 324 Neutron Avenue.

'Well?' she says.

'I'm thinking.'

'What about?'

'About whether I can get a flight home direct from Las Vegas, instead of having to go all the way back to Boston.'

'But aren't you going to go to Atomville?'

'No.'

'Why not?'

'Because I've had enough. The whole idea of coming here was stupid, a total waste of time. I'm going to come back to Whitby, throw myself on Andrews's mercy and ask him to give me back my job. And if he won't then I'll go somewhere else, get another job, a better job. I've had enough of this.'

'But . . . but you can't give up *now*.'

'Why can't I? I've crashed my hire car, I'm about to overrun my visa, I've lost the ashes and I no longer give two shits about finding Jack. I've found out all I need to know about where he went after he left, and as far as I can tell he went completely off the rails. I don't need to be his son. I don't need to be anybody's son. You're the only one who matters to me Liz. Not some dead father I didn't see for twenty years who was never a father to me anyway.'

Okay. So I've told her. But I couldn't help myself.

For the next few seconds Liz says nothing, which gives me all the time I need to reflect on the stupidity of what I've done.

'I really think it would be a big mistake to come home now,' she says, her words arranged like furniture, her tone as spacious and measured as Miles's loft apartment. 'I think you need to find out what happened to him. You do. Cooper, you owe it to yourself to go to Atomville. I'll send you money, if you need it.'

'Money's not the issue here. You don't understand. I'm going crazy – the whole thing's crazy! All it's doing is opening up old wounds.'

'They'll never heal until you find out who sent those ashes.'

'And how would you know?'

Another thoughtful pause. 'Because I'm your friend, that's how.'

It's my turn to think, I realize. But somehow I don't manage it. 'But do you love me?' I blurt, even though I understand with perfect clarity that it's absolutely the wrong thing to say.

'Cooper, I . . .'

'It's alright. You don't have to answer. I was only joking anyway.'

'It's not that . . .'

'But do you?'

Now the pause is longer. Now the pause is long enough for it to qualify as silence.

'Yes. Yes I do, but . . .'

'But only as a friend, right?' No point in holding back now, is there? I mean, I've already blown it. Might as well go all the way. 'I mean, not as much as Andrews. It's Andrews, isn't it, that you really love?'

'Cooper really I . . .'

'Isn't it?'

'Th . . .'

'Deny it. Go on!'

'It's not true, Cooper.'

'It's not?'

'It's not. It's not what you think. He's just my boss.' Her voice sounds strained, emotional. 'It's not what you think.'

No? Well you know what? I don't believe you. Because I don't understand, Liz, I don't understand how you can love me enough to track me down, to risk your job, to ring me long distance in the middle of the night, but not love me the way I want to be loved. 'Are you alone Liz?' I say, finally able to insert a wedge in between thought and action. 'Or are you calling me from work?'

'Of course not.' Defensively. 'I'm calling you from home.'

But whose home? That's the question.

'I'm worried about you Cooper.'

'Don't worry. I'm fine. Honestly. And I'll go to Atomville.'

'You will?'

'Yes. If that's what you think I should do.'

'It is.'

'Okay. But listen. I'll do that. But I don't want you calling me any more. You understand? I don't want you checking up on me, or running credit searches on my dad or risking your job for me. Just keep the fuck away, okay. Just keep the fuck away from me.'

And I don't hear what her answer is because before she can say anything I've put down the handset and traced the phone lead to where the socket is located down behind the bed and pulled it out from the wall.

That's it for sleep. My room's too claustrophobic to lie for ever on my bed, so I get up and go for a wander round the darkened motel corridors, up an outside staircase and onto a tiled roof terrace where a few plastic tables and broken loungers loll beneath the stars. I decide to spend the remainder of the night up there, staring out at the looming mound of Salt Mountain to the near north-east, the glow of Las Vegas to the distant south-east and the atomic sunset that is the even bigger glow of Los Angeles to the south-west.

I miss my music. Now the shock of what I told Liz on the telephone is passing I'm starting to wonder if that's the only thing I really miss about England, if that's the only thing I really wanted to go home for. Not Liz, not my job, but my Quads. It's taken me over six years to assemble those grey boxes. I've sacrificed holidays, evenings out, shit, I've even sacrificed relationships to save the money to buy them. And it's not just the money. It's the time, the time I've spent stripping them down, reconditioning them, rebuilding them, learning about every facet of the system . . . I've practically retro-engineered the fucking things. And sad though you may think it is, it feels to me like my one genuinely creative act, the single thing I've done for its own sake, the one thing I've managed to bring into this world that is purer than myself.

I used to find that sort of satisfaction in programming computers, but that changed when I went to work for DERA and it became a job. And I was hardly likely to find personal fulfilment of any kind at Featherbrooks. So I started getting into this idea of the perfect sound, pursuing it with the kind of stubborn obsessiveness I usually associate with my father. Because sound, sound can put you somewhere no visuals ever can. It's the most powerful sense, except for maybe smell, but there's not too much consumer-end hi-fidelity equipment in the shops for that right now (unless you count Miles's Smeg, which I suppose you might). I mean, you would not believe some of the recordings I've heard on people's systems as I've trolled around the country hunting down obscure components. Close your eyes and you are there, absolutely there, sitting on a bed with Robert Johnson or next to Glenn Gould on his piano stool or in some smoke-smogged bar with Charlie Parker or in the studio with Michael Jackson and Quincy Jones. It's incredible; you drop right out of time, you travel to a place you couldn't possibly have ever visited in a way that a century ago would have been utterly inconceivable. Every whelp of the guitar strings, every suck of breath . . . you're so close you're almost inside the fucking musicians themselves, you're probably hearing what's going on better than even they ever did. That's what high-end audio means. Exstasis. Getting free of time. Getting free of your ugly, useless self.

Which is why I miss it. Because here I am on this fucking rooftop in the middle of Nevada and I might have travelled physically further than I ever have before but I'm feeling more lumbered with myself than ever. This is what music allows you to escape from, this body, this planet, this world. I mean look at it. Look at these lights pulsing on the horizon like giant boils. It doesn't take much imagination to see how the sprawls that foment and fuel them will continue expanding outwards until one day they'll have unfurled themselves across the entirety of Nevada and California. And you don't need to be raving and apocalyptic to see how the global climate change that their pollutants and emissions have already helped to trigger would by that time be causing the temperature to rise, the water that keeps these cities going to disappear, and the biggest urban zone in the history of mankind to collapse in on itself. Within decades its inhabitants will abandon it, perhaps for lands newly revealed by the retreating icecaps, and it'll be left to crumble slowly back into the desert. In a century or two there'll be nothing left but the ruins of a handful of buildings, the residual patterns of the tarmac grids and, standing stripped of context like the temples in those ancient Mayan cities where the forests got chopped down for miles around and living there became untenable, a single monumental burial mound, attended by a dwindling coterie of increasingly confused and incoherent priests. And silence. Gorgeous, timeless silence, fuller and more pure than any music could ever be.

I feel a clarity, suddenly. The alcohol seems to have left me, taking with it the depressive fug I picked up at the protest camp. I'm not going to Atomville just because Liz says I should. I'm not that impressionable – and I don't need to impress her any longer either. I'm going because I don't believe Jack gave up on art, like Dungarees thinks he did. Stubbornness, single-mindedness – that's the trait that he and I have most in common, and so I know in my bones he wouldn't've given up. He took the granite block to Atomville because for whatever reason he thought that was the best way to move his project forward. He wasn't just idly sketching horses' skulls to while away the time. Those sketches were studies for the carving he wanted to make, I'm sure of it. I don't know what it was about Atomville that particularly attracted him, but something did. Maybe it wasn't even his second choice, maybe I've got it the wrong way round. Maybe Salt Mountain was the detour.

It seems perfectly possible, suddenly, that Atomville was where he was always headed, all along.

So that's where I'm headed too.

Aurum foliatum

Atomville

Arriving in Atomville is like arriving back at the source. Power is close by: you can feel it, an almost imperceptible hum that shimmers beneath the stage set of the silent, baking streets. This is the ur-Featherbrooks, the Platonic original, the distillation and essence of the nuclear imperium. Here I am in the heart of a desert, hundreds of miles from anywhere, nothing but sagebrush and scrub for three hours in any direction, and what do I find but a utopian suburbia, an irrigated oasis of shingled houses complete with white picket fences and trim green lawns, neatly arranged around a nexus of chainstores, mini malls, mega malls, fast-food franchises, rows of gleaming medical centres and lots of banks.

This town is a dream of perfection. The sidewalks – capacious and unblemished, disinfected by the sun – are too clean to be walked upon. They border wide, chocolatey roads, delicious blacktops that remain unblemished by the swish saloons and boxfresh SUVs that roll noiselessly along them, serenely transporting their occupants from one air-conditioned environment to another, cocooning them from the merciless, radiating sun.

But this is only the beginning.

Check it out. The motel I'm staying at is another two-storey prefab like the one in Jackass Flats. It's centrally situated on the strip mall that runs north–south through town. It has Hawaiian decor in the lobby and a kidney-shaped swimming pool in the parking lot. And it's named Tomsk-43 after one of those secret military science towns they had behind the Iron Curtain, which is apparently the local idea of irony. More bizarrely still, in reception there's a little fishtank set to one side of the counter, a single goldfish inside of it, swimming round and round. Its eyes are little balls of cloud and I think it might be blind. Which would be a very peculiar coincidence.

Right next door to Tomsk-43 is the Nukem Solarium & Massage and after stopping by to make an appointment for a neck rub I run the Honda through the car wash at the Atomic Body Shop. I have

a coffee at the Electron Espresso, pop into the Half-Life Hardware store to hunt for a US/UK electrical adaptor, contemplate a drink in the Tank Farm Tavern, window-shop for Italian sofas at Fission Furniture ('For all your furniture needs') and peruse the fine selection of previously owned housewares on display in Melt-Down Mary's Thrift Store. Then, passing by the local high-school football stadium (whose team is called the Bombers and whose logo

is a mushroom cloud), I go over to the Edward Teller Memorial Library, where I pick up a local street map and spend a few minutes perusing the forty-foot mural of a B52 bomber painted along the building's western side.

Don't imagine religion stands in opposition to all this atomic evangelism. The church, which stands on the corner of Proton and Argon, a little way west of the Uptown Mall (which dates from the 1950s and has a steel model of a helium atom topping off its sign), is clearly a popular place – even on a weekday like today its parking lot is glutted with blue LeSabres and two-tone Cadillac coupés. But its windows are laid out according to the geometrical relations of the Balmer series, the spectral dark lines you get when you burn a pure sample of any element and refract the light the flame gives off through a prism, and pinned to its outside wall is a strange steel artwork depicting the abstract forms of a man, a woman and a child flying like angels upwards and around a trinity of atoms.

I'm really going to love it here.

I spend the afternoon taking a boat trip up the river. According to Lucille, the Tomsk-43 receptionist, it's the best way to see the Areas, which is the vast patch of desert just to the north of Atomville where all the production and processing of the plutonium actually takes place. From what she tells me, there was some kind of dispute back in the 1970s between the US Coastguard and the Department of Energy over who had access rights to the stretch of the Chiawana that ran through the nuclear site, and the argument got right out of hand. Both parties ramped it up until it went all the way to the Supreme Court, who ruled in favour of the Coastguard. To get back at the DoE for challenging them they made it public access, which is how come anyone can walk up any day they want and take a cruise – or a jet-ski, or a kayak – right through the middle of one of the most sensitive installations in the entire world. You can even camp on the river bank as long as you don't go above the high water line. Take one step past it, though, and you're likely to get shot.

I join the tour at a small marina located at the southern end of town, just past a giant Marriott hotel called the Chiawana Inn. There's eight of us on the boat in all: me, a Donny Osmond look-alike tour guide called Graham, who's doing this in between studying for his zoology degree, an identikit retiree couple called Gene and Ruby, and a Promise Keeper and his family (wife, two kids). I know he's a Promise Keeper not because he's got a caterpillar-thick moustache that twitches when he talks like it wants to scurry off his face (though that might be a clue) but because he's wearing a cap that has the words 'Promise Keepers – We Jump For Jesus' stitched across its peak. When I ask him where he got it he says at the King Dome in Seattle, when he took his vows.

'So what brings you to Atomville?' I ask.

'We're movin' here,' the Promise Keeper tells me proudly, crushing his skinny wife against him as he does so. With her ivory skin and trembly smile she's very fragile-looking. Presumably, before he became a Promise Keeper he used to beat her up, and she still looks scared of him. 'Gonna move right in here, set up a Christian school. Ain't that right, hon?'

'Uh huh.' The wife tries hard to look enthusiastic, but doesn't succeed. 'We searched the longest time before finding the right place,' she squeaks.

'And right here's where we found it. We were looking at property only yesterday.'

'Oh yeah?' I say. But I don't pursue the matter. I shift my attention to the boat we're in, a sleek green launch, one of those ones that's powered by water jets. It moves slowly away from the bank but the river's big and wide and once we're out in the open Graham gives it some throttle and it speeds across the water, skimming off the surface and scaring up little coveys of duck and wild geese.

I move away from the other adults and up into the prow of the launch with the Promise Keeper's kids. A boy and a girl, maybe twelve and thirteen, they're standing with their hands on the rail, sunlight on their faces, wind in their hair, like Kate Winslet and Leonardo DiCaprio in *Titanic*. I slot in beside them and adopt the same pose. The hotel's already far behind us and now we're coming alongside what my map says is Rutherford Park, four or five hundred yards of trees and lawn on which some kind of major activity is happening. Tents are being erected, bunting's being hung, and

when I glance at Graham he's pointing in that direction and shouting at Gene and Ruby that it's the preparations for tomorrow's fair.

On the right bank, almost directly opposite the park, a giant tongue of water tumbles from a square concrete irrigation ditch; a little further to the north, laid out across the flood plain and fenced in by ranks of poplar trees, are what look like cherry orchards, the arcs of hundreds of irrigation sprays frozen in the air above them, each projecting its own little hologram of rainbow light.

But soon we leave all that behind as well. It's a glorious day. The milky overcast of yesterday has been burnt off by the sun and the sky is blue and cloudless, pure as a computer screen. I close my eyes and will myself into the sensation of speed, of flight. My body feels weightless, my shirt ripples around me and the bands of sweat round my waist evaporate taking with them the nervousness I've been feeling at the prospect of visiting Jack's old house in Atomville. Soon I'm thinking of nothing except the motion of the boat and the breeze on my face. I'm getting much better at letting go of things, I've noticed. It's a habit I think it would be worth my while to cultivate.

I keep my eyes closed until the engine dies and the hull smacks across the water, one, two, three, four times, then settles. I look around. The river's narrower here than it was, maybe eighty or a hundred yards across, and there are stony shoals stretching up the middle towards a series of small islands. The water shimmers turquoise between crumbling ten-foot cliffs. And looking across at us from one of them is a spaceport from a 1950s Dan Dare comic. At least, that's what this collection of white and silver buildings looks like to me.

Then a swerve of feedback whips out from the boat's PA and Graham's voice booms out across the Chiawana. 'Well, good afternoon everyone,' he says. He's standing in the stern talking into a hefty microphone, the twin images of our tour group reflecting in the mirror lenses of his Randolph Aviators like they're twin TVs. 'On behalf of Chiawana River Tours I'd like to welcome you all to the Atomville Areas Nuclear History and River Wildlife Tour.'

Back to reality. Graham explains that this is Three Area, the oldest installation on the facility, now used mainly for scientific research, most of it non-military. We gawp for a while as he points out its various component parts, then he engages the throttle and we chug onwards up the river, through some shallows, past a couple of long thin islands sacred to the local tribes.

After pausing to look at some wildlife – an eagle on a pole, a porcupine snoozing in a tree – we round a bend to the sight of two identical buildings standing side by side.

'That's D-Reactor,' Graham says. 'When they finished building it they found a crack had developed in the core, so they had to junk it and build the whole thing all over again right next door. A little further and you'll see C-Reactor, and B-Reactor after that. B-Reactor was the the first plutonium reactor they built here, the first one ever built – not counting the Chicago Pile.'

'So why didn't they call it A-Reactor?'

Graham chuckles like he knew this was a question someone was bound to ask. 'They called it B-Reactor so that if the Nazi spies found out about it, Hitler would think there must be an A-Reactor too. It was supposed to be knocked down and buried as part of the clean-up, but a lot of the old-timers here – including a bunch of guys who actually worked on it – they felt it should be cleaned up and preserved as a national monument.'

'Which it should be,' says the Promise Keeper. 'I mean, that building changed history for the entire human race. You can't knock it down.'

'Kinda looks like a church, don't you think?' says the Promise Keeper's wife.

I look round, expecting to see her staring at it dreamily, but she's not; she's standing staring and hugging herself with her arms, even though it isn't cold.

Graham gets us back to the marina by five o'clock and though I'm subjected to an unexpected moment of last-minute panic when the Promise Keeper, in a hideous bout of evangelical pseudo-friendliness, asks me for my email address (a request I manage to deflect only by making up some story about my service provider going bust, a lie that sticks out a mile), the overall effect of the river trip has been to put me in the correct mindset to stop prevaricating and go and investigate the address that Liz has given me.

Consulting the map I picked up at the library, I drive due west into a narrow zone of storage depots, superstores and factory outlets that quickly melds into a nexus of suburbs straight out of *The Wonder Years*. The streets here are silent and deeply shaded, screened from the unforgiving sun by rows of healthy-looking chestnuts and sycamores beneath whose boughs all these boxy, shingled, pastel-coloured houses sit surrounded by carefully groomed lawns and primped and tended shrubberies. If it wasn't for the arid spine of what my map says is Eagle Mountain flashing in and out of view between the trees and wooden eaves I'd be hard pressed to imagine I was within a hundred miles of any desert, not least because in many of the driveways expensive speedboats balance primly on their trailers and lend the place the feel of a marina waiting for the tide. The sense of stillness is made still more intense by the background hiss of garden sprinklers and the softly echoing shouts of kids bicycling away down side streets and

never quite glimpsed full-view – signs of life that seem almost artificial, as if the whole neighbourhood is an elaborate, semi-organic façade that masks the workings of some enormous and inconceivable machine. Until, that is, I roll up outside 324 Neutron Avenue, which is the address I've got for Jack.

I know that he'd been living here even before the Honda comes to a halt. While the surrounding houses are all painted delicate shades of dove-blue, peach or lemon this one is the colour of old leather. The window panes are cracked and filthy and held together with masking tape, the frames around them rotted through; the yard is wild and overgrown; a waist-high mesh of metal chainlink stands in place of the standard-issue white picket fence. It's a disaster, the black sheep of the street. Everything about it reminds me of my childhood. Like it or not, it feels to me like home.

With the light fading fast behind me I walk up to the door and press the buzzer. Nothing happens – surprise, surprise – and so I knock. I wait a while, slap at a large mosquito that's trying to settle on my shirt, knock again. As I raise my arm to make what's going to be my final knock before giving up and going away the door swings open and a woman hurries out to greet me holding two capped glass beakers both filled with a liquid that looks suspiciously like urine.

'Here you go,' she blurts. 'I'm sorry – we forgot to put them out this morning. We're still getting the hang of the way things work round here!' As she speaks her heavily pregnant belly swells forwards towards me and her hefty thighs wobble mightily inside a pair of khaki sweats. A lumberjack shirt hangs open from her shoulders and her navel pokes out from beneath the hem of her punished blue vest. What warms me to her though is the giant pair of Mickey and Minnie slippers cushioning her feet.

'Um, I don't think you actually want to give those to me,' I say cautiously.

'I don't?' she says, using her free hand to push a clump of tawny, corkscrew hair back from her face. Her fingernails are ragged and ingrained with dirt and her forearms are splashed with streaks of paint – I've clearly interrupted her in the throes of decorating. Through the open doorway the lower rungs of an aluminium stepladder descend into what I can see of the corridor behind her, rucks of dustsheet and curls of discarded wallpaper twine around its legs. 'You're not the guy?' With a protective reflex she pulls the sample bottles back against her breast. 'Then what do you want? You got something you're trying to sell?'

'I'm looking for my . . . I'm looking for the person who lived here in this house before you. Am I right in thinking you've only recently moved in?'

Now she looks truly suspicious. Can't say I blame her, seeing as how my general lack of social instinct is making me sound like a tax inspector. I explain that it was my father who lived here previously, that he just died, that I hadn't seen him since I was a child, that I'm trying to discover whether or not he had any other relatives. Once again the appeal to family proves to be the one to make.

'Well,' she says, still a little wary, 'okay, but I don't know if I can do much to help you out. Me and my husband, we just moved in alright, but as far as we know from what the realtor told us the place had been empty for a good two or three years. It was a repossession see – the vendor was the bank. We wouldn'ta bought it but on account of Mike's getting relocated here and us needing somewhere quickly for the baby.' She glances at her stomach and I do the same and for a moment the smile comes back into her eyes. 'And no offence or anything, but when we took it on it looked it too. I mean, neglect. We're having to do everything to it, and I mean everything . . . I'd invite you in to have a look but I'm on my own and to tell you straight there's not much to see. We've had everything stripped right out. It's just a shell.'

I nod and look away, stare over at the next property for a second.

'I'm sorry hon. Why don't you drop by tomorrow afternoon when Mike's here? I'm sure he'll show you round.'

'Yeah,' I say. 'Maybe I'll do that. You wouldn't happen to have the name of the realtor would you? Maybe I can go and see him in the meantime, find out if he knows anything about why it was repossessed?'

'It was a woman who we dealt with,' she says, correcting my assumption. 'But the office is easy to find – it's right in town, just up from the fire station.' She gives me the name and the address, 1056 Lancaster, scribbles it down for me on one of those curls of wallpaper. She's much more helpful, much more friendly, now she's found a way to bounce my problem onto someone else.

I spend an alcohol-free evening watching HBO and the next morning, Saturday, at 9 a.m. I pull up outside the estate agent's office all ready for the next stage of my quest. But it's not to be. The office is closed, and the index card Blu-tacked to the inside of the little window set into the entrance door informs anyone who cares to read it that the proprietors have gone to Florida on holiday and the office won't be open again for business for another ten days.

Frustrated, I return to Tomsk-43 to regroup. In reception Lucille is sitting behind her desk and chatting on the phone as she was when I went out half an hour ago. But whereas half an hour ago she had a loose nylon cleaner's poncho draped around her boxy body, now she's dressed like Anne Boleyn. I wait patiently for her to finish her conversation so I can ask her for my key.

Finally, she puts down the phone. 'Hey Cooper!' she shouts, even though I'm only three feet away. 'How's it going? Your room okay?'

'I love it, thank you,' I say. 'It's really very nice. It's really a very nice place you have here. Honestly.'

'Well, we like it,' she says.

'And so you should.'

I can't keep my eyes from flicking to her clothing, and she hoists her bodice self-consciously and pats down some unruly pleats. 'Whaddaya think? I only just finished it last night. It's taken me months – I had a terrible time with the trim.' She moves her shoulder forwards to show me her left sleeve; above the elbow it's one big puff of satin patterned with dozens of tiny blips of what look like molten polystyrene. 'They're all genuine river pearls,' she says, 'and I sewed on every one myself.' Lucille's lips are deflated and loose, like the rucks of crushed velveteen on her dress. When she speaks she reveals the teeth behind them to be long, yellow and strong, like those of the rabbits I kept as a kid. 'I know what you're thinking,' she says now, after a brief pause to see if I would stare some more (I do). 'You're thinking – why exactly is she dressed like something out of the sixteenth century?'

'It did cross my mind,' I say, turning a little pink.

'Well, I can't say I blame you. If I was from out of town, I'd be thinking the exact same thing. But it's okay, I haven't gone crazy. It's for the fayre.' She pronounces the 'y'. I mention something about seeing the preparations for it from the boat; she says that's right. 'Last night was the official opening, but it runs all weekend. The whole town goes.' She hunts around behind the counter and produces a flyer. 'Ye Grande Scientifick Fayre of Olde Atomshire,' says a pseudo-gothic, carved-wood font. 'Comes of age!' say some cartoon-fiery letters.

'It's the fayre's twenty-first anniversary, is what that's referring to,' Lucille says. 'It's a local tradition. You should come along, join in the fun.'

Taking the flyer from her I examine it more closely. Designs and symbols, some chemical, some alchemical, surround an oval lithograph of Galileo. On the back is information about parking and dress code and the various attractions on offer. These include pig roasts, 'Live and Re-enacted Experimentations, including a Demonstration of the Principle of Acceleration', a mead bar and market stalls stocked with 'the Verry Latest in Pendulums, Spyglasses and other Scientifick Innovations'.

'You know what, Lucille?' I say. 'I think I might just do that.'

At the Fayre

The fayre's about four blocks east of where I'm staying, in the tree-rich park bordering the Chiawana. An unbroken wall of canvas tents hides whatever's going on inside but the tents themselves are a bit of a giveaway. Square and squat yet also elegant, with low roofs peaking at a single point, gently flaring walls and pennants flying like little dragons from the central pole, they're of a style I'd describe as 'late Crusade', the kind of tents you'd expect to see if you showed up at a joust. The street leading down towards the park is cordoned off and strung with bunting and banners beneath which a couple of hundred people are milling about, families mainly. Kids ride on their fathers' shoulders while moms heft camcorders or propel monster buggies about. Teenagers mooch together in clumps, exchanging complex handshakes and performing skateboard stunts. With the exception of the teens, pretty much everyone has some kind of vaguely medieval costume on, even if it's only a felt hat with a pheasant feather poking out of it or a pair of yellow tights like Errol Flynn's. The sun is shining. The river is blue. The trees are green. A medieval knight glides past on a pair of rollerblades. It's a summer Saturday, a small-town event. Everything is as it should be.

Except for the white Subaru I walk past on my way towards the entrance. It looks like the same pickup but I can't be sure – when I saw it last I didn't get the registration. This time I'm not going to make the same mistake. Trying to look as innocent as I can, I stop beside it, memorize the plates, glance in through the window. The blue flask on the passenger seat, the red cap on the dash. That clinches it.

Okay, well, two can play at that game. I glance around to make sure no one's looking then drop to one knee, unsling my backpack and dig around for a piece of paper – a petrol receipt – and a pen. 'I'm watching you,' I scribble. Then I fold the paper into quarters, trap it underneath the wiper and hurry on in the direction of the park.

Along with everybody else I queue up at a line of hay bales and wait my turn to pay. Two monks are taking money and stamping people's hands. Though there's only a few people in front of me the queue moves slowly, and as I near the front I realize there's some more complex transaction going on.

'How much?' I ask, when my turn comes.

The first monk, who's younger than me, looks me up and down. 'That all depends.'

'On what?'

'Well, you can't come in looking like that. There's a dress code, see.'

'You telling me they didn't have shorts in the fifteenth century?'

'Sorry pal. You'll have to hire a habit. It's the rules.'

The other monk – a girl whose straight blonde hair is largely hidden by her cowl – gives me a sympathetic look. 'They're very nice,' she says. She has a gluey mouth and a long undulating nose that's raw around the nostrils. 'Just like ours. Real felt. Not scratchy or anything.'

'No exceptions?'

'None.'

'Not even for a foreigner?'

'Nope.'

'Okay. How much?'

'Day hire? Seven shekels, plus a twenty shekel deposit.'

'Shekels? Won't dollars do?'

'Everything inside the fayre you have to pay for in shekels.'

'Most people order theirs before, by mail,' explains the girl, sniffing. I think she's got a cold, which is maybe why her hood is up.

'It's a bit late for that,' I say. 'Can't I buy some here?'

'Yeah, but you won't get such a good exchange rate.' She pulls a pocket calculator out the folds of her robe and starts tapping away. 'It's only 2.3 to the dollar and then there's commission. Oh, and sales tax.'

'Are you serious? And I can't get in without doing this?'

Both monks shake their heads. I stand there for a moment looking from face to face, trying to work out whether or not I'm being taken for a ride. Their faces are the picture of monkish innocence, but is anything ever what it seems? I can't decide.

'Hey buddy, get a move on will ya? You're holding up the line.' That from some burger monster standing a few paces to my rear. Three hundred pounds and a goatee beard, his name strikes fear into frozen patties from Salt Lake to Seattle. I'm quaking in my boots.

But then I remember the last fight I had and open my wallet and start unloading bills into the eager palms of the monks who do their calculations and pass me back a sandwich of folded felt and a pouch filled with small pewter discs. While he stamps a circle with a dot at its centre on the back of my hand the boy asks me where I'm from.

'England,' I say, assuming he's being friendly.

He's not. 'That way,' he says, pointing not at the main entrance to the fayre but to another, smaller, tented entrance to his left.

I swallow my smile and go the way I'm told; inside the scarlet draperies two knights await, one male, one female.

'Shoes please,' the woman says.

'What? Don't tell me I've got to hire sandals too?'

'Security,' she says, and thumbs behind her to what I hadn't seen: an airport-style x-ray-machine-and-metal-detector combo, manned by two more knights and a tall man with a gingery crop, stocky build and tight little moustache whose more minimal costume of chinos, leather jerkin and fez doesn't stop him looking like the archetypal cop.

'You've got to be kidding.'

Clearly this was a phrase she used herself quite recently, probably yesterday afternoon about five o'clock. 'Do you want to come in or don't you?' she snaps. Around the edges of her plastic breastplate I can see the stains of sweat beneath her armpits, which is when I realize how hot it is beneath the canvas and how much less she's enjoying this than me. So I remove my trainers and hand them over along with my bag and then divest myself of coins and metal objects in order to pass through the detector.

After I've collected all my stuff I'm directed towards a little screened anteroom marked with the international symbol for the male of the species where, alongside a pageboy having trouble with his tights and the burgermeister from behind me in the queue, who's squeezing himself with some difficulty into a padded tunic, I don my robe. And then, finally, I'm let into the fayre.

There's lots to see. There's a big chessboard painted on the grass, with human players wearing moulded plastic hats appropriate to their rank and team and two people perched high on umpire seats on either side, ordering them about. There's a mocked-up Leaning Tower of Pisa, constructed at an angle out of scaffolding and wrapped around with a giant plastic drapery painted with the colonaded windows of the original, from whose summit a party of men in frockcoats are dropping combinations of sacks of flour, bricks and cannonballs into a large sandpit squared out on the ground below. There's a bunch of horses available to ride, and a blacksmith working shoes for them at a little smithy. He's bald, and pierced and stripped to the waist; smoky rivulets of sweat decorate his caramel-smooth back. There's a roped-off area down on the riverbank where a retinue of knights are hoiking on their armour in preparation for a sword-fighting tournament. There's even a small outdoor theatre, where two men in doublet and hose are performing what's billed as a marathon version of *Galileo's Dialogue Concerning the Two Chief World Systems*.

Despite the supposed strictures of the dress code, there's an incredible variety of costumery going on. If you look vaguely like you've just walked out of a jumble sale some time between the fall of the Roman Empire and the battle of Waterloo then, it seems, you're basically okay. More strangely, it seems to be a semi-rule that everyone has to try to talk in a kind of pseudo-archaic English. All the time I'm catching snippets of this peculiar 'Ye Olde'-speak – lots of *prithee*s and *verily*s and *sire*s. It's very odd. On the evidence before me I'd say the Atomvillians have got a pretty vague idea of European history. But then why should they have a good one? I mean, what the fuck use is it to them? The world they rule with their satellites and their corporations and their oil pipelines and their weaponry, what does it need to know about who won the Wars of the Roses or what people were wearing on their feet when the first Bible was printed or what Thomas Browne had to say about funeral rites? All this stuff is meaningless except insofar as it helps the machine keep rolling, and it doesn't, not really, except for what you can extract from it in terms of myth and bullshit, tall stories to keep people thinking they've got some kind of individual worth beyond what they can be punished into producing or corralled to consume. When Henry Ford said that history was bunk he wasn't trying to deprive us of something – he was trying to tell us the truth of what he could see was coming. He was trying to do us a favour. Fat lot of thanks he got. All anyone ever gives him is the blame. But then that's human culture for you.

But back to shopping. There's a huge variety of stuff on sale.

Mostly it's pseudo-scientific tat like gyroscopic toys, liquid thermometers, executive pendulums and plasma balls (one of which, I'm ashamed to admit, I actually bought once from an Innovations catalogue, though even I couldn't bear the ugly-looking thing on my coffee table for more than a few weeks). Several tents are devoted entirely to the sale of telescopes, including some beautiful antiques, all brass and polished hardwood with absolutely astronomic price tags (no pun intended) dangling from their tripods. The customers don't seem dissuaded though, and everywhere I look plastic's changing hands with lightning speed (clearly shekels have their limitations). Makes sense – an educated, scientific community stuck all the way out here in the desert, far from mainstream society and its accompanying light pollution? Stargazing's bound to be a popular pastime. But then again, New-Agey stuff also seems pretty big – I might as well be at bloody Glastonbury given the number of stalls flogging perfumed candles and mystic crystals and iron-banded wooden boxes and embroidered cushions from Rajasthan and silver charms from I don't know where, probably from Mexico or China or Shitstain, Indiana.

What I'm finding more enticing are the various foodstuffs on offer, advertised by the aromas blending in the still, summer air: candy apples and home-baked brownies and fresh apple juice and homemade hamburgers and pecan pies and hot chestnuts. There's even one guy roasting an entire sheep on a big steel spit; the rich smell of its charring flesh oozes out across the grassy square, bulldozing all the other, lesser odours in its path and triggering sudden and debilitating hunger pangs in this punter at least.

I want, and I'm on my way to get when something even more important than food catches my eye. In the shade of a large awning, propped up amid an uncharacteristically elegant display of astrolabes, lenses and mineral samples, is a framed print showing the same square-in-the-circle design that was etched into

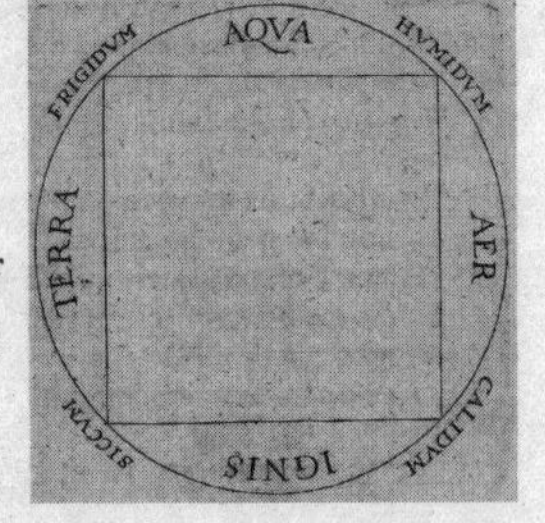

the lid of the coffee canister. Executing a Tron-like turn I swivel through ninety degrees and motor through the flow of foot traffic to get a closer look.

The stallkeeper is short and plump, with a smooth, stretched look about him like someone has just given him a compressed-air enema. While I peer at the print he hovers nervously, scenting shekels. His buck teeth are tinged with sepia and when he breathes he wheezes slightly like he's stopping all that air from trying to escape. His werewolf eyebrows form a single mantle above a pair of thick trifocal spectacles and there's a rim of orange eczema around his patchy, pan-scourer hair, like someone's pulled off a clump of it and used it to Vim around the edges of his face. He's wearing a white shirt, saggy black loafers, towelling socks, a pair of extravagantly tooled and decorated lederhosen and a pocket protector clipped into the pocket of his shirt, pens lined up in it like starlings on a power line. An übernerd, if ever there was one. Incredibly, he also wears a wedding ring, which suggests the terrifying implication that somewhere out there is his female counterpart.

'What's it mean?' I say, pointing to the symbol.

'That's ner-not for sale,' he says, stuttering a little and looking like I'm going to bite him. 'Der-display only.' Oh, okay. So maybe he wasn't scenting shekels then. What did he think – that I was going to steal it?

'Fine,' I say. 'I don't want to buy it. I just want to know what it means.'

'It's al-ker-chemical. Like that wer-one,' he says, pointing to the circle with the dot in it on the back of my hand.

'What's that mean, then?'

'Ger-gold.'

'Oh, right. Well that I could've guessed.' I don't know why I'm being such a bully. Maybe because it's so unusual for me to meet someone who's obviously even more nerdy and Asperger's than I am myself. 'I've seen this before,' I say, pointing back over at the woodcut, 'but it was slightly different. The square only had three sides and there was an eye drawn in the middle.'

'I der-don't know anything about that,' he says. 'But ther-this one, it's a schematic representation of mer-matter. The suh-*circulus quadratus*. The thinking originates in ancient cher-China about fer-four thousand years ago, the Doctrine of the Two ker-Contraries, what was called wer-*Wu-hsing*. In the beginning there is only ker-chaos, and then comes order via the separation of er-opposites like earth and water, der-dark and light. These principles were often identified as ger-gods – sun god and mer-moon god usually.'

'Osiris and Isis,' I say, reminded of what Jack said in Cox's interview.

'Per-precisely. These ideas came to the Egyptians from the cher-Chinese, then down to har-Haristotle, who redescribed it like in the der-diagram: four elements, der-divided into pairs, from which all else was made. And arising out of these, fer-four properties: hot and cold, wer-wet and dry.'

'And in the centre chaos?'

'That all depends. Per-possibly. But you shouldn't really think of it as being like the per-Periodic Table. The elements aren't like elements in the modern sense. They're more like ster-states, with the fifth element, the agent of ter-transformation, underpinning them, though many followed her-Heraclitus in supposing that the fuh-fifth element was itself a kind of fire. They thought that wer-when you applied fuh-fire to something it was ter-transformed into its constituent elements, see? Take wer-wood. Wood was thought to have been made from a particular mer-mixture of air, earth and water, because when you burnt it the ser-sap ran out – wer-water – smoke was given off – air – and you were left with er-earth – or ash.'

'Oh,' I say, and I'm just working out how to escape this the world's most boring man when something much more interesting shows up.

'Good morrow, kind sirs,' she says, with a deep and fairly gracious curtsey. 'Could I tempt thee to a sprig of gypsy heather for yon buttonholes? At the lowly price of a single shekel, 'tis a bargain verily and no mistake.'

The stallkeeper guffaws like this is the funniest thing he's ever heard. He and the girl clearly know each other. They exchange a few sentences in this ludicrous dialect everyone's affecting, laughing all the while, and she slots a purple heather twig wrapped in a small trumpet of baking foil between two of the many pens jammed into his pocket. He stammers an embarrassed thank you – I doubt he's used to getting much attention from such young lovelies. But then again, nor am I. He's not the only one who can't think of anything to say.

Fortunately she's on gypsy-autopilot, and she reiterates her offer of a sprig of lucky heather.

''Twill bring me luck forsooth?' I manage finally. All that *Lord of the Rings* nonsense I used to talk with Miles – I knew it would come in handy one day.

'Sire, it surely will. I tell no lie when I sayeth that sporting my lucky heather will place you high in fortune's favour.'

I want to tell her she's a buxom wench but manage to restrain myself. 'I liketh your shoes,' I say instead.

'My buskins of speckled cordswain? Why, thanking you. I makethed them myself.'

'Dideth you?'

'Yeth, I didth.'

'Ith that a lithp?'

She's grinning now, and the whole world seems suddenly much brighter. Come on Coops – you can do it. Ask to buy the girl a drink. 'Prithee verily fine lady of the heather, wouldst it pleasure ye to share a mug of mead at yonder tavern?' Oh yeah. Rocking.

'Oh jesteth not! Such a noble knight as thou most clearly art cannot care a whit for a lowly gypsy such as I?'

'I most surely can, and shall. Come, and drinketh with me.'

Without a hint of hesitation she smiles and nods and takes my arm and we skip across the grass together to the bar and settle down on bales of hay and order cups of mead, a drink which turns out to bear a suspicious similarity to root beer.

That wasn't so hard now, was it?

She's called Kelly. She's from Atomville but has been away studying palaeontology at the University of Wisconsin. Now she's back here to do research for her PhD. If I told you how hot I think she is, you'd probably have to wipe the page.

'I don't understand,' I say. 'Why have you come back here to do your research?' We've dropped the cod-Elizabethan accents, I'm pleased to be able to report.

'Oh, there was an important find here a few years ago, while I was still in high school – a local fisherman found a skull half embedded in the bank of the Chiawana, hardly any distance from where we're sitting right now.' She points lazily in the direction of the marina where I took the river trip.

'A skull?'

'Uh huh. They thought it was a murder victim to begin with, maybe someone from the forties or something, but then someone carbon dated it and found it was from ten thousand years ago, like during the last ice age.'

'No way?'

'Yeah, it was too cool. And it started this big controversy, because when someone remodelled the face using forensic techniques they found it had Slavic features.'

'What's so controversial about that?'

'Well, because, see, the skull could be proof that the Amerindians weren't originally from here, like their myths all claim. It shows they were immigrants, who came down from what's now Russia over what's now the Bering Strait when it was covered by an ice sheet, and when the ice melted found a corridor that led southwards and gave them access to what became America.'

'So their myths are myths. So what?'

'No, you see, it's important because their myths are what they mainly use to claim rights of ownership over lots of their ancestral lands round here. So if the myths are wrong, then they have no natural rights over the land; they're immigrants just like the rest of us, and they have to share.'

'But they're sharing already, right? I mean, they were pretty much forced to.'

'Yeah, but you should see how many resources are tied up in the courts fighting the claims. It's such a waste.'

'And that's why you got into palaeontology? Because of this?'

'It's one of the reasons. I mean, you know, I wanted to do something where I could make a difference.' She pushes back a braid, slurps on her root beer. Her nose alone is worth a thousand poems. Don't get me started on her hands, her eyes, her lips . . . and of course her breasts, pushing against the fabric of her tunic like twin symbols for gold. 'What do you do?'

I'm about to answer when a line of monks who've been conga-ing around the park pretty much since I arrived file past us, chanting a low chant they're clearly under the impression bears some kind of resemblance to traditional evensong. Given the context, this isn't remarkable enough to put me off my stride, conversation-wise. But what happens next is, because as they draw level with us the hindmost monk breaks away from his brethren and comes towards me and Kelly holding something in his outstretched hand. I look up and watch him almost absentmindedly, presuming he's going to hand me some kind of pamphlet, until I realize his pace is quickening and his purpose becoming increasingly intent. Then, before I can react, there's a rush of air at my ear and two knights power past us at a run. They charge the monk and with perfect coordination hook him beneath the arms and haul him backwards in the direction of the exit, and in the process his cowl falls from around his head. Underneath, the monk is wearing wraparounds and a red baseball cap. It's the driver of the white Subaru.

'Hey!' I shout, jumping to my feet.

He lifts his head and points his long right forefinger. 'The Amesbury Archer awaits!' he cries. And then he's gone, dragged from the scene like Gandalf by the Balrog, his removal presided over by the same guy in the chinos and the fez I'd seen hovering around in the security tent. To make the whole thing just that bit more sinister everyone in the vicinity now starts to applaud, apparently in the assumption the whole thing was some kind of performance laid on for extra authenticity. All except one person, a plump and moderately elegant woman dressed in pointy purple slippers and a sort of chiffon sari, which billows out around her as she puffs across the grass in our direction.

'Kelly!' she blurts when she finally reaches us, in between making a big deal of being out of breath. 'Are you okay?'

'Sure Mom,' Kelly says. 'We're fine. Nothing happened. Oh – this is Cooper.' Her eyes shine as she says it and she can't suppress a smile. I'm really in there, gotta be.

'I'm honoured to meet you. Cathy Trevisan. That's Cathy with a C.' She sticks out her hand and we shake. Her grip is soft. Perhaps a little scaly.

'What was all that about?' I ask.

'Oh that – nothing. Just a security thing. It's all fine now.' She pulls her lips back and runs her hands across her forehead to wipe away imaginary sweat. 'But you're English,' she says, with a final gasp.

'Would you like me to remove my shoes?' I say.

'I'm sorry?'

'Nothing. Private joke. I've been having a fine time chatting to your daughter.'

'Oh, have you? Good. She can be very charming when she chooses. So – what brings you to Atomville, Mr Cooper?'

'Yes, you never told me – what brings you here?' Kelly parrots, still grinning away. You know, I think she might've really fallen for me.

'It's Mr James, actually. Cooper James. That's James with a J,' I add, unable to resist. For a moment Cathy Trevisan blinks wildly, not quite sure which way I mean this. 'I'm here looking for my father,' I say hurriedly, to reassure her.

'Looking for him? Have you lost him?'

'You could say that. Actually he's dead.'

'Oh, I'm so sorry.'

'Don't be. Really. We hadn't seen each other for nearly twenty years,' I say, laying it on a little thick for Kelly's benefit. 'But then I . . . I got news of his death, but it was all a little vague so I came here to try to find out more about what happened to him.'

'And he lived here in Atomville?'

'That's right. He was an artist.'

'An artist?' Cathy's hand flies up to her mouth, as if to push the phrase back in. She and Kelly turn to each other in unison and their eyes widen together, apparently operated by the same set of wires. 'But, but you don't mean, you don't mean Jack Reever . . . ?'

'That's right. How . . . ?'

'But what . . . what a strange coincidence.'

'So you knew him then? You knew my father?'

'Yes, of course. Very well.'

'Well, I mean . . . do you know what happened to him?'

'You mean to say you don't know?'

I wish people wouldn't say things like that. 'No, I don't. As I said, that's why I've come. That's what I've been trying to find out.'

This time Kelly and Cathy don't look at one another. This time Kelly looks at her feet and Cathy looks away. Unlike when she ran, now Cathy is perspiring small beads of sweat that cling to the fine dark hairs on her upper lip. Kelly shuffles a little, clears her throat. 'I think you should tell him, Mom,' she mutters quietly.

Cathy nods and takes my hand in both of hers, and I have the vague impression she's trying to ingest me.

'There was . . . an accident. A bush fire – it was very violent. It cleared the desert for miles around. Your father's studio was caught up in it. By the time the blaze was brought under control no trace of him remained.'

Dinner at the Trevisans'

Cathy insists I come and eat dinner with her family that evening, and after a trip back to Tomsk-43 for a change of clothes and a shower that's where I go. The house is a stone and stucco building in an exclusive-looking suburb about ten blocks from the park, spacious and supremely tidy, dressed with white carpets and white leather furniture. Out back is an impressive deck, carefully cluttered with a hardwood chair-and-table set and a barbecue that looks like something filched from the bridge of the Starship Enterprise. Beyond a varnished rail the garden, steeply graded and dense with ornamental trees and bushes, leads down to the river. At the water's edge a jet-ski and a smart speedboat nuzzle up against a private jetty.

Kelly and Cathy are busy when I arrive, preparing food in the steel and marble kitchen. They don't want me to help so they hand me two Cokes and send me out onto the deck, where Cathy's husband Todd is piloting the barbecue between the planets.

'You must be Todd,' I say, standing like a lemon with our drinks. I want to hand him his but I can't, on account of how he's bent almost double over his advanced piece of cooking tech, deeply fixated on some kind of widget.

'Just give me a minute here . . .' he says. I wait. 'Bingo. That's got it.'

He stands up, presses a sequence of milled brass buttons and a long horizontal panel covered in micropores ignites in a waft of electric blue. And that's when I recognize him – he's the bloke from the fayre, the one with the fez and moustache. The policeman.

'Heeeey,' he says, wiping his hand on a freshly laundered rag before offering it to me. Instead of shaking I pass him his Coke, which he accepts with an 'oh right, thanks'.

'You must be Cooper,' he says as finally we press flesh. 'I've heard a lot about you – mainly from my daughter, if I might say so.' He nods back in the direction of the barbecue. 'Sorry 'bout that. Small blockage in the feedpipe; been giving me hell for weeks. Can't seem to find a minute to ream the darn thing out. How's it going?'

'Yeah. Good.'

'You enjoying yourself here in our little town?'

'Yeah, you know. It seems nice. I mean, I only just arr– '

'And you had fun at the fayre? It's kind of an Atomville tradition.'

'It's great.'

'Well, we like it. And Kelly tells me you're staying over at Tomsk-43?'

'That's right.'

'Fine choice. Lucille, who runs the place? She's an old friend of ours. But then everyone knows everyone in this town. It's one of our favourite things about it.' He turns and projects his voice back towards the kitchen – 'Hey, Kelly! Five minutes and I'll be ready for those steaks! Don't know 'bout you but I've got a hunger on. And we want to get done with eating before the fireworks start. We usually get a good view of them from here. Atomville does the best fireworks in the state. Lot of the guys here, they treat it as kind of a hobby. After all, most of them spend their lives building fireworks that'll never get launched. Or that's what they hope!'

This is the same kind of neo-Imperialist black-humour joke that lots of the Americans at Featherbrooks like to tell and Todd plainly thinks it very funny, at least if how much he's laughing is anything to go by. I laugh too, and Todd goes on to tell me how, when Atomville was promoted from a glorified barracks to a proper town back in the 1950s, they fired Stinger missiles off the top off Eagle Mountain to celebrate. 'Before my time, of course,' he says. 'But it must've been something to see.'

I nod enthusiastically and then, thinking the ice has been broken, I ask Todd what he does.

'Sorry Cooper, but I can't tell you that. I'm on Q-clearance. You understand. I mean, you're one of us, right? Which facility is it you work at again? Cathy did tell me . . .'

I remind him. Needless to say, I don't mention the small problem I'm having with my job.

'Oh right. Yeah, that's in Yorkshire, right?'

'That's right. You know England?'

'My son was posted there for a while. He was at Greenham Common around the time they shipped the missiles out and the dykes got it closed down. Not that I've got a problem with lesbians – as long as I can watch! Just kidding, Coops. It's just that I don't agree with their politics. I mean, what do these people think they're going to achieve, clogging up the access roads to all our military bases? It's beyond me, I'll tell you that for free.'

'We have a lot of problems with protestors at Featherbrooks too,' I say, embarrassed by the memory of my little outburst the last time I went into work. Suddenly I feel an urge to take up the silver sword of justice (or maybe the silver skewer, there being several lying within easy reach) and defend the rights of sexual minorities to chain themselves to fences around the globe in misguided pursuit of a more caring, more peaceable, more equitable society. Fortunately I manage to suppress it – anything else would be completely out of character.

'By the way,' I say instead, 'I wanted to ask you. That man who got thrown out of the fayre, who was he? I mean, he didn't actually seem to have done anything wrong.'

If Todd is bothered by my picking up his involvement in the incident, he doesn't show it. 'Oh, you don't want to worry about him,' he says, picking up a grill plate that's been leaning against one of the chairs and slotting it into position over the flame bed, 'he's just a local crazy, a troublemaker. He used to be a member of the Society for Creative Re-enactment but got himself banned from all their events a couple years back when he tried using the fayre as a platform for one of his political hobbyhorses. I mean, there's a time and a place for all that stuff, but people's leisure time sure ain't it.'

'No.' I'm wondering whether to tell Todd I've seen the man

before, in Salt Mountain. I've been assuming he was something to do with the authorities, someone who'd been put onto me by Fioravanti or by Featherbrooks – the timing wasn't quite right but then who was to say he hadn't been tailing me since I left customs in Boston? But if he's not, if he's some Atomville-based protester type, then what's he been doing following me across three states? And how in hell did he know I was in Salt Mountain in the first place? 'You wouldn't happen to know his name, would you?' I ask.

Todd gives me a look like I've just dropped a hammer on his foot. 'His name? Now what'd you want to know his name for? Tell you the truth, I can't even remember. Lemming, something like that. It's really not my department.'

This makes up my mind. There's no point in telling Todd anything; I already know as much as he's going to share with me.

'Where's your son now?' I say, in order to say something.

Todd smiles proudly, indicates space with a wave of his arm. 'I don't know, exactly. Probably somewhere over Iraq. Oh, cool. Here comes the meat.'

After Cathy's said grace and we've all had a chance to load our plates with food and comment on the quality of the cooking I open the conversation by telling of my slightly fruitless visit to Jack's old place.

'You went to the B-house?' Cathy says, surprised.

'B-house?'

'A-house, B-house, C-house, all the way on up to F,' Kelly pipes. 'The houses in that suburb were all prefabs, built to predesigned floorplans and erected during the war. They were the original "tract" homes; I mean, back then this place was basically one huge factory.'

'Still is,' jokes Todd, and me and Cathy chuckle dutifully, though Kelly gently chides him not to be such a cynic.

'Like the reactors?' I say, referring to the lettering system. I'm keen to stay onside with Kelly, for obvious reasons. But my remark has the opposite effect: save for the fizz and crackle of bugs cannoning into the grill of the electric zapper on the wall above our heads the deck falls completely silent and tangible coldness displaces the balmy air. For some reason I feel guilty, as though by finding something out about Atomville for myself I've committed if not a crime then a serious breach of etiquette. 'I took the river trip,' I say apologetically. 'You know, down by – '

'Oh yes,' says Cathy quickly, recovering her poise. 'Isn't it excellent? I'm so glad, it's one of our best tourist attractions. I was going to suggest that Kelly took you, if you hadn't been already.'

'I'd go again,' I say hopefully, but though I glance at Cathy's daughter she's too busy slicing up her entrecôte to reciprocate.

Embarrassed, I hurriedly explain about the woman now living at the B-house, who didn't know where Jack had moved to.

'I doubt she would. Jack rented that place when he first came to Atomville but he moved out of there and into the studio, a couple of years back I guess it must be now. He couldn't carve stone here in town – too noisy, see – and he couldn't afford to rent a house and a workspace both. So the house had to go. I guess it's been sitting empty ever since – there's not much call for rentals here. It was kind of gnarly, too.'

'So he *was* carving stone then, while he was here?'

'Yes, of course. What else would he have been doing?'

'I don't know. It's just that this friend of his I met in Salt Mountain said he'd practically given up art.'

'Protester, was he?' chomps Todd, shoving a large frond of lettuce into his mouth and making his moustache look more like a caterpillar than ever.

'That's right.'

'Figures. That he'd be talking out his ass, I mean.'

'There's no need for obscenities, thank you Todd,' snaps Cathy. It's funny the way the two women treat Todd, like he's neither husband nor father but a child for whom they share mutual responsibility. An image pops into my head of Cathy and Kelly recast not as mother and daughter but as lesbian lovers. The image becomes quite alluring, once I've got the angle right.

Alluring enough for me to have to dispel it asap. 'So how did you and Jack meet, originally?' I ask Todd benignly, hoping for some man talk.

But Todd disappoints. 'Cathy met him first,' he says, immediately deferring to his wife – a reaction which serves only to enhance my fantasizing, not erase it as I'd hoped. 'You knew him a while before I did, hon.'

'That's right, I did, I did.' Cathy adopts the pose of someone remembering. She's very performative, I've noticed. 'Someone must've invited me to one of the lectures he was giving, because at any rate I started going to them. So it was most likely just by luck, I guess. Another coincidence. Still, Jack was always going on about just that, wasn't he? The power of coincidence. He probably wouldn't've seen it as coincidence at all but indicative of some higher meaning. But then that's artists for you. I guess they see things that just sail right past us normal folks.'

But I'm not interested in Cathy's encomium to the suprahuman sensibilities of practitioners of the plastic arts. It's this idea that Jack gave talks I want to know about. 'Jack gave lectures?'

'That's right. It was his way of introducing himself into our little town. It was very clever of him, really. He came here not knowing a single soul, and of course doing what we do here this isn't the most welcoming of communities, so he approached the various societies and associations – you know, the Rotarians, the American Nuclear Society and so forth. In fact, I know exactly how he started, because he told me once and it's obvious now I think about it; he approached the Masons on account of how he was a mason himself, a real one! And they had him give an after-dinner presentation, and that led to another somewhere else, and pretty soon he'd done the circuit and of course that way he got to meet nearly everyone who was anyone in town, since we all of us are on one or other of these wretched committees!' She says it like it's understood that while this is a cross she and her fellow committee members have to bear, it's one they all bear gladly – a small guilt-relieving penance for the affluence of their lifestyle. That's when I realize who she reminds me of. It's Janet. Give or take a few vagaries of accent the same damn words could just as easily have come out of her mouth. In fact I'm pretty sure they have done, and on more than one occasion.

'And these after-dinner talks, these lectures, what were they about?'

Cathy looks surprised, as if the answer should be obvious. 'About art and science! About how the two disciplines had been separated since the Renaissance, about how it was important for the future of mankind that they should be brought back into contact with one another. Though of course he focused on sculpture and atomics, those being his areas of specialty. They were wonderful talks. Erudite, entertaining . . . he was very knowledgeable your father, and had a wonderful sense of humour.'

She finishes and waits for a response but right now I don't have one. At the top of my neck, right where my skull sits and pivots on my atlas vertebra, I can feel a headache building. Headaches usually work from the outside in, at least in my experience. But not this one. This one's moving centrifugally, spreading through my cortex like a pipette of ink dropped in a glass of water, irreversibly staining tissue as it spreads. On the plate in front of me half my steak is sitting going cold, its juices already congealed into a greasy, viscous glaze and something similar must be happening to my expression because now Kelly leans towards me, touches me lightly on the arm, asks if I'm okay.

'What you've got to understand,' I say, 'is that all of this is a total mystery to me. Atomville – it's absolutely the last place on Earth I expected Jack to be. I realize you're down on protesters, and understandably, but back when he was still a part of my life that's exactly what Jack was. He and Stasie – my mother – they were the type who hung around outside the gates. And now I find that fifteen, twenty years down the line he's giving a pro-nuclear lecture tour to the people who are responsible for producing half the world's stockpile of weapons-grade plutonium. No offence. And what I want to know is, why this transformation? What happened to him to make him change sides like this?'

Cathy nods slowly, apparently thinking all this through in

contrast to the others, who both now go into tension-avoidance mode and start to clear away.

'To be frank with you, Cooper, I have no intention of trying to speak for Jack. After all he's no longer with us, and it would be extremely insensitive of me to try and do so, even if he was. And of course I didn't know him outside the context of his time here in Atomville. I really didn't know anything about his background, and we didn't have the kind of relationship where he would tell me things of a personal nature about himself. But I don't think I would be misrepresenting him if I told you two things that I know for sure about the Jack Reever that I knew.'

'Please,' I say, perhaps a little pathetically (but now my headache is really starting to kick in). 'I'd really appreciate it.'

Cathy nods, wipes her mouth with her napkin, folds it onto the table and generally composes herself. Then she speaks. 'First, ever since I knew him your father was very careful to define himself as neither pro- nor anti-nuclear,' she says carefully. 'He felt, I think, that to ally himself with either camp would be a mistake – he told me on several occasions that he wanted his art to rise above the clichéd terms of polarized political debate, and I remember this because it was one of the things that first convinced me that what he had to say was worth listening to. And second – and I'm afraid I can't help you out on how he came to think like this, but it was certainly an opinion he also expressed to me on various occasions – he'd come to realize that many forms of so-called protest action are quite pointless and often actively counterproductive. With such a complex issue as nuclear energy, an issue which transcends the political and the physical, which in so many ways pushes at the very edges of what we as a collectivity of human beings can be said to know, what Jack had come to realize was that much protest is deconstructive, when what the situation required was people – and not just scientists and politicians and people like you and me but lay people, artists – to be constructive, to bring something new to the debate rather than just rehearse the same old paradigms. So I'm sure I'm not presuming anything, Cooper, when I tell you that one of the reasons your father had come here to Atomville was that somewhere along the line he'd made the decision to leave behind that school of thought, which says so much but in fact achieves very little, and instead devote his time – and his art, and his life as it turns out – to focusing in on one situation and one situation only and really *changing* something real.'

I nod, even though I'm not completely sure I'm following her logic here. 'Which was?'

She reaches for her drink. 'I think Jack was dedicating himself to trying to imagine – and, through his art, communicate – how a solution to the spent-fuel problem might look.'

'Well that at least makes sense,' I say. And then, suddenly afraid that Cathy might think I'm referring to her little speech, I add: 'Because before I came here I visited Salt Mountain – and before *he* came here that's where Jack was.'

Immediately Cathy pounces. 'Oh, Salt Mountain!' she says, looking to the heavens as if that was where she'd like to send it, hurtling off on the back of some giant rocket into deepest space. 'Jack was *furious* at the guys down there. They wouldn't take him seriously, wouldn't even talk to him, he said. It's a very typical attitude, with the newer installations. But Atomvillians have been around a long time now – we have a sense of history, a sense of wider community commitment than places like that, places that just sit behind their fences and totally isolate themselves from any local concerns, haven't yet developed. I'd say it's totally indicative that the first sympathetic ear Jack found in the nuclear industry was here. See, since the break up of the Soviet Union the Areas has shifted away from plutonium production and warhead manufacture to concentrate on clean-up, containment and improved reactor design. You won't find anyone here who'll deny that in the fifties and sixties especially we caused a mess. We did. A lot of the technology was rough and ready, a lot of it was real dirty, a lot of stuff that shouldn't have escaped into the environment did, and now we've got to clear it up. And that's fine. I mean, we want to do that! The money's there – Congress already put through a 30-billion-dollar package earmarked for that purpose. There's still some plutonium being made, of course. Our warheads need servicing and maintaining, the ones we've still got left. But that's not the main issue any more. Not now. If you drive out to the Areas – and you will, I'm going to take you – you'll see the old signs about this being a nuclear facility have been pulled down and replaced with ones identifying it as a site of Environmental Restoration and Waste Management.'

'Well, okay,' I say, still feeling contrite in the wake of my little outburst. 'I mean, I can see how Jack would want to get behind a major environmental restoration effort.'

To my complete surprise, Cathy erupts. 'It's not okay at all! It's a total whitewash! And I'll tell you why. One word: "waste". As in "waste management". *That's* what's wrong. *Because it isn't waste.* To call it that is to completely capitulate to the people who'd like to shut us down. I've fought and I've fought to have that word taken off the signs and off the literature, and I'm fighting still. It's a typical piece of Washington bodging by consensus politicians concerned only with protecting their own position. Ask anyone here in Atomville, anyone who actually knows what they're talking about, and they won't call it waste. To them, that's almost an insult. The term is "spent fuel", or "transuranic product". And that's not some "collateral damage"-type euphemism either. It's simply the correct description. Because what's sitting out there in the tanks and ponds is not waste. It's an incredibly valuable resource, which one day science will discover a way to use. And this is something your father understood.'

'He did?' It seems extraordinary. My father, the man who thought all science was evil, who tried to discourage me when I developed an early enthusiasm for maths, an expert on the long-term uses of transuranic product? It's about the most unlikely thing I've ever heard.

'Absolutely. Jack was trying to conceive of an art form that would do justice to the problem of long-term transuranic storage in all its difficulty and complexity. It was a subject that no other artist of our era has even dared approach, mired as most of them are in their anti-science and anti-enlightenment discourses of political correctness. And yet it was something that was so desperately needed here, in this community of engineers and physicists who, brilliant minds though they may be – and let me just boast here that Atomville has the highest average IQ of any community in the country – often have little or no idea how to communicate to the outside world just what it is they're trying to do. I've spent my working life looking for ways to bridge that gap. And Jack had more potential to forge that link than any person or project I've ever seen before or since. We both thought so, didn't we Todd, the very first time we saw him give that presentation? We just thought, this man is the key. Didn't we?'

Todd, who by this time has set an array of foil-wrapped bananas to baking on the grill, glances in our direction and nods a slightly diffident affirmative. Kelly, meanwhile, is nowhere to be seen. She's back in the kitchen, presumably. I kick myself that I didn't take the opportunity to help her clear away. Not for the first time my continuing pursuit of a solution to the conundrum of the ashes seems like the significantly more pointless option of the various available alternatives.

'And so we gave him a lot of support because we felt that his was just the kind of fresh thinking that was needed here,' Cathy continues. 'It's hard to believe but scientists can be culturally very narrow in their views. The system encourages them to ultra-specialize, and they often lose the ability to think outside the box. Jack's art was capable of helping change all that.'

'How?' I try not to sound incredulous, but it's hard not to when Self-Heating Soupspoons and Mark IV Studio Reactors are spinning round inside my head. 'I mean, just what was this great piece of art he was working on that was going to succeed in making a difference where generations of scientists and government policy-makers have failed?'

'Well, it wasn't like it was one thing in particular. I'm not naive enough to think that one piece of art could do all that and neither was Jack. As much as anything his real talent was for communication, for reframing the debate in terms of new ideas. To my way of thinking, his work managed to link human with geological time in a way that anyone could understand – black-clad art-world types, nuclear boffins, even ditsy public-relations mavens like myself.' She laughs at the quirk of fate that's left her sitting centre frame and shifts a little in her seat.

'But he must've been working on something. I know he came here with a large granite block. Was he using that for anything? A huge thing, you couldn't miss it. You say he had to move out to the studio in order to carry on with his carving? Was he carving that?'

Cathy meets my gaze and blinks. 'You know, I do vaguely remember something, now you mention it. But most of my conversations with Jack about his work stayed on the theoretical level. And I never went to visit at his studio.'

'So maybe there's something out there?' I say. 'I think I'd like to go and see.'

'Are you sure? I don't think there's anything – it's just a ruin. And it might be upsetting for you.'

'That's why I want to go, Cathy. If that's where Jack died, then I want to see. You know, pay my last respects. Upsetting is sort of the point.'

She reddens, finally caught out. 'Yes, of course. Well, Todd will take you, won't you Todd?'

'Er, sure,' says Todd, this time without looking up.

'I'm more than happy to go alone if you'll just tell me . . .'

'Don't be silly, Todd will take you. It's the least that we can do. How about tomorrow morning? Todd, you pick Cooper up, take him out there, then you can bring him back over here for lunch.'

'Really, I don't want to impose.'

'Now you listen up Cooper James! It's no imposition. You'd be imposing if you didn't let us host you while you're here. You're Jack's son! It's the very least that we can do. Todd will run you out there in the morning, and on Monday I'll take you out to visit SOFFT.'

'Soft?'

'S-O-F-F-T. It's an acronym. Supra-Ordinary Fast-Flux Test Reactor. Actually its full name is SOFFTER, but we call it SOFFT for short.' She smiles at me, not maven now but mother. 'It's sort of the town pet.'

'Bananas are done,' says Todd. Then the air splits open to the south and the whole sky fills with light.

'Yay!' says Kelly, bouncing cutely back out onto the deck. 'The fireworks have started. How completely cool!'

Despite the lack of any Stingers the display is still extremely good. Waves and waves of . . . well, you've seen fireworks before, I'm sure. And somewhat surprisingly, rather than make my headache worse they help it dissipate. So when the final giant plume has glittered down across the desert and Kelly asks me if I want to take a walk down by the river, I definitely do.

We tramp down across the lush lawn and turn right at the jetty. There's a path here that leads along the bank, very secluded, very quiet. We walk in silence until we get to where someone's built a rustic-type bench by nailing some planks across a couple of old tree stumps. Here we sit, listening to the clacking of the ducks.

'So Todd's not your dad?' I say, eventually. Over the course of the evening I'd kind of worked this out.

'Oh, no. He and Mom only got married a couple of years ago, though they were dating for a while before that, off and on.'

'So what happened to your real father?'

'He moved to LA.'

'D'you see him much?'

'Oh you know. Now and then. Not too much.'

'You miss him?'

'Not really. He never really liked me.'

'He never liked you?'

'No – not really.'

'Why not?'

'I guess I wasn't pretty enough.'

I don't believe her. 'Fathers aren't supposed to judge their kids on looks.'

She shrugs. 'That's how he was. He only likes pretty women. He organizes beauty pageants. That's his job now. He always did it as kind of a pastime but now it's all he does. Since he left me and Mom he's been married twice, and to beauty queens both times. The first one was much too young for him and she was a real bitch. The new one's a bit of an improvement, though I can't say I like her much.'

A couple of the ducks that have been making all the noise flutter up out of the water and land near us on the bank. Even in the half light I can tell there's something odd about them. The first one has a deformed beak, which stops too short and won't close properly. The second has a withered leg and half a wing.

'Jesus,' I say. 'That's pretty extreme.'

'Oh,' says Kelly, 'don't worry, they're all like that round here. Everyone always thinks it's the Areas but it isn't, it's the pesticides. The river's full of them, from all the irrigation.'

'Really? Nice.'

I dislodge the sod I've been kicking at and it falls into the river with a plop. From across the water comes the hooting of an owl. It's dark now, proper dark, though the desert sky's so clear and shows so many stars that it looks like there's a city in the sky, an LA of the stratosphere, its streets and malls and towers all picked out in lights. Kelly shivers a little, entwines her hands and holds her arms straight down in front of her. I wish I had a coat to give her, but I don't.

'Thanks Kelly,' I say.

'For what?'

'For introducing me to your parents. They're being so nice and helpful, I can't believe it.'

'Oh,' she says blithely, 'that's okay. You looked like you needed help.'

'I did?'

'You seemed kind of lost.'

'Oh. And that's good?'

'I guess so.'

I don't know what to say so I say nothing. Kelly releases her arms and swings them back behind her, making her breasts push out against her blouse. I try not to stare at them. I think I fail. Those alchemists knew what they were on about.

'I'm cold,' she says.

Why, I've no idea, but this makes me feel helpless, completely at a loss.

'Well, maybe we should go back inside,' is what I say, if you can believe it.

'Oh,' she says. 'Okay.'

She turns and I troop along behind her, nurturing a feeling of dismay. Was that the moment, I'm left thinking. Did I miss it? It finally occurs to me that I could have protested the decision, said something funny, suggested an entertaining way to get her warm, but now of course it's too late to do anything because the moment's gone.

Visit to the Studio

The next morning Todd comes to Tomsk-43 to pick me up and take me out to what's left of Jack's old studio. We drive for maybe two miles beyond the last buildings in Atomville, nothing between us and the low brown hills on the horizon except a single railway line that curves across the desert about a mile beyond the north-western city limit. There's a sign here says 'Dead End'; beyond it the thin tar carpet unrolls across the contours bordered by a couple of scraggly rows of irrigated trees; beyond them stretches an immensity of red dirt undulations, their Martian aspect softened by a low, dense scrub. A few dabs of flattened, high-base cumulus hover foamlike on some invisible bank of cooler air that's snaking its way east. The view is framed by two matching series of low and interlocking hills. Apart from that there's nothing. No fences, nothing. It should feel alien to me but it doesn't – I've been here many times before, hugged the contours in my speeder playing *Star Wars Rogue Squadron*. The Tatooine level looks just like this.

'Is that the Areas?' I say, pointing out into the empty expanse.

'Uh huh.'

'What's to stop you just walking in?'

Todd laughs. 'Just try it. There's what we call concentric circles of defence. The desert here is full of concealed cameras and movement sensors. If we stopped our vehicle, within five minutes there'd be a patrol car on its way to check us out. At this stage it's all kept pretty low key, more or less civilian. But if we stepped off the roadway and started walking into the desert, they'd let us come, let us get deeper into trouble. If we got as far as that low hill there,' he says, indicating a brown bump about a quarter of a mile away, 'a chopper would set off and within a few minutes we'd be picked up. And we still wouldn't've got a sniff of the real lines of defence, the tanks and missile silos and machine guns that really guard the place.'

'Oh. I see.' Almost exactly like *Rogue Squadron* then. It all seems incredibly desolate, but then remoteness and isolation always was Jack's thing – that's remained a constant, if nothing else. Maybe living out in the desert like this is like living by the sea – all about the planet, about moods and weather, about wildlife maybe. About silence. Art. About anything except other people.

'I thought you worked at Featherbrooks? Don't they have the same deal there?'

'Maybe they do. No one's ever told me. But it's a much smaller installation. Mainly we've just got a good old-fashioned fence.'

Without any warning the hardtop branches out into a small matrix of throughfares that have been laid like a grid upon the desert. There's two or three completed steel-frame structures here, along with the metal skeletons of several more, but mostly the spaces between the thick tarmac bands are either concrete blanks or patches of grey desert pocked with rabbit holes.

Todd negotiates the maze. 'Guy from Spokane, he put this operation together about eight, ten years back. There was a fashion for a while of trying to set up little independent manufacturing operations off the back of this franchising experiment that the DoE was running, and he got himself permission to throw down this little plot. But of the five tenants he started with three never showed up and the other two went bust, so that was that. Bank called in the loan and the place lay derelict. The only thing here now is a chemicals company that operates out of those two sheds handling the city's toxic-waste disposal. The place Jack took had been an auto-repair shop, but the guy's wife ran out on him or something and he took to drinking. Pretty soon he went broke. Which was good for Jack, I suppose. Anyway, we're here.'

Here is a smoke-blackened chainlink fence. Stacked up against the fence, like balloons held in a net, are dozens of tumbleweeds. They're piled so high you can't see what's inside, so we get out the car and walk round to the gate, to which is pinned a sign.

'Jack's idea of a joke,' Todd says.

I'm looking at the sign, thinking how perfectly it fits with what I've learned of Jack, when something strikes me.

'Weird that it survived the fire,' I say.

'Yeah, you're right,' Todd says, sounding genuinely mystified. 'Must've got caught up in one of those cool vortices you sometimes get.'

I murmur agreement – it's part of international nerd culture, to know these things.

There is a lock but it hangs broken from a length of rusted chain. Todd pushes through the gate and I follow him around the dune of tumbleweeds towards the contemporary equivalent of those burnt-out lots in the ghost town just outside of Jackass Flats. What was once a steel and aluminium building is now a pile of molten, twisted wreckage; a jagged skeleton of girders juts up from the blasted concrete, caging in a mess of corrugated iron, metal wiring, charred household detritus – a toilet bowl, a stainless steel sink – all dredged around by a thick silt of shiny black ashes the colour of wet slate.

A little awkwardly Todd describes how the workshop and living areas were divided up, the rough positions of Jack's desk, his drawing table, Thoth's basket, the cooker and the fridge. He tells me how my father used to sit outside on a beaten-up old easy chair of an evening, reading by the light of a storm lantern, how he used to sleep on a flat board laid over the sink unit which because of his bad back he preferred to sleeping in a bed. It seems a stripped-back and minimal existence: basic, independent, unemotional.

'Must've been some blaze,' I say stupidly.

'It was a bush fire.' Todd extends an arm and waves it slowly across the desert. 'Ripped right through this whole area over here. That's why the ground's so clear – see how there's no cheat grass or Russian thistle anywhere? That's what got burnt up. It was hot enough to melt the fence, look, which is how all these tumble-weeds blew in.'

I nod but don't reply, just gaze around.

'And nothing was left of him at all?'

'The fire was pretty fierce.'

'But there must've been teeth, at least?'

'Jack wore dentures, I'm pretty sure.'

'Bones, then.'

Todd shrugs. 'Not that I know of. But you'd have to speak to the police.'

I nod and cast another look around the ruin. Then something strikes me.

'Wait a minute. Where are all the sculptures? Where's the granite block?'

'Hey, you know, I don't know,' Todd says. 'I hadn't thought about it.'

'Well, do you remember what any of them were?'

'Not really. I mean, art's not quite my thing. You'd have to ask Cathy.'

Tell Cathy, ask Cathy – Todd's beginning to sound like the original hen-pecked husband. 'But you'd been out here, right? You must have seen some of what Jack was working on? I mean, was there anything big, sort of table-sized, maybe like some kind of giant horse's skull?'

Todd's standing staring blankly in my direction, jaw slack, mouth hanging open about half an inch. Slowly at first then quickly faster, like in *Tetris* if you don't touch the controls and let the blocks just fall, a look of recognition piles up on his face.

'Er, yeah, I think that's right; there was kind of a big carving out here, sort of yay tall, some kind of plinth thing with a skull on top.'

'A horse's skull?'

'Could be.' He doesn't sound too sure and I wonder if he might be humouring me. The idea makes me unaccountably angry.

'So where is it then?'

'Someone must've stolen it.'

'Stolen it?'

'Maybe it was kids, from the neighbourhood.'

I gesture at the emptiness. 'What neighbourhood?'

'Well, you know. Kids come out here all the time for keggers, that kind of thing. Who knows what they get up to.'

'But it was solid granite, right? You'd need a fucking crane.'

'Hey, Cooper, I don't know, okay? I'm sorry.'

The anger boils over into fury and I can no longer hold it back. 'You don't know? Jesus Christ! Did anyone actually give the remotest kind of a shit about what happened here? I mean, there's no body, no marker, anything of worth's been stolen. What the fuck is going on?'

Todd steps up to me and grips my shoulders, then holds me in a forced half-hug. 'It's okay to be hurt,' he says, missing my point entirely. 'I would be too. But you've only been here a couple days. Give us a chance, we'll help you find closure with this. And you know, it's not true that Jack was allowed to pass away without acknowledgement. We came down here and held a vigil for him, and he was remembered in our church. We're not heathens you know, we're Christian people. And stop me if I'm speaking out of turn here, but I think you've done an amazing thing by even coming here. You didn't need to do this. You didn't owe him anything. Way I see it, Jack did a darn low thing, running out on you and your mom like that. Have to say that if I'd known that about him, I think I would have found it much harder to build a friendship with the guy.'

But I'm not impressed and I extract myself from Todd's embrace and turn away. I wish I'd come out here alone. The rest of my my journey I've made in isolation but now, when it really counts, I haven't got the solitude I need. I should've insisted on them giving me directions; I shouldn't've come out here with a stranger, however well intentioned he might be.

To put some space between us I step over the corrugated metal sheets that formerly clad the walls and roof but which now lie gnarled up and pathetic, like the leaves of a dying plant, around the low breeze-block perimeter, clutching the flowers I've come to lay. The debris is substantial, jagged with corners of plasterboard and charcoaled fittings, booby-trapped with trip wires of molten flex. Here's some iron brackets, there's an oil drum filled with steel stone-carving tools. Here's a frazzled computer disk, there are the ashy effigies of several books.

And there's an Eye of Horus, scratched into a patch of naked concrete.

I kneel down to examine it, run my fingers along its curves and grooves. There's no doubt that this is Jack's work – I don't believe for a minute there's anyone else round here capable of carving something as intricate as this. Not neighbourhood kids at least, and that's for sure. But when was it done? Just before the fire? Or when he moved here? It's impossible to tell. All that's certain is that the area around it has been cleared away. Someone wanted me to see it. And I have a feeling they'd probably rather I didn't mention it to Todd.

I stay down there for a while longer looking at the emblem until my knees begin to hurt. Then, making sure they lie just so, I lay the flowers across it, get back on my feet and head back over to where Todd is waiting, back turned, in quiet acknowledgement of my need for privacy.

As we sit down to lunch I give voice to a new theory I've got about the fire.

'What if the fire wasn't an accident?' I say. 'What if the fire started at Jack's studio and spread outwards, rather than the other way. What if Jack set the fire deliberately?'

'What're you saying?' Cathy asks, her voice a trifle querulous.

'I'm saying maybe he committed suicide.'

Everyone seems a little shocked by this.

'I don't think that's the kind of thing that Jack would've done at all,' says Cathy hurriedly. 'I mean, he wasn't the least bit depressed. Was he Todd?'

Todd shakes his head, looks grave. 'Not to my knowledge, though I didn't see a great deal of him towards the end. Still, hard though it might be for us to accept, I don't think we should deny the possibility. Which of us can see inside another's head? These things happen. And the fire was very fierce. I guess it's worth considering that Jack did set it himself.'

'You don't really think so, do you hon?' Cathy says. It's a little weird, having seen her be so dominant, to watch her play the simpering wife like this. I guess there's a more complex dynamic to this marriage than I realized.

'No, darling, I don't think so, not really. It seems like a lot of trouble to go to. I mean, if things get that bad, most men would find it simpler to just – ' With thumb and forefinger Todd mimes firing a pistol upwards through his jaw, angled so the trajectory of the imaginary bullet passes directly through the centre of his brain, making Cathy and Kelly grimace. 'And I think the police would have picked up on any evidence of arson – it's the kind of thing they're trained to look for, if only because of pressure from the insurance companies. I've gotta say I think you're barking up the wrong tree there, son. Kelly, would you please say grace?'

Kelly gives me a worried look and does as she is told, and for a minute the conversation's halted as we all bow our heads.

We raise them and lunch gets underway, but as Cathy carves the meatloaf she's prepared and Kelly pours us all water from the jug Todd leans over and says to me in what he clearly imagines is some kind of whisper, 'You know, you had kind of an emotional experience back there at the studio, amigo. You sure you're up to this?'

I presume it's lunch he means, the patronizing bastard. I haven't quizzed the Trevisans about the ashes yet because it's so obviously not the kind of thing they'd do it seems almost rude to ask. But their *Stepford Wives* complacency is beginning to piss me off;

something in me wants to give them all a slap. 'You know someone sent me a canister of stuff that they claimed was Jack's ashes, don't you?' I say suddenly, apropos of nothing.

Todd's surprise is vehement and complete. Now there's no more whispering. 'What? Who sent you that?' he says. His bluntness is gratifying, after the way he hedged around my suggestion that Jack committed suicide.

'That's what I was hoping you might be able to be tell me.'

'This was sent to you while you were staying here in Atomville?'

'No. Back in England.'

'I don't know anything about it,' Todd says, sounding suitably appalled. 'It sounds like kind of a sick joke to play. Who would do a thing like that?'

'I've no idea. But presumably, if Jack really died in the studio, they're not real ashes, they're just scrapings from the floor. If they bear any relation to Jack's remains at all.'

'I don't know. I guess we'd need to take a look at them.'

'Yeah, well, that's going to be a little tricky.'

'You didn't bring them with you?'

'I did. But they were confiscated at customs. I think they thought they were anthrax or something.'

'Oh my,' says Cathy, like I just told her I've lost my car keys. 'Don't you just have all the luck? Why didn't you tell us about this earlier?'

'I don't know. It seems so dumb . . . but I think I was embarrassed to.' This isn't the real reason of course, though there is a grain of truth in it.

'But that is just absurd!' she says, when she's extracted all the details. 'How dare they! Those immigration officials, they think they can do anything they like. I can't *tell* you how many stories I have heard . . .' And she proceeds to tell us some of them, tales of stately US matrons getting shaken down for drugs and friends with foreign spouses being asked if they've got explosives in their shoes. As she tells her tales her outrage grows until it drives her up from the table and over to the telephone. She jabs at the keypad then snags a toothpick from the dispenser on the table with which to probe at a bit of meatloaf sinew that's got jammed behind her upper right canine while waiting for the number to connect.

'Carl? That you Carl? Oh, hi darling. It's Cathy. How's little Martha getting on? She had that nasty dermoid removed okay? Yeah? Oh that's great. You must be so relieved. Uh huh. Uh huh. Oh right. Yeah – look, Carl honey, I'm real sorry for calling you on a Sunday like this, but something's come up that I need to run by you. See, right now we've got this charming young man from the UK staying with us' – here she winks at me – 'and it turns out he's Jack Reever's son! You remember Jack, don't you? Yeah – that's right. In that fire. That's right. Well Cooper, that's Jack son, he's travelled here to the US to lay his father to rest. And you are never going to believe what those morons at Boston immigration did when he flew over here from London . . .'

She proceeds to tell Carl the whole sorry saga, with so much elaboration about my good character and purity of intent that I begin to sound like a medieval knight carting a shard of the one true cross back from the Holy Land in the hope of founding a cathedral. By the time she's finished I've almost begun to believe her myself.

When she's done she sits back in her chair and deflates gently. While she does, silence reigns.

'Carl says it won't be a problem. He'll see to it tomorrow,' she says.

'Erm, thanks,' I say, not really knowing what she means. 'That's very kind.'

'Don't mention it. It's the least that we can do. How's the meatloaf?'

'Oh, excellent.' I say. I think that piece of sinew's gone.

Over dessert Todd asks me cryptically if I'd like to see his basement, and while I'm helping Kelly clear away and load the dishwasher with dishes (which in this household seems to be used not so much to clean as to sterilize if the extent to which the crockery must be rinsed before it's allowed inside of the machine is anything to go by) I ask her to clue me in. She rolls her eyes. 'Todd's hobby,' she whispers. 'I won't spoil it for you Cooper, but let me tell you you're pretty honoured. He doesn't take just anyone down there, you know. It must mean he really likes you.'

'Not as much as I like you,' I want to say, but instead I ask her if she'll have dinner with me that evening.

'Sure,' she says, breezily. 'You have any place in mind?'

'I wanted to check out that Atomic Ale Brewpub,' I say. 'I had a look at their menu the other day when I was passing and it looked pretty interesting.'

'It's okay.'

'Fine. How about I pick you up at seven?'

She agrees but before the conversation can progress Todd reappears.

'Hey Coops,' he says. 'Leave that. Come with me.'

He leads me through a doorway and down a set of concrete steps into a basement smelling of laundry and lined with shelves stacked with normal basement-type stuff. A small anteroom to the space we're in contains a washing machine and drier, a drier that's steadily clanking the moisture from a drumful of clothes, but there's another doorway here as well and this is the one Todd's attending to. It's set with a heavy-duty metal door that looks like it belongs in a crack den or a bank vault and which is fitted with a digital keycode lock. While he punches in the numbers I politely look away, turn my attention to the complex venting system spaghetti-ing the ceiling. Jokingly I ask if it's to get rid of radon gas. But it turns out that's exactly what it is. 'We're so damn careful over in the Areas now, and it would be the supreme irony for me to get cancer from working in my den!' he says. Indeed it would.

The lock clicks open and he ushers me inside. The moment I enter I discover the nature of Todd's hobby.

Todd's a gun nut.

'Welcome to my armoury,' he says. Nodding, I gaze around at the rifles and pistols racked up on the walls of this cuboid concrete bunker, at the little cabinet of trophies, silver cups and little pewter statuettes of shooting men and running dogs.

'Nice,' I say. Calmly.

'Jack liked it too.'

'He did?'

'Sure. He used to come down here all the time. In fact, it was your old man got me into making my own ammunition. He knew all about that kind of stuff.'

'Not when I knew him he didn't.' I think for a minute about this latest of Jack's many metamorphoses. Gunpowder. It figures. The *Pirotechnia* has a big section on how to manufacture it. 'He must've picked it up from Cox.'

'Cox? That the guy Jack knew in Graniteburg?'

I nod.

'Yeah, Jack mentioned him once or twice. Machine-gun expert, right?

'That's the one.'

'Well, I've not got any of those old World War II Vickers or anything like Jack said *he* had, but I have got this.' Todd crouches down and pulls a black attaché case out from underneath the workbench, thumbs the two combination locks to the correct alignments, then flips the lid to reveal a foam interior carefully shaped to hold the kind of weapon an Imperial Stormtrooper might have slung about his neck.

'The Heckler & Koch MP5K,' he announces. 'A *Maschinenpistole* in the purest sense of the word. The K stands for Kurz.'

'As in Colonel Kurz,' I say, but once again the joke is wasted.

'Right. Exactly. And as you can see it lives up to its name. It's basically a cut-down version of the full-sized MP5 sub-machine gun, which is the classic of its genre. This model was designed at the request of Hechler & Koch's South American sales rep back in 1973, who'd spotted a gap in the market for dignitary protection. The briefcase is just a gimmick really.' Todd wets his lips and points out a trigger concealed in the case's handle. 'Try and fire it from the standard carrying position and you're likely to put holes in your own leg as much as anybody else's, which is why this particular model ended up as a hot collectors' item. But remove it and attach the shoulder stock and you've got a highly effective, easily concealable assault weapon. Jack and me, we used to go shoot this baby off over at the range just south of here. We could run over there now, if you like, loose off a round or two. Ever shoot a gun before, Coops?'

'Er, can't say I have,' I say, deciding not to mention the several hundred hours I've clocked up playing *Time Crisis*. I doubt they count.

'So now's your chance. Choose your weapon.'

Todd is grinning like an idiot, knowing that the range of killing machines on offer – six rifles, give or take, plus some fifteen handguns, not to mention the MP5K – is guaranteed to intimidate. Indeed it does; avoiding anything that looks even remotely like it might be able to do some damage to anyone, I pick out the smallest gun on offer, a little black automatic pistol that's barely bigger than my palm.

'Beretta .25 automatic, huh?' he says, taking it from me and releasing the empty clip. 'The model favoured by James Bond.'

'Really?' I say, thinking I've made a good choice after all. 'Cool.'

Todd grins a fanatic's grin. 'Until *Dr No*, when the Armourer pointed out it was a woman's gun and M told him to replace it with the Walther PPK.'

'Oh.'

'No stopping power. It'll drill a hole in you, but unless you hit a vital organ that's about the limit of it. Still, a good choice for target practice, and a perfect learning gun. Though I think you'd have more fun with this.' He fetches down a small, snub-nosed revolver and hefts the hunk of silver metal in his palm. 'This is the Taurus 617 .357 Magnum – an exciting little gun. Not much bigger than your Beretta there but it packs a much much bigger punch. If you shoot yourself in the foot with this one, it'll blow off half your leg.'

I look down at the object in my hand and picture myself maimed accordingly. Todd wants me to experience a frisson of excitement from the possibility, I know he does, but what I get instead is a stomach lurch and an aftertaste of meatloaf.

'Er, thanks Todd,' I say, suppressing a gassy burp and passing back the weapon. 'Maybe some other time?'

Quite frankly I'm much more interested in spending the rest of the afternoon alone getting mentally and physically prepared for taking Kelly out tonight.

We are star shampoo. We live in, we are of, the lightest, most extraordinary foam. The universe is foam. The sun, those stars you see slowly tumbling through the night, they are bubbles; when they explode they shower suds far out into space. Planets are the hairballs, spun together by the plughole of gravity. We . . . God knows what we are. The little petrol glints of soap upon the strands of hair, probably. Meaning atoms must be like the steam rising off my arms and shoulders, and sunlight like the spray of water from the shower head . . .

This analogy really isn't working.

I get out the shower and use three towels to dry my body off, then I fix myself a large Jack Daniel's and Coke. I'm excited. I'm going on a date.

'It's that outrageous scene where Anakin's mother explains that her son is the result of a virgin birth that seals it. Suddenly the little huddle of mud and stone igloos we're sitting in isn't Tatooine anymore – it's Bethlehem, but sort of relocated to somewhere in California. I mean, Lucas has three kings showing up, or two kings and a queen, who arrive in their spaceship bearing gifts: a power pack, the R2-D2 droid and . . . well, okay, so the third gift isn't actually handed over in that scene but it's presumably a light sabre, and no doubt Obi-Wan's going to give it to Anakin in Episode Two. And Anakin is *such* a Christ-like figure. I mean, think about it. He's a slave for starters, right, just like the oppressed Jews of biblical times, and he has a talent for mechanics to rival the young Christ's for carpentry. Qui-Gon Jinn even presents him to the Jedi council as his candidate for the chosen one for God's sake, like he's the Dalai Lama. And all of *Star Wars* is a play-out of the myth of the chosen one in any case, this whole thing about the difference the lone but true-hearted sword-fighter can make. It's the same thing as *The Matrix*. It's all religious myth.

'But in the end my question is, given all of that, is the story really offering us an alternative to the evil-empire bureaucracy the rebels are trying to defeat? Or is in fact this myth of a chosen one a prerequisite for that bureaucracy's very existence, something the masses need to sign up to in order for them to accept and accept again the dictates of bureaucratic rule, which doesn't necessarily change that much regardless of who's nominally "in charge"? Because who is Anakin/Christ/the Dalai Lama but another feudal lord, another manipulator who uses the techniques we now call spin to proclaim his right to rule as Jedi Knight, Sun King, Star God, when the fact of the matter is he's just another annoying Californian teenager with a mother fixation, an elevated idea of self and a truncated moral sense that allows him to exploit vulnerable tendencies in other people's emotional make-up without worrying himself about the pain he might be causing? I mean, who?'

I slap the table, sit back, sip my drink and wait for Kelly's answer. But I'm not sure Kelly has one. Certainly she's looking at me very blankly, an expression I take to be indicative of confusion or even mild shock. It makes me wonder if perhaps I made a mistake in ordering a third pint of the Plutonium Porter, which according to the drinks' menu 'ain't no beer for wimps!'

'But doesn't Anakin become Darth Vader anyway?' Kelly says. Poor Kelly: she's trying, she really is. But it's not the same as talking to Liz. Liz would understand what I'm getting at. Liz would be able to engage me at the level I'm working on.

In semi-despair I stare out of the window. An astonishingly violent sunset is in progress – it looks like a severed aorta spraying blood across the sky. The air conditioning's brought on a clammy feeling in my flesh, the seat I'm in is uncomfortable and angular and rubbing every pimple on my back. My groin feels damp, my heart is racing and my glasses keep on slipping down my nose. This is where the self-hatred usually kicks in.

I finish my drink and pay the bill and we get up and head out to where I parked the car. Save for a rash-red rim of light irritating what we can see of the horizon, the sunset's almost dead.

'Well, thanks for dinner,' I say.

'You paid for it.'

'Oh, yeah.'

'. . .'

'. . .'

'Are you sure you're okay to drive, Cooper? You have drunk quite a lot.'

'Oh, that's nothing in England,' I reply stupidly.

'Todd says everyone there's an alcoholic.'

Momentarily I bristle, ready to defend the dignity of my countrymen. But then it penetrates my drunken skull that Kelly might be joking – and also that by Atomville standards Todd's probably right.

'Do you like me Kelly?' I blurt out suddenly.

'Yes,' she says, 'of course I do.'

'Would you let me kiss you?'

Why I ask this I have no idea. This isn't something that you ask. It's something that you do.

'Cooper, I'm not sure if . . .'

But she doesn't get to finish because I've grabbed her and crushed my lips against her face.

'Cooper! No!' She squirms away, shakes me off like I'm a rampant labrador trying to fuck her leg.

'Oh God,' I say, a furious remorse instantly outswelling my desire. 'Oh God, I'm so sorry. I didn't mean . . .'

'What were you thinking?'

'I don't know, I just thought . . .'

'What? That you'd just *rape* me, right here in the parking lot?'

'No, not at all, I –'

'Or what? That because you bought me dinner I owe you some kind of sexual favour, now?'

'Of course not, I wou . . .'

'I mean, what kind of behaviour *is* that?'

'I don't know, I wasn't thinking, I'm not normally like this, I think I might have had too much to drink.'

'I think you might be right.' And after taking a moment to shrug her clothes back into place and smooth down her hair she turns and starts to walk away.

'Hey – where . . . where are you going?'

'Back to the restaurant. To order a cab.'

'But I'll drop you home . . . I'll behave now, I promise.'

'In the state you're in? Do you think I *have* a deathwish? No thank you. Goodnight.'

Then she's gone. I'm left standing alone, in the dark, in the parking lot, feeling like the world's biggest prick.

I am – and I've often heard it said – a master of seduction. Did I tell you that?

The SOFFT Machine

The next day it's just me and Cathy – me, Cathy and the secret embarrassment I'm lugging round after the drunken debacle of a pass I made last night. Cathy comes to pick me up promptly at eleven, but before we can drive out to the Areas we have to visit the Federal Building to get me organized with a security pass. This involves a fair amount of waiting around, not least because my host has to have a lengthy chat with everyone she meets. It's almost as bad as being dragged along to one of the charity events that Janet and Matthew used to organize in Nottingham – all performance politeness and enthusiastic conversations about sweet FA.

When we do finally get underway it's along a six-lane super-highway that leads north out of town and straight into the desert.

'Why such a big road?' I ask, noting the conspicuous absence of any other cars beside our own.

'Oh, you should see it first thing in the morning,' Cathy replies.

'At least thirty thousand people commute along it every day. Even with this many lanes there's always a traffic jam.'

'Why don't they build a shuttle train?'

She looks at me like I'm insane.

Feeling European and out of touch, I stare out the window for a while, drawing solace from the clear intention of the asphalt powering on through the sagebrush in front of us to wrap itself around the entire planet. Soon we pass a sign that says 'You are Now Entering a United States Nuclear Reservation', though Cathy tells me this is just for show, that we've technically been inside the reservation ever since we left the city limits. A little further on we pass another sign. This one is more novel: it features Superman standing arms akimbo with cape billowing astride the words: 'Security is an Individual Responsibility. Be an Individualist.'

'Great, huh? They're all original, from the 1950s. A few years back they were going to be torn down, but we got up a petition and managed to get them renovated instead. It's amazing what you can achieve if you get organized. And here we are.'

She takes a turn marked 'SOFFTER' and steers us down a minor tributary of the mighty artery along which we've been travelling. We drive another mile or two in silence, and I'm just beginning to get my first pangs of childish 'are we there yet?'-style impatience when a pure white curve billows up between the ragged canyons. In a didactic and slightly grating tone, Cathy informs me that the perfect hemispherical dome is bigger than that which caps St Peter's 'in Rome'. Surrounded on three sides by yellow blockhouses with squat black stacks of heat-dissipation vanes perched on their roofs, it certainly looks like a cathedral or a temple of some kind.

Once out the car I get a better look at the reactor compound. In the north-east quadrant squats a large long yellow building that could be an IKEA superstore; beyond this a large crane on caterpillar tracks is parked up beside a row of eight-metre-tall white drums, each of which has a big orange radiation marker on its side. The whole thing is fenced all around with dual fences between which zigs a no man's land of security walkways, sonic motion

detectors and guard-dog runs. There are watchtowers and a barracks. Whoever's in charge of protecting this place, they're not taking any chances.

'Before we go inside I want you to see our visitors' centre,' Cathy says, and leads me in the direction of two blue Portakabins. 'Jack was very fond of it. He used to come up here a lot.'

We walk up the wheelchair-access ramp and step inside. Here, behind a small faux-wood Formica reception desk positioned just inside the door, an elderly lady sits. She wears a grey wool cardigan over a pressed barley-coloured blouse and, somewhat incongruously, a pair of raspberry sweatpants. When she sees us enter she dons the large pair of mauve-framed spectacles that hang from her neck by a silver chain and, on recognizing Cathy, greets her enthusiastically. Pleasantries are exchanged while I sign the visitors' book. Then in we go.

The exhibition kicks off with a tall glass cabinet crammed with SOFFT memorabilia. There's some photos of the construction site, a nice hexagonal chunk of basalt from the bedrock into which the foundations were dug, some examples of the radiation dosimeters and film badges the workers use, a few self-congratulatory industry certificates for excellence of design and operation.

I point at a shelf busy with cups, plaques, pennants, that kind of thing. 'Those look like sporting trophies,' I say, thinking back to the cabinet in Todd's armoury.

'That's exactly what they are. They're from our very own softball league. Each reactor sports a team, and we have a little field over by the river.'

Fair enough. Next to the cabinet is one of those baize-covered mobile displays. It's covered with pictures of animals and plants, graphs and pie charts, photocopied journal articles. This, Cathy explains, is one of their environmental projects. 'Big parts of the Areas have been untouched by man for over fifty years. There's a lot of rare plants out there, and recently we got funding to study them – this summer for the second year now we've got a bunch of botany students flying in to do work for their PhDs. And you see these elk?' She grazes one of the seven-by-fives with a lacquered fingernail. 'Well it's now been demonstrated thanks to studies done here in Atomville that the characteristic migration patterns of these animals wasn't genetically programmed as we thought but enforced by man. Three or four centuries ago elk were a plains animal, exclusively. It was only the arrival of more people that drove them up into the mountains in the winter. Now the land's available again they're free to get back to their natural habitat and that's just what they've done; they stay down here all year round, along the banks of the Chiawana mostly, the only elk in the country that've been able to do that.'

We move on. Now we've had a double dose of homey feel-good stuff we're apparently ready to be exposed to some info on what's actually happening here, a task that's wisely been entrusted to a happy cartoon atom that looks like it's moonlighting from playing lead blackberry in a Ribena ad. The atom bounces across a series of wallcharts while merrily informing us in words of no more than one syllable exactly what a fast-breeder reactor is (which is a reactor that creates more fuel for itself as a by-product of its own power-generating processes, in case you didn't already know).

I put it to Cathy that what the display is describing is nothing less than the mythical perpetual motion machine. 'Exactly!' she exclaims, entirely oblivious to my sarcasm. 'You know, you are *so* like your father. That's *exactly* the first thing he said when I first explained SOFFT to him.'

I'm not sure what I think of this, so I ask the obvious question. 'Does it work?'

She laughs but doesn't answer. She points instead to a photograph of bright metal plates fitted together in a honeycomb fashion. 'This is the cap of the reactor. Isn't it beautiful? Like all the components in the core, these are manufactured to within a tolerance of about a thousandth of an inch out of low-swell stainless steel, because that's the only material that'll cope with having high-pressure liquid sodium pumped through it at enormous temperatures. Isn't it strange how the shapes are so similar to the way the basalt has formed in the bedrock, these hexagons? That's something that Jack spotted immediately but just hadn't struck the rest of us. It takes an artist to see that kind of thing.'

'Why are they hexagonal?'

'Because the breeder blanket assemblies that sit underneath them, holding the depleted uranium ready to be transmuted into extra fuel, they're hexagonal as well.'

I feel like pushing her but she's already moved on. Oh well. At least this time I got an answer, even if it was utterly meaningless.

'Take a look at this. Jack was *obsessed* by it. He used to drive out here just to study it.' Bending forwards I peer at the object in question. It's a short length of metal piping made, according to a small information card resting inside its fishtank-like display case, of 316 stainless steel. About eighteen inches long and six or eight in diameter, it's heavily insulated and it has temperature sensors wrapped all around it. But apart from the fact that it's clearly very sophisticated and just the kind of thing you'd expect to find in a nuclear reactor, I can't see anything extraordinary about it at all, apart possibly from the fact that the pedestal on which it sits is very pretty – prettier than you'd expect for a museum display. The four edges have been bevelled slightly and the machinist's put a polished curlicue pattern all the way across its upper surface.

'See the finishing?' Cathy asks. 'Another thing none of us noticed but that Jack straight away picked up on. It's called knurling, and was an old way to get oil to fit between two tight-fitting metal components. He said these days it's no longer used, on account of our developing improved lubricants, but it's very difficult to do and that whoever made this pedestal was using it as a way to show off his machining skills. Ain't that just fascinating?'

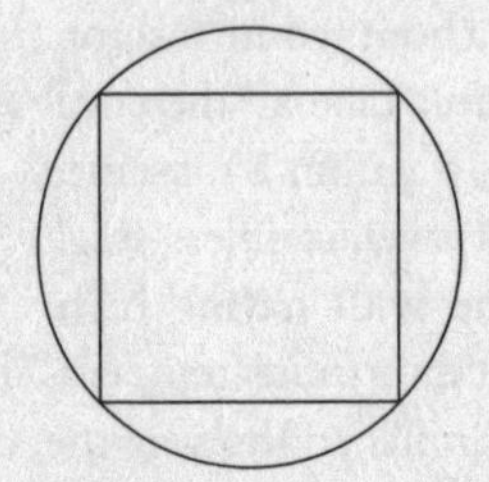

It is, but I can't see it being sufficient reason to keep him coming back. And I can't see what would be either, not until I move around to look at the pipe from the other side and I catch sight of what is etched into the back corner of the pedestal.

This is beginning to freak me out.

When we're done we say goodbye to Eileen and walk down to the entrance hut, which bears a strong resemblance to the one they used to have at Checkpoint Charlie. Behind a bulletproof screen there sits an official, a slate-faced woman in a light-blue shirt and navy slacks whose general demeanour hasn't been improved by the addition of a badly straightened broken nose and a brown leather eyepatch similar to (though rather cleaner than) the one worn by Cox. Taking a disdainful glance at my documents she hands me three more forms to complete. While I fill them out, wondering all the while if anyone from the Federal Department back in town has bothered to get in touch with immigration yet and found out that my visa expired today, Cathy hovers nervously. The official is the first person I think I've come across in Atomville who she seems wary of. Or maybe it's not her at all but the two guards lolling against the drab khaki walls, staring at us through their mirrorshades and fondling their various items of weaponry like they're bondage whips. Thanks to my afternoon being enlightened in Todd's basement, I can tell you exactly what these are. Between them they are carrying: a 12-gauge semi-automatic shotgun with magazine; an M-16 airborne assault rifle with flash-suppressor; an Uzi with three spare clips hanging from its carbon-fibre-reinforced sling; and two Beretta 9mm service automatics.

When I'm done Cathy fetches down two hard hats from a rack. 'Not too stylish, I'm afraid, but rules are rules.' We put them on, walk out the back door of the guardhouse and follow a concrete path across a gravelled quadrangle towards a door with a scrolling LED readout fixed above it. 'The reactor is currently in Mode 1 . . .' the readout says. 'Reload 2 days ahead of schedule . . . TOTAL quality is our goal . . .'

Inside the door there's something I recognize. 'I know this green,' I say to Cathy. 'It's the exact same colour they use to paint the corridors at Featherbrooks. We had a staff lecture on it once – it's been scientifically selected to instil a sense of calm and alertness in the viewer.'

I'm being sarcastic but Cathy beams. 'That's right!' she says. 'I knew that you were one of us. Hope you're feeling alert!' We both laugh though the comment isn't funny and we've still got forced smiles plastered stupidly across our faces when we arrive at a second pair of security guards, more lightly armed than their colleagues in the entrance hut. They're manning a set of peculiar cubicles with glass walls and floors and metal holes in which I'm told to place my hands.

'You want me to take my shoes off too?' I ask, but the guards don't get the joke, thinking I'm referring to a sign I hadn't actually noticed but which I now see pinned up on the wall behind them.

'Everyone's checked for radiation both coming in and going out,' Cathy explains. 'It's standard safety procedure. You'd be amazed how often the detectors in nuclear facilities get triggered by someone bringing in contamination they've accidently gotten off some piece of source material outside. Your father being a prime example. First time he came here he set all the alarm bells ringing. We had to go get him scrubbed down, throw his clothes out, everything. Turns out he'd been keeping his trousers in the same drawer as an old tin of radium paint he'd picked up somewhere and then forgotten about. He was a liability, alright.' She says this in a nice way, smiling at the memory. I think that Cathy was actually really quite fond of him, though they must've made an unusual pair. The Jack I knew would have thought she was the devil. Stasie too of course, though that goes without saying.

The lights in the cubicles click on for a few seconds and then click off and the guards motion us through. We walk along a corridor, go up a concrete stairway, turn a corner and arrive before a large steel door with a small bulletproof window set into the wall beside it. 'First stop, the control room,' Cathy says. The door's equipped with a key panel not unlike the one on Todd's private armoury; Cathy punches in a code then stands by the window so she can be seen by whoever's on the other side. 'The door's on a timer,' she explains. 'When it opens go through quickly. If it's open for more than thirty seconds, Rambo and company'll show up and then you'll really see some paperwork.'

Inside, the control room's not what I'm expecting. I was thinking square and white and ultra-modern; what I'm seeing is semicircular and decorated with that thin-strip wooden panelling that was big in kitchens in the 1970s. Everywhere there are dials and banks of knobs and blinking lights, but they're all quite ancient-looking and disturbingly analogue; they don't seem quite up to doing the job required of them. The place smells weirdly sweet – of sesame oil, or caramel perhaps – and there's a purring background hum full of clicks and stutters and other gentle noises of the kind made by happy machines. There are also – bizarrely – three orange lava lamps, sitting on a special shelf of their own beneath the steady gaze of a mini-cam. The overall impression is halfway between a porn set and a submarine.

'Lava lamps?' I say.

'They generate the random numbers we need to seed our encryption codes,' one of the controllers explains. 'Plus they look nice.'

After we're done with the control room we take a trip down into the guts of the operation. Back down the stairs, along another corridor, through another security checkpoint and we're traversing a thin catwalk threaded through a 3D chaos of fretted pipework while Cathy expounds on the operations of the liquid sodium as it zips all round us at temperatures pushing seven hundred degrees. Some of the piping is thicker than my torso, some of it thinner than my finger. I feel like I'm wandering round around the blood vessels of a giant leg. It's a bit reminiscent of my feeling that night at the gold mine, that the forest was a single giant plant that I was trapped inside of.

The catwalk carries us over to a big oval door that – again – looks like it belongs inside a submarine. I say it looks like an airlock, and Cathy explains that's exactly what it is.

'Another of our safety measures,' she says proudly. 'The other side is the containment dome, and it's kept below atmospheric pressure so in the event that there's a breach, air rushes in instead of out. Simple but effective.' She could be talking about a new greenfly spray she's just bought for her garden roses.

Around the airlock entrance there's a safety and surveillance zone marked out with black and yellow tape. The door itself is marked with a giant radioactive warning symbol and the word FISSILE written all around it in mango red. A laminated safety message has been fixed to it at eye height. Please take note of the following alarms, it says:

1. A 'howler' ('Ah-oo-gah! Ah-oo-gah!') signifies a gamma leak.
   Run, do not walk, 300 feet from containment.

2. A 'gong' ('Gong! Gong!') signifies a fire.
   Leave calmly by the nearest normal exit.

3. A 'telephone' ('Bring! Bring!') signifies a phone call.
   Answer promptly, and listen carefully.

I mention that instruction three seems a tad obvious.

'Safety first,' Cathy replies, without irony.

We step into the airlock, wait for a minute while the pressure adjusts, then step out through the far door into what feels like the open air. Far above us the containment dome curves away like an internal sky. From the rim of the hemisphere Klieg lights bright as tiny suns glare out, illuminating a forty-foot fuel-rod insertor/extractor robot I'd seen photos of in the visitors' centre and a two-hundred-and-fifty-ton monster gantry lift which spans the space like an ogre squatting for a dump.

'Impressive, huh?' Cathy yells above the din, sweetly unaware that I'm busy reimagining it as the world's largest latrine. The floor is immaculate, slightly convex and tiled with hexagonal tiles of 316 stainless steel plate. An outer ring of tiles have a different finish to the rest and have purchase points set into their surfaces. 'Those are the breeder blanket assemblies, under those,' says my guide, pointing to them. 'And in the centre is the core . . .' We circumnavigate the beast on a curved steel walkway similar in construction to the catwalks in the Electroworks (except that those were straight) and then pass directly over the core on an aluminium gangway that's designed to be swung out of the way when the cranes need access. Despite the fact that there's nothing much to see beneath us save the groovy metal floor, I still get the feeling

I'm crossing an abyss. 'It's like the stone bridge in Moria,' I mumble at the din, and not for the first time I think of the monk who was dragged away like Gandalf and wonder if that's in fact the way the answer to the mystery of the ashes lies, rather than on a magical mystery tour around this giant machine.

The gangway takes us to a second airlock door, this time ajar, on the other side of which is a narrow spiral staircase. Down we go, clanging round nine, ten, eleven revolutions, Cathy calling warnings about not going too fast lest we start getting dizzy, until we arrive at the bottom and another door. 'Interim Examination and Maintenance Cell: Authorized Personnel Only,' the plastic door tag says.

'Here we are.'

Here is a room that looks a bit like a recording studio, the way it's crammed with control panels and workstations and walled on one side with a massive sheet of yellow-tinted glass. There, however, the resemblance ends. Instead of musicians and their instruments, the window lets onto a huge steel-clad cylinder that extends, as far as I can tell, straight down into the ancient basalt substratum below our feet. A stainless-steel tube about forty feet long and honeycombed with little portals dangles in the centre; all around it, like a family of praying mantises cornering a hapless stick insect, six or seven remote-controlled manipulator arms hang in spidery repose.

'That's the MOTA,' Cathy says. 'Materials Open Test Assembly, in the jargon. And that's a six-foot waffle of leaded glass and mineral oil between us and it, which is why the lighting's a little peculiar. Each of those fifty-six pockets takes a canister, and each canister can take a sample of any material we choose. Once the canisters have been prepared and inserted, the MOTA is raised up right into the core of SOFFT where it's exposed to the neutron flux for precisely calculated periods of time. By varying the length of that exposure we're able to take elements apart and rebuild them pretty much however we want. We can transmute any element into any other, give or take.'

'Even lead into gold?' I say, wondering between bouts of utter amazement if I've finally located the hinge on which Jack's transformation from wannabe alchemist to amateur nuclear technician might have turned.

'Even lead into gold,' says Cathy, her voice a balm.

'That's incredible.'

'It certainly is. Jack thought so too. First time we brought him here he said it was the most beautiful thing he'd ever seen, "the final realization of all the dreams of alchemy". And that's a direct quote.'

Direct quote or not, elements of the puzzle I've been piecing together over the past fortnight are falling into place. 'You say you can transmute *any* element?'

'Within limits, but yes.'

'So presumably you can also transmute dangerous elements – and make them safe?'

Cathy's smile is like a sunrise. 'Ah, Cooper, you're your father's son alright. I knew it would be worthwhile, bringing you here like this. You see this is exactly the power – the crucial importance – of fast-breeder technology. Forget burial – this is the solution to the problem of nuclear waste. See, not only can we can take the spent fuel from any normal nuclear reactor and separate the uranium and plutonium out for reuse as fuel in a fast-breeder such as SOFFT, not only can we take the by-product of that fuel once it's been used and after processing put it back through the machine, but we can also take the isotopes that you can't process, the really nasty ones, the ones that have no industrial or medical use, the ones that are going to sit around being supertoxic for tens if not hundreds of thousands of years to come, and change their neutron content. We can't quite get rid of all the by-products this way, but we can in theory reduce them in volume about a hundredfold and cut the storage time of what's left over from tens of thousands of years to about five or six hundred, which is much more manageable. And we can do all this in machines that also generate electricity. It's the answer, and this is what your father understood. For years he'd been thinking about how to address the "waste problem" ' – this time Cathy makes the quote marks with her fingers – 'with his art, and when he saw the MOTA and understood SOFFT's full potential he realized he'd found the technology he'd been looking for to enable him to do just that.'

'Do just what, exactly?'

'He wanted to take a small item of highly radioactive waste, transmute it in the MOTA into a substance that had a radically shorter half-life and incorporate it into one of his sculptures.'

What she says makes me think of the teddy bear in the cemetery at Graniteburg, the one with the little girl inside. 'So maybe that's what he was going to do with the granite block?' I say. 'Carve it into some kind of container and put some of the transmuted waste inside?'

'Maybe so. It was certainly the kind of thing he talked about.'

I take a moment to reflect on this. What was the idea here? Did Jack imagine he could transmute himself in this machine, use it to turn him into the great artist he presumably aspired to be? Did he see here the possibililty of some kind of reconciliation of Biringuccio and alchemy, ecology and nuclear science, some kind of resolution of all his inner contradictions? After all, if Cathy was right about the capabilities of SOFFT, then the nuclear industry's back-end problems were indeed over; it could move on from being everybody's favourite nightmare and become the kind of high-output/low-impact energy provider it had been first promoted as back in the 1950s.

I'm not sure. There's something here that all seems too pat, too convenient. I just can't see my father as some kind of glorified nuclear PR, however profound the changes he'd undergone since returning to America. It's not that I don't think he wouldn't have bought into the technology – maybe he did. But I just can't see him making art that was that straightforward, that conceptually functional. It wasn't him. He wasn't that . . . he wasn't that *obvious*.

'Machines,' I say. 'So presumably that means you're going to need more than just the one?'

'Of course.'

'But then that's a lot of plutonium you're going to be carting around. Really a lot. What You're proposing is an entirely plutonium-based energy economy.'

'So what's wrong with that? We're much better at it than we used to be. Reactor design is better, storage and transportation are better. We've got it down. And we *need* more plutonium, in case you hadn't noticed. You work on Nuclear Missile Defense. What do you think's going to power the satellites? Solar panels ain't gonna do it. Not for rail guns. Not for any laser that's powerful enough to knock out a missile.'

I shy at this, like a horse that's used to being blinkered. And I *have* been blinkered – I put the blinkers on myself. Always childishly maintaining that I don't know what my job is – what's that about? I know damn well. I might not understand the exact use to which my code is put but there's no question that it ends up as part of the system Cathy's talking about. I wouldn't have taken the position otherwise. The whole idea was to stick a finger up at Jack, wherever he might be, do the thing that he would have most despised. It's about time I grew up and admitted it.

'But to have so much plutonium in circulation, isn't that asking for trouble?' I say, hoping to appease the gremlins of guilt busy sinking their teeth into my neck. 'What about the health risks? The risk of theft? And all the work you need to do to separate these isotopes out from one another, you can't help but contaminate . . .'

Before I can get to the end of my sentence I'm being showered by a cascade of opinion and statistic; I've hit another Cathy-mine, it seems. 'Oh, but it drives me nuts how much crap is talked about the harmful effects of radiation in the environment! I can recommend to you a paper written a couple of years ago by some friends of mine, one of whom is the most respected health physicist in the country. This is a bunch of people who did a *proper* examination into the *actual* effects of radiation exposure, going to a native community in South America where because of a lot of granite in the area the background radiation in their homelands was two or three times the world average. And you know what they found? They found that these people lived longer, healthier lives than normal people! What they found was that radiation higher than background in non-excessive amounts can actually be good for you. It's to do with the radiation stimulating antioxidant effects in the cells which protect against damage from other, more intense forms of radiation. It's a fact commonly accepted all over the former USSR, where they don't have the prejudices we do.' Cathy's eyes are wide and glazed as she beams this wonderful factoid across to me. Then she blinks once, twice, nods sharply, blinks again, drops her mouth into a pucker of pity and concern, and changes mode: from PR back to mother. 'What you don't understand,' she murmurs, 'is that the people working here, they're heroes. If anyone's going to save the planet, it's them.'

I nod myself, unnerved – I'm yet to get used to Cathy's lightning-fast transitions. 'Yeah,' I say.

This time, thankfully, she doesn't reply, and the two of us fall silent for a while, perhaps to better contemplate the awesome forces at work just a few metres above our heads. Forces harnessing the trapped power of the sun. Forces splitting and swapping atoms between elements and transforming them into one another in ways of which the alchemists could only ever dream. And then we make our way over to the SOFFT cafeteria, which is the same as all cafeterias everywhere, where we consume the exact same lasagne and fried potatoes I eat at Featherbrooks at least once a week, usually on Thursdays.

The Riddle of the Stones

After lunch Cathy drops me back at Tomsk-43 where I burst into reception to find Lucille standing behind her counter like the barman in *The Shining*. She's changed out of that dumb-fuck Anne Boleyn get-up she's had on all weekend and is back in her uniform of pink T-shirt and nylon poncho, the latter cinched around her ample waist by a utility belt holstered with canisters of Pledge and Windolene. She looks like Batman's aunt.

In her hand she's got a brown envelope, which she's pointing at me like a gun.

'Someone left this for you,' she says.

I half take, half snatch the letter from her. 'Who?'

'No idea. I found it pushed under the door there, about an hour ago. Person who left it didn't even come in. Which is pretty psycho, if you ask me.'

'I didn't, but thanks anyway.'

Lucille looks surprised – I've been nothing but sweetness and light to her since I arrived. Ignoring her I turn my attention to the letter. My name is scrawled across the envelope in biro, nothing else. I tear it open. If it's anthrax, well, too late. Anyway it isn't, it's a note. Handwritten. Badly. Scarily badly. '*The AMESBURY ARCHER awaits you at STONEHENGE*,' it says. '*COME SOON if you want ANSWERS to your QUESTIONS. Come ALONE. Tell NONE of your Atomville friends. NO ONE is to be trusted. Signed: A FRIEND.*'

Okay. Well, this is unexpected.

'Something important?' asks Lucille.

'Er . . . no. I don't know. Not really.'

'Well, it's sure enough stopped you right in your tracks,' she says, with an air of satisfaction.

'No . . . it's nothing. Just something crazy, a joke maybe. About Stonehenge, of all things.'

'Stonehenge?'

'That's right.'

'What, *the* Stonehenge?'

'Yeah.' I let out a nervous laugh. 'This person wants me to meet them there. Which is pretty stupid, considering where it is.'

'Why? You've got a car, aincha?'

'What?'

'It'll take you about forty minutes, this time of day.' Lucille bustles out from behind her desk, goes to the rack of tourist pamphlets, pulls one out and hands it to me. 'Here ya go. It's up on Eagle Mountain; there's a track. There's a map on this, shows you the way.'

She's not wrong, either.

The journey takes me out of town in a direction I've not been before, west along the Kokanee river – a Chiawana tributary – and through a great swathe of irrigated maize. The plants sprout from the ground in the middle of an otherwise almost completely barren desert, like someone's found the genetic code for the skeleton warriors that grew from the dragon's teeth in *Jason and the Argonauts*. But these aren't rogue warriors, fending for themselves on some patch of rocky land. They're a well-trained army, a honed feeding machine. Born into regiments, they push out through the soil, encouraged to grow straight and true and uniform by wheeled sprinkler arms which parade across the fields like robot sergeant-majors, monitoring their charges and moistening them with scientificially proportioned rain.

Beyond the fields the road curves around to reveal the full-grown army pounding off to war in the form of a column of gigantic pylons. If you didn't know better, you'd probably assume that the matrix of overhanging wires slung between their massive shoulders is carrying power out to Portland or Seattle, surplus power produced by the plutonium reactors. But this isn't the case. These wires are bringing power in from the big dams further south along the Chiawana. Plutonium reactors don't produce energy, they consume it, and in vast amounts only matched by the quantity of cooling water they hoover from the Chiawana then dump back boiling hot, enough to raise the temperature of a forty-mile stretch by several degrees centigrade, which according to Graham the boatman is sufficient to kill the eggs of spawning salmon. They're like colossal leeches that suck the lifeblood water and power from the landscape they're supposed to be there to protect. An army of robot skeletons alright.

Come alone. Well, I'm coming.

We went to Stonehenge several times but the last time we went is one of those childhood memories that's stuck in my head like a glass shard from a shattered hologram, lodged among the folds of cortex like some piece of war-wound shrapnel that the surgeons judged too dangerous to remove. Minuscule and fragile, for years it's lain there too painful to probe and too painful to forget entirely. Most of the time it lies pretty much dormant, a cyst pulsing quietly at the very edges of my consciousness. But catch it in the right light – the operating-theatre illumination thrown by a coincidence, a chance meeting, a smell, a piece of music – and it flashes back the scene coded into its crystals in perfect amber detail while spearing its way another few millimetres towards the centre of my being.

We're riding horses, is what we're doing. There's some festival going on – what I can't remember, probably some solstice thing. But anyway, we're riding horses, Stasie, Jack and me, riding horses along a road across Salisbury Plain some distance from the stones. But they're there, definitely, off somewhere to the left. There are deep browns and golds but also purples going on, there is shadow, and there's that perfect ambience of temperature you get when a still, flawless summer's day has got hot enough for the heat to carry over long into the night and the setting sun is dead ahead of us and flashing into my eyes as Jack bobs from side to side. So the stones are over on my left, and somewhere on the right there's the campsite where we were staying in the VW and it must've been where Jack had got the horses from, borrowing them from some bloke who'd been using them to give kiddy-rides all day, bargaining a couple of hours of free-range riding time for I don't know, a bag of marijuana or a carving or a signed Stasie record or something, I've really no idea. It was just another Jack thing, the kind of surprise he liked to drop on us. The world's greatest improviser since John Coltrane, Stasie used to call him.

Anyway, so there we were heading down this road or rather country lane, Jack in front and me in the middle and Stasie bringing up the rear, and Jack was telling us one of the stories from when he was a cowboy, stories he told all the time because he knew they were a winner as far as us kids were concerned. And this particular story he'd almost certainly told before – at least, in this memory I don't remember the feeling of hearing it for the first time; the feeling I remember is more that of comfortable boredom, of being reassured, of being told again something that I already knew for certain was the truth.

What he was talking about was this serious crush he'd had on a buckskin quarter horse. It was spring and they were cutting half a dozen horses out of the herd of sixty or so the ranch maintained to be 'broken' – made into saddle horses. This was voluntary extra work, done on Sunday afternoons. Jack drew Babe, the buckskin mare in question – a two-year-old who had never had a halter on or been closer than a hundred yards to a human in her life.

She took a while to break but three months later, by the end of June, he was riding her every day. 'She was still real skittish and it took my full attention to ride her but I had such a crush on her,' he said back over his shoulder as we clip-clopped down the road into the sun. 'She was so fast and could turn on a dime and so pretty with her black mane and tail and speckled dun hide. And I had two hundred dollars of my own saved up and soon enough I started getting this crazy idea of buying her.'

The idea didn't seem the remotest bit crazy from where I was sitting. 'Why didn't you?' I remember saying, mystified. 'I would've done.'

'Oh well,' Jack said, sounding in just those two words happier than he'd sounded for months, 'when you're young everything seems black and white. But you grow up a bit, you start to find that all the things you were so sure about, they just bleed into one another, that the world's made up of greys. That's just how it is. And I guess that maybe this is the moment I started learning that for myself, on account of how I'd been saving my pay because I had this unrealistic, uninformed idea that I wanted to go to art school, and I guess at the end of the day that's what I wanted more, even though it didn't feel like it at the time. I mean, the going price for a young, green-broke quarter horse was two hundred bucks and a cowboy with his own horse was worth a hundred and fifty a month so this was a career opportunity. And even the boss knew what a crush I had on this mare and hoped I would buy her and then stay on. Fit young cowboys were hard to come by. It was gruelling, hard work – day after long day – blistering hot in the summer, bitterly cold in the winter. And yet it was so real, so right there in your hand. It was a temptation to stay right there for ever, that's for sure.'

'You should've stayed,' I said, pronouncing judgement.

At this Jack turned in his saddle to look right at me, the sun like a halo round his head. 'Yeah, well, if I had then you wouldn't be here,' he said, hair on fire, eyes glittering and emitting light. 'So maybe I made the right choice in the end. But it sure didn't feel like it at the time. I remember saying goodbye to Babe, my arms round her neck, crying like a baby. And she stepped on my foot, the bitch, though that was perfectly in tune with the love–hate relationship we had. And then I dried off my tears with my neckerchief, left my plain, no-nonsense bat-wing chaps hanging on a nail in the barn and caught a ride with the foreman of the neighbouring ranch over to Lincoln where I found myself in this cavernous, empty train station with a one-way ticket to Seattle. Sixteen years old and everything I owned in a duffel bag.'

And that's it, freeze frame. I don't remember any more, it just stops right there on that image, with Jack turning back around on his saddle and the sun bursting into my eyes as he moves his head. Which is a little odd, considering how all this must have happened after the whale and the bulla and the gold-mine raid, must have happened later on that summer, and I remember all that other stuff clear enough. Sixteen years old and everything he owned in a duffel bag. Twenty-nine years old and everything I need in a suitcase. Not quite so romantic, is it? Wonder if I'll ever tell my kids this story? Wonder if I'll ever have any? Not at this rate, I won't.

The thought makes me think again of last night's fuck-up with Kelly. Christ. If I carry on like that, I would say the chances of my ever reproducing are minuscule at best.

What a mess.

Soon enough Eagle Mountain is sloping up out the earth before me like a giant tarpaulin. With about half a mile to go the road starts curving away from it but then I see the 'War Memorial' sign that Lucille told me to watch out for. Pulling off the highway I turn onto a gravelled track, and from here on in progress is slow. The Honda's not built for this kind of surface, and in order not to completely wreck the suspension I have to weave between the labyrinth of ruts and humps just like everyone (with the notable exception of Miss Banner) used to have to do down our old driveway.

The track starts zigzagging up the slope and as I meander round the curves I begin to get a clear view right out over Atomville and beyond. The town is a long sparkle on the desert, the irrigated fields and parks surrounding it lending it the character of an oasis, a glass and emerald brooch. By contrast the Areas are undefined, a void identifiable by the almost total absence of roads, buildings, crops. Still, as I climb higher I see a couple of things I recognize: the Pantheon-dome of SOFFT; the chimneys of B-, C-, D- and F-Reactors down by where the Chiawana etches a massive omega into the weary earth; and the long oblong forms of the old chemical separation plants, according to Cathy the largest buildings on the planet at the time they were constructed.

The day I got here I discovered – thanks to another of Lucille's pamphlets – that a weird connection between Jack and me was hidden in this landscape. I looked for it during the trip out to SOFFT but I couldn't see it; now, though, it's finally revealed. See the way the undulations in the desert run in parallel, in those kind of wide striations? That's because in the last ice age there was a huge lake north of here called Lake Missoula, about half the size of what's now Alberta. The lake was dammed along its southern side by a three-kilometre-high wall of ice and when the planet began to warm the ice began to melt and the wall collapsed, sending countless billions of gallons of water in a humongous flood right through this area, a flood so powerful it carried boulders weighing hundreds of tonnes down with it, boulders which ripped right into the basalt bedrock.

When the temperature dropped again the dam refroze and the lake refilled, ready for the same thing to happen all over again – and again, and again. This – what they call a channelled scablands – is the result; basically the features you get at the bottom of any streambed but magnified thousands of times. There's only a few examples of it ever happening. One of them is here; another – the biggest – is the outflow channels on the Lunae Planum on Mars, north of the Valles Marineris. And the third is a place called Newtondale, which is just south-west of Featherbrooks and somewhere I go hiking all the time. Bizarre, huh? Father and son, both wandering alone in the nearest thing Earth has to offer to a Martian landscape. Genetics or coincidence? Call this number to cast your vote (calls charged at 50 pence a minute).

And I'm just wondering about this, and that, and Babe, and Jack drawing all those pictures of that horse's skull, and whether that all ties up together somehow in this mysterious granite sculpture that no one seems to know anything about, when I zoot up the last little bit of dirt ramp and arrive at the top of Eagle Mountain. And there it is, right there in front of me, plain for all to see. Jesus Christ. It really is.

I park the car and skirt around the monument, too wary of being ambushed by whoever it is I'm meeting to get close to any of the stones. Not that they're stones at all – even from this distance I can see the whole thing's actually made of concrete, tonnes and tonnes of it, cast in giant moulds with rippled inner surfaces designed to lend some kind of authentic stone-effect to the finished product. Stonehenge. Once in ruins, now rebuilt – in America, of course. Stonehenge, and a white pickup truck.

So. He's here then. Whoever he is.

'Hullo?' I shout. There's not a breath of wind and my voice carries easily. For a moment all is silence, and only the chirrups of cicadas hidden in the patches of brittle grass come back to answer me. But then he steps out from behind a bluestone into a block of sky framed by the standing stones like it's something he's been practising.

'Yo,' he says. And he stands and looks at me and smiles. He has a shocked look – it's not an expression; it's just the way his face is made: wide-eyed, open and unblemished. Young even, though he's got to be my father's age.

'It's you,' I say, 'who left the note?'

'That's right.'

'And sent the ashes.' This time it's a statement.

He pulls the red cap from his head and weaves his fingers

through a matted weft of icy-looking hair. 'How'd you know?'

'The handwriting. Same on the note as on the tin.'

He smiles. 'Well done.' His eyes are like silver coins spinning on a pair of cracked old cue balls; he shucks out a hand even though I'm standing at least six yards away. 'Nick Lemery,' he says. 'At your service.'

'Yeah, right,' I say. 'You owe me a job.'

It's very weird. For the best part of a month now I've been dreaming of this moment, dreaming that when it came it would be some kind of showdown, that maybe I'd even have to fight. But now it's actually happening I don't feel remotely confrontational. Part of it is Lemery, I think. He's not like Cox or Patrick Belin, headstrong types a bit like how I remember Jack to be, crazy maybe but with a powerful craziness. Standing there in that oil-stained Massey Ferguson cap with his trousers tucked into his rubber boots all the Gandalf associations from the fayre are immediately dispelled. He doesn't look powerful. He looks . . . helpless, sort of.

Doesn't mean I trust him though.

'Why all the "Come alone, don't tell anyone" malarky?' I ask, not yet ready to give up my six-yard headstart in case I need to run away. 'Why all that crap? And why did they throw you out of the fayre? What are you? The fucking Unabomber?'

'I'm a farmer,' he says, 'and a good friend of your father's.'

'Did he tell you to get in touch with me?'

No reply.

'Did he tell you to follow me?'

Silence.

'What about the fire? Was it an accident?'

A shrug.

'Oh fuck this.'

I walk past Lemery into the circle of the henge, sit down with my back against the altar stone. I'm no longer the remotest bit afraid of him. No one this irritating could be remotely dangerous. Not unless he's trying to annoy me to death.

He follows me into the centre, squats down on the gravel facing me. 'You *are* like your father, you know. I didn't think you were, but you are. You've got his same impatience.'

This doesn't seem to me to merit an answer so I don't give it one. But this pleases Lemery and a Botox flush of self-indulgent happiness pumps his features and eases the fissures of anxiety from his face.

'You know what they've just discovered at Stonehenge – the real Stonehenge, I mean, in Britain?' he asks.

'No,' I say, 'but I've got a feeling you're going to tell me.'

'An alchemist. The Amesbury Archer they call him, on account of his being buried with fifteen arrows and this big old bow.'

'Oh yeah?'

'That's right. He was buried in a barrow right by the processional avenue with three copper daggers and five beakers and his bow, and the gold jewellery he was wearing on the tresses of his hair – gold which he most probably worked himself. From the patterns of isotopes in his teeth they know he came from Central Europe, maybe from Switzerland or the ancient mining region of old Bohemia. But he'd travelled west to Salisbury Plain and there his knowledge of metals made him powerful. Knowing how to transform lumps of rock into sharp, pure metal? That counted as magic then. Who knows? Perhaps it was his idea to bring the first bluestones from Wales. He died four thousand five hundred years ago, so the timing would be right.'

I look again at Lemery's grated and embedded nails, the callouses embossed onto his palms, his torn and tired shirt, the two-dimensional farmer logic etched dully on his pupils. 'What exactly are you trying to say?'

'What do you think alchemy's about?'

I slump a little further down the altar stone, resigning myself to yet another dose of Jack-related madness. Fuck, how depressing. It's just what I thought back in Cox's kitchen, that there'd be nothing but a heap big pile of idiocy waiting for me at the end of this most pointless of quests. 'Look, I've heard all about it. About the bread and the beer and the purification of the soul and the transformation of matter. And it still makes absolutely zero sense.'

'Well that's because you've been looking at the symptoms, at the side effects. It's like I said to you, what's a farm for? And you told me, it's for driving tractors. You'd be missing the point.' For the first time Lemery does the whole glance-about-to-check-no-one's-listening thing. I've been expecting it for a while but this is the first time he actually does it. He signs to me to lean towards him and juts forwards himself, trapping me in the guillotine of his breath. A framework of hops, a spotlight of sweetcorn, a broad blade of bacterial decay, it scythes neatly through my neck. 'What it's about,' he creaks, 'is utopia. The bringing into existence of the perfect society, the perfect city.' He leans back, half lowering his eyelids like he expects me to kiss his hands in thanks for the gift of this knowledge.

'Oh piss off.'

'You don't understand?' he says.

'What's to understand?' I say.

'This,' he says. And with his index finger he draws *circulus quadratus* in the gravel. 'Recognize it?'

'Of course I do – it's on the coffee canister, you fucking know it is. And just about everywhere else I look. It's the alchemical diagram of the structure of matter. The five elements. I know all about it.'

Lemery smiles sort of secretly. 'That's one interpretation. But there's another, just as valid. You see, the symbol can also be interpreted as signifying a golden fortress. The perfect city. The New Jerusalem. After all, a brick from the City of God, isn't that what the fifth element is? The philosopher's stone, isn't that what it was supposed to be?'

'Who knows.'

'Look,' he says, scrubbing out the symbol he drew in the gravel and then smoothing down the stones to make a fresh slate, 'it's quite simple.'

Famous last words.

'Back in ancient times, before Babylon and Ur, there were just villages stretching out in loose trading networks and patchworks of territory across the plains. And in these villages everybody worshipped good old Mother Earth along with a whole bunch of weather gods and animal gods and, of course, the Moon, who was the most important deity of all of them because it was light from her that made it possible to hunt. That's how everything was organized, by these gods. Chieftains and shamans would take on the personality of one god after another – rain god, pig god, corn god, leopard god . . . whichever was most propitious for the survival of the tribe. But then someone came up with this new idea. What if there was only one god and it was the sun? With all these local gods, nothing could ever get organized, nothing could ever get done; it was far too complicated, you could never please all of them at once, you spent your whole time appeasing one or other of them. But if there was one god who ruled over all of them, and a chieftain could come forward – a sun king – who could talk directly to him and thereby embody his power here on Earth, why, then that would give you power over gods, people, animals, weather. Everyone.'

'One ring to rule them all,' I say, thinking that I liked the explanation that Jack gave in his interview with Cox, that the sun god came to the fore because of climate change, much better than this lame conspiracy-theory version of events.

'Exactly.'

'I meant it as a joke.'

'It's not a joking matter.'

'Sorry.'

Lemery sniffs, squats down again and, after waiting for a moment to let me wonder if he's contemplating whether or not to bother with me, he draws another circle in the grit. 'And what the sun king takes as his symbol is not an eagle's feather or a leopard skin or a corn tiara but of course a circle. The first abstract idea. Representative of the sun itself but also suggestive of unity and perfection – after all, the sun is the single perfect thing, the single uncorrupted, unchanging thing that is immediately obvious to everyone. It's too perfect to look at, even. But it doesn't stop there. It's a symbol of something else as well.'

'A hole?' I say, but like Cathy and apparently everyone else in this town of mental cases Lemery's had a sarcasm bypass.

'Protection. A wall. A stockade. You want to build a wall for protection, a circle's the easiest form – easiest to build 'cuz it uses least materials, easiest to defend on account of there aren't any corners for the enemy to hide behind. So. Two circles, sun king and settlement. Sooner or later these two things are going to come together. And then what do you get? If you examine the archaeological remains of all the earliest cities in human history, you find they have three basic structural elements in common.' With his grubby index finger Lemery draws a line inside the ring. 'They have a palace, where the sun king lives.' Then he draws a second line, perpendicular to the first. 'They have a temple, where all the priests hang out. These are the brains of the operation, the guys who predict the seasons and eclipses and things like that, holy knowledge by which they can demonstrate they're in touch with the great god of the sun – and thereby control the actions of the sun king, who as often as not is just a figurehead.' Now he draws a third line, to form three sides of a square. 'And then they have a granary, which is where they store the food they bring in in the form of taxes, and which is where they get their *real* power, the power to feed people when they go hungry. These three things plus the circular wall equals a citadel. Stick a bunch of houses round the outside,' he adds, drawing a second, slightly larger circle round the first, 'and hey presto. City. That's how it begins.

'Remind you of anything?'

It does, as it happens. 'Stonehenge,' I say, impressed despite myself and intrigued a little, too, though I try my best not to sound it. 'But why then does the canister marking only have three sides of the square, while the ones on the Studio Reactor and the woodcut both have four?'

'Because Jack started out working with the *circulus quadratus* but then he got into this idea that that was a corruption of an even older form, the symbol that was in itself a city if you marked it on the earth in the appropriate place. And all this stuff in alchemy about trinities and three into one and the transformation of the soul, that's what it's all in reference to. Because this symbol, it was effectively a spell that did transform people, from villagers into subjects. It was very powerful and it spread like a virus and it transformed a loose society of subsistence farmers and nomads and hunter-gatherers and what we call civilization was born.'

'But what's this got to do with anything? What's it got to do with Jack being here in Atomville?'

'Have you been listening to anything I've been telling you? Your father was a *magician*; he was here to cast a spell.'

'My father was a romantic and a depressive who fucked up his life then committed suicide when he couldn't live with what he'd done.'

'Is that what you really think?'

'That's the way it looks to me.'

'Then you've not been looking very hard.'

'Who the fuck are you to tell me, you fucking freak? How the fuck would you know, creeping round behind my back in Salt Mountain like some kind of half-baked spy, leaving stupid messages, talking about magic and spells like some kind of Harry Potter nutcase, sending me my father's remains without even having the decency to tell me what they were!'

'I had to make sure you came.'

'So why didn't you just send me a fucking invitation, like any normal person would've done?'

'I did.'

'It was hardly *normal*.'

'Jack wasn't normal.'

'I suppose not. Normal people don't wander round the desert casting spells.'

'Here they do.'

I don't regard this remark as meriting an answer so I don't give it one. Not that this bothers Lemery. He stands, walks a few paces over to a bluestone, waves his arm in the direction of the Areas.

'Look at this place. All that knowledge, all that alchemy, this is where it ended up. For four thousand years it drifted around and got lost and mixed up with other stuff, the brewing and baking and metalwork, the Christianity and mysticism, all that shit, until the alchemists finally got their act together and gave up breathing in all those mercury fumes and developed chemistry and discovered themselves a new holy trinity: proton, neutron, electron. You don't think calling the first atomic explosion "the Trinity Test" was an accident, do you? These guys knew what they were doing. Their bombs and reactors unleashed the power of the sun down here on Earth: a real sun god, no longer just an abstract idea. Reactors, reprocessing plants, warheads – these were the new palaces, granaries and temples. This was a whole new level of sun kings and priests. Throw a security cordon all the way around it, build a dormitory town to house the workers, and what have you got yourself? I'll tell you what: the New Jerusalem.

'Did you know Atomville is where the tract home was invented? Well, it is. And it proved very successful, the perfect home for those who wanted to settle outside the walls of this new citadel. No surprise that as the atomic powerbase grew the tract home spread throughout America. It was a sign – for those with eyes to see – that a new state was forming, a state within a state. By the end of the 1940s the requirements of the nuclear industry, the public face of this secret state, already dictated political policy in this country. And still it grew, went transnational, until by the 1960s, what with its arms races and power stations and the multitude of its spin-off technologies, the exigencies of the atomic sector were dictating governmental policy for half the globe. Have you any idea how much it's cost us, this great nuclear experiment? A *trillion dollars* since 1945 in the US alone. I mean, you can't even *conceive* of it. It's not a state anymore, it's a fucking empire. It pump-primes a good proportion of world's major economies and controls millions of jobs and the destinies of billions of people, and all because the product it creates is so dangerous and toxic that its existence as an institution is guaranteed for thousands and thousands of years in order to take care of it. Plus, of course, it's not answerable to anyone; no one can touch it. Democratically it's completely unaccountable. It wasn't voted in, it can't be voted out. It owns half the newspapers and magazines in the country, and now that General Electric's bought NBC and CBS has been acquired by Westinghouse it's got TV as well, so there's no chance it can even be criticized any more, at least not from within this country. You ever hear of the True World Government, Cooper? The Society of the Golden Dawn? The Illuminati? The Hermetic Brotherhood of Light?'

'Yeah, sure. I watch *The X-Files*.'

'Fuck *The X-Files*,' Lemery hisses, shaking loose a Warholian head of hair. 'Fuck *The* fucking *X-Files*. *The X-Files* is for losers and for idiots. What I'm talking about, what I'm telling you, this stuff's for real.' He jabs his outstretched fingers in the direction from which I'd come. 'See Atomville, see the Areas out there? See how there's almost nothing visible on the surface? You wanna know why that is? It's because 90 per cent of it's all *underground*. You don't believe me, I've got maps, I've got copies of plans like you would not believe. I've been studying this for years. Forget Tibet, forget fucking Atlantis. This is where they hang out. This is the City of the Sun, the City on the Hill. This is the New Atlantis, my friend. *Atomville*.'

You know what? I have no time for this. It doesn't freak me out, it doesn't even mildly peturb me. Compared to the 'revelations' about the way the world works I've had dumped on me over the years by Stasie this barely makes the grade. 'Yeah, right,' I say. 'And this underground city of yours, don't tell me – it's inhabited by lizardmen from the sixth dimension.'

Lemery gives me this look like I'm the crazy one. 'What? What in hell are you on? Is that more *X-Files* bullshit or what is it? I'm serious here, Cooper. I'm talking about real people with real power. Power that your father challenged. Like the Amesbury Alchemist four thousand years ago, he came from the east with new ideas for how the people here should go about things – for how they should think about time, and the world and their environment. And to start with they ignored him. Then, when they saw he had something to offer, they tried to exploit him. And then, when he showed them he had power of his own, power to bring fuel rods from Europe like his ancestor had gotten bluestones from Wales, well, then they got scared.'

'Wait a minute. What fuel rods?'

Lemery blinks at me. 'You know, the fuel rods. The breeder blanket assemblies.' But still I look blank – I've no idea what he's talking about. 'You mean to say you don't know? Bill didn't tell you?'

'Tell me what?'

'I thought you'd been talking to Bill Valentine. At the fayre.'

'Who's Bill Valentine?'

'Damn.' He looks away, fits his hair back inside his cap. 'This is all back to front.'

'What fuel rods? I thought Jack was working on a granite sculpture designed to store transmuted waste?'

'Yeah, The Herm. He was working on that when he got here. But he'd moved on.'

'Moved on to what?'

'To bigger things. But there's no point talking to you now.'

The farmer steps outside the bluestone circle, starts walking back in the direction of his truck. Scrambling to my feet I follow him. 'Why not?'

But he doesn't answer, just keeps on going to his vehicle, climbs inside, starts the engine.

'Hey! Wait! You can't just disappear on me now. What fuel rods?'

He reaches over to the glove compartment, starts rootling round for something. When he's found it he passes it through the open window. It's a business card, oil-soiled and dog-eared.

'Here. Dr William Valentine. This is his address.'

'Who's he?'

'Just go and see him.'

'And then what?'

But Lemery's already gone. With a scrunch of tyres and a giant fart of exhaust and dust the truck swings around and bounces off across the plateau. A moment later its red tail lights have slipped down behind the lip of hill and there I am, alone, staring alternately at the business card and the slow disc of the weakly setting sun, wondering what on earth that was all supposed to be about.

'Oh Cooper!' bellows Lucille the second I walk into reception. 'Your friend's here.'

'What friend? I haven't got any friends.'

'Well, you've got this one and she seems very nice. I told her you'd gone off rubbernecking so I didn't think it would be long before you were back. She's waiting for you out by the pool.'

The pool is small and kidney-shaped and in a fenced enclosure that juts out into the motel's parking lot, as I think I mentioned earlier. The fence is tall and wooden so when you're in the pool you don't realize you're in the parking lot. But still.

I walk down the corridor towards the entrance, dodging the maids' cleaning wagon and trying to work out why it is that Kelly's come back. Last night I thought I'd scared her off for good. Maybe she's come to give me a mercy-fuck.

Which would be nice.

But the person sitting waiting for me on a plastic deckchair by the pool isn't Kelly. The person sitting there isn't cream-complexioned with blonde blonde hair and white white teeth and bitten-cherry lips but has skin like expensive oiled wood, a cowl of straightened hair and an air of fluttery self-absorption I've often tried to emulate. The person sitting on a plastic deckchair flipping through a magazine and sipping from a can of Fresca is the last person I expect to see. The person sitting flipping sipping – is Liz.

'Cooper! Finally.'

I say nothing, at least not straightaway. I just stare for a while from the safety of the doorway. Then I say:

'I thought I asked you not to call.'

'I didn't call, I came,' she says.

'I don't get it.'

'I took some leave.'

'Why?' I mean, I don't want to look a gift horse in the mouth here, but.

'Because when we spoke on the phone I thought you didn't sound yourself. I was worried.'

'Enough to fly all the way out here to find me?'

She nods. She's wearing a pair of Gucci sunglasses I've never seen before – she must've bought them at the airport. They're very dark and hide her eyes completely.

'In case you haven't noticed I do actually care, Cooper.'

This should make me happy, it really should. But it doesn't feel right.

'So what's happened? You fallen out with darling Doug?' I say. I'm testing her, trying to hit a nerve.

Bullseye. 'How many times do I have to tell you he's not my fucking boyfriend?'

'So what is he then?'

'He's my *boss*! Look, I came to find out if you were okay because I was worried about you. Really worried – so worried it's giving me an ulcer. But if you don't want me here, I can get right back on a plane and fly back home again. I got the flight on Air Miles anyway. It's not like it'll cost me anything but time and what's left of our friendship.'

Which isn't much, she might've added. But she doesn't, and now I'm feeling guilty for trying to throw it all away.

'I'm sorry,' I manage eventually. 'Really. It's just that everything . . . it's all been so fucking weird.' And then, pulling my eyes up from where they've been rolling round the rubber toecaps of my Converse: 'It's really good to see you.'

'It's good to see you too.'

'Do you want to come up to my room? I can make you coffee. There's a machine.'

'You don't drink coffee,' she says.

'Yeah, well. Things change,' I say.

Bill Valentine

I tell Liz about the all-round far-outness of Atomville, about going to Jack's old house, about the fayre, about meeting the Trevisans, about being driven out to the studio where Jack died, about the missing artwork. She agrees with me it's odd that a two-tonne hunk of granite should vanish just like that. She asks me about losing the ashes which she says I mentioned on the phone though I don't remember it, so I tell her about what happened to me at customs. Then I realize that it's getting late and if I want to follow up on Lemery's suggestion that I go and see Bill Valentine, I've got to go now. I ask Liz if she wants to come. 'Sure,' she says, like I've just asked her to come with me to the supermarket.

'Is this the car you crashed?' she asks, as we approach the Honda.

'That's the one.'

'Jesus. Did you tell the rental company?'

'Nope. Actually, I haven't spoken to them since I left Boston. They were expecting the car back ten days ago. They're probably wondering where I am.'

'You mean you just ran out on them? You complete and utter imbecile. You do realize technically that's Grand Theft Auto, that you could go to jail for what you did?'

'Really? Shit. I just thought they'd charge my credit card. Tell you the truth, I haven't really thought about it. I've sort of had other things on my mind.'

'Haven't the police been in touch?'

I shake my head, open the passenger door.

'Well, that's a total miracle,' Liz says, getting in. 'Hadn't you thought they might be? I mean, it was easy enough for me to find you in Jackass Flats.'

I don't answer this till I've gone round the other side and got into the car myself. There's a little algorithm chugging away inside my brain, trying to factor out.

'And here,' is what I say, once I've put my seat belt on.

'Yes,' she says, 'and here. Though this was harder.'

'But not impossible.'

'No. Clearly not.'

I start the car and manoeuvre out of the parking lot. I know which way we're going; if the address that Lemery gave me's right, Bill Valentine's house is right around the corner from Jack's old place on Neutron Avenue.

'So how did you find me? There's more than three motels in Atomville. Don't tell me you ran a check on my credit card.' I mean it as a joke but she doesn't reply. 'You didn't, did you?'

'It's a Fifth Amendment issue.'

'Fuck Liz, what're you like? A month ago butter wouldn't melt, now you're turning into a regular double agent.'

'Don't say that.'

'But it's true! And also quite impressive. I mean the first time was pretty crazy, but twice in one week . . .'

She looks away from me, out the passenger window. 'I guess once you've crossed the line the first time the rest comes easy. Let's not talk about it, okay?'

'If that's what you want.'

'It is.'

But the whole thing gives me a childish buzz of excitement and I'm not quite ready to let it go. 'Me Mulder, you Scully, right?' I say, trying to press some buttons, get a grin.

'Don't, Cooper. It's not funny. You shouldn't make a joke of it.'

'I'm just trying to cheer you up.'

'I'm fine. It's you I'm worried about.'

'Me? What's wrong with me?'

'I don't know. You're not yourself.'

'I dunno,' I say. 'I feel okay.'

'But that's just it. With everything that's happened, you should feel terrible.'

'Maybe I'm in shock.'

'I know you think you're being ironic but I'd say that's a distinct possibility.'

'Oh come on.'

'No, seriously, break it down: in the last couple of weeks your father's died, you've lost your job, you've taken off halfway round the world without telling anyone when before you couldn't even go to the corner shop without discussing it in at least three emails, you've had all these problems with the ashes and the car and everything, and you're experiencing an apparently total lack of emotional response.'

'I've had emotional responses,' I say, thinking of my attack on Dungarees's son at the Salt Mountain protest camp.

'Well, okay, you don't have to listen to me. But from where I'm sitting you're acting completely out of character. It made more sense when you were yelling at me down the telephone.'

I sit, grip the steering wheel, stare at the empty road straight ahead. Why is there no traffic?

'So maybe that's a good thing. Maybe all these things that have been happening, maybe they are having a big impact on me. Maybe they're changing me in some fundamental way, and that's what you're seeing. Perhaps I'm just jettisoning twenty years' worth of neuroticism. That was after all the whole point of this trip.'

'But I liked you the way you were before.'

Yeah, well, not enough. 'Well that's nice of you to say so Liz, but the fact is that I didn't.'

'You didn't like the way you were?'

'No. I hated myself. I wasn't happy.'

'And you're happy now?'

'Right now I'm nothing. But that's okay. Maybe someone, somewhere has decided that it's time for the life of Cooper James to undergo some structural renovations. And since the forces involved seem pretty impressive, I'd say there's no point in fighting them. Might as well go with the flow.'

'All new Cooper?'

'That's right.'

Liz turns away from me, sits back in her seat and looks straight ahead down the empty street in front of us. 'I think you need to find out what happened to your dad,' she says, and her voice is tight and perhaps a little frightened and also a little cold.

You can tell Bill Valentine's house belongs to a friend of Jack's because although it's the exact same type of house as all the others in the neighbourhood, it's the only one with a large and pointless pile of earth dumped in the driveway. I park the Honda opposite and we get out and walk up and ring the doorbell. When a minute has passed and no one's answered Liz suggests that no one's home. But I point to the car sitting next to the mound of earth, engine still ticking quietly from recent use and ring again and this time I hear footsteps. Then the door swings open.

The man who's opened it I recognize – he's the really unattractive bloke who was selling the woodcuts at the fayre.

'*You're* Dr Valentine?'

'I'm very per-pleased to meet you, Cooper. Uh-uh-again,' he says, extending his hand and beaming a smile as if to say: who else could I be? 'And per-please . . . ker-call me Bill. Ner-Nick Lemery called and ter-told me you were ker-coming. Ker-come on in.'

We do as he asks and soon enough we're seated side by side on the sofa in his messy living room. He sits opposite in a brown fabric-covered bucket chair and says nothing for a while, staring at us – at me, mainly – through those thick spectacles of his. I feel a bit like a prize specimen, a rare moth freshly netted by a lepidopterist.

'Juh-Jack's son,' he says finally.

'Yeah, well, here I am. What's all this about some fuel rods?'

'Ber-breeder blanket assemblies,' he corrects. 'You ner-know what they are?'

'I've been to SOFFT.'

He smiles. 'Ker-Cathy gave you the tour?'

'That's right,' I say, embarrassed though I don't know why. 'So what about them?'

'We wer-were importing some, Jack and me.'

'You were *importing* them? Where from?' If I sound incredulous, well – wouldn't you be?

'It's a ler-long story.'

'I'm listening.'

Bill grins excitedly and smooths his trousers with his hand. He's clearly been waiting to tell his tale for quite some time and now his chance has come he can hardly contain himself. 'I used to work at suh-SOFFT,' he says, 'I'm a ner-nuclear engineer. Pipework was my sper-specialty. I helped develop the ter-technology they use for per-piping liquid sodium round the core – for ker-cooling it, you see. But I retired three yuh-years ago, just before Jack arrived in Atomville.'

Once again my brain starts going click-click-click. Bill + Pipework is what I'm thinking. Bill + Pipework = . . . ?

'And you got to know him how?'

'Through the ber-B-Reactor Preservation Committee. You've heard of ber-B-Reactor? Well of course it was der-decommissioned long-ago, but there's a Committee that I suh-sit on made up mainly of retirees like myself, der-dedicated to its preservation as a national mer-monument. They wanted to demolish it, you see, ber-but we've been fighting to get it officially rer-recognized as a World huh-huh-huh-Heritage Site. The ker-Committee Secretary invited

Jack to ger-give a luh-lecture at our monthly meet, and we got ter-talking afterwards. It turned out we had a ler-lot of the same interests in ker-common.'

My little equation suddenly solves itself and I ask Bill if he was responsible for putting together the knurled display piece in the visitors' centre. His face lights up.

'That's right! That was mer-mine. Jack had seen it, too – that's what got us ter-talking. I think he was the only per-person who ever ner-knew what it really meant.'

I nod, pleased with my detective work. 'And the assemblies?'

Bill nods back. 'Let me sher-show you something.'

Moving with all the grace of an outpatient on lithium he gets up from his seat and wheezes over to where an aged television and precariously balanced VCR sit atop a short oak cabinet which is home, it transpires, to a litter of videotapes. One of these he selects – by what criteria I've no idea, since few of the tapes have either labels or boxes – and feeds it into the machine, though some experimenting with cables and sockets and remote controls is also required before a picture can finally be encouraged to appear.

We're in a large banqueting hall or conference centre; a dinner's going on. Long tables filled with suits run in parallel towards a back wall, in the centre of which is a podium at which a man dressed in black tie is talking. The camera's elevated to maybe one and a half times human height and set on wide angle, giving an overview of the scene. The podium's small and distant; there's some kind of logo or insignia marked on it but we're too far away to see exactly what it is.

'What's this?' I ask. There's no sound yet.

'It's a vuh-video of a lecture Jack gave to a conference we had here, about three years back. It's how the whole importation got uh-underway, initially. Wer-watch.'

I turn back to the screen and as I do the camera zooms a little, not quite right up to the podium but far enough forwards so I can see the logo printed on the front.

'That's the SOFFT logo,' I say.

'The conference was a fer-fund raiser for the fast-ber-breeder programme. SOFFT's been under threat for suh-several years now. The DoE thinks the per-project's been a failure, fer-far too costly and impractical, and they want to cut the grant and mer-mothball the reactor. Cathy Ter-Trevisan's been ger-going crazy trying to find another way to ker-keep the thing alive. The ker-conference was her idea – she thought maybe if they flew in ner-nuclear experts from ker-Canada, France, Japan and juh-Germany and ser-sold them on the research value of what was happening huh-here at SOFFT, then they might ker-come through with some independent funding.'

'But why did she want Jack to speak?'

'She ther-thought he'd be excellent PR, an uh-uh-onside artist to help woo the ker-culture-crazy Europeans. And he wer-wooed them alright, only not in ker-quite the way she huh-had in mind. Huh-here's Jack now look . . .' Fumbling with the remote, Valentine brings up the sound just in time for us to hear the dinner jacket ask us to please welcome our speaker for the evening, Mr Jack Reever, artist. He indicates stage right and there's applause and the camera jerks a little as if to pan but then it doesn't and a small bespectacled man with a buzz cut, dressed in a sports jacket, drab tie, white shirt and ill-fitting trousers, walks in from the side of the frame. To begin with I think it must be a mistake, that Bill's forwarded to the wrong part of the tape. It's not until he takes the microphone that I recognize him.

It's Jack. 'God! He's so . . . he's . . . he's so fucking *old*.'

Liz says nothing. Nor does Bill. They're listening to Jack who by now has begun to speak. Bill looks radiant; Liz has an expression looks like she's taking notes.

Good evening, everyone. My name is Jack D. Reever and I'm the after-dinner entertainment. Now, I know that you've all had a couple of days packed with lectures and meetings, and you've just had a good big dinner courtesy of the fine chefs here at the Chiawana Inn [light applause] and that what you'd probably like served up now along with your coffees and brandies is a good comedian to lift the world from your shoulders for the next half hour or so, especially those of you who've travelled halfway round of it to be here. But I'm here to inform you that, due to an unfortunate oversight in what was an otherwise flawless piece of conference planning, when the time came to book an after-dinner speaker it was discovered that the budget had altogether run dry. And comedians don't come cheap, whatever they may tell you. So in their wisdom the organizers decided to go for, well, not quite the next best thing but certainly the most economic option they could think of. They booked a sculptor. Me.

'This is too much,' I say. 'I'm not sure I can deal with this.'

'What's the matter?'

'I haven't heard his voice in twenty years! And now he shows up looking like a nuclear engineer . . . er, no offence,' I add, remembering our host.

'Well, give him a chance,' Liz says. 'If you get too freaked out, just say.' Then she reaches over and takes my hand in hers.

So what's a sculptor got to do with SOFFT? I hear you asking. What's a sculptor got to do with fast-breeder technology? What's a sculptor even doing in Atomville at all? Well, it might surprise you to hear that even as a child I was real into nuclear technology – maybe more so than a lot of you sitting out in the audience today. I know what you're thinking, you're thinking that sounds like one messed-up kid, and you'd be right – though of course I'm a little older than many of you out there, or I look older, anyway, and back in my day it wasn't so unusual for boys especially to be given nuclear-chemistry sets as Christmas presents, like the one my father gave me. It would be unbelievable today but in the 1950s the PR around atomic stuff was all positive. I mean, you'd hear Edward Teller speaking on the radio about the great leaps forward that were just around the corner in this marvellous new atomic age, giving the hard sell about his plans to use hydrogen bombs to excavate a huge harbour up in Alaska to serve the fishing industry and help exploit the oil. It wasn't until Peter Sellers turned him into Dr Strangelove that people began to sit up and think, though I guess that what it made you guys think is that Peter Sellers has got a lot to answer for.

At this the audience laughs uneasily and Liz grips my hand a little tighter. If it's meant to calm me down, this gesture, it's not working. I mean, I've wanted to hold Liz's hand pretty much ever since I first met her but if it ever happened (which I didn't think it would), I'd sort of hoped the circumstances would be rather different. As it is it feels all wrong. I'd imagined her grip as warm, caressing, loving. But her skin is cool, her bones angular and metallic. So far is the experience from what I had in mind, in fact, it almost makes me shiver.

In any event, I got given this kit made by the Porter Chemical Company. 'Safe! Harmless! Exciting!' said the box. 'The Story of Atomic Energy with Safe Interesting Experiments.' Right. So they'd put inside some little pieces of uranium and radium and this thing called a spinthariscope that you could take into a dark room or closet and close the door and use to see the tracers given out by radium decay. I mean, it hadn't seemed to occur to anyone that if this stuff had done for Madame Curie, they probably shouldn't put it in the hands of pre-teens.

The laughter's more confident this time; Jack's beginning to win over his audience. But if he's winning them, he's losing me.

'He never told me that,' I say. 'He never told me that about when he was a kid.'

But there you go. Still, it hasn't given me cancer – yet. Worst thing that happened was I left the uranium near the old man's Brownie and fogged up a film he'd just finished shooting. But I guess I got pretty hooked on the stuff because a few years later I worked up what I called 'An Experiment in Radiation Genetics' and entered it for the Fifth Annual Seattle Science Fair. I'd got the veterinarian who looked after my parents' dogs to show me how to operate the x-ray machine in his surgery, and then I'd got these eight breeding pairs of hamsters, poor things, and blasted them with x-rays to see what the effects on their offspring would be.

The best way to describe how the audience is laughing now is probably uproarious. The best way to describe how I am feeling, on the other hand, is incendiary.

By the third generation I was getting mutations, though whether it was due to the radiation or the in-breeding it was impossible to tell. I mean, I don't remember doing much in the way of a control. But still I won the Veterinary Medal for my efforts, though what the judges thought of me I'll never know. If some kid today did what I did, he'd probably be packed off to reform school within about thirty seconds but these guys, they were no doubt real into Edward Teller and thought I was going to be the Oppenheimer of radiation biology or something. I'm willing to bet that none of them figured I was going to quit school at the end of the year and run away from home to be a cowboy.

So that's one reason why I'm here – my weird and twisted childhood. But there are other reasons too, one of which, naturally enough, is sculpture – though we'll get to that – and another of which is the yin to nuclear science's yang, and that is: alchemy.

And I've sat silent long enough.

'This is bullshit! It's completely different!' I explode, jerking my hand free of Liz's grip.

'To what?' she says. She sounds shocked.

'To the interview he did with Cox, back in Graniteburg. It's a different version of his childhood, a completely different story of why he started to try to make nuclear artworks, everything!'

'People are allowed to change.'

'Change, perhaps, but not to completely reinvent their past.'

'Maybe he's just being economical with the truth. Maybe he didn't think the stuff he told Cox was suitable for this audience.'

I jump up and hit the stop button on the VCR. 'Or suitable for Stasie and me.'

'Don't switch it off! It hasn't even got started yet!'

'Sod that. I already know exactly what he's going to say. He's just going to witter on about alchemy in order to justify using the technology at SOFFT. It's what Cathy Trevisan told me when I went out there. I didn't really believe her then, but now I see it's true. He's completely sold out to the system.'

'You can talk.'

'What I've done or haven't done is irrelevant here,' I snap. 'I can't deal with this. My father, an apologist for the nuclear industry!' I stare at the others for reciprocation of my anger but Liz looks worried and Bill looks plain embarrassed. 'You know, I've travelled halfway round the world to find out what happened to this arsehole and what do I discover? That he was just that – a fucking arsehole. I mean did he actually have a soul? Was there anything he had inside himself he put any value on at all?'

'Well, of course there was,' Liz says stupidly.

'Why "of course"? Look at the evidence. Since I've got here I've met . . .' I think back to the beginning of my trip, count the names off on my fingers one by one: 'Max Depaoli, Cox Macro, Phil Metzger, Patrick Belin, the hippy guy in the dungarees, Todd and Cathy, Lemery, the good Dr Valentine . . . all these people so completely different that if you put them in a room together, they'd be at each other's throats within thirty seconds. And yet somehow they all completely identified with Jack, thought at one stage or another he was the best friend they'd ever had. But he had nothing in common with any of them!

'It's the same thing over and over, and where it started was with me and Stasie. It's . . . it's like he had no centre, like he just morphed into whatever people wanted him to be, then once he'd taken what he needed he'd betray them and turn his back on them and just take off. He was like some kind of chameleon or shapeshifter or something. It makes me want to spit.'

I'm on my feet now, shouting down at Liz and Bill, their expressions no longer either worried or embarrassed but slack with the bovine blankness of people who've been unexpectedly confronted with a chunk of information extremely difficult to process.

'I didn't mer-mean to upset you, Cooper,' Bill stammers eventually. 'I ther-thought you'd be per-pleased.'

'Well, I don't know . . . I don't know what I feel. I mean, my father gave up everything to pursue this damn artistic ideal of his and now here he is junking all his principles. All the way through this trip I've been thinking well, he may have abandoned his family but at least he stuck by what he thought was right. But it's all bollocks. He didn't believe in anything at all.'

'No,' says Bill, shaking his head a little desperately. 'You der-don't understand, it wasn't like that . . . he never did the transmutation he was ger-going to do at SOFFT. It was ker-cancelled.'

I hear this loud and clear but I'm too worked up for it to stem my outrage. 'Why? If he was so chummy with Cathy and everyone?'

'Because of what her-happened that ner-night. At the ker-conference.' Bill insists, pushing with his hands at the air around him.

'Jack's lecture, see, the Europeans and juh-Japanese absolutely luh-lapped it up. When he finished he was swamped by people huh-handing him their business cards.'

'Lucky him.'

'Well, yer-yes. Because one of them was a German ner-nuclear executive called Herr huh-Hühnerstall, who was one of the most important people at the ker-conference. He worked for ker-Kraftwerk, the German conglomerate, and for twenty years he'd been in charge of building the KFFR–2573, the biggest fer-fast breeder in the world. He invited Jack to have a drink with him, and over per-port and cigars he explained that though he'd fer-finished the reactor on time and under ber-budget, while he was awaiting ratification in the buh-Bundestag for it to be switched on an environmentalist ker-campaign turned public opinion against the whole ter-technology. At the last mer-minute the government changed its mer-mind and instead of being told to throw the switch huh-Hühnerstall got an order to start dismantling his life's wer-work. And now here he was at this conference with all these reactor components to get shuh-shot of.'

'So?' I say, rubbing my eyes, trying to take this in, vaguely aware that it's my turn to feel bovine.

Bill giggles. 'Ther-that's just what Jack said *he* said, too: "So wher-what's this got to do with me?" And what Hühnerstall rer-replied was, "Well, maybe I've got something that'll be yer-useful to you in your art. Perhaps if you could mer-meet me tomorrow for ber-breakfast, we can wer-work something out!" Well, Jack couldn't believe his luh-luck. He'd been trying to get his hands on ner-nuclear materials for years and now here was some ker-crazy German guy offering them to him just like that! He ler-left the conference, drove back to the fer-french-fry plant where he was wer-working nights to pay the rent, did his shift, ker-clocked off at six a.m., and then der-drove back to the hotel where he used the rer-restrooms to change back into his suit before ger-going up to breakfast in huh-Hühnerstall's suh-suh-suite. And over ker-coffee and ker-croissants, Hühnerstall gave him the ter-twelve ber-breeder blanket assemblies.'

Bill takes care to impress upon us the immense significance of this event. Not since the inauguration of the Manhattan project in 1940 had anything remotely like this ever happened. No private individual had ever been legally granted the rights to possess this kind of nuclear material. Maybe somewhere deep in one of the former Soviet republics there's a ganglord with a stolen warhead or two. But to have such a thing granted legally? If Jack accepted, he'd become the world's smallest nuclear power.

'And did he accept?'

'Of ker-course he did. Her-how could he say ner-no? And it certainly ker-caused a storm. No one here wer-wanted him to do this, and I mean ner-no one. Everyone was fer-furious, and within a week suh-SOFFT had changed their mind about the ter-transmutation. Said they were still going to let him do it, but that they were ger-going to have to levy a small charge.'

'How small?'

Bill pauses, smiles. 'Uh-eighty mer-million der-dollars.'

'Jesus.'

'Exactly. Juh-Jack was very upset. Really insulted. What did they expect him to do, he said, her-hold a stoop sale? He got a bunch of flyers printed up, "Transmutation fer-Fundraiser and Barbecue," and per-pushed one through the door of every DoE exec in town. Ner-needless to say, they didn't see the juh-joke. But ther-that was Jack. He was ber-brilliant, especially when he had his ber-back against the wall.'

'You were really fond of him, weren't you Dr Valentine?' says Liz.

Bill blushes. 'We were fer-friends. And even though I used to work for suh-SOFFT, it made me really angry, wer-what they did. It wer-wasn't fair, to string him along like that and then to cher-change their minds. So I told him I'd help him with the importation. It suh-seemed the least that I could do. And unlike a ler-lot of people, since I was already retired I had nothing to ler-lose'

'That was good of you.'

'Well, mer-maybe, but I have to say if I'd ner-known what I was ger-getting into, I don't think I'd have volunteered. There was no fer-formal procedure for an individual to do this kind of thing, and Jack had to ger-go through the same procedures as if he were a major corporation like juh-General Electric or Westinghouse. But they have huge staffs and big ber-budgets at their duh-disposal. For one man on his own, especially one as per-poor as he was, it was ner-next to impossible. Even with me huh-helping him it took us nearly two yer-years to ger-get it done. There was so much paper-work you ker-can't imagine, and every time we thought we'd ger-got near the end of it there was mer-more. Jack suh-sold pretty much everything he had to ruh-raise the money. In the end he even had to sell his huh-house, which is how come he ended up living out at ter-Todd's studio.'

'The studio is *Todd's*?'

'Der-didn't he tell you? He'd ber-been a part-investor in that industrial estate out there, then when it didn't wer-work out he ended up with some of the fer-finished units as compensation. It was standing empty, so he told Jack he could stay there, if he luh-liked. It was ver-very kind of him, especially since we'd become almost like per-pariahs in Atomville by then.'

'But I don't get it. Why would he do that? I mean, if Jack had fallen out with SOFFT?'

'Ber-but Jack didn't fall out with ker-Cathy. It wasn't her who mer-made the decision about the ter-transmutation. She still wer-wanted it to go ahead. She was as angry as he was about the fee. Ber-but there was nothing she could der-do.'

'So why didn't they tell me all this? I mean, Todd took me out to the studio himself. And you'd've thought Cathy would've mentioned the importation, when she took me out to SOFFT.'

'Maybe they were embarrassed,' Liz suggests. 'Maybe Todd thought if you knew he owned the studio, you'd try to hold him somehow responsible for the fire.'

'I dunno,' I say, shaking my head. 'It doesn't make any sense.'

I look at Dr Valentine to see if he has a better explanation but all he wants to do is tell us about the morning the breeder blanket assemblies arrived in Atomville. 'They shut down half the town with ruh-roadblocks,' he says, rubbing his palms up and down the thighs of his polyester trousers with excitement like a child on Christmas Day. 'There were ger-guards everywhere; they even put machine guns on the tops of some of the ber-buildings. Your fer-father and me, we took official delivery of the consignment over at the ker-Kraftwerk compound off of Oppenheimer Way. Had to open the ker-crates, check for contamination, sign about thirty forms. Jack said it was like taking delivery of twelve Egyptian mer-mummies, for all the fer-fuss there was.'

'But where did he keep them after that? Surely he couldn't store them at the studio?'

'Oh no. Of course not. That really wouldn't have ber-been allowed. No, they were kept in ter-trust for him by Kraftwerk, in their uh-underground facility. Jack had to go there every month, to ker-carry out the radiation safety checks.'

Bill stops talking and stares at me expectantly, like he's waiting for me to say something stunning and momentous. But what it is I've no idea. Maybe it's an apology for my earlier outburst but I don't think so. It's not that kind of look.

'So what did he want to do with them once he'd got them?'

He raises his eyebrows and lifts his hands, soft hands, puffy, the hands of an office worker. Hands like mine, not hands like Jack's. 'I don't know. They had them tied up in so much bureaucracy I don't think he could do anything.'

'So why did you bother to import them, if he couldn't use them in a work of art?'

'Wer-well we der-didn't realize that, to stuh-start with. And when we fer-found it out, we ner-nearly gave up on the per-project. But then juh-Jack said, "Well, you know Bill, I ther-think we should ger-go ahead regardless. Maybe it's enough to just import these der-damn things anyway." '

'So he thought the importation *was* the artpiece?'

'That's rer-right. At least, ther-that's what he told me.'

As we're leaving Bill asks us to wait, says he has something for me. He disappears off into another room and when he returns a minute later he's holding not just the picture of the *circulus quadratus* I saw on his stand at the fayre but also the block it was printed from.

'These were juh-Jack's you know. He mer-made them.'

'He did?'

'That's why I wouldn't suh-sell the print. Ber-but I think he'd mean you to huh-have it now. And the wer-woodblock.'

I protest that I couldn't possibly take them but Bill insists. 'If yer-you want to ther-thank me, make some mer-more prints from it and suh-send me one. He had his own interpretation of wer-what it meant, you know, the suh-*circulus*. Ver-very interesting. That fuh-first conversation at the ber-B-Reactor Preservation Committee meet, this is wher-what we talked about when he found out that it was me that mer-made the pipe. Wer-what if the four outer segments are the four fer-fundamental forces and the square is matter, he said. Because then, you see, it's mer-matter itself that's really the fuh-fifth element; it's muh-matter that doesn't actually exist. Only the four fer-forces – strong nuclear, weak nuclear, electro-mer-magnetic and gravitational – only they exist. The forces are like fields of ter-tension, and atoms are what happen when they intersect. Atoms are like ner-knots or nodes in the forces' fer-fields; when they're tied up nice and tight like ker-carbon or any of the elements in the middle of the per-Periodic Table they're very stable. But the higher up the Table the looser the ner-knots become until you reach the ones like uranium or ter-tritium, the unstable ones that huh-have this special tendency to come untied. If you think of mer-matter as being like a giant ker-carpet weaved of the der-different kinds of forces, then radioactivity's like the fraying tuh-tassels at the edge. Jack yer-used to say that yer-you and me and plants and stars and all that mer-makes up material existence, that's like the per-patterns on the carpet. And what I always used to tell him was, ther-that's right Jack. And ther-that's why it's sensible to ker-keep back from the uh-uh-, from the uh-uh-uh-edge.'

Bill has to use all his willpower to conjure this final word; when it comes he hurls it from his palate with spittle-spraying force.

'Sounds like good advice,' I say, resisting the temptation to wipe the spattered wood-block on my T-shirt. Then I realize that far behind the lenses of those bulletproof spectacles he's wearing tears are pooling in the gutters of Bill's eyes.

On the way back to the motel I ask Liz where she's staying.

'I've taken a room at Tomsk-43,' she says, apparently surprised I haven't already worked this out.

'What?' I say. 'Thought you'd keep an eye on me?'

She laughs. 'Maybe.' She sounds relaxed. I think she thinks I'm flirting with her – and she's enjoying it. I say nothing for a minute while I guide the Honda through a junction, just feel the tension in the air between us. It's a different tension from what we've had before. I even think it might be sexual.

'So when we get there, what're you going to do?' I ask.

'Oh, I dunno,' she says. 'Take a shower. Unpack.'

'You're not unpacked?'

'Not yet. I thought I'd wait till I could find you first.'

'Oh right,' I say. 'And then what?'

'Well I'm kind of hungry. You want to go get something to eat?'

'Sure,' I say. 'But what about after that?'

She thinks I'm flirting with her, she really does. 'After eating I'll go to bed, I guess,' she says, flirting back.

'Really?' I say.

'What?' she says. 'Cooper? What?'

'Because that's not what I was thinking you might want to do,' I say.

'Oh?' she says. 'And what exactly were you thinking?' There's so much static in the car my right shoulder's starting to shake.

'I was thinking . . .' I say, glancing into my blind spot and starting to indicate, 'I was thinking that before you go to bed you might be planning to fill out a PS-6.'

Like the car's been touched to earth the static's gone and the tension with it, the sexual tension anyway. I've flipped Liz round, reversed all her polarities and there's a different tension now, wholly repulsive, tangibly metallic.

'Fuck you Cooper.'

'No Liz, fuck you. Don't you get it? As long as you're filling out those fucking forms you're spying on me. That's the basic truth of this situation. It doesn't matter whether you broke the rules to help me out, or that you came here for the best of reasons. As long as you're filing PS-6s you're part of that machine and all your good intentions, they're irrelevant, because your actions don't belong to you.'

'That's not true . . .'

'It *is* true! Why do you think I always get so angry when you get all anti-establishment at work? Because you only do it *at work*. It's only there you feel you can be yourself. Every time you leave the building it's like they've got a CCTV camera installed inside your head and you turn into this kind of automaton.'

'How can you say that, when I came all this way . . .'

'Don't you realize? They *wanted* you to come all this way. As long as you're here you're their eyes and ears: Andrews, Daniels, all the rest of them. Look what Jack was doing! They're desperate to keep an eye on me. God knows what I'm likely to get up to, Jack Reever's son, loose in America on his own. Fuck's sake, Liz. I bet they made it easy for you, didn't they? Two weeks off at three days' notice? How often does anyone get to swing that? Last time I wanted a week's holiday I had to book it eight months in advance and even then they moaned. Think about it.'

Liz sits silently for a moment. Sniffs.

'I lied about the credit searches.'

'Andrews authorized them, didn't he?'

'Yes.'

'You've got to choose, Liz.'

'Choose?'

'Me or Featherbrooks.'

But she doesn't, not right then, and we get out the car, walk across the asphalt and go up to our respective rooms without exchanging a single other word.

Ken

Next day I wake suddenly at eight, alone, limbs spavined, face buried in a puddle of drool, spat forth from a nightmare in which I was trying to save slightly-smaller-than-life-sized Japanese businessmen and housewives from the blast at Nagasaki. It was – in common with the majority of my nightmares – structured like a psychotic video game. There was I, a relative giant, running to and fro across a street of wooden houses trying to catch these kimonoed women as they charged past me, fleeing the mushroom cloud pustulating in the middle distance. Shock waves came in one after the other, each more destructive than its predecessor. The damage began with a mere knocking over, then came superficial burns, then the clothes went, then the skin. There were seven shock waves before the blast itself finally hit, and when it did the true pointlessness of the game – which had been sort of hovering behind the whole experience in the way that true knowledge often hovers in dreams – finally revealed itself as all those I'd saved as well as those I hadn't got transformed instantaneously into white-on-black shadows against the nearest wall. And then of course the walls went too, which was the moment I awoke.

This town, I think, when I've taken a hit on my inhaler and brought my breathing under control, is getting to me.

I get up, pee, and as I flush the phone starts ringing. I walk back into the bedroom and pick it up.

'Hi Cooper.'

'Kelly?'

'I hope I didn't wake you up.' Cold as ice.

'No, not at all. I've been up a while.'

'Oh, good. Well anyway, I just called to let you know your father's ashes have turned up. I've got them here at the house. They're waiting for you.'

'Oh. Great.' I surprise myself by how nonchalant I sound. 'I'll be there in an hour.'

I shower and pull on some clothes, and hoping I don't bump into Liz I slip out through the Tomsk-43 reception, say a quick good morning to Lucille and walk down to the local Denny's to get breakfast, picking up a copy of the *Atomic Bugle* from one of those newspaper dispensers they have everywhere on the way. I'm just sitting there perusing it while tucking into the Early-bird Critical Pile – short stack, two eggs, bacon, hash browns, bottomless coffee, $3.99 – when what should materialize right outside my window but the bull bars of Nick Lemery's Subaru. He is not alone – with him is a big black bloke dressed in chinos, Hush Puppies and a red plaid shirt.

While they walk round to the entrance I prepare to look relaxed; for some reason, I've no idea why, my heart is pounding.

'Mind if we join you?'

'Be my guest.' I motion for them to slide their way around the other side of the semicircular banquette that curls around the table, though right now another round with Lemery's the last thing I want.

'We're not disturbing you?'

'Me?' I fold up the paper. 'No, not at all. In fact, it's quite reassuring to know you're still following me around.'

Lemery chews his lip. 'Actually, I'm not. Not any more. The woman at the reception in your motel said we might find you here.'

'Three cheers for Neighbourhood Watch,' I say, extending my hand to the newcomer. 'Hi. My name's Cooper.'

He shakes. 'Hello. Ken.'

'Hi Ken.'

'Hi.'

Ken is tall and quite imposing-looking with the same goatee beard and dead man's stare as Eriq LaSalle.

'Ken's a helicopter pilot,' says Lemery. 'He's someone I wanted you to meet.'

'Someone else.'

'That's right.'

'I met Bill you know, last night.'

'I know.'

'I thought you might.'

'And he told you about the importation?'

'He did. But I don't see what it's got to do with anything.'

The waitress comes over; Ken and Lemery order coffee. She brings two cups, fills them. Lemery primes his with creamer and lots of sugar, Ken just sips his neat.

'Poor Bill. He never did quite work it out,' Lemery says, stirring in a second sachet of white refined. 'See, among all the nine zillion pieces of paperwork he and Jack had to fill out to get the things shipped over was a document concerning the appointment of a Radiation Safety Officer, someone who'd be responsible for the safety of the assemblies when they finally arrived. Normally several people on shift rotation would do this job, but of course Jack didn't have the money to employ a team like that. So he put down his own name for RSO.'

I shovel a mouthful of pancake into my mouth. 'So?'

'Well, the RSO has to be within twenty miles of whatever he or she's responsible for at all times, in case there's an emergency or a leak or something. Which meant that once the assemblies were here Jack couldn't leave Atomville. Not unless he wanted to break the law and lose his legal rights of ownership.'

'Couldn't he apply for some kind of waiver? Get people to stand in for him temporarily?'

'He could, and did. But they always found some excuse to turn him down. It was their way of punishing him for crossing them.'

'But the assemblies were being held in proxy storage anyway. Surely it was just a technicality? They wouldn't've enforced it.'

'Technicality schmecknicality. One Friday, after he finished the importation, we got in Jack's truck, planning on driving over to Seattle to celebrate with some of his old artist friends. We were headed west on the highway, not far past the Eagle Mountain turn, when a cop from the Atomic Patrol pulled us over. We thought a brake light must be out or something, but he took down Jack's details and verified who he was, then told us . . .' Lemery pauses to pull a pair of frameless supermarket spectacles and a folded sheet of official-looking paper from the pocket of his battered purple bodywarmer, '. . . and I quote: "that the holder of Radioactive Materials License WN–10407–1 shall at all times make him- or herself available within a twenty-mile radius of the above specified radioactive material(s) in order that she or he be available for emergency-evacuation procedure coordination of local population in the event of leak, spill or any containment violation as specified in WAC 246–273 'Emergency Evacuation Procedures', paragraph 13, subsection 3, either in person or in the form of a qualified and authorized substitute, to be authorized at least one brackets one month in advance according to the procedure specified in WAC 246–281 'Radiation Safety Officer Procedures: Delegation'." See? Clear as mud.'

I lick my lips and nothing happens. My last bite of pancake's turned to sawdust in my mouth. I can't seem to swallow.

'So what you're saying is . . .'

'When they realized they couldn't stop him doing the importation they fixed it so it turned into a kind of trap.'

Okay. It's going to take me a minute or two to get my head round this. And I'm feeling short of breath again. Short of breath and frightened, suddenly. Frightened enough for my bowels to loosen and a cold violent tingling to start up in my hands and feet.

'What do you mean, a trap?'

'Just that! A trap! He couldn't leave Atomville without losing everything he'd worked for. Which might've been okay if then they hadn't started persecuting him, making it impossible for him to stay. But that's where Ken comes in. Right Ken?'

Ken clears his throat. 'Right,' he says. He looks very serious.

'Ken works for one of the security operations here,' says Lemery. 'He's a helicopter pilot. Armed patrol, emergency rescue, that kind of thing.'

Ken allows himself a grin. 'Or that's the theory. But it's not what I spend most of my time doing.'

'So what's that then?' I ask, putting down my fork and pushing away my half-eaten meal.

Ken looks at Lemery, Lemery looks at Ken, Lemery nods. 'Hunting coyotes,' Ken says, pronouncing it the American way, without sounding the 'e'.

Not sure how I'm supposed to respond to this, I say nothing.

'Look,' says Lemery impatiently, 'back in the forties and the fifties the scientists just didn't know what to do with all the radioactive sludge and shit that came out of their production plants. So what they did was, they dug these big trenches out in the scablands, lined them with concrete, filled them up with liquid effluent and capped them off. But only the sides and lids were concrete. Not the bases. The idea was the waste would react with the dirt, form mineral salts and hold itself there in suspension. But of course, as any schoolchild could've told them, it didn't really work – the crud just kept on leaking down toward the water table. They were designed so that the effluent would seep out from under the sides and form mineral salts and to some extent they did that. And the mineral salts that did form, well they caused another problem.

'The animals that live out in the desert, they need mineral salts to survive. It's like why you put a salt lick out for cows. You just gotta have it. And we have this one animal out here in the reservation which is kind of a desert badger. It's just a little bigger than a raccoon and it's got a long bushy tail and these big old claws and it's a mean burrower. And these badgers, what they do is tunnel down beside the concrete and lick up the salts from where they've been leaching out from the bottom. Doesn't take long, of course, for them to get sick and die. And so pretty soon you've got a bunch of deep burrows tracked through with radioactivity with a bunch of badgers laying around at the bottom of them, very dead.

'Next thing you know the jack rabbits arrive. These guys, they don't miss a trick. It doesn't take them long to figure out here's a whole heap of prime real estate lying empty. So they move right on in, start a family. Or at least they try. But they don't get too far before they're not feeling too great either. Give them a month or two and they're wandering round the desert in a daze, their nervous systems all shot away with metastasizing cancers. And that's where our friend the coyote comes in.

'For him, it's Christmas. Here are a whole bunch of rabbits stumbling around in the cheat grass, too sick to run. So he just cleans up and lays back in the sun patting his belly. But soon he's thinking: "Hey, you know, I don't feel so good." Which is not surprising, since by now there's all this plutonium headed for his long bones and his brain, because that's what plutonium does. From then on thinking anything gets kind of difficult, which it would for you if you had a lump the size of an orange in your skull. But he's still aware enough to know that something's out to get him so he does what his instinct tells him to and starts off running. Fast as he can he runs away, over the hills and far away – coyotes can cover a whole lot of ground when they really want to. In fact they migrate. Not many people know that, but it's true. Of course, normally, they keep well out of us humans' way. But with big tumours clogging up their brains they forget to do that, and next thing you know you've got Mr Coyote leaving a trail of plutonium-laced coyote shit right down Main Street, USA, at least until he gets hit by a truck and torn apart by the neighbourhood cats who go home and cuddle up next to little Jane and Johnny. You get the picture?'

'Fine,' I say, trying to ignore the churning in my stomach. 'But I still don't see the problem. Put a fence around the trenches, spend some of the 30-billion-dollar clean-up budget on draining them out and cleaning them up. End of story.'

'Oh yeah,' Lemery scoffs. 'Simple. Apart from, some of these trenches they've actually lost. They got covered over with sand and Russian thistle and general desert crud and now they don't even know any longer where they are. Hey, it was twenty years ago, you can't expect anyone to keep records all that time! That's like back into the Stone Age! So no, they don't clean them up. What they do is . . . well, you tell him, Ken.'

Ken reaches over to the dish of condiments, snags a sachet of Sweet'n'Low, tears the paper open and pours the white powder out onto the place mat in front of him, watching it intently all the while. 'What they do is, a couple of times a week, dawn or evening is the best time, they have me take the chopper out, couple of guys with rifles in the back there, and we go hunting.' All his gravitas is gone; he looks and sounds like a guilty schoolboy.

'You go out and shoot the coyotes? From a helicopter?'

'Round here it's kind of a perk.'

'A *perk*?'

'Yeah. It's only the high-up guys, the top agents and department heads and stuff, it's only them who get to come ride shotgun. They take it in turns, bring guests, they even have a little competition going – trophies, the whole deal. For them it's one big kick, high-octane fun. And one of the guys who comes with me most often is Todd Trevisan.'

I knew it before he said it. The statuettes in Todd's basement bunker. Not dogs. Coyotes.

'Todd?'

'You know him, right?' he says, looking up, recovering some dignity. 'Nick said you knew him.'

'Yeah. I know him.'

'Did he tell you what he does?'

'He said he couldn't. Q-clearance.'

'Right enough. Well Todd's security – same as me, but higher up. And part of what he does is training. He's a trainer, trains agents basically. That's Todd's gig. These CIA and FBI recruits come in, one of the things they need to learn is covert operations. You can't teach that in a classroom. You have to send them out in the world, have them practise on real people. Stake out the house, take photographs, put in phone taps, that kind of thing. So most times Todd comes out hunting with other colleagues, trainees, whatever. But this one time, not long after your father had done his importation, he comes with this guy from Washington, someone who he's trying to impress. But the guy is not impressed. Not at all. Certainly not by Todd's tacky hunting trip – he couldn't give a shit. He's after bigger game: the chance to put the screws on Todd, for starters. He waits till we're up in the air and flying and then he says – and I can hear him loud and clear, over the intercom – he says, "So Todd, what you gonna do about this artist?" '

'And clearly they're talking about Jack,' Lemery interjects, 'I mean, there aren't exactly a whole lot of artists living in Atomville; your father was kind of a local celebrity, a little bit. Sorry Ken. Go on.'

'And Todd says: "Well, it's difficult. I mean, he's kind of a friend of my wife's." And the guy says: "So don't tell your wife. Just get rid of him. Scare him off. Get him out of Atomville. I don't care how you do it, just get it done." '

'But Todd was renting Jack his studio, right?'

'Right, exactly,' says Lemery. 'But he did that as a favour to Cathy before Jack imported the assemblies, back at the stage when no one conceived the possibility of him actually pulling off anything like that. But now things have got out of hand and Todd's running scared, because if this guy figures out he's actually helping to house this thorn in the side of the DoE, he's out of a job.'

'So what did he do?'

'What didn't he do, is more like it. He roped in a couple of his lesser-brained trainees, told them to go do some basic psy-ops stuff – break into Jack's place, move stuff around, tap his phone in an obvious fashion, follow him around. "Disorientate and demoralize" is what they call it. Which is what they did. Except of course Jack couldn't leave. Not unless he wanted to lose the assemblies and spend a spell in jail into the bargain. So they upped the stakes. Got enthusiastic. First they stole The Herm. And then . . .'

'And then they killed his dog,' says Ken.

'Thoth?' I say weakly. A horrible thought is beginning to form behind my right ear. I feel it physically, immediately, a violent pain in my cranium, like someone's trying to trepan me with a laser mounted on a satellite five miles up in space.

'Yup.' Lemery. 'Poisoned him. It was about the worst thing they could've done. That dog was the nearest thing Jack had to . . .' The farmer stops himself just in time but he can't hide his embarrassment. 'Man, he loved that dog,' he continues, a little more quietly. 'It was old as Beelzebub and so bad with arthritis it could hardly make the trip across the room to reach its water bowl, but the two of them had been together for years – ever since Jack's time in Graniteburg. It kinda sent the guy to pieces. He got in some supplies, a gun, barricaded himself into the studio and waited for them to come for him . . .'

'Shit,' I say. 'Holy shit.' The pain in my head has become almost unbearably intense. I force air into my lungs, brace myself against a rush of panic. My hands have gone completely numb with pins and needles; the world is bending in around me. I feel nauseous, dizzy, my legs have gone to sleep. 'What're you saying? That they couldn't scare Jack off so they tried to burn him out?'

'I'm not saying that they tried,' hisses Lemery. 'I'm saying they succeeded.'

'You can't just go around making those kinds of accusation,' I protest. 'Where's the proof?'

He doesn't blink. 'Stashed under a tarpaulin in Todd's garage. That's where. Plain for all to see.'

That's it. Without another word I run for the restrooms, lock myself into a cubicle and sit down on the toilet lid. Double over, grab my ankles, put my head between my knees. Try to breathe. It doesn't work. My lungs are filling up with sand, my heart's vibrating like a fire bell, I'm starting to shake. Panic is taking hold of me. I pull my inhaler from the pocket of my jeans, fumble it, send it skidding across the floor and into the next cubicle, then spin around and lift the toilet lid and vomit up my breakfast in a series of jerking, inverse gulps.

By the time I get back to the table Ken is gone and Lemery is waiting with refilled cup of coffee and a plan.

The plan is more than averagely insane.

'You want to take back The Herm and transport it out into the Areas?'

'Yes.'

'Why?'

'It's what Jack would've wanted.'

We're standing out in the Denny's parking lot by the Subaru, which I now see has been fitted with a serious-looking hoist. 'It is?'

'Look – what do you think he wanted to do with those assemblies once he got them?'

'I dunno. Bill said he didn't want to do anything – that importing them was an end in itself.'

Lemery shakes his head. 'No, that's all crap. That's just one of the stories Jack threw up as a smokescreen.'

'Then maybe he wanted to transmute them in the MOTA, make them harmless?'

'That wouldn't have worked. Apart from the fact that they'd already turned down his application to do a transmutation, the MOTA can't handle anything that large – it struggles with anything much bigger than your thumb. They'd have had to build a reactor specially, and even then it would be pointless – the fuel rods were full of depleted uranium, which isn't even all that radioactive.

'No. What he actually wanted to do was encase them in granite and use them to build a monument, a nuclear Stonehenge, right over there in the middle of the Areas where they've poured all that shit into the soil.'

'Another warning marker?'

'Yeah, but it was more than that. It was a spell, an alchemical spell. It was to be like a new citadel, see, placed at the heart of the old one, and designed to short-circuit and transform its power.'

'And how was that supposed to work?'

'Hey, search me, I don't understand these things – Jack was the magician. He tried to talk me through it on a few occasions but it was way beyond my limited comprehension. But that's what he wanted.'

'And? You think dumping The Herm out there will be some kind of miniature version of this spell?'

'Something like that.'

'You're crazy. And in any case, how're you going to get it there? It's only like the most secure piece of desert on the planet.'

Lemery grins, removes his cap, wipes his brow. 'That's where Ken comes in.'

'What? You're going to get him to fly it out there with his helicopter?' I scoff. I'm joking, naturally.

'Yup.'

Oh. 'And how're you going to convince him to do that?'

'He's already agreed. In fact, it was his idea.'

I'm surrounded by lunatics. It's official. 'He'll lose his job.'

'It's lost anyway, once news gets back that he's been seen here in Denny's talking with you and me.'

'You mean . . . ?'

'Right. We have to do this now. Today.'

I consider this for a moment. 'And what if I don't agree?' I say.

'Well, that's up to you. Just so long as you realize that Ken'll lose his job in any case and your father will be denied his proper final resting place.'

'Er . . . how so, exactly?'

'The Herm. It's hollow. It was originally designed to store a piece of transmuted waste. Except there is no transmuted waste.'

'So?'

'So Jack redesigned it to take something else.'

'What?'

'I think you know.'

I turn away from Lemery for a moment, stare across the hot hood of the Subaru at the cars cruising past on Oppenheimer Way. There's something inexorable about the logic of all this, something that's impossible to resist. For that reason alone I feel like I ought to say no, enough, no more. But I don't. I'm too tired. I want it to be over. So I do what I always do. I give in. I mean, what difference does it make? It's no madder than anything else that has happened to me in the last few weeks.

'Okay.'

'Okay? You're sure?'

'Yes, I'm sure. You can do it. You have my permission.'

'I hoped you'd say that. Thank you.'

'Don't mention it.'

'So where are they now?'

'The ashes? At Todd's, funnily enough.'

'So what're we waiting for? Let's go.'

'Alright,' I say. But as I pull open the passenger door and climb into the front seat of the pickup truck I certainly don't feel it.

'So why, anyway?' I ask as we roll north-east towards the Trevisans' place, keen to talk about anything except my father's final days. 'Why you and Jack? How come you ended up being such good friends?'

'Oh, that,' says Lemery, changing up to fourth. 'I make it my business to get to know everyone round here. I'm in the protest racket, see.'

'But why do you care so much? No one else does.'

'Yeah, well, I'm not your politically motivated protestor, driven by high ideals. For me it's really simple. For me it's personal.'

I watch the road, guessing that if I wait he'll tell me why.

He does. 'It's like this. I was born in '47. I had an older brother born the year before, born deformed and dead. Me, I popped out the following year, also deformed but basically alive. I've had major surgery, I've had cancers, I've had boils, sores all over. My thyroid is all screwed up, I've been on thyroid medication, I was in and out of hospital as a kid with what I now know was radiation sickness but what back then we always called the 'flu. I was in the hospital in an iron lung in the special unit where they would bring the workers that got burned or crapped up – before they built the Paracelsus Medical Center they would bring the workers over to my hospital in the next county so they didn't show up on Atomville's health stats. I was on that floor for eight months in the iron lung and I'd watch 'em bring these workers in and a few days later wheel 'em out with the sheets up over their faces.

'And not only workers but kids were also dying. We had a lot of kids dying on that ward. Found out later that paralysis can be induced by massive thyroid failure and we had a whole floor full of kids with that. Thought for a long time it might be the pesticides that were being introduced, us farmers having used so much of that shit we've messed up the Chiawana good and proper, over and above what the nukers have almost. So we thought it might be the pesticides. But there was no proper data, and after a long time spent looking I decided to do my own piece of research on this, find out for myself.'

'Why didn't you just move away?'

'Good point. Why didn't I? I mean, that's what any sensible person would've done. But I'm not sensible, never have been, always been as stubborn as they come. Who knows, maybe that's part of the damage they did to me. Brain damage. So I didn't move away. Instead what I did was go walkabout to a whole bunch of other farming communities just like ours round here, communities where they use the exact same rigs and sprays we do. And what I found was they haven't suffered anything like a fifth as much as we have. See, you've got the ionizing radiation, you've got the pesticides, you've got the caesium in the water, you've got the iodine-131 in the water too, okay? And it's all in a bowl, what we call the Chiawana Bowl, this big depression formed by the glacial scablands the other side of Eagle Mountain. And all that shit, it settles right into that depression, and it's the young that get hit first. You remember your graduating class in high school?'

I look at him, away from the red Pontiac Firebird I've been watching hover towards us like something out of a Sega pre-gameplay montage. 'What?'

'The kids you went to school with. How many of those kids are dead?'

I think of Jake and Max, of Otter, little Leaf and Jaycey. What ever happened to them? Why did I never bother to keep in touch? 'No idea.'

'Make a guess.'

'I dunno, really. Maybe one or two.'

'Right – traffic accidents, suicides, the normal attrition rate for humans. The class I graduated from – and this was a local school, in an area where people stick around while they grow up, so I know – had twenty-seven kids in it, and not just local kids – a lot of them were the sons and daughters of military personnel, brought in here from all over the nation, people of indiscriminately mixed genetics, in other words. The only thing we had in common was the food we ate and the milk we drank and the air we breathed. And of those twenty-seven kids, exactly one half of them are dead. Now, today. One half. And from heart trouble and cancer mostly, hardly any accidents. At school, kids were always having nosebleeds and most of us had polyps in the backs of our throats. I remember some – Tammy Rider and Sandy Kelpster and Maggie Bean – they were good girls, they're all dead. They were the ones that ate their vegetables, drank their milk. Us bad-ass little boys who snuck bags of Planters Peanuts and cans of Pepsi instead of having fresh stuff for lunch like we were supposed to, who ate Twinkies and bananas and Babe Ruth candy bars meaning that we didn't get as much of the local produce in our systems like the others did, we made it through.'

I should feel sympathy, I really should, but I've heard all this before. We get it all the time at Featherbrooks, though there it's microwave radiation they all harp on about. I know it would be better just to agree with Lemery, to let it ride, but I can't help myself. 'It seems like a lot of effects to come out of the stuff that's in the soil in the Areas,' I say. 'And at least now the problem's being acknowledged. At least now they're doing this big clean-up.'

Lemery looks at me like I'm something he's found clinging to the sole of one of his rubber boots. 'Sure, Cooper. That's right. You're absolutely right. Look how responsible they are. "Oh, look at us, we made a mess but hand on heart we admit it, give us 30 billion bucks, we'll clear it up." Sure. Give *me* 30 billion, *I* could clear it up, and a whole lot faster. They've already spent 2 billion, just shuffling paper. Not to mention . . . and well, whatever. It's too late now. Heads up. We're here.'

The Ashes Return

Lemery has parked some way down the street from Todd and Cathy's house; through the windscreen I can just see Todd's SUV squatting in the driveway. I get out and walk up to the house and ring the bell. There's a short lull and then Kelly swings open the door.

Face to face for the first time since the other night, I'm not sure which of us is the more embarrassed. In the end it's she who breaks the awful silence. 'Cooper? Are you okay? You look awful.'

'I'm fine,' I say, and without waiting to be invited I walk straight past her and through into the living room. The package is sitting on the coffee table; it's large and square and it's plastered in security stickers and clearly didn't come by normal post.

'You should have seen the forms they made me sign when it arrived,' she says.

'You got a knife?'

'You want to open it?'

'There's something I want to check.'

She fetches me a utility knife from the kitchen and I carve into the package, extract the coffee canister and pop the lid. It strikes me once again how heavy it is, how carefully it's been reinforced with an extra layer of sheet metal inside, not just on the sides but on the bottom too. Opening out a copy of the *Atomic Bugle* that's lying nearby, I tip the contents of the canister out onto it, into a little heap. Then I start sifting through the dust and debris with my fingers while my host looks on in vague disgust.

'What are you doing?'

'Looking for something.'

'What?'

'I don't know, till I find it.'

I carry on sifting for a while. There's all sorts of crap in here. Lots of grey dust for sure, but also bits of charcoal, various porous chunks of what I guess is bone, strands of wire, a couple of fragments of white porcelain, a bit of molten plastic, a tiny screw, all mixed up in a heavy granular particulate that has a kind of reddish or ochre tint. If Lemery really scraped all this up off the floor like he said he did, then God only knows how much of it is Jack.

'Palaeontology,' I say suddenly. 'That means you look a lot at bones, right?'

'I guess,' she says. She's sitting on the white leather sofa opposite, flipping through a copy of *Cosmopolitan*, pretending to ignore me.

'Here,' I say, rolling one of the larger chunks of matter free and carrying it over. 'What does this look like to you?'

'Well, it's a fragment of bone, Cooper. Please put it away.'

But I don't put it away. Instead I hold it out to her. 'Can you take a proper look? Please? Can you tell me if it's definitely human?'

The question's weird enough to kick-start the academic portion of her brain and with an 'okay, I'm going to humour you' expression she stops freaking out, takes the bone gingerly between thumb and forefinger and moves over to the window where there's better light.

'It's difficult to be sure,' she says. 'I mean, I thought it was maybe a knuckle or something. But now I'm not so sure. I think it's more likely a leg joint of some kind. From a coyote maybe. Or a dog.'

'A dog?'

She nods. 'Yeah, maybe. It doesn't look human, anyway. The human skeleton's the only one I really know, and I can't fit this in anywhere.' She shudders and hands the nugget back, nerd retreating, girl returning to the fore. 'How'd that get mixed up with . . . with the rest of it?'

'I don't know,' I say, pouring the ashes back into the canister and sealing up the lid. 'But I've got a pretty good idea who might.'

'Who?'

I jerk my head backwards in the direction of the French doors at the far end of the room, through which a shadowy figure can be seen moving across the deck.

'Todd?'

'Yeah. Todd.'

I'm out on the deck again, with Todd and his interstellar barbecue; he's planning on searing some fresh tuna steaks for lunch. Kelly's done her usual trick of bringing us some Cokes and then disappearing back into the house, though on this occasion I think it's because she senses something unpleasant is about to happen. She might just be right. Beyond the lawn the river glitters. The day is pushing onwards and it's getting hot, hot enough that my hands are starting to itch.

'Long way from the sea,' I say, 'to get fresh fish.'

'I know a guy. Once a week he has it flown in express delivery. On ice.'

Using a specialized-looking wire brush, Todd's brushing stubborn charred flesh residue from a heat fin. It's an intricate operation.

'I hear you've been hanging with Nick Lemery,' he says.

This throws me off my stride. 'How d'you know?'

'It's my job to know.' Todd stops brushing, blows some debris free, brushes again, blows again, then begins to fit the fin back into its position. 'I don't mean to pry, Cooper,' he says. 'I apologize if it seems that way. But you've got to watch out for Lemery. He's been causing problems round here for years. He's an extremely unstable personality.'

'You think he's bad, you should meet my mother.'

'I'm serious. This isn't a joke. Lemery's a listed security threat.'

'So was Jack, from what I hear.'

Now the heat fin's fixed Todd is trying to reposition the grill plate but it won't clip back into its allotted place. Unable to find the fit he's trying to force it and the effort's making him sweat. Suddenly it shears sideways and catches his thumb, slicing a triangular lid of skin from the tip.

'Darn!' he says, and just manages to stop himself from giving the barbecue a kick. Blood wells up from the wound and drips expensively down onto the decking. 'Kelly!' he yells. 'Can you bring me some Band-Aids out here?'

He sucks the thumb, then wraps it in the rag he's been using to wipe his hands. The rag quickly turns red. My own hands are itching more and more and also turning red, though I doubt it's out of sympathy. And I don't think it's the heat. I must've got something on them in the toilet. Bleach, maybe. It's either that or nervous tension.

'What did he tell you anyway?' Todd snaps, making no attempt to hide his irritation. 'Lemery.'

'That he's had his life ruined by the pollution from your reactors.'

'Screw that. It's all bullshit, you know. He's been trying to bring a case against the DoE for years. But he hasn't got a leg to stand on.'

I shrug. 'That's not how it looked to me.'

'What d'you mean, that's not how it looked? You think that one meeting on a mountain with a crackpot puts you in a position to judge?'

What, do they have CCTV cameras hidden in the stones up there? 'He showed me documentation,' I lie. 'It looked pretty open and shut.'

'I suppose he didn't tell you that half the people round here have already *received* compensation for any health difficulty they might have had any time in the last forty years, whether it's related to the Areas or not. Lemery's whole problem is that he didn't get any of it, that's all. And didn't deserve it, either.'

'Why not? Wasn't he affected?'

'Did he look ill to you?'

He didn't, but I've no intention of admitting it. And I don't have to because at that moment Kelly appears, clutching a large and professional-looking medical kit which she unzips and opens out on the picnic table, revealing enough gear to equip a small ER. Unwrapping the rag from Todd's thumb she examines the cut, winces sympathetically, then sluices it with iodine. 'The only part of Lemery that was affected by anything was his brain,' says Todd, gripping the thumb around its base with the fingers of his good hand in an attempt to stem the flow of blood. 'The man's an idiot.'

My hands are so hot they're like an alpha source, radiating waves of anger and frustration. I should confront him now, while he's at a disadvantage. And while Kelly's here – I could use a witness. But my nerves have all iced over and my heart is racing and I prevaricate by picking up the rogue grill plate and slotting it into place. 'You had it the wrong way round,' I say, half to myself. And then I lose my temper.

'Jesus Christ! Don't you get it? Lemery is not the point! Why didn't you tell me about Jack and the assemblies, Todd? Why not? Or the monument he wanted to build. How come you and Cathy forgot to mention that? And what about poisoning his dog? And setting fire to his studio? With him inside? What about that, *Todd*? Or was that just bad shit that happened in the past?'

'Now wait a minute . . .'

'Cooper, how dare you!' Kelly bursts out. 'Since you got here my parents have shown you nothing but kindness, generosity . . .'

'They've shown me nothing, Kelly. They've shown me a PR exercise. Ever since I got to Atomville all I've heard is spin and half-truths.'

'That's not true . . .'

'Oh no? And I suppose you're also going to tell me that it's not true that you didn't bump into me at the fayre by accident, that your mother didn't ask you to come over and talk to me, get acquainted, get her an introduction, without letting on you all already knew perfectly well who I was. Aren't you?' Kelly gulps air at this, looking for all the world like the blind fish in the Tomsk-43 reception. 'Why don't you ask your stepfather what he's got hidden in the garage, Kelly? Go on. Ask him.'

But Kelly doesn't answer, just throws down the medical kit and runs into the house.

'You asshole,' Todd says, when she's gone.

'What's in the garage, Todd?'

'I don't know what . . .'

'Why don't you show me what you've got hidden in the garage? Come on. You know what I mean.'

Todd stares at me with murder in his eyes and lips white as the spittle gathering in their corners. Then he gets up and walks into the house. I follow warily, assuming he's showing me the door. But he isn't – what he's doing is exactly what I've asked.

The garage is spacious and very organized. Shelves of tools and DIY equipment line one wall. There are three parking bays, one of which is occupied by a silver TVR sports car, but there's still room enough for a full-sized ping-pong table, a large white freezer, a work bench and a man-sized object with a tarpaulin draped over it. A ghost.

It's by this that Todd is crouching, unknotting the rope laced through the metal eyelets in the hem. Once it's loose he pulls the shroud away, causing the material to give off a sharp, whining screech as it rides against the granite underneath.

'There it is,' he says.

And there it is indeed.

The Herm stands a little under six feet tall from pedestal to crown. Its five-foot frustum sits on a three-inch base and shoulders up to a stylized carving of a horse's skull, the focus of the piece. The skull sits imperiously in its high stone collar, its raking angles dropping backwards into eye sockets that look almost like they've been carved to take fitted wooden dowels. The contours and surfaces are smooth and delicate; the teeth are bared and toothlike. It has an animated air about it, like it's not a solid thing at all but a costume with someone hiding inside of it, some kind of shaman or high priest. It's how you imagine Death would dress for his attendance at the feast.

'You see how it's gotten blackened all over like that? Well that happened in the fire. I didn't *steal* it. I took it after, for safekeeping.'

'Which is why you told me it had been nicked by neighbourhood kids?'

Todd flushes now, and hard. 'Yeah, well, I didn't really trust you then.'

'You didn't really trust me? *What the fuck was there to trust*? I'm his fucking *son.*' I'm so blocked with anger I can hardly think. 'And you fucking killed him.'

'No I didn't. I did not. It's not what you think – I wasn't even there. And my people didn't start that fire . . .'

'Fuck off Todd. Don't . . . don't waste your breath. Does this thing open the door?' I point to an industrial-looking rubber button mounted on the back wall not far from where I'm standing, and when Todd doesn't answer I reach over and give it a punch. Sure enough, electric motors whirr into life and the steel sections of the door start slowly upwards, letting desert air blurt in. When the gap has widened sufficiently I walk down through the empty bay, down the drive and out into the street where I give Lemery the signal to move in.

By the time we've got the Subaru backed up to the garage Todd has disappeared. With me guiding him, Lemery eases his vehicle alongside the TVR. He's just about got it into position when Todd returns with a rifle held across his chest. Immediately Lemery kills the engine and all is quiet.

'And just what in hell do you think you're going to do with that?' Todd says, gesturing at the pickup truck with the gun stock.

'Take back what's mine,' I say.

'Oh no you're not.'

'Oh yes I am.'

'Well then I'm going to shoot you, for threatening my property.'

'*Your* property?'

'Yes, mine. That sculpture counts as collateral on my studio. It's my property and no one's gonna take it from me.'

'Let it go, Todd.'

Another voice, coming from behind the Subaru. Cathy. Hands on hips, she strolls into the garage looking as relaxed as if she'd just found us all sitting round chatting over a cup of tea.

'Please tell Todd to put down the gun,' I say.

'Todd, put the gun *down*.'

'But honey . . .'

'But nothing. You're not going to use it, so put it away.'

Looking like a child who's been told to switch off his video console and go and give Granny a kiss, Todd leans the rifle against the wall. Instantly Lemery switches on the engine and starts to operate the hoist.

Todd moves forward to protest but Cathy holds a hand out, stops him. 'Let them take it. C'mon. It belongs to Cooper really. You know it does.'

'I dunno. Jack cost me a whole bunch of money . . .'

'Todd, enough. We'll discuss this later.'

For a moment everyone stands around looking foolish, disarmed by the speed with which Cathy's defused the situation. But I'm not done yet.

'It was all an act, wasn't it? The fayre, Kelly flirting with me, everything. You knew I was coming all along.'

'We heard something about it, yes.'

Fioravanti. I knew it was a mistake, taking a pop at him like that. 'So you set me up.'

'We didn't set up anything. We decided to be friendly, that was all. The fact that we had some warning you might be coming is irrelevant.'

'So it's okay for you to lie to me, is what you're saying.'

'I think you're overreacting.'

'Overreacting! Your husband steals my father's work, your daughter pretends to flirt with me . . .'

I'm close to tears and Cathy sees it. She moves towards me, shouts my name, puts a hand out and grips my shoulder. 'Cooper! Cooper! Calm down. Calm down a minute.'

'I am calm!' I shout back, assuming she's going to contradict me yet again. 'Can't you even listen?'

'No – wait, you don't . . . it's your hands. What's wrong with your hands? There's something wrong with them. Are they okay?'

Confused by her concern, I break off from my litany of crimes to examine them. In the face of so much bullshit I'd forgotten the redness and the itching. But now, all along the palms and fingers I see the skin's begun to blister.

'I dunno,' I say dully. 'Maybe it's sunburn.'

'Doesn't look like it. Have you been in the garden?'

'No – I didn't leave the deck. Why?'

'I thought it might be poison oak.'

I run the events of the morning through my mind, wonder momentarily and slightly stupidly if it might've been something I ate in Denny's. And then I realize what it is.

'Lemery, you fucking moron,' I say through tears. 'When you scraped those ashes up you didn't get Jack! All you got was what was left of Thoth and a pile of fucking extract of Fiestaware! They're radioactive! That's why they got confiscated at Logan. They should've bloody kept them!'

Lemery looks over from where he's making the final adjustments to the chain cradle he's rigged up round The Herm and smirks pathetically. 'Sorry Coops.'

'Sorry!? Look at my fucking hands!'

'I think we'd better get you to the hospital,' Cathy interrupts.

'You'd better take the ashes too,' Todd adds quickly. 'They'll need to analyse them.'

'No! The ashes go with him. Do you think you can manage that, Lemery? The canister's on the coffee table in the living room.'

'Sure. I'll take good care of it.'

'You'd better. Assuming there's anything of Jack left in it at all.'

For the first six or seven minutes me and Cathy drive in silence. I'm waiting for her to apologize, explain, something. But she says nothing. So in the end it's me who speaks.

'You are aware,' I say, 'that your husband's a fucking psychopath? That it was him – or whoever takes his orders – who set the fire? That it wasn't an accident?'

'I'm afraid it was. No one meant for it to happen.'

'I don't believe you. I think they tried to harass Jack out of Atomville, and when that didn't work they tried to burn him out.

Except they didn't count on him being stubborn enough to refuse to budge even when they'd turned his home into a bonfire.'

'That's just not true. I refuse to believe that Todd would ever sanction anything like that.'

'Then who did? Jack? You think he set the place alight himself? But I thought you didn't think him capable of suicide. Not unless you drove him crazy first by using the assemblies to trap him here in Atomville and then trying to run him out of town. I mean, how's that for a catch-22?'

'Cooper, look, I just don't know, okay? I honestly don't know. You have to understand that I regret Jack's death as much as anyone – he was a close friend, really . . .'

I bark out a sardonic laugh. 'Fuck, I'd hate to be your enemy.'

'. . . and we told him time and again it was madness to go ahead with the importation of the assemblies. We knew the DoE would find someway to stop him getting away with it; he was never going to win. And as for the idea that we – whoever "we" might be – had some kind of coordinated plan to get him to commit suicide – *that's* what's crazy. You're talking about different operations, sourced from offices thousands of miles apart, not communicating, pursuing different aims. It wasn't a coordinated thing. And this whole saga about him not being able to leave town, it wasn't as bad as Mr Lemery has no doubt made it sound. It might have been technically the case, but it was hardly like if he had gone to Seattle for the weekend he would've been arrested. They might have stuck him in a cell for a day or two, long enough to give them an excuse to formally divest him of his rights to legal ownership, but that would've been the worst of it.'

'That's still plenty, if you ask me.'

She waves her arm dismissively. 'He'd gone through much the same thing at Salt Mountain, he told me so himself. He knew the score. And even if he'd held onto the assemblies he was never in a million years going to be allowed to build the monument he wanted.'

'How d'you know about that?' I snap, furious that Cathy's out-playing me.

'Because he told me! Jack couldn't keep a secret for five minutes, except maybe from Bill Valentine, who's anyway incapable of imagining that anyone might ever have something to hide. Forget that the projected budget was in the region of ten million dollars, an impossible amount of money for him to raise. Even if he had by some miracle gotten hold of something approaching that kind of sum, he'd still have needed the DoE to grant him a patch of land out in the Areas on which to build the thing. And even if it'd wanted to do that – which it absolutely didn't – it's simply not allowed. The government can't give up any land it owns without putting it out to tender, and most all the land out here is sacred to the Native Americans. The moment any of it came on the market they'd have a much better claim on it than Jack Reever ever could. It just wasn't going to happen.'

Cathy's incredible. I'd thought my position was unassailable but after just two minutes of sparring with her I can already feel my moral certainties beginning to ebb away. 'It might've done. Maybe he could've made some kind of agreement with one of the tribes or something.'

'Oh get real. It was politically unacceptable. The guys who run this place, they play hardball. Their first priority is the continuation of the industry, and they're just not going to let through anything that gets in the way of that. These people are extremely focused and extremely powerful. There's no way they'd let anyone like Jack come close to threatening them, not even for a minute. He was in way over his head, and he didn't know when to quit.'

'Exactly. So you tried to burn him out. To make him leave. Like you did to David fucking Koresh.'

'Listen, you can't lump me in with some FBI idiots who got trigger-happy five states away. Me or Todd. Todd's my husband.'

'Todd's a psychopath,' I say again, but this time around the term doesn't seem to carry so much weight.

'Well, you're entitled to your opinion.'

'He poisoned Jack's dog,' I say, aware now that I'm starting to sound petulant.

'No one *poisoned* it. It probably died of fright when those dumb recruits he sent over to give Jack a scare bust into the studio. It was about a hundred anyway. Get your head out of the sand, Cooper. Since 9/11 the political climate here has changed. The kind of thing Jack was up to, right now it can't be tolerated. It was the end of the road for his project. Todd was just trying to get him to move on before someone with a lot less sympathy turned up and arrested him on suspicion of nuclear terrorism.'

'Oh, I see. So you were doing him a favour.'

'I know it's hard to believe but that's right, we were. We were his *friends*, Cooper. Not Johnny-come-latelies like Nick Lemery, who no doubt hasn't told you of his long track record of problems with the truth, not to mention the law.'

'Please. This is bullshit. Save your breath. Really. I've heard enough.'

Cathy shrugs and says nothing and the lights turn green and we roll forwards and travel about a quarter of a mile down the highway.

'You know . . .'

I sigh loudly, turn to look out the window.

'. . . I was just going to say that this place we're going to, I don't know if you have health insurance, but if there are any bills Todd and I will pay, okay? It's the least we can do.'

'I don't want your help.'

'But we'd like to help.'

'It won't change anything.'

She laughs at this. 'You're a tough one, aren't you Cooper?'

'I didn't used to be,' I say, and then the sky-filled mirror windows of the Paracelsus Medical Center slide up on the right and we turn into an entrance bracketed by a lush, boxy hedge and a steel sign that says 'Emergency'.

Once we're in the building Cathy doesn't mess around. It takes her only seconds to marshal forces: a nurse here, a doctor there, access to a diagnostic suite, reservation of a private room. Exhausted by the events of the past couple of hours, I allow them all to push me here and there like a broken marionette.

The man who attends me is youthful, thirty-six maybe, with a head of cherubic blond curls which I see when he bends down to examine my hands are just starting to thin out at the pate. It's a radiation burn, he thinks, though it would be easier to know for sure if he could give the source material to the rad-team they have on site.

'This is Atomville,' he says, offended, when I tell him that I've sent the ashes off elsewhere. 'We have procedures for this kind of thing. It's not like we don't know what we're doing.' His attitude is patronizing, the way he wants me to feel like I'm in trouble, like I've been playing with fire and I've burnt myself and now the grown-ups have had to come and help clear up my mess. He has no idea. He doesn't understand a thing. But neither I nor Cathy bother to explain. What would be the point?

But what the hell, it doesn't matter. He soon leaves anyway and Cathy with him, and I'm left alone with a nurse who bandages my hands and puts me on a drip and makes me take a handful of pills which she says are painkillers and iodine. I'm sure I'm supposed to listen to her carefully but I'm feeling completely disassociated from what's going on. The nurse, the pills, the doctor – they all seem two-dimensional, like figures on a computer screen. Right now I can't be troubled with them, or with the ashes, or with anything in Atomville, not at all. My mind's busy with something else, something that I've never been able to reduce to any kind of logic, a problem I've never been able to solve. Something that happened to me a long, long time ago, the last time my hands felt like this. Though on that occasion it wasn't radiation burns. It was stinging nettles.

I started to tell you about it before, in fact, but I set up an escape route (which of course I took). I always set it up that way, and I always bail out before the telling. I always have done. But this time I'm not going to. This time I'm going to tell you – finally – the truth.

You see, it's not the case that I can't remember what happened after the horse ride at Stonehenge. I can remember perfectly. It's just that I never wanted to remember, that's all. Never wanted to let myself. Because what happened is this.

After we returned the horses we packed up the camper van and drove back down to the commune, maybe an hour and a half, two hours away. I think Stasie must have played a gig the previous evening and we'd travelled down and spent the night. But that bit I really can't remember and it's not important anyway. What is important is that we got back home around eight o'clock, had some dinner, spent a normal evening messing around doing nothing in particular and then went off to bed. And maybe it was too warm or something but anyway I couldn't sleep. I'd been on a bit of a high all day I think, getting Jack and Stasie all to myself like that, but being back in the commune and seeing Moon again had brought back the feelings of jealousy and now there I was in our room, tossing and turning in my little bed while all around me the other boys were fast asleep.

I'd had quite a few nights like this that summer, and my customary response was to slide my hand down the gap between my bed and the wall, flip open the loose skirting board and take out the bulla. And so this is what I did. I took it out, unfurled the leather thong, and examined the small bone in the half light. But I was bored of it now; the feelings of guilt my possession of it inspired far outweighed the meagre satisfaction I got from the fact of it being mine. So I wrapped it up again, put it back in my hiding place, and then pushed back my blankets and stood up on my bed, peeking out the little garret window that was let into the roof above my head to see what I could see. And what could I see? A light flickering out from the section of the barn that housed Jack's workshop, that's what.

Well, here at least was entertainment. Jack was up and doing something – fooling with his metalwork, most probably. Shoving my feet into my gym shoes I pulled on my coat and shuffled out the room, down the stairs and through the kitchen and out into the night, certain that, since my dad and I were once again buddies after our man-to-man chat on horseback at Stonehenge, he'd be more than happy to take me down onto the beach for a bout of stargazing.

I went through the gate and trundled down the track that led across the field to the barn, rubbing my eyes and hurrying a little

– even though I didn't have far to go it was scary being out there on my own and I'd be happier when I was cocooned within the sanctuary of the workshop. I rushed on, my attention more on the possible horrors lurking in the shadows that lay behind me than on what lay ahead, and I had my hand on the latch of the heavy wooden door before I heard the voices. Or rather, before I heard her voice. Hers? Shannon's, of course.

With a young boy's sense of melodrama I froze and held my breath, not sure what I should do. She wasn't supposed to be here, I knew that much. She was supposed to be back in the United States. Did this mean the two of them were continuing their love affair in secret? But the voices coming from the other side of the door weren't love voices, at least not in any way that I understood. The voices on the other side were arguing. Unpleasantly.

Shannon was accusing Jack of something, or that's the way it seemed. She was very upset. She kept asking him if he was in love with her and he kept saying no, and then she said she'd trusted him, and then when he said nothing in reply she demanded he tell her what was she supposed to do; did he really want her to go back to America and get a termination?

I didn't know what a termination was. I didn't care. I didn't even stick around long enough to hear Jack's answer. What I did instead was run, run like I did that night at the Dolaucothi gold mine. Once again I ran until I tripped but on this occasion I landed not in a nestlike hollow lined with leaves but hands first in a bed of ancient, vicious nettles. And yet I didn't cry out; I didn't make a sound – my head was that full of Shannon being here I'm not sure that to begin with I even realized what I'd done. And when the pain came I welcomed it. It was like a mark of honour, a medal awarded for the accomplishment of a daring deed. Because this time I'd run away not in fear but in pure exultation.

Shannon had come back after Jack had sworn to Stasie the two of them were never going to set eyes on each other ever again, and I had found this out. I had one thought in my mind and one thought only: now I had the means to attract the same kind of sympathy and attention that Moon had got after he'd blurted out to my mother that Jack and Shannon were having sex. That there was absolutely no rational component to this notion didn't worry me. After all, just that afternoon I'd found myself back in my father's favour and I even had the bulla in my possession. But the fact of Jack having given it to Moon instead of me *even though it had been Moon that had told Stasie about him and Shannon* still burned really deep, and somehow I couldn't let go of the idea that to be a man, to be respected by your elders, you had to be capable of betraying them when confronted with the demands of a higher, more important principle or truth.

Truth. What did I know about truth? Me, who'd stolen from my best friend and lied about it too, lied so shamelessly that I'd started to believe my lies myself. But this kind of self-knowledge was a long way away back then, and at that moment I was happier than I'd been for weeks.

Completely oblivious, now, to the phantoms of the night, I crept back to my bed and lay fully clothed beneath the sheets, brain spasming with the fantasy I was concocting for myself. What a complete cretin I was, what a selfish little fuckwit. I didn't understand anything, not a single thing. All I could think was that I had to hold out till morning, though morning seemed an impossible length of time away. It doesn't seem to me, now, that I fell asleep but at some point I must have done – I can't believe I spent the whole night awake, I would have gone insane. Unless of course I already was, which is quite possible, considering what happened next.

The first thing was that Tom came banging on our door, yelling at us all to get up from our pits, just like he did every other day of the week. In an instant I was rabidly alert with the momentousness of what I was about to do. I held on till Max and Moon and Jake had all got up and left the room, and then I checked my hands. I could already feel them throbbing hard, of course, but the visual impact was going to be important. And it fulfilled all expectations: my skin was blotched and ugly, my fingers swollen and beestung. When I finally came down to breakfast – having dawdled until I was sure as I could be of the maximum possible audience – Stasie spotted them immediately.

'*What* have you done to your hands?'

'I fell in nettles.' I said, like it was obvious. I looked around the room. Jack wasn't there. He must've still been upstairs.

'When?'

'Last night.'

'When last night?'

'When you'd all gone to bed. I couldn't sleep so I went out to the barn . . .'

This is the point at which I started crying. In the crude excuse for a plan I'd concocted the night before I thought tears would come in useful, but now the time had come I didn't need to act them. Here I was, in the moment, and I was genuinely upset. Events were tumbling out of my control, and knowing that I'd already tipped the rock that was any minute to start its slow, unstoppable rumble down the hill towards our little house, this was terrifying. I suppose I could have stopped there, said no more. But I didn't. I couldn't. So I carried on, gave that crucial little extra shove, even though I was no longer convinced that what had worked for Moon would work for me as well. But it didn't matter. I was experiencing a kind of vertigo. I'd dared to go right up to the edge of the cliff and now I had to jump.

'What on earth were you doing out at the barn?'

'I heard voices. I went to see. Daddy was there. With Shannon . . .'

That was enough. Just that. Stasie didn't want or need to hear any more. She filled in the blanks all by herself and Jack didn't last the day. He was packed and gone by nightfall, and suddenly I was all alone and surrounded by people telling me I mustn't worry, I mustn't blame myself, that soon he would be back and things would be okay. It was the second time I'd got what I thought Moon had had, only to find it wasn't quite the same as what I'd thought.

And I never saw Jack again.

I'm in a room, alone, shoes off, lying down on a bed. The nurse has gone and the room's all dark except for the glow given out by a purple-coloured nightlight thing, the luminous dial of the clock opposite and the little red stand-by LED on the wall-mounted television. My hands no longer hurt. Nothing's happening.

Hollow is how I feel. Numb. Like my soul, my most inner being, has self-aborted and slid out down my trouser leg. I remember the drawing Chrys did of me in Stasie's living room, my 'aura painting'. I now realize it wasn't the junk I thought it was. It was utterly perceptive and correct. That was who I was, this is who I am, even though I couldn't see it at the time. Poisoned, rotten, surrounded by lies and darkness and filled up with them too.

I lie here for a long time, staring at the LED, trying to comprehend what I've just told you, wondering if I'm actually awake or not. Then there's a knock at the door and Cathy's head floats in.

'How're you feeling Cooper?'

'I'm fine,' I say. But the words come out blurred and indistinct.

'Why didn't you tell me about the car?'

'Car?'

'The hire car. You know it's listed stolen.'

'Oh that. Yeah.'

'Well the police are here. They want to talk to you about it.'

'Oh. Okay.'

'Shall I tell them you'll be ready to talk to them, in what – maybe an hour?'

'Yeah.'

Cathy stares at me. 'You don't seem to be taking this particularly seriously.'

'I've got other stuff on my mind.'

She sniffs, looks disapproving. 'There's also a problem with your visa, apparently. We'll need to see your passport.'

'Fine.'

'Do you have it with you.'

'At the motel.'

'Well you're going to have to go and get it.'

'Okay.'

'One hour.'

'Right.'

'Goodbye Cooper.'

'Bye.'

She gives me one more disapproving look and then she goes. I feel groggy, dreamy, not sure whether all of that just happened. Not sure how much I care if it did. None of it really matters now, in any case. My quest is over. I've found who sent the ashes. I no longer want my old job back at Featherbrooks. I'm no longer in love with Liz. I've even sorted my father out with a fitting memorial, or Lemery has at any rate.

Lemery. I look at the LED again and blink, feeling more awake. I have the strange sensation of something falling like a stone from my head down to my stomach (doubly strange because I'm still lying down on my back). If Jack died in the fire, how did Lemery know to send the ashes? What, did Jack give him the canister and cut the eye into the concrete first, then tell him: Look here Nick, things are getting out of hand with these damn agents; if anything happens to me, I'm going to die right here, on this symbol, and you've gotta scrape me up and send me to my son?

Bollocks. That never happened. Lemery's not been telling me the truth.

That piece of farmer scum.

I'm awake now, awake and up, feet in shoes, scrabbling with my laces through the bandages. I can't manage bows so I do knots, sit on the bed to wait out a headrush, then go over to the door.

But it's been locked.

It is a crock of shit, and it smells as of a sewer.

Urn Burial

I've never forced a window before. Fortunately the Paracelsus isn't built for high security and the hinge restrictor built into the frame gives on my third shove. I'm on the first floor – the second floor if you're American – but the bushes below, the same ones we drove past coming in, they look like they'll break my fall. I've got this image in my head of the members of the A-Team jumping off the tops of buildings – legs straight out before them, half sitting up – and landing on the roofs of cars. It always looked like fun. I contemplated trying it once in Nottingham, using the privet hedge that ran past my bedroom as a crash pad, and I got halfway out the window before the hedge began to look altogether too spiky and uncrashpadlike, and I decided to give up. But now I have no choice.

I cast around the room to see if there's anything that might be useful to me. There isn't. I consider tying bedsheets together into a rope and using that to make good my escape, but it'll waste time and with my hands the way they are I don't think I'd be able to grip it hard enough – or even tie the knots.

The window ledge digs into my thighs. I don't quite see how the A-Team managed it, to get into that sitting position. It seems to me you'd have to take a running jump which isn't possible, not here anyway. Poised upon the edge of the abyss as I am, the ornamental hedge suddenly looks far less inviting and comfortable, just like the privet did before. Beneath the deceptively soft duvet of leaves thick and gnarly branches, brutalized by years of vicious trimming, fork up in vicious Vs which could have been specifically designed to spike the genitalia of plunging males.

The ground's really quite a long way off.

In the brief moment of my fall I see myself from inside the hospital, over the shoulder of an orderly sorting through a card file or fetching a couple of sample bottles from a cabinet. I'm that moment in a slapstick comedy when, seen only by the camera, the hero tumbles past a window like a sack of potatoes and lands in a cloud of twigs and dust and leaves. In a film it's funny. In real life it hurts. A lot. In real life the hero can't move for several minutes. In real life the hero bleeds.

How come when I was twelve I was so much more sensible about this kind of thing?

I hurry through Atomville in a crouching run, dodging behind walls and bushes whenever possible. Past the Balmer Church I go, past the Federal Building, past the library with its B52-bomber mural on the wall. I don't know what to think any more. I don't know who is wrong, who is right, who's telling the truth, what the truth itself might even look like. *It is a container of excrement and 'tis very strong, such that no one may abide it*. I'm in my own video game, in my own movie, but unlike the fantasy production of your everyday media-saturated fat-arsed suburban loser someone somewhere's actually watching this. Twenty-four hours a day, seven days a week, somewhere the video's rolling, somewhere I'm being rendered. I'm in *The Truman Show* – *The Cooper Show* – but in this version there'll be no big bubble to rip through at the end, no goofy escape by boat, no dramatic finale and easy conclusion, no chance to go back to the last save point. In this version, I could travel twice around the globe and never find the director, never catch a single viewer in the act. In this version I've no hope of ever finding out who's trying to help me out, who is trying to trap me, who is lying, who is telling the truth.

Because everyone is lying. They can't help it. The truth is that there is no truth. No one here really has any idea what is right and what is wrong, what is bad, what is best. No one really understands too much of anything. It's just a mess. And I've always hated mess, always had the feeling that mess is somehow out to get me, always had this suspicion that one day mess would tire of the logic I'm forever trying to impose on it and just rise up and sort of glub me out. Look out Cooper. Here it comes. *It is a vessel of fertilizer, and none may abide its strength.* Run, run. Keep on running. Run like you've never run, not since you were a child running through the Cornish woods, fleeing an old mining museum your father was busy breaking into, not since you ran from Jack and Shannon in the barn. Push out your legs, puff up your lungs, let them carry you. It feels good, it feels right. It clears your head, flushes out the fear, helps you take control. Run, Cooper. Run, Ash. Go on. Run. *For it promoteth growth. And it is very powerful.*

When Liz opens the door I shove past her and push on into her room.

'Cooper . . .' She sees my bandages, my face red and pouring with sweat, my torn clothing, the knotted laces on my shoes. 'Wow. What happened to you?'

'Get your car keys. I need your help.'

'Only if you tell me what's going on . . .'

I look her in the eyes. 'Please. Get the keys. We haven't got much time. I'll tell you all about it on the way.'

But I don't. Beyond what's necessary for me to give directions, during the drive out of Atomville we don't talk at all. I'm not quite ready yet.

The gateway's right opposite the water tower just like Lemery said it was, and since the water tower's the only feature of any significance along this stretch of highway we find the turn-off to the farm without any problem. Beyond the gate the gravel track takes us across a stretch of plain, then up a low hill to where a house and several barns stand sheltered on three sides by poplars, the fourth side left open to give the house a fine view back across the way we came.

Lemery's truck sits parked out front, The Herm standing beside it still wound around with ropes and chains. But there's no sign of Lemery himself.

Liz pulls up, applies the break, switches off the engine. 'Okay,' she says, 'we're here. So. What's going on?'

I listen to the silence. The engine tinks. 'Have you made your mind up yet?'

She turns and stares out the window. Maybe she's looking at The Herm. Maybe she's looking at the house. Maybe she's looking at the trees.

'What if I haven't?'

'Then I get out and you turn the car around and you drive back to your life and you and me, we never speak again.'

'That simple?'

'You're the one who has the choice, Liz. Not me.'

'So what's about to happen now, it's that important?'

I sigh and wish I smoked – now would be the perfect time to light a cigarette. 'In the big scheme of things, no, it's pointless and irrelevant. But to me it's important. It's the most important thing.'

She waits, leans back in her seat, looks up at the roof, closes her eyes. 'Okay, then I choose . . . you.'

'You do?'

'Yes.'

'And you'll leave your job?'

'I can't promise that. But I won't tell them anything.'

'They might not let you have the option.'

'Then I'll leave.'

'Cross your heart and hope to die?'

'Cross my heart.'

'I hope you're not lying to me.'

'I'm not.' She opens her eyes, leans over, kisses me firmly on the cheek. 'Cross my heart and hope to die.'

I feel my face heat up as hot as my hands were earlier and probably as red. We sit staring at each other for a moment, embarrassed by our sudden intimacy.

'Then . . . okay,' I say.

'So?' she asks, ever the efficient one. 'What's going on?'

I breathe out, feel some of the tension leave my body. 'What's going on? Well, for starters Jack's not dead.'

And then it all comes out. Well, most of it, at least.

We get out of the car and walk up to the house in search of Lemery. I'm about to pull open the fly screen and try the front door when I see him stretched out on the porch's ancient swing seat, fast asleep.

I go over and shake his shoulder. 'Wakey wakey.'

'Cooper, hey.' The farmer jerks upright and sits for a moment, head in hands, elbows on knees, willing himself into consciousness. The completion of this process apparently isn't possible without his cap, hanging on a nail nearby. He reaches for it, pulls it on. 'What time is it?'

'Five.'

'Shit. Ken should be here any minute. Hey, how was the hospital?'

'Fine,' I say. 'Where are the ashes?'

'In the truck.'

'You haven't put them inside yet?'

'No. It's a two-man job.'

'Good. Let's do it now.'

Liz and I wait in silence on the porch, watching the flies, while Lemery goes inside to get us all a drink of water. Then we follow him over to the Subaru. He climbs inside, backs it up, brings down the hydraulic arm, and when the hoist is low enough I slip it through the lifting loop he'd rigged up earlier and give him the thumbs-up to haul away. The engine whines, the tyres knuckle down into the dirt and The Herm rises a few feet into the air. I signal to him to lock it off and I get down on my hands and knees to have a look-see underneath.

'Four bolts. We'll need some kind of wrench.'

Jumping down from the driver's seat, Lemery comes over with a socket set plus a couple of hefty blocks of wood which he sets out below the dangling form. He gets the right sleeve on the second try, fits it to a handle, starts loosening the bolts. They're oiled and perfectly aligned and they undo easily. When he's got them turned out about halfway off he hands the wrench to Liz with instructions to screw them out completely while he and I take the weight of the granite base.

'Ready?' I say, once the bolts have gone.

'Ready,' he says. Together, we waggle the thick slab from side to side. For a moment or two it feels like it will never shift, then suddenly its weight rams down into my hands and makes me gasp. For the first time I'm glad of the bandages I'm wearing; without some kind of padding I don't think I'd be able to keep my grip.

We manage to set the slab down on the wooden blocks just before my strength gives out, and I pause, hands on knees, to allow the oxygen back into my arms and hands and back. It's hard to believe I'm actually here with the sculpture, finally. I look into Lemery's face, then into Liz's, and for a moment all the lies and secrets are forgotten. Around the edges of my eyes I feel the prick of tears.

Liz smiles very slightly and puts her hand up to my arm. 'Well done, Cooper,' she says. 'You made it.'

I don't say anything, just stare into her pupils, trying to see what's really hidden there.

'Come on then,' says Lemery.

'Yeah, yeah.' Where it's lying across the blocks the slab forms a natural seat and I sit down on it and peer up the arse-end of the sculpture to see what we've revealed. There is indeed a cavity, just as Depaoli said there was inside the teddy bear Jack carved in Graniteburg. Circular, about ten inches in diameter and fully occupied.

With a little bit of encouragement whatever's jammed up there soon comes sliding out.

It's a stainless-steel flask, very heavy, about twenty inches tall and beautifully made: a perfect cylinder of metal with just the finest of lines about a quarter way down its length where the lid begins. It's decorated all over with the same curlicue pattern as I saw on the little pedestal out at SOFFT and the top is engraved with the Eye of Horus inside the three-sided version of the *circulus quadratus*.

I hand it to Liz and ask her to unscrew the cap – what with the bandages, my hands can't get a proper purchase on the metal. She has to trap it between her feet to get it turning but once she gets it started it comes off like a dream. Just before she removes it altogether, she stops.

'You don't think . . . you don't think there's anything dangerous in here do you?' she says, glancing at my dressings.

'No.'

'You're sure?'

'I'm pretty sure. Want me to do the last bit?'

'No. It's okay.'

Or so she says. But as she makes the last few turns she screws up her face and leans away, just like I did when I opened the canister in the security office back at Featherbrooks. But nothing leaps out and, unharmed, she hands the open flask to me. I take it and peer into an inner cavity about four inches in diameter and polished to a mirror sheen. At first I think it's empty. Then I realize there's something small and soft and brown lying right down at the bottom. Lifting up the flask, I tip it out and let it drop onto the ground.

It's a thin strand of leather thong bound round and round. I bend down, pick it up, carefully undo the knot. The leather, soft with age, unravels easily. At the centre, fastened to the thong in the manner of a pendant, is a tiny curl of bone.

'What is it?'

'It's a tympanic bulla,' I say, croaking the words out past the lump that's swelling in my throat. 'I told you about it, remember? It's the one Jack cut from the whale and gave to Moon.'

'And now he's given it to you?' Liz says softly, imagining she understands.

He must have known I had it all along, must have known all about my lies, my avarice, my jealousy, my hiding place. He must've come and taken it when he left, after I betrayed him. 'That's what it looks like.'

I can't help it. Tears have overtaken me. I have to turn away.

Lemery steps up, puts his arm around my shoulders. Liz comes round in front of me, takes my bandaged hands.

'The Amesbury Archer had a son, you know,' says Lemery. 'He was buried nearby and he wore the same gold in his hair. He was born in Britain. Just like you.'

'Shut up, Lemery. That's not what this is about.'

He opens his mouth to speak, closes it again. 'Okay,' he says.

'Jack set the fire, didn't he?' I say, throwing Liz a warning look. The farmer nods. 'And he wasn't inside when it went up.' Lemery looks at me, then down at the ground. 'And he's not dead.'

'I guess not.'

'So are you going to tell me what really happened?'

He wrinkles his nose, clears his throat, pulls his hat a little firmer down onto his head. 'It was Thoth,' he says, eventually. 'That was the breaking point. After they killed Thoth Jack knew he couldn't carry on – and he knew they'd come again, keep coming till he left. So he fixed them up a goodbye gift. He rigged the studio with fertilizer bombs and trip wires and incendiaries and every night for the next few nights he snuck out on his belly into the desert and camped out in a sleeping bag. Then one night: boom. He sat and watched the fire awhile, then came up here like we'd planned. I had an old jalopy waiting for him; we'd fixed it up with out-of-state plates and a stuff bag in the back filled with clothes and some of his personal effects. And off he went.'

'Where?'

'I honestly don't know.'

'He's going to live out the rest of his life on the run?'

'He doesn't have a whole lot of life left to live. All that messing around with radioactive materials, all the cigarettes he smoked . . . it came with a pretty heavy price. He had real bad cancers growing all through his body. And you know Jack – he wasn't one for health insurance and he wasn't going to get well again on Medicare, and anyway, it was almost certainly too late. He just wanted to make sure the few months he had left, he could live them free.'

My next question's obvious enough. 'Why didn't you tell me? Why the wild-goose chase?''

'That was Jack's idea. He wanted you to figure it out for yourself. If you couldn't – or didn't want to – he thought you'd be better off thinking the same as everyone else.'

'Why?

'I don't know, Cooper. Guess that's between you and him. Maybe he didn't trust you with the truth. Not until you'd had a chance to see things from his point of view.'

'Not trust me with the truth? But I'm his *son*.'

'Yeah but, the last few years, you've been kind of sleeping with the enemy, right? And Jack ran out on you. For all he knew you could've hated him so much the minute you found out he wasn't dead you'd run straight off to Todd and company, tell them to go start looking for him.'

So. I escape one guilty piece of the past and find myself snagged by another. That seems to be the way life runs. I blink and let my gaze run away from Lemery, down the hill, away through the opening in the trees to where a cloudy stain of sun is setting over Atomville while all around the Earth – the ribbon of the Chiawana, the vast tracts of the Areas – is slowly falling in and out of focus. I have the sensation of being alone on the prow of a ship, my ship, right on the apex of a giant bow wave, no other vessels in sight, nothing ahead of me but the rippling sea and only the sun, the moon and the stars to help me navigate. I feel like this for a long time and for a long time nothing happens until gradually I boomerang around and come back into myself and realize I'm breathing, breathing naturally, easily, breathing deep clear breaths down to a part of my lungs I'd forgotten existed, a part of my lungs I've not managed to use for close on twenty years.

And then, clattering across the sky, slicing up the space around us: the unmistakable sound of rotor blades.

The helicopter circles, once, twice, then comes into land about thirty metres from the farmhouse. It's a Black Hawk with an open side and wheels instead of skids. The wheels hit the dirt and Ken jumps out and does a crouch-run across the yard to where we're standing. Strangely formal, we all shake hands but it's impossible not to see the fear and urgency stamped upon his face.

'So are we gonna do this thing?' he shouts to Lemery above the racket.

Lemery doesn't answer, looks in my direction.

'It's fine by me,' I say.

Then Ken asks me if I'd like to go along for the ride.

I shake my head. 'I think I'll stay here, thanks.' I want to tell Lemery that it's not really anything to do with me, that Jack's not even in there, that if he thinks it's the right thing to do then he should do it, that he knew my father so much better than I did. But why say these things when we all already know they're true? I've found what I was looking for and more.

All that remains is to reassemble The Herm and get it ready for its final journey. The ashes are still sitting on the back seat of the Subaru and I get them and pour them into the flask and seal it, taking care this time not to get any of the powder on my hands. Then I slide the flask inside its cavity and while Ken and Lemery lift the pedestal Liz and me fasten on the fixing bolts.

When we're done Lemery manoeuvres the sculpture into a suitable position and then waits beside it while Ken brings the helicopter round and holds it in a hover directly overhead. A winch comes inching down; Lemery hooks it to the chains. When he's done he backs off and gives a signal and slowly, very slowly, Ken starts to haul it up. Inch by inch it rises up into the air, and then when it's about ten feet from the fuselage the aircraft begins to turn and pull away.

Up over the poplars it flies, across the chessboard of crops and arid steppe, across the river busy with early-evening motorboats, around the edge of Atomville and deep into the secret belly of the Areas. Off to some patch of ochre earth lost among the toxic labyrinths of all those forgotten trenches that it will watch over for ever like Jack always meant it to, standing silent as a scarecrow and lonely as a sentinel for ten thousand years until the Areas are gone and the USA is gone and everything else that is familiar to us now is beyond history and forgotten, until my children's children's children, and Liz's children's children's children, and Lemery's, and Cathy's, and Ken's, and Bill's, and Pat's, and Cox's, and, yes, maybe even Todd's, until one day they come back to this place and find it here, alone and waiting for them.

The three of us stand watching as the T formed by the helicopter with The Herm beneath it slowly disappears from view. It's a gradual process. First the T becomes a line, then the line becomes two dots, then the two dots merge together and grow ever smaller until at last they start to blur into a shelf of leaden cumulus well on the way to being transmuted by the sunset into a slab of purest gold. I'm squinting now; the helicopter's almost entirely gone from view; this is the last of Jack, my father, that I'll ever see.

I wave.

So do the others. Then Liz takes me by the hand and Lemery leads us back into the house, where we make coffee and wait for the police.

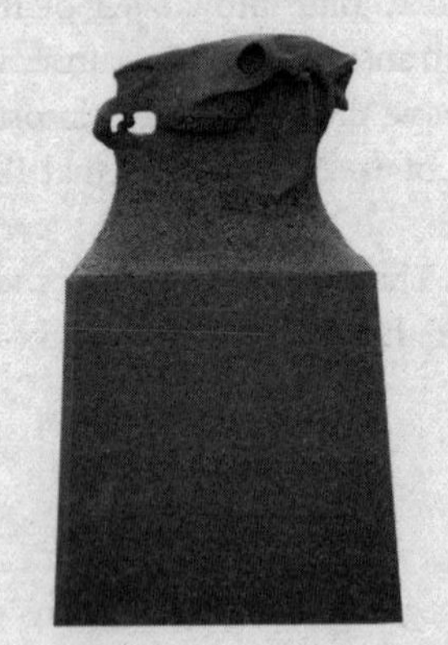

Author's Note

This book is based on a true story.

If this book were a film, that's probably the line the studio would be inserting about now (or more likely earlier, in the short gap between the fading title credits and the moment when we hear the first line of dialogue). And there would be me, the disgruntled author, sitting in the audience at the premiere (having not been invited to view any of the rushes or private screenings), fuming silently (and later loudly, and probably drunkenly, at the party after my fifth glass of wine) that this wasn't right at all, it wasn't 'based on' but 'inspired by', and then not by a 'story' but by an artist's 'life and work'. And then some kind soul would no doubt pat me on the back and shove me in a cab and dispatch me off into the arms of the night – or at least to someplace where I couldn't do any more damage than I'd already caused.

But that's not happening, at least not right this minute. Right now it's Monday morning and I'm stone-cold sober and yet to have even my first cup of coffee and as much in control of my existence as I ever get to be, and I'm going to take this opportunity while I can. So. 'This novel was inspired by an artist's life and work.' The artist? James L. Acord, sculptor, who first came to my attention thanks to a lecture he was giving at London's Royal Institution in February 1998. A great lecture, some said, even an epoch-defining event, though one which, despite being invited and determined to attend, I contrived to miss by writing the wrong date in my diary. Fortunately I managed to make up the loss by wangling an introduction to this singular American, getting drunk with him and then spending most of the following two days in various hotel bars and pubs, various drinks in my hand, listening with something approaching wonder (and occasionally touching incredulity) as he spun a series of increasingly extraordinary tales about his fifteen-year quest to make art out of nuclear waste.

I was captivated, and by the end of that weekend I was sure enough that I would remain so that I asked Acord how he'd feel if I used some of the stories he'd just told me as the basis of my next book. And he must have thought there was absolutely no chance of my ever getting off my arse and actually doing it because he said, 'Sure, why not? Be my guest,' or words to that effect.

He did stipulate one condition, however, and only one. I could interview him as much as I felt was necessary, I could tap him for facts and contacts and advice, I could even make his artworks an integral part of my text if I wanted to (which I did; it's what I've done – oh, and the illustrations heading up each of the three main sections are his as well, though he did those specially for the book), but I should never, on any account, ask him to read the finished product lest it make him regret his generosity and faith in me. And so I won't do that. But what I will ask, Jim, is that you read this single page, just so I can be sure that you know what a pleasure, an honour and an education it's been, working with you as an artist, getting to know you as a human being.

By lending me his life, of course, Jim Acord also lent me his friends, acquaintances and colleagues, many of whom I've come into contact with over the past few years and all of whom, without exception, have greeted me with the kind of frankness and trust of which a writer dreams. In particular I'd like to thank Carey Young for rightly surmising that James Acord would be 'right up my street'; all at The Arts Catalyst for bringing Jim to London in the first place; Bill Happel for lending me his cabin in Vermont; Jed Brignal and friends for hospitality and aura-painting; Simon Franklin for tips on how to run a nuclear reactor; Wanda Munn, Gerry Woodcock, John Stang, Bob Schenter, Russell Jim, Jerry Williams, Norm Ackley, Frank Gaylord, Tom Bailie and Greg and Debora Greger for unspun insights into the life of a US nuclear facility; Philip Schuyler for doing all the spade work on the real story of Jim's life; and Tom Putnam, Brian Freer, Arthur Aubry, Linley Storm and most especially Philip, Judy, Alex and Julia

Munger, without whose hospitality, kindness and trust this book would have been neither started nor finished.

In addition thanks are due to: Drew Heinz and all at Hawthornden House for giving me the time and space to get the book out of a particularly stubborn hole it had fallen into; Marion Mazauric and all at La Laune for a similar donation further on down the line; Jonny Geller and all at Curtis Brown for their ability to play the long game; Leo Hollis, Mary Mount and all at Viking for piling their chips up on my number; Amit Gupta for timely title advice; Jann Turner for hiking hills to the accompaniment of my beta-version rants; Dave Wark, Lise Autogena, Liz Bailey, Armin Medosch, Jon Bradshaw, Peter Carty and Ian, Indira and Steve for various bits of research help; and family and friends too numerous to mention for services and favours too varied to list. Though it may not always seem it, writing a novel is in fact a group activity, and the writer only ever gets to jump off the cliff of his or her project on account of all those good people prepared to line up and hold the rope (usually while quietly shaking their heads at the reckless spectacle being played out before them). It must be hard sometimes, I realize. But thank you.

In closing I'd just like to say – in case it's not already obvious – that Jack D. Reever is not an attempted portrait of the artist James L. Acord and that the various interpretations of Reever's art given in this book are not to be understood as commentaries on Acord's art (even on those various occasions when the art object in question happens to be pretty much identical). Jim Acord loaned me his life and work to use as a frame across which to drape my own fiction, and that's what I've endeavoured to do.

Hope you found something inside to make it all worthwhile.

James Flint 2003